Unfamiliar Territory

Unfamiliar Territory

A Novel

Mary Smathers

CARMEL BY THE SEA, CALIFORNIA

Book Design by *the*BookDesigners
Cover images used under license from Shutterstock.com
Map by Joe LeMonnier

Library of Congress Control Number: 2025904178

ISBN # 979-8-9906745-0-9 (paperback)
ISBN # 979-8-9906745-1-6 (e-book)

mks publishing
Carmel by the Sea, California
www.marysmathers.com

First Edition
Printed in the United States
10 9 8 7 6 5 4 3 2 1

*In loving memory of my mother and grandmother—
resilient women who met the challenges of their times
with grace and fortitude.*

With gratitude to the prolific correspondents of
19th-century America—letter writers, diarists, and
journalists—whose eloquent and descriptive accounts
offer us a window into the past.

CASTRO/BRENNAN

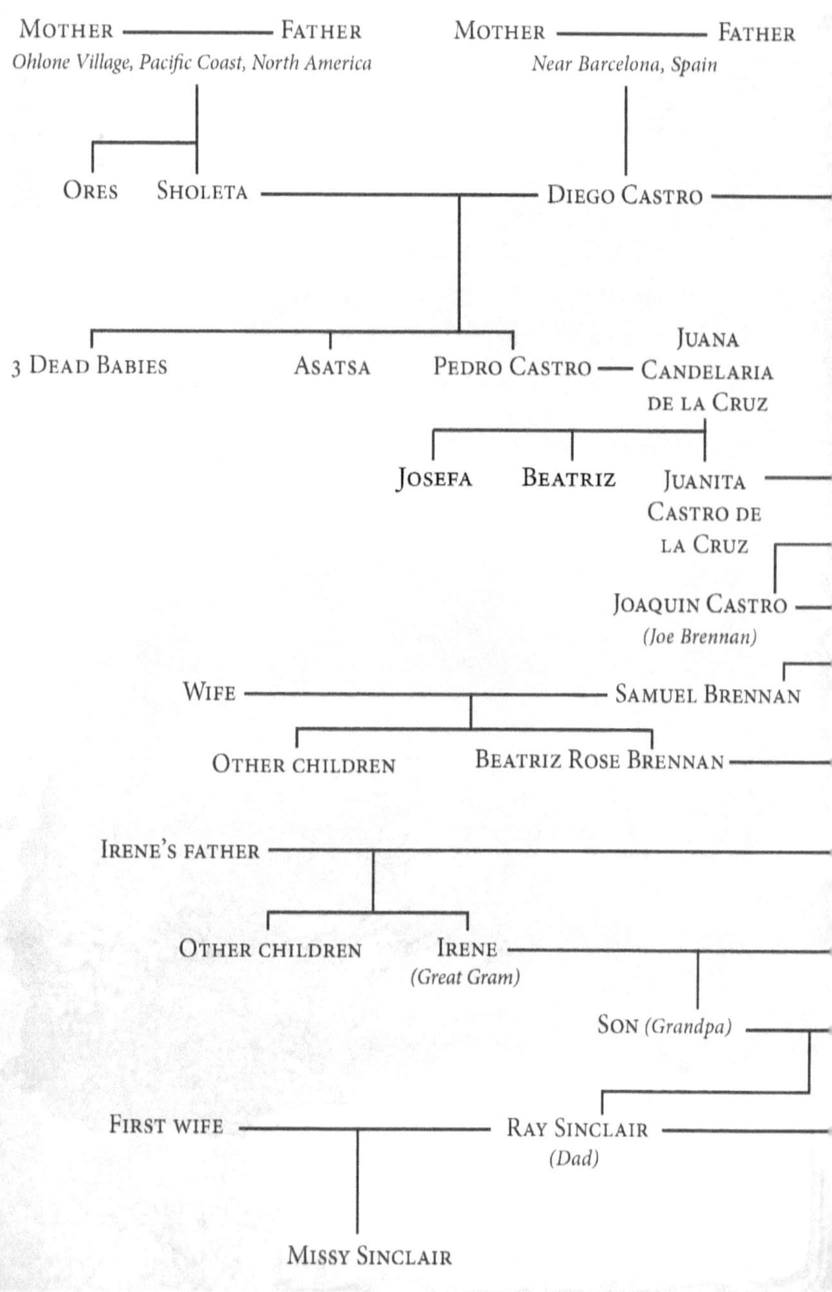

FAMILY TREE

Mother
Don Sebastian Altamirano
Sinaloa, New Spain
Maria Joaquina Altamirano
5 More Children
Beatriz Castro Altamirano
9 More Children
Captain Malachy Brennan
Mrs. Brennan
5 Other Children
Elizabeth Brennan
3 Other Children
Lover
Husband
Irene's mother
(father unclear)
Other Children
Husband (Mr. Sinclair)
Wife
Second Wife (Momma)
Nicole Beatrice Sinclair

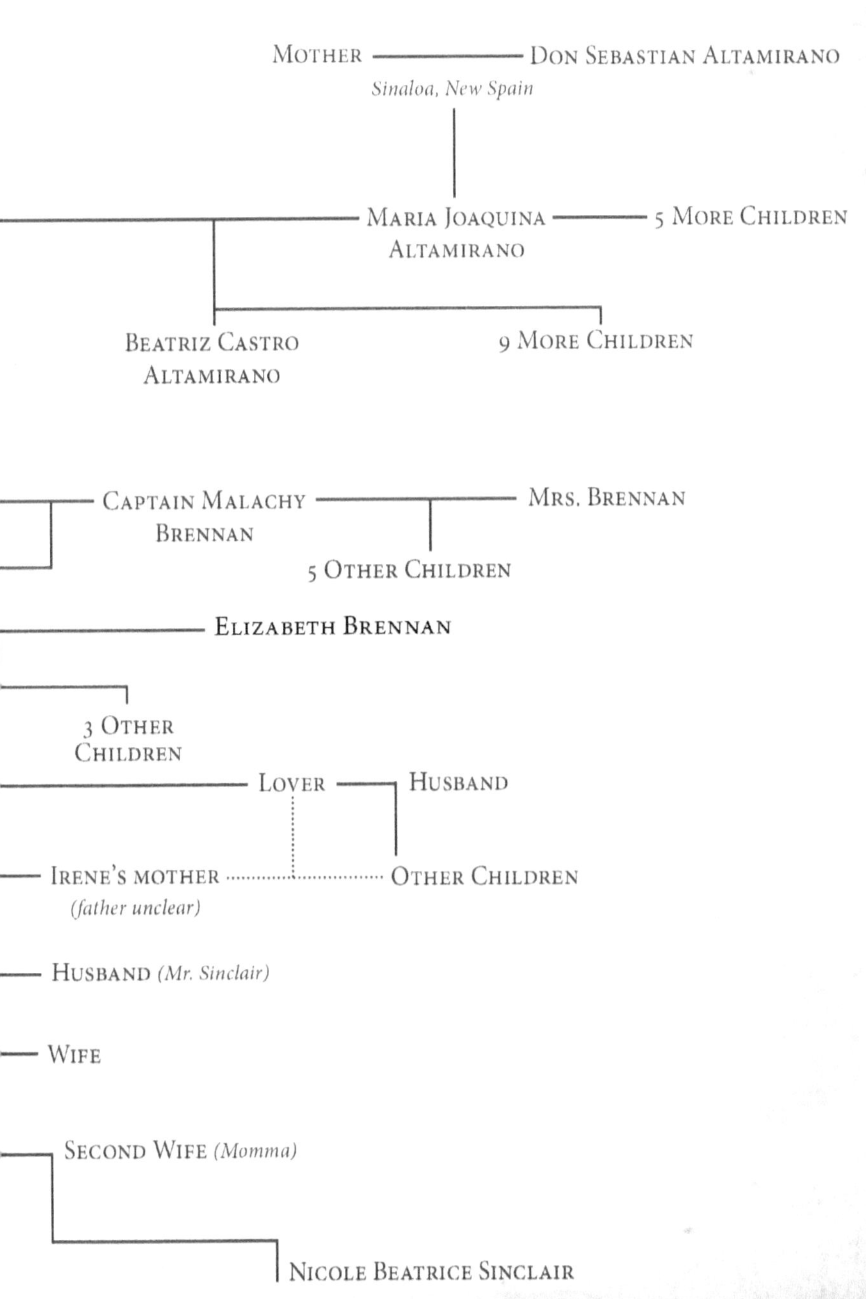

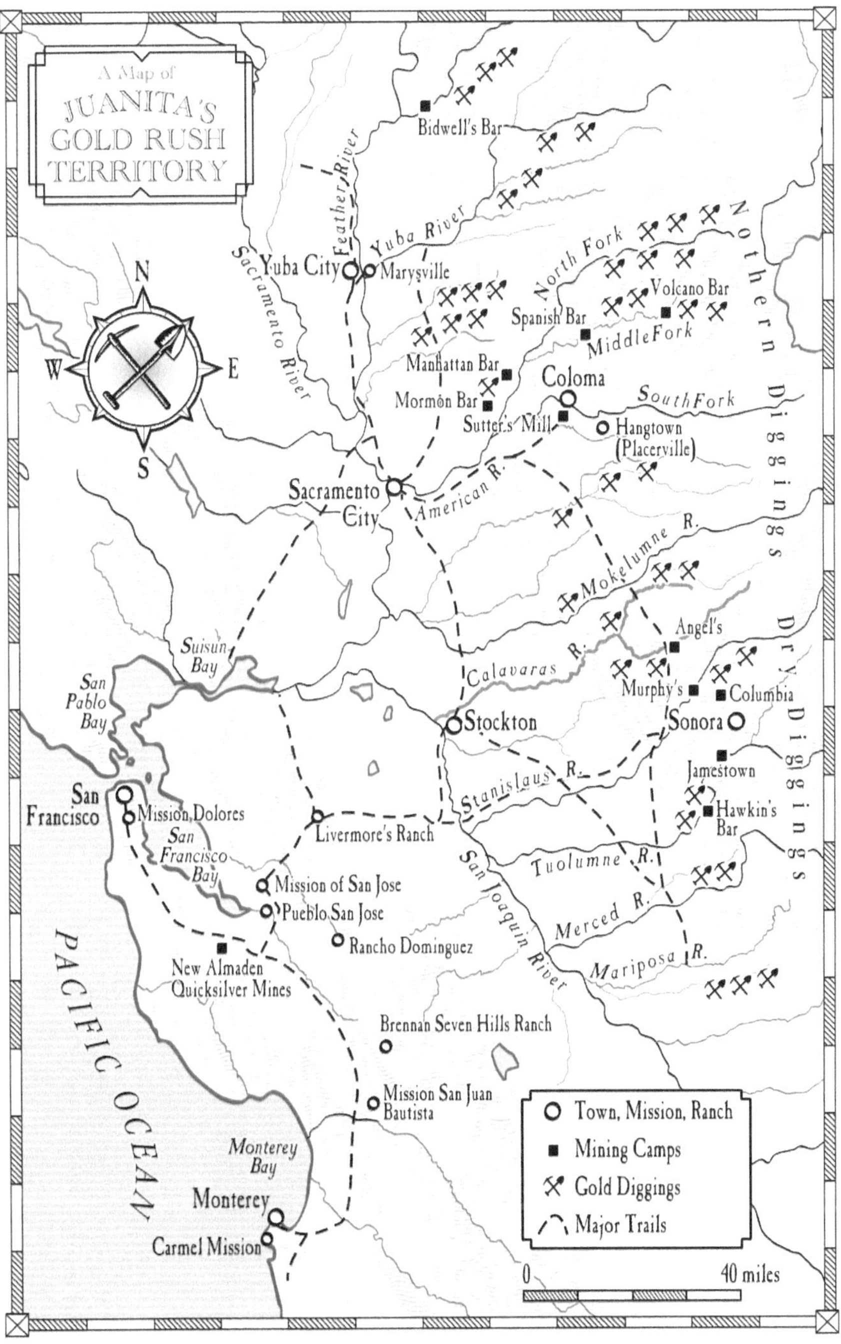

A Map of
JUANITA'S
GOLD RUSH
TERRITORY

N
W
E
S

Feather River
Yuba River
Sacramento River
Bidwell's Bar
Yuba City
Marysville
North Fork
Spanish Bar
Volcano Bar
Middle Fork
Manhattan Bar
Coloma
South Fork
Mormon Bar
Sutter's Mill
Hangtown
(Placerville)
Northern Diggings
Sacramento City
American R.
Mokelumne R.
Angel's
Calavaras R.
Murphy's
Columbia
Sonora
Suisun Bay
San Pablo Bay
Stockton
Jamestown
Hawkin's Bar
Dry Diggings
San Francisco
Mission Dolores
San Francisco Bay
Livermore's Ranch
Stanislaus R.
Mission of San Jose
Pueblo San Jose
Tuolumne R.
Rancho Dominguez
San Joaquin River
Merced R.
New Almaden
Quicksilver Mines
Mariposa R.
PACIFIC OCEAN
Brennan Seven Hills Ranch
Mission San Juan Bautista
Monterey Bay
Monterey
Carmel Mission

Town, Mission, Ranch
Mining Camps
Gold Diggings
Major Trails

0   40 miles

Flight

January 1850

Juanita Castro de la Cruz galloped toward the *El Camino Real* main road, flying under the ranch's gateway sign no longer bearing her family's name, heart thumping with every *thud, thud* of the horse's hooves. How quickly could she ride up to the gold diggings to reunite with her son? How long before the new *yanqui* owner discovered she'd stolen his favorite horse?

Tugging Canela's reins and kicking her flank, Juanita turned north toward her sister's *rancho* above Pueblo San Jose. Her thick black hair, surprisingly free of gray strands despite years of loss, bounced in its knot beneath her *sombrero*. The day's waning light cast a hazy, rosy tint in the distance and shadows formed along the road. She wrinkled her nose at the dank air filling the shaded patches. Must get to the Dominguez ranch before dark.

Surely her sister and brother-in-law would welcome her. Her younger sister would be appalled at the treatment the new boss had inflicted. And her brother-in-law, still a well-connected Don, would have creative ideas for finding Joaquin. Thank goodness reliable Beatriz lived close by. Josefa, her other sister, had disappeared from Monterey over a year ago, her husband obsessed with gold fever, like so many.

She spurred hard and gripped the reins tighter to speed on, operating on survival adrenaline, more to leave the past behind than with a clear destination. She had no idea where Joaquin was or how to find him in this new California. He'd apparently sent her letters from the gold fields which the new owner had purposely destroyed.

Juanita passed the Rancho Dominguez gate and steered the chestnut horse toward the large adobe as the sun slipped below the rolling horizon. Slowing to a trot to catch her breath, she noticed their sign was faded, the "O" in Dominguez missing. The sign hung crooked, the "Z" dangling toward the ground.

Several muddied, gray cows ambled along the road, no *vaquero* in sight. She pulled on Canela's reins to shoo them into the meadow, clicking to the horse and *ya, ya*-ing at the cows. Unfamiliar with Juanita or her horse, they were reluctant to obey. One bull stopped, perfectly still save for huge eyes unblinking in defiance. She persisted, turning Canela around to the bull's backside, one way, then the other, to get the stubborn animal to budge. Finally, he grunted and loped toward the green grass.

Hmm, I have to be the cowboy, she mused as she adjusted her riding jacket, smoothed her skirt, and wiped the sweat from her face with a sleeve. She should look presentable upon surprising her sister and brother-in-law. She couldn't reveal she'd just sped in frantically on a stolen horse. No need to scandalize the relatives—the circumstances of her unexpected arrival would disturb them enough.

She scanned the shade below overgrown trees for a hitching rail and finally found a mossy bar, the watering trough rusted through. After tying Canela, she found a ladle and bucket at the well around the side of the house. The mare drank noisily while Juanita hammered their formidable redwood door with her fist.

"Beatriz, it's me, Juanita," she called. No answer. Was that a noise inside? She knocked again, then swiveled the iron latch and shouldered open the heavy door. No flowers adorned the entry table as was customary in their childhood home and in all the fine *haciendas*. The fountain in the central courtyard was dry, the decorative tiles cracked and peeling off the terra cotta base. Stringy, brown bougainvillea vines draped off the second-story balcony, devoid of a single green leaf or magenta bud.

Rather than a gleaming, welcoming house reminiscent of the days her parents and grandparents owned the Castro hacienda, the grounds and interior appeared worn, neglected. Where were Beatriz and Agustín? Where was their staff? Where were the cowboys keeping track of the herd?

As she peered down the hallways, she heard loud, angry voices. A door slammed. What were they fighting about? She could only hear fragments.

" … sell more …"

" … find that map …"

A hallway door squeaked open and her young nephews in nightshirts peeked out. Then the door suddenly shut and the little ones scampered off, their stocking feet whispering across the tiled floor. No more shouts. Just an eerie quiet.

She reached the library door. "Beatriz, are you okay? It's Juanita. *Qué está pasando*?" she asked as she knocked, then went in. Chilly air took her breath. No fire in the hearth, only a few tapers flickering in soot-coated wall sconces.

Beatriz sat on a green velvet sofa with a carved wooden frame, an exquisite piece she'd had shipped from Spain to decorate one of the most elaborate adobes on the El Camino Real. Papers lay across her lap. Every desk drawer was open, with notebooks, documents, maps strewn across the knotted redwood surface. Formerly neat shelves were in disarray, as if an earthquake had shaken the formidable room and dislodged all its contents. Juanita knew the earth had not been quaking recently. This mess was man-made.

Beatriz had always maintained a proper residence as benefited the important Don Dominguez she married when the situation deteriorated at Rancho Castro.

Beatriz looked up in desperation, tears streaming. Surprised, Juanita took her into her arms as she glanced around for her brother-in-law.

"Oh, Juanita, I'm so embarrassed for you to see the house, us, like this. We need proof of Agustín's grant. There's a Commission . . . hire lawyers, speak English, lose it. And Agustín wants to sell my dresses." She began to sob.

Juanita had heard rumors of a Land Commission coming, requiring *Californios* to prove ranch ownership to the new state government. Land they'd lived on for generations, much of it granted with a wave of the king's hand or a governor's proclamation in one document issued two, three or four generations back. Occasionally, only on a handshake.

For generations, the Dons had branded their cattle and kept their mostly Native cowboys busy herding livestock within their granted tracts. Spanish and Mexican gentlemen took pride in a strict code and in legendary hospitality—there was no need for contracts nor formal paperwork to conduct business, not when Alta California was populated with only a few thousand non-Native souls. Juanita's family's land had been marked by a river, a cluster of sycamores, rock formations, and an especially effluent spring. Juanita's grandparents, Don Diego and Doña Quina, and her parents, Don Pedro and Doña Candelaria, were gracious hosts to all who stopped at their grand estate on forty-eight-thousand acres of rolling hills and fertile pasture lands, orchards and gardens. Neighboring ranchers, military leaders and governors, priests and English explorers, French scientists, Boston merchants and Russian trappers . . . they were all provided with delicious meals, a comfortable bed, and the latest news. For almost a hundred years, questioning the Dons' titles was unimaginable, insulting.

But the US War of Invasion had changed everything. Enormous Alta California would soon be an American state, under a government based far across the plains. Yes, Mexican ranchers were used to a distant ruling power—in Mexico City, and before, even farther away in Spain—but for generations, they'd benefitted, profited even, from a governing authority which mostly ignored them.

This new master, one of a different language, religion, culture, and never-ending thirst for land, did not appear likely to ignore its latest prize. And the battle now raging on whether to admit California to the United States as a slave or free state brought even more attention to the latest star being added to Old Glory. Gold and land were everything.

Agustín growled from a dark corner. "What are you doing here, Juanita? You can't just barge in. Beatriz, you'll do as I say."

Surprised, Juanita pulled Beatriz in tighter. "I had to leave. With Mamá gone, there was nowhere to go. I've got to find Joaquin."

"We've got our own problems right now." Agustín shook his head and left out the side door, the slam startling the sisters.

Not the welcome she'd imagined. The family closeness of her childhood and comfortable predictability of four generations of ranch life had been disrupted by cattle plague, debts, the American invasion, and war. Her family gone, Rancho Castro in the hands of a yanqui, her son off in the gold fields with no communication for almost two years, Juanita felt unmoored. With Mamá's passing, there was no reason to continue working for the ranch's new owner. But here, Beatriz and Agustín appeared lost in their own troubles.

Juanita guided Beatriz to stop crying, clean up the paperwork and pile it on the desk. She sat her on the sofa and, holding her sister's hands, asked for an explanation. Calmer now, Beatriz detailed how they needed to raise funds to pay a translator and lawyers so they could prove ownership of the rancho at the Land Commission hearings starting soon.

"We don't have gold dust or those new coins. A little of the old silver, which no one wants anymore. We just have land. The hacienda, the cattle . . . you know. We trade here. There's no gold in our creeks. So Agustín wants to sell the clothes and china, candlesticks. Even the furniture. Anything the yanquis want in San Francisco, in the new towns."

"But what about the land grant? Don't you have—?"

"That's just it. The grant from Portola's days went to a relative who had no children and gave the land to two feuding nephews. Their sons divided it and Agustín got his share from his father, one of those sons. But there really weren't papers. No way to prove his distant uncle and heirs passed it down legally, or to whom, or what the property boundaries are. Agustín's father got shot in the skirmish up north. He'd joined the Bear Flag revolt. Got mixed up with the wrong people."

Juanita squeezed her sister's hands as she tried to make

sense of this unexpected bad news. She'd left in a such a hurry and assumed Beatriz and Agustín's large estate would help her reestablish a stable family life, maybe even become a home after finding Joaquin. She had nowhere else to go. How naïve she'd been. So involved in her own problems.

She grimaced. "I guess we'll have to sell something to pay these lawyers. What else do we have? This is home. This is all we've got."

Beatriz looked at her clearly then, puzzled. "Wait, what are you doing here? Can't you stay there? I know Mamá's gone but they need you to run the ranch."

"No, I'm never going back. Malachy came to find me after Mamá's internment. He let it slip his horrible wife destroyed letters Joaquin must have written to me from gold country. I've always hoped he forgave me for sending him away, that he understood why. But now …"

Beatriz gasped. "How horrid. So malicious. Then I'm glad you left those terrible people, those spoiled kids. You were so good to stay with Mamá."

They crossed themselves and hung their heads in a silent prayer to their beloved mother lying at peace alongside their father in the Castro family cemetery, now inaccessible to them. The cruelties mounted.

"But I did get the rancho producing and selling cattle again," Juanita said. "Now the wretch will have to manage on his own. He has no idea how to operate a rancho."

"Stay with us," Beatriz said, putting her hand on Juanita's arm. "Help us translate any papers and speak at the hearings. We only know a few words, but your English is so good."

She hesitated. "I can't stay, *hermana*. I've got to find Joaquin. He'll wonder why I never responded to those letters."

"You had no choice. He looked too much like the *patron*. That jealous wife would have figured out her husband was Joaquin's father."

As a young teen, Joaquin had quickly grown taller than the other stable boys, his hair turning lighter with an auburn tint, until he looked like Malachy Brennan, the scoundrel who'd abandoned her after an impassioned love affair fifteen years before. In an especially heartless twist, Malachy had returned to buy their debt-ridden ranch, then kept her as ranch manager. Her confused mother refused to leave, insisting she be buried in the family plot on the hillside above the hacienda.

Fearing the greedy, ambitious wife would eventually detect the resemblance and toss them off the ranch with nothing, Juanita had married off her sisters, sent Joaquin away and tried to protect her mother. It had been excruciating watching Mamá fade in confusion as she struggled to wash kitchen pots and pull sheets taut, while Juanita rebuilt the ranch business for someone else's benefit.

"Juanita, you must stay to help with translating," Beatriz said, wiping her tear-stained face and straightening as if filled with new purpose. "You're crazy to even think about the diggings. Do you know what it's like? Cold and rainy or very hot. Rocky, hilly, no buildings. Rough living. You don't know if Joaquin is still there. I got one letter from Josefa. It sounded awful."

She rummaged through the bottom drawer of a small desk and handed a stained, worn paper to Juanita. No date or location was listed at the top.

Dearest sister Beatriz—
I miss you and life on the rancho and the Monterrey
bakery so much. Despite the hardships and losses we

*suffered losing Papá, losing the rancho to pay his debts,
and poor Juanita and Mamá turned into slaves for that
nasty family . . . it all pales in comparison to the difficulty
of life in the diggings.*

*The gold is mostly a dream, but since it is a dream you
see at least once a month, it's hard to let go of ambitions.
But don't be fooled, the gold and the dream are fleeting.*

*There are only men here. And they keep pouring in.
Sonorans and Chilenos, Black men from the southern
states, Yanquis from New York, Boston, Ohio and places
out East we've never heard of. There are Frenchmen and
Irishmen with red hair and beards. I've even seen some
Chinese. Remember the Kanakas we used to see on the
wharf in Monterrey? They're here too.*

*I've only met a few women in all these months
since we left home. A Native woman who cleaned in a
makeshift rooming house, another who washed and
sewed miners' clothes. One was a doctor's wife who
was not happy to be dragged along but the doctor was
very busy. One baked bread and pot pies filled with
vegetables and chicken when she could get them. When
she cooked, men lined up outside her tent for hours
after slogging in the rivers all day. Not much but
hardtack, salt pork and whiskey in the diggings.*

*There are no buildings, just canvas tents and mud
and more mud. You sure could build beautiful adobe
out of it all, but none here know how. They just prop up
canvas for shelter. The miners spend all day in the rivers,
panning, lifting rocks, scraping through the mud, then
digging some more. I've seen only a few tiny cabins. Since
miners move so often to grab another claim or find an*

untouched spot maybe canvas does make the most sense.

Anything you want costs at least five to twenty times the price you'd expect. And the drinking and gambling does not stop. Mamá and Abuela would be appalled by the volume of sinning here in mining country.

Oh, almost forgot to mention, Charles had a chance encounter with our nephew, Juanita's boy, in a doctor's tent. Goes by Joe now. Said he wasn't hitting any gold strikes and so might head to Mexico if another bad winter sickened him further. Charles thought he seemed sad from the losses—his grandfather, Castro Rancho, his mother, a life with horses. Still, he seemed determined to prove his manhood before returning to family, even declining Charles' offer to stay in our tent until he recovered. As Charles said, "At least that boy's got the touch with horses. He'll find his way even if he doesn't hit a pocket mine."

Truthfully, we're thinking about leaving the Bars after a bitter winter here. We both suffered with terrible illness. Sadly, I lost another one. My third miscarriage—just like our mother. Perhaps we'll go to Marysville to start a bakery. And a warehouse. The muleteers constantly carry tools and supplies throughout the diggings. I will write when I have more news.

Don't come here. Stay where you are on your beloved rancho with Agustín and the children. The rancho life is what our family knows and loves. The diggings are not fit for any man, or woman. Loving regards to Mamá and Juanita.

Your dearest sister,
Josefa

Juanita's eyes scanned the words, the handwriting, the stains on the worn paper trying to imagine Joaquin's daily life. Recovered from illness? Did he have a log hut or a canvas tent? Her mind whirled with images of him suffering through winter storms, or discovering a nugget the size of an acorn, or lying in the dirt afflicted with cholera or scurvy. She hurled a torrent of questions at her sister. When did this arrive? Do you have the envelope? Oh dear, she doesn't know about Mother's passing—how will we inform her? Why didn't you ever tell me you'd heard from Josefa and there was news of Joaquin?

Beatriz groaned in exasperation. "The envelope is gone. But why didn't I tell you about this letter? Come on. Mamá's rosary was the first time I'd seen you since my wedding. I know Mamá was terrified to go anywhere, how she faded under the new owners. But you could have brought her here to see us. Her own grand babies, hermana."

Juanita felt the accusation like a stab. Maybe she'd prevented them from being kicked off the rancho, but at what cost? Her son lost to her for almost two years. Her mother's mind diminished and now she was gone, too. And her sister, who she'd thought she'd set up for comfort by marrying her off to an established Dominguez, was now struggling to keep their land.

Beatriz did not stop the scorching harangue. "You want family, Juanita? You have to sacrifice for it—look what I'll have to do to help Agustín keep our ranch. Sell all of this." She stretched her hands out toward the once lavish library. "You're always so self-absorbed, so independent. Where's your duty to family? And don't you have any sympathy with our sister miscarrying again?"

"How dare you! Of course I do. And of course I have duty to family. I stayed with our ailing mother. I found you and

Josefa good husbands to get you out of that house. I protected our family."

"Maybe. But you sent your son away. Now you have nothing. The Alta California we knew, where we were raised, is gone. Extinguished. How are you going to be independent now?" Beatriz tossed the letter on the sofa and hustled out the door with an aggravated groan, leaving a disturbed Juanita alone in the cold library.

Later, after offering a mug of cinnamon-spiced chocolate in place of any dinner, a cold and mostly silent Beatriz escorted her sister to a guest bedroom. Juanita thanked her and refrained from asking about a diminished kitchen staff or absent vaqueros causing cows to wander. She would think more clearly in the morning. Her father had taught her to gather as much information as possible and analyze all options before making decisions. Had he done that when he started borrowing money to replace the cows lost to cattle plague? Her mind would not quiet.

When she heard fighting down the hall, she opened her door to listen.

"We need clothes to wear, dishes to eat off, Agustín. You can't empty this house completely."

"You've got to accept reality. We don't need so much. One pair of shoes is plenty. The Dons are not having grand parties now."

"Where you planning to sell my things? At the bordellos in San Francisco? I don't want my dresses worn by French prostitutes. I've heard what's going on up there."

"Come now, Bea. There are fashionable hotels which could use our china. Yerba Buena—I mean, San Francisco—is no longer a lonely *presidio*. It's become a city. With theaters and shows and wealthy men who demand finery."

"What about your clothes, your boots?" Beatriz's voice rose up an octave in anguish.

"Of course, with so many men we'll also sell my clothes, tools, and riding gear. And your sister needs to help. We can't feed another mouth without something in return. She can tutor the children in English since we had to send the yanqui tutor away. Translate. That'll be critical. Juanita can stay if she translates."

Juanita crept closer to catch every word, tiptoeing along the wide hallway, across the terracotta tiled floor.

"She wants to find Joaquin," Bea explained. "Up in the diggings."

"Completely ridiculous. She's a fool. How will she do that? There are thousands there now, coming in from all over. He could have left the gold area or died of cholera for all we know."

"What a horrible thing to say. Don't you understand her wanting to find him? What if it was one of the boys?"

"She sent him away. She's got to live with it."

"*Qué barbaridád*, Agustín! How ugly can you be?"

Juanita heard a crash. A glass or a vase? And furniture toppling onto the tiles.

"And you're not giving my dresses to prostitutes!" Beatriz yelled. "What would my mother say? They never should have secularized the Missions. Look what's happened ever since."

Juanita returned to her room. Sleep was impossible, so she opened the pale blue shutters and breathed in the cool night air, heavy with another rain on the way, and searched for stars, the moon. Any brightness. The ink-black cloud cover was pin holed with scattered twinkling stars but provided little consolation for what lay ahead. Clearly, Rancho Dominguez was not a solution to her predicament.

Beatriz would dutifully follow her husband's lead, even as she argued with him. True, Juanita spoke English, but could she really assist them with legalities in the new California? Proving their land title could take months, or years. Maybe it was selfish, but she had to find Joaquin, no matter how foolish an errand Agustín declared it.

However, her brother-in-law's idea to sell fine clothes and kitchenware in San Francisco for cash was smart. Luxury items from England, France, Boston, and Hong Kong were expensive. Those with means from the Mexican-era economy had the desired goods right here in Alta California. No need for the folks in Yerba Buena to buy off the wharf. And with her small collection of Mexican silver losing its value by the day, Juanita needed gold dust and the new US dollars if she were to have any chance of survival. The bartering economy was almost extinct.

Pale candlelight spilled out from a window below. Agustín still must be rummaging through his study. She pulled her dress back over her underclothes and headed down the colored *azulejo* stairs.

Agustín barely glanced up from his desk. His once handsome face betrayed the stress he was under; early age lines spread into his cheeks, wrinkles settled above his thick eyebrows, and his luxuriant black hair was thinning prematurely.

Juanita took a deep breath, then plunged in with her proposal. "Look, Agustín, I know you think I'm foolish for wanting to search for Joaquin, but I'm going up there one way or another. Before I leave, I'll translate proclamations, maps, whatever you need. And I'll take the first load of clothes up to San Francisco if you let me keep a share. I'll bring back gold dust and try for yanqui silver too."

Slamming down a book, Agustín gave an indignant sigh.

"San Francisco's no place for a respectable woman. Drunks and gamblers everywhere. Shacks for brothels and saloons with barely dressed French girls catcalling in the streets. Monte tables on every corner. You can't imagine."

Juanita started to protest. "I'm sure you exaggerate . . ."

He shook his head with a pained grimace. "When the ships come in, the wretched pour off with no civilized place to recover. There's disease. Filth in the streets. Men living in abandoned boats in the harbor. There's lines at the mail stop, bedraggled miners hoping for letters from Boston or some German town, others arguing as they send gold dust to loved ones they abandoned. There's men selling picks and axes. Others searching for flour and whiskey. There's no way to protect all that gold—just pistols and rifles and machetes."

"But—" Juanita tried to stop the tirade but Agustín continued, as if in a scornful trance.

"Steamships take these desperate, barely clothed souls up to Sacramento, Marysville, and Mudville—new towns just sprung up. You see destitute miners returning with nothing. Then there's those with nuggets and pouches full of the gold dust who just gamble and drink it away. It's a chaotic, inhumane place barely fit for any man, and certainly not a woman. You're not going there. You can stay here, translate documents and act as translator at the legal proceedings." He gestured to an old *plano* with drawings. "I know you've run a rancho, but I'm in charge here. No interfering in our affairs."

Juanita quickly swallowed her pride, trying to keep defensiveness out of her voice. She attempted to sound grateful. "I'll translate the plano for you but go see Don Guillermo Arnell. In Monterey. Ask his advice. He was a friend of our father's. Papá took me to his English classes and I had him tutor Joaquin before he closed his school. He's translating the state constitution for the yanquis. They respect him. But go before they send him off to the new capitol in San Jose or to that Washington out East."

Agustín, sullen, nodded slightly. "I'm sorry you heard me and Bea arguing. I've a duty to save my family's land. I can't keep the household the way she's accustomed. Being part of the US requires we operate differently. Can you get her to see that?"

"I'll do what I can," she said. "My sister understands her duty. My parents trained her well."

Early the next morning, perplexed, guilt ridden, Juanita went to the stables to think, deciding she could at least muck the milking stalls for her struggling family.

She knew her homeland was growing and was now the United States. But how different could it really be? How hard could it be to find an auburn-haired Joe who knew English and Spanish? Someone would know him. From Josefa's letter, she figured there was probably a Hanford Bakery in Marysville now. Her sister might know where Joaquin was these days.

She tossed oats in the feeding box as a treat for the horses, who looked as if they hadn't received much attention lately. Several cows mooed low, begging to be milked. She grabbed a pail and stool from the corner, guided one in the stall and got started. As she squeezed hard, then soft, to get the milk flowing, she mulled over the situation. Could she use these skills in this new California? She watched curious mules stroll by, smelling the oats, then heard clatters and stomping in the shed.

Mules! That was it. Josefa's letter said mule trains constantly transported food and equipment to the miners. She could become a muleteer and get supplies to the gold fields.

And Beatriz's dresses to San Francisco.

After the last cow was milked, she kicked the stool out, grabbed a pitchfork and threw hay out to the mules. She grunted as she scooped and tossed, sweating and wiping her brow frequently. To not be questioned, she'd have to go as a man. Much safer and far less noticeable.

Having lived and worked with men her entire life, Juanita was confident she knew how they acted, how they moved, and sometimes how they thought. She could even ride like a cowboy. Though her father never knew, as a teenager she'd pushed her thin dress up over a pair of men's pants she'd pilfered from the bunkhouse. It was an adjustment to steer the horse with one leg on each flank, but quite a reasonable way to ride.

She was confident she could impersonate a man and drive a mule train. Canela and three or four of Agustín's mules, loaded saddle bags and travel boxes with items from the Dominguez hacienda would be her path to San Francisco and then up to the Bars. Wherever that was.

"Oh, there you are," Beatriz said, coming around the corner of the shed just as Juanita chased the last cow out to the grassy field. "What are you doing?"

"I decided to be of some use. I'll translate Agustín's documents, but then, Bea, I need your help." Juanita offered to take clothes and valuables to the city, telling her she would return with the gold dust and silver before heading northeast to the mining area. "You keep most of the coins but let me keep a share, for the trouble. I need my own silver."

Beatriz laughed, scornfully. "What will you do up there? Wash clothes? They need cooks but none of us Castro girls ever learned. Why don't you go to Uncle Francisco or Aunt Beatriz? The relatives felt terrible about what happened to

Rancho Castro."

"No. After Papa died, not one aunt or uncle offered to help with the debts. It was me alone. I'm going one way or the other." Juanita paced through the stalls.

Beatriz, frustration twisting her voice, said, "You're completely *loca*." Then she kicked the milk bucket over, steaming white liquid spilling into the straw, stomped out of the shed and up the hill behind the great house.

Stunned, Juanita sat down hard on the milking stool. She'd tried honesty with both Beatriz and Agustín, her only remaining family, but to no avail. Now, she felt forced to plan and go, alone, without their knowledge. She just knew Joaquin was out there. She had to find him.

After two nights of surreptitiously collecting fine dresses, silver cutlery, china place settings, men's and women's shoes, small blacksmith tools and even a few hats, Juanita made final preparations to leave. Beatriz had not spoken to her since the milk shed spat, forcing Juanita to eat alone or with the Native servants, which was convenient for packing up Dominguez family items without their knowledge.

Knowing more than a few phrases in the local Rumsien Ohlone language, Juanita was polite, speaking the servants' native tongue to keep them distracted from her real purpose. Her grandmother had always treated the Natives poorly, but, in contrast, her mother had admonished the three sisters to treat their workers with respect. "Thankfully we brought them to God," her mother would say, "but do be sensitive to what a change the Spanish arrival was for them. And always be a Christian model for them to follow." Juanita did not allow herself to wonder what her religious mother would think of her now, planning to sell her sister's belongings in secret and disguising herself as a male muleteer.

A Native servant had told her Agustín was riding to Monterey to meet with Don Guillermo Arnell today, just as she'd suggested, so it was time to leave. She loaded the saddlebags and satchels to the brim, rolling clothing tightly and wrapping tools, silverware and china plates between the fabric. She had selected four mules, along with Canela, the mare she'd stolen when she fled the Seven Hills Ranch. She was a thief already. And stealing a man's horse was the biggest sin of all. Borrowing Agustín's mules, and loading up clothing and cutlery without their permission, was just another step toward the hell her mother, and the priests, had described in florid detail.

After sealing the lid on each travel box, Juanita tiptoed into the storage area off the blacksmith shop where her brother-in-law stashed his saddles and bridles, hoof tools and whips, chaps and *reata*, the long, coiled leather for roping cattle. She searched the gear for a regular saddle, leaving the side saddle in exchange. Then she stuffed a machete under a leather strap and a pistol in her bag.

She chopped her long tresses with sheep shears, then tucked her crudely cut shoulder-length hair up under a borrowed cowboy sombrero. She wore trousers cinched with a leather belt and a man's poncho, the style vaqueros used in the coldest months. She kept the shirt loose; good thing years of work and sadness at her family's losses had shrunk her once voluptuous breasts and slimmed her formerly curvy waist. She practiced a man's swagger and reminded herself to use a full arm to shake hands, deepen her voice if she had to speak. But say little. Mostly just nod.

Juanita didn't expect anyone to ask but felt it important to have a story in mind regarding her search. She'd say she was looking for Joe, her nephew, although she had no idea what last name he was using. When she'd sent her son away from the rancho at fifteen, she'd just told him to use only English and become Joe, an American. If asked, she'd report the fictitious nephew's parents had died, leaving land near San Jose which might have quicksilver on it, and she had to tell him about his inheritance. That sounded believable.

When the kitchen was empty of Native workers, Juanita left a letter on the table.

Dear Beatriz and Agustín—
I translated the planos and map and left them on your library desk. I'm traveling to San Francisco to sell some of your dresses and shoes, china and tools. I will return in a week with the gold dust and US silver dollars. I've borrowed several mules.

When I return, I would like a small portion of the proceeds and I'd like to borrow a mule or two. I will then be off to the gold diggings to locate Joaquin.

I need to find him before he gets dangerously ill or abandons gold mining for Mexico, where it will be extremely difficult to find him.

Beatriz, for this first round of selling, I was careful to take only the dresses collecting dust in your armoire, and the china and cutlery you don't use every day, since there are currently no fandangos planned.

I am sorry for any consternation my actions may cause. I am doing this to assist you with the Land Commission and to raise some funds for myself, since I have nothing.

> *I do not want to be a burden and will take my
> leave soon after returning to Rancho Dominguez with
> the proceeds.*

> *Juanita*

Since the mules carried a heavy burden, more than the usual saddle bags and boxes, Juanita kept Canela to a slow amble. She also carried dried meat and dried fruits, a gourd of water and a flask of whiskey; while she had not developed a taste for the strong spirit, it completed her disguise.

What had she become, this Juanita dressed as a man in the new California? A traitor to her sister and brother-in-law? She'd return with their funds, but she was borrowing their mules, selling clothes and household items without their knowledge or permission. Was she turning her back on her family and heritage? Or was she being a savvy survivor in the new normal?

As she rode off as Juan the muleteer, likely facing dangers she could not even fathom, shame dripped into her sadness, mixing into a toxic compote. It would take a lot to get back into the good graces of her sister, who hadn't wanted to sell anything, and Agustín, who didn't think the city or gold mines suitable for a woman.

She traveled until almost dark, then stopped at the Pico family's house down a pine tree–bordered lane. She hitched the animals to a rail and called out to the two-story adobe-and-wood house with glassed windows framed by forest-green shutters. Remember, you're a humble muleteer stopping by, she told herself, albeit one with a family connection. She planned to present herself as a Dominguez relative.

A Native servant opened the kitchen door but quickly

disappeared. A stern-looking older man greeted her and listened to the family names.

"You're an Argüello? We know them from Mission San Diego days. You can stay in the milking stalls with your horse and mules."

He closed the door. No conversation or offer of a warm meal included. As Juanita returned to the animals, she heard window shutters pulled closed tightly. Sure wasn't the hospitality of the old days. She shook her head at the changed landscape. But was she so innocent herself?

She tied the animals in the covered stalls and settled under a *poncho* in the corner, where she nibbled a little dried beef and swallowed sips of water from the gourd. Then she lay her head down on a straw pillow and contemplated her circumstances until exhaustion consumed her. Her legs were sore from the new riding style. She drifted off.

Ssssssss, rattatat, hissssss.

Canela snorted. The mules stomped. Suddenly, she startled awake. What? There it was again, a hissing, past the mules. She got to her knees, slowly, then up to her feet, and tiptoed over to the machete in its saddle holster.

Hissss, rattatat, sissss . . . the straw stirred. She muttered calm words to the jittery animals as she crept closer.

Riding hills and trails, valleys and riverbeds, there were always snakes. Rattlers, threatening. Garter snakes, harmless. In their habitat, she let them all be. But in the milking stall, with her horse and mules spooked, there was only one action to take. When the straw rustled, she took three quick steps forward, then flashed the machete down, chopping off the snake's head. Her heart pounding, she pushed aside the loose hay and saw the body. Right decision—it was a rattler.

What other dangers lay in the days ahead? It could be a long week before returning to Rancho Dominguez with a stash of silver.

To Mission Dolores

January 1850

Juanita woke in the straw with the insides of her legs chafed and aching, unaccustomed to riding like a man. She fed Canela and the mules handfuls of hay—yet another thing she was stealing—before heading to San Francisco's Mission Dolores, where she figured she could convince an aging priest in a distressed church to exchange shelter for labor.

The Mission dairy had lost Native workers since secularization, the war and gold fever. She knew well these beleaguered priests burdened with caring for a dying system, remembering her painful exile in the decrepit Mission Santa Barbara, pregnant and treated as the lowliest domestic at the order of her parents. Her experience could be useful now, although it was not one she relished repeating as her mind had attempted to gauze over that torturous year. Alone, freezing in a tiny cell, she'd done little but scrub floors and cast iron skillets, never receiving word on whether her father would forgive her straying with the handsome Irish woodworker and accept her back into the family.

Fortunately, she and baby Joaquin were welcomed home to Rancho Castro with the understanding she would help manage the ranch, raise her son and become obedient and devout. She complied. Now, with Californio ranching days fading into a Mexican past, Juanita was in unknown territory. But she knew Mission priests.

The mules moved slowly through the valley, the endless verdant hills on either side dotted with ancient oaks. When the little mule train stopped for a midday rest by one of the creeks, she scratched her arms and neck. Fleas in the milking stall had bitten all night and she was covered in red welts. At least the pants protected her legs, she thought, as she absently leaned down to scratch an ankle bite.

When they continued northward, a breeze caught the grasses and sycamores along the creeks. As she approached the tail end of the bay, the wind strengthened, blowing her poncho and flapping the *sarapes* over the mules' pack boxes. To the west, puffed, cottony fog rested on the ridge line then sailed down the slope toward the valley floor. A chilly dampness coated them. She pushed the mules on.

As the afternoon sun ebbed, the hills descended into the Mission's fields and *potreros* for the dairy cows. It grew swampy, with creeks and large sand dunes poking through the marsh. Birds squawked and squalled overhead, as if announcing their arrival. Willows swayed in greeting as the ragtag group finally arrived at the Mission Dolores courtyard.

Juanita tied up the animals, unbuckled the heaviest mule boxes and went inside, where a mildew smell greeted her as she clomped her boots on the floor, leaving a trail of mud and sand on the sanctuary bricks. Oh no, I need to clean the floor, she thought automatically, then remembered she was a man. Her mother used to admonish vaqueros who entered the house without cleaning their boots. Perfect for her disguise.

She went looking for the padre, her legs sorer than ever. How long until she'd get used to the male saddle? An elderly priest in a threadbare robe, holes at the hem, frayed rope belting the fabric, emerged, wiping his mouth and blinking repeatedly.

"May I help you, *muchacho*?" he asked, a slight slur to his speech.

He's a bit drunk already and it's not even dark yet she noted. Regardless, she immediately pulled out her most obsequious Spanish—appropriate for an important church leader—explaining she needed a place to stay, would sleep in the paddock with her animals and trade milking and cleaning stalls for the hospitality.

"Oh, you're a Californio. I'm Father Mateo," the priest mumbled. "Of course, you can stay, young man. I'm tired of all the yanquis and my English is not so good. Stay in the empty stall by the herb garden," he gestured, each word more slurred than the last. "Get your mules watered, then come eat with me. I could use Spanish conversation." Then he ambled off toward the living quarters, mumbling to himself. No notice of the muddied floor.

At the meager supper of rice and beans topped with an egg and slice of cheese, Juanita questioned the priest on how to sell her wares in San Francisco. He never answered, just said she could stay as long as she wanted and work as a cowhand. Most Native vaqueros had left long ago and he only had one novice priest. While he frequently housed Sonorans and Californios if they committed to two weeks of work, they usually ran off to the mines before the fortnight was complete. There were always more chores than workers.

He was delighted to converse in Spanish. Sure, a few Californios passed through, but mostly it was yanquis jumping off the boats or dragging in on the wagons. And they weren't good Catholics! San Francisco had become a city of sinners, full of brothels, saloons, and gambling houses, but he hoped to purify them, get them back to the church.

"Are you holding mass, Father?"

"Well, no, but I can do confession. There's no mass without a collection plate or parishioner donations. Everyone wants to get rich, not give to the church! Plus, all these migrants are Protestants, from the East, from European countries." He laughed halfheartedly as he took a sip of wine. "The French prostitutes sure aren't coming to confession!"

After thanking God for the dairy and gardens, he explained they sold milk, butter, cheese and vegetables to the city's vendors. "The novice and I can't do all this alone." But there were a few miners now returning from the diggings. "It's not easy up there. Many come back with empty pockets. Couple of 'em gulped down the Mission milk like it was gold itself the minute they rode in. They don't all have dust or nuggets and need a way to make an honest living. Awful lot of that monte gambling 'round here. What's your name again? Jose? Got any skills for them rivers? Know how to pan?"

"It's Juan," Juanita explained as the priest's eyelids got heavier, "And I don't plan on panning for gold. I have things to sell in San Francisco. Clothes. Boots. Where's the best place to do that?"

"Smart man," Father Mateo said. "A whole lot of sinners 'round here, Jose. But they gotta eat too. So keeps us in the gold dust, and them new coins comin' in. You can help with deliveries but don't stop at the monte tables. I don't take to gamblers staying at the Mission. You hear?"

After leaving Father Mateo's supper, where she'd gathered little information, Juanita ventured out to explore the Mission's neighborhood. It felt good to stretch after two days riding in the unfamiliar style. The soreness reminded her to walk like a man. She pulled her hat low over her eyes and kept her belted pants and shirt loose.

Juanita had always been curious, a trait which led her into childhood mischief but also motivated her to study her father's atlases and history books. Her grandmother had encouraged the tendency, including her on trade expeditions and at dinners with sea captains and scientific explorers at Rancho Castro's famous long redwood table. But people were no longer just passing through Alta California. They were building homes and businesses.

Crude wooden structures bearing saloon signs were clustered alongside the muddy road. No glass anywhere, only shutters or cloth covering the windows. Tents and canvas tarps lined the sand dunes, drooping in the heavy mist. Where was the adobe? Why didn't they build with mud bricks like her countrymen built the missions and presidios? Although almost abandoned, the Mission Dolores sanctuary was still standing at eighty years old.

She crept on, aiming for the raucous noise in the distance. Red, hand-painted lettering announced the Hotel Potrero. A young Native woman, dark hair tied with a faded red velvet ribbon with red lips to match, called out from the hotel doorway in broken Spanish.

"Need a place to stay? We got rooms here, mister," she called. "Come in out of the fog, honey. We'll warm you up right quick."

Juanita waved her whole arm to signal no, rather than finger-wag like a woman.

Candlelight was spilling through cracks in a neighboring building's slats. More red letters announced *"Monte, Faro Mesas Aqui!"* with *Here* and *Ici* painted underneath the Aqui.

Yells and laughter, catcalls and grumbles, shouts and clattering furniture slipped through the thin pine boards. She heard hands banging tables, dealers shouting instructions, patrons cursing in multiple languages, and coins clinking—the sound of gambling.

Though she'd heard about gambling's evils from her parents and priests all her thirty-seven years, Juanita had never been to the monte or faro tables. She was determined to see the sinning for herself.

The second she stepped inside a disheveled woman with bare shoulders and hitched-up skirts approached. Her slurred words were worse than Father Mateo's and Juanita smelled whiskey on her breath. She shook her head and the woman stumbled off. Not a single other woman was visible in the crowd.

Candle smoke mixed with the sour tang of weak beer, sweat, and leather. Crude canvas window coverings kept out the cold. Feeling slightly dizzy, she pushed a makeshift curtain aside to breathe in chilly air.

Men bustled across eight pine tables, pushing at each other, throwing cards, yelling, swilling a drink, pounding gold dust pouches on the table. It was so loud she could not have had a conversation even if she'd wanted one—which she certainly did not. But Juanita was fascinated.

She'd been to fandangos where hundreds of Mexicans danced and sang, drank and smoked all through the night. But those had included women and fine gentlemen proud of their respectability and community standing. There was a limit to how wild fandangos got. Debauchery was discouraged.

This, however, was a swarm of men, body heat, and alcohol-fueled competition. She'd never experienced so many men in one place with no women present, and the tension and combativeness only heightened as the evening wore on. Gotta learn to act this way to be a convincing man, she told herself.

Juanita watched for an hour, ordering a whiskey with one of her sister's Pioneer Coins to not look out of place, and shaking her head when invited to play. Clearly, there were huge amounts of gold dust and US silver changing hands in the saloon. Yet the chaotic gambling hall did not look like a market for her fine dishes, cutlery, hats, or ranch tools. Maybe her brother-in-law was wrong about selling fine things in the city. Where were the women who would want her sister's silk dresses?

When she returned to the Mission yard to arrange a stall for the animals and a place to sleep, Father Mateo's novice was calling for "Jose" through the paddocks.

"The padre wants you to come back in for a brandy. He's lonely for Californios and Spanish. He's worried you were out gambling. Did you win any of those silver half dollars?"

"Don't gamble. And it's Juan," was all Juanita managed to utter. She wanted to rest and focus on what was next but she needed this priest's knowledge and access to anyone with gold nuggets to buy her wares.

Thankfully, Father Mateo was more alert than he had been at dinner. When she entered his simple sitting area, he had two small glasses and a brandy bottle waiting.

"You out at the monte tables?"

"Just getting acquainted with the neighborhood, *Padre*. I don't gamble. I'm here to sell fine clothes. Know where I can find customers? Not around here, I don't think."

"You'll see the true San Francisco soon enough. Maybe next week go down to the wharves but watch out for cheats and thieves and liars. They're everywhere. But I need you working here first."

Father Mateo began reminiscing about times before the gold seekers flooded in, not allowing her to make it a conversation. She was simply an audience for his loneliness and misery.

". . . had a big funeral for Leidesdorff before the gold fever. The whole city came to the Mission for it, did a full mass— must have been four hundred here. He built the City Hotel, you know that? And from the West Indies, imagine? Yes, it was a fine time, before the gold madness. Jose, my friend, this city's been declining ever since.

"We've got some Catholics coming in now, but them Irish and French aren't coming to Mass. They've got no morals, just looking to get rich quick. Why, they even had a horse race here, out in the fields behind the Mission. Leidesdorff put everyone up to it. Now a couple of them rich fellows want a racetrack. More gambling. The devil's games they play in those saloons."

Fearing he'd go on all night, Juanita thanked him for the brandy and said she'd see him in the morning after milking time. As she was walking out, she tried for one more piece of information.

"Father Mateo. I so appreciate your hospitality. You know so much about San Francisco. I'm looking for some family members. Would someone in San Francisco know a bakery couple, the Castro-Hanfords? Perhaps you knew my uncle, Pedro Castro? Many travelers stopped at his ranch in the time before . . ."

"Hmm, sounds familiar. Oh yes, I remember the name. Didn't he lose it all, his rancho, to some Irishman? What was it, gambling debts? Such a loss and to a yanqui. We Californios, we're disappearing. The Americans don't want us around, but they sure want our land."

Juanita grabbed the door frame to steady herself, horrified to hear such a tale about her hardworking, religious, serious father who had never gambled a day in his life. And from a priest. The Castro name had always been respected, one to carry with pride.

"No, it was the cows, Padre. They got sick, the cattle plague. Pedro Castro did not gamble."

But the padre didn't hear her in his brandy-fueled haze as he meandered to his cell for the night.

Juanita milked cows, cleared manure, and weeded winter vegetables for several days before the Padre released her to explore the wharf and heart of the new city. He advised leaving her horse as someone would steal it. Better to take a mule or walk.

"No one steals horses, Padre." She swallowed the bitter irony.

"They do now. This is not your Alta California. The Dons are not in charge. These greedy foreigners might fancy your mare as a quick ride to the diggings. The ones who come in on the wagons are in decent shape, if they don't get the cholera or chopped up by Indians. They usually got a mule. But the ones off those ships—they're sickly, desperate. Your horse would be a lucky find."

Juanita decided to walk. She carried three saddlebags stuffed with men's trousers and shirts, shoes and tools, and threw in a silk scarf and an elegant slip to show off the women's wear. Though she did wonder if Father Mateo was eyeing Canela for himself or to sell to a local hotel owner or gambler. Or those racetrack people.

Carrying the heavy saddlebags, her pants rubbing her thighs, she slowly walked the three miles to the commercial district through sand and mud. While still strange to be in disguise, it was easier to slog down the rough track in trousers than in her customary long dress. As she traipsed toward the bay, she could smell the briny air.

Suddenly, her right leg disappeared into a sinkhole. She yanked hard and her foot came out with no boot. Arms up to her elbows in the morass of silt, salt water and sand, she finally retrieved it.

As she hobbled toward the water's edge to wash out the filthy shoe, a horrific smell hit her—blood and offal. The water line was red with animal debris, pieces of hair, fat and flesh floating in the foam. What was this? She looked for a clean patch of water and saw corralled cows alongside a shed in the distance. A slaughterhouse built right on the water, likely so the tide would clean out the waste. Though she was far from squeamish, she thought this arrangement, while clever, might turn a few stomachs of those travelling the Mission Road.

Suddenly, a Chinese man approached, resembling sketches in books in her father's library. She knew Kanakas from the ships docked in Monterey and she'd traded with tall Russians with flowing beards and trappers from French Canadian northern territories. She'd even fallen in love with a reddish-haired Irishman and welcomed pale sea captains from Dover and South Hampton at her father's table. But a Chinese . . . never did she imagine she'd one day meet someone from such a remote land here in Alta California.

Trying not to stare, she cleared her throat and nodded to the man with a welcome in Spanish and then English. He had a long black braid and wore a wide-brimmed hat, and a frayed produce basket hung on his back. He didn't stoop from a heavy load so perhaps he was returning from selling Father Mateo's produce at the wharf. This man would know the best market in San Francisco.

He smiled at her greeting, but raised his shoulders in confusion, clearly not understanding either language. Juanita smiled, thanked him and walked on.

Where had he come from? Off a ship? Were there more Chinese here? Wait, her sister had written something about Chinese miners in that letter from gold country. It must be hard to get along without understanding the two main languages. Then again, the Natives had done it for generations. Surprises and mysteries continued.

As she strode on, Juanita decided she'd need to freshen the bargaining skills she'd learned from her grandmother. Abuela Quina had repeatedly reminded her many grandchildren that it was important to always watch for thieves and cheats and assume everyone is trying to steal from you. Strike a hard, but fair, bargain—you must be sure to give something, too. No one would trade with you if you offered up poor quality or didn't honor your commitments. What would Abuela think of this new California? Perhaps it was best her grandmother had passed away before so many overwhelming changes transformed the land she had settled.

A group of Natives approached, heading toward Mission Dolores, and she asked in Spanish where men's clothes were sold. They pointed down the trail and mentioned the Men's Emporium near the docks. Finally, the Mission Road ended at a swampy waterline with a wharf area, hills and enormous sand dunes facing the bay's edge.

A forest of tall ship masts ribboned the shoreline and extended, row upon row, into the harbor. In the distance, past the tangle of sails and timber, several islands sprouted up through the currents.

Canvas tents, browned with mud, spilled down the slopes. She could see pine-board shanties barely held together with rusting nails, straw and mud patching the gaps, and crude outhouses leaking open sewage into the road. Every corner had a saloon or a gambling hall. Dry goods stores, boarding houses, and tent-covered mess tables lined each street between the bars. As in the Mission neighborhood, she marveled at the absence of any stable structures. It was as if playful children had thrown together an encampment of sticks and cloth, but these were grown men living and working and drinking.

Most shocking was the mass of people. Men of every size, ethnicity, and age moved in a frenetic dance where the only steps were acquire, spend, gamble, and drink. Lawlessness permeated the atmosphere. Teenage boys scraped through the mud in front of facades labeled Wells, Fargo & Co. and City Hotel and US Mail, searching for a golden sparkle. Pistols and knives hung from most every belt, and grime coated most every man. Juanita couldn't help but note all the untrimmed beards and sweat-soaked hats.

She saw Kanakas from the ships in Monterey, Mexicans from the Sonoran mines and southern provinces, Chinese with thin braids, yanquis with yellow, red, or dark hair, a few Black men from the islands or the southern states, pale faces from Cornwall and France, joking Irish, Californio cowboys with sarapes, and Natives in sarapes pretending to be Californios.

And the noise was deafening, nothing like the tranquility on her former ranch, thousands of grassland acres inhabited by cattle and a few vaqueros, rabbits, and elk, bears, wild boar. The old Spanish Presidio's adobe fort sat quietly on the hill above it all, as if an audience watching the cacophony and chaos below.

This mess was it? Sleepy Yerba Buena of a few hundred sea merchants and Mexican soldiers had transformed over just a few months into Gold Fever San Francisco, a mass of thousands expelling noise and stench, swirling in greed, desperation and excess. Juanita pulled the poncho up over her nose to block the smell of marine air mixed with manure and wet sand, damp wool and leather, horse and human sweat—a uniquely San Francisco stink.

Gold Fever San Francisco

January 1850

In awe, Juanita wandered down the path, boot squishing, stepping carefully to avoid rocks, manure and sink holes. She dodged the hawkers down Market Street and headed toward the ships crowding the wharf. Then she turned and looked back, transfixed by the sheer volume of people, tents, and shacks lining the hills. She'd never imagined anything like it, nor read of such a place in her father's history and geography books.

As a child she'd visited Santa Barbara with her grandmother when it was just a cluster of adobes circling the Mission. Monterey remained small, and mostly abandoned, during the gold strikes and US takeover. This bigger port was nothing like sketches and descriptions she'd read of great cities like Boston and New York, Paris and London. This conglomeration of humanity in disorganized chaos was no longer a town, not really a city, and certainly not grand.

Juanita pushed through the crowd and kept her head down to avoid the saloon and card-game barkers, marveling that all manner of entertainment was available in the middle of the day. As she explored the crudely cut streets, she spied open fires with men cooking under tarps or wooden overhangs. Remembering her mother's strict rules—cooking exclusively in the adobe fireplace, iron pots and utensils only—these thrown-together kitchens looked ripe for fires. Men sat at long pine boards and rough-cut benches eating whatever the cook served. She peeked into boarding houses and saw rows of wood slats, some empty and others with men passed out in all their clothes. Men were everywhere.

Outside one saloon, the Pioneer, a crowd gathered as the barker yelled, "French girls just in off the *Sea Serpent*! One ounce entry!" Ah, so the girls were in the saloons. Near the water, in sloppy structures no more substantial than ranch milking stalls, she saw prostitutes pushing curtains aside to invite men in.

She finally made it to the docks, where the schooners and frigates were either bursting or sat empty and now used for storage, a hotel, or saloon. Recent arrivals brimmed with kegs of whiskey and burlap sacks of rice, beans or flour. Workers unloaded timber and bricks too. Mules and men hauled over-loaded wagons up the endless hills.

While Juanita found the bustling metropolis fascinating, it was also overwhelming. Too many people. She was used to wide stretches of unpopulated land filled with circling hawks and deer grazing in the shade of sycamores and black oaks. As a teenager, she'd enjoyed the days when she could ride from sunup to dusk and never see another soul, checking in with her family only at the supper table. San Francisco was the complete opposite.

She had no intention of staying in this place longer than necessary. She'd collect as much gold dust and as many coins as she could accumulate and then move out of this human swamp. Plus, she'd promised Beatriz she'd return with the silver in a week. Only a few days left to sell everything. She continued exploring.

Small shops lined the road offering blankets, sarapes, boots and pants. An assay office—the freshly timbered front still pink and oozing amber sap—rose up next to a hand-lettered sign reading "Montgomery Street."

"How much you want for those saddlebags, *hombre*?" shouted a shopkeeper. "Ain't none in town these days, so I could give you several ounces for 'em."

"Not for sale," she called, enunciating her English, striding to the assay office. A guard with a rifle glared as she walked in. Startled at hissing behind her, she turned to see a Californio wearing thick gloves dangling a twisting rattlesnake. Those shoving toward the front of the line cleared instantaneously, as if by magic. She waited, watching the cowboy hurry to the back and throw the snake into a small black safe.

Once she reached the counter, the assay officer laughed at her Mexican silver.

"Where'd you get those coins? You a Californio? Well, ain't you out of luck. Where's your pouch of gold dust? Got any nuggets?" She shrugged.

"How will you get the rattler out of there?" she asked, nodding to the safe.

"When the Wells driver's ready to haul gold to Boston, we got our ways. Can't help you, man. Next!" he called out to the fidgety crowd.

"Where's the Men's Emporium?" she asked the miners jostling to stay in line. Most shook their heads but one pointed up the hill.

As she walked on, she wondered how she would ever find Joaquin in the pandemonium. No one seemed to sit still in this city. She promised herself from now on she'd ask every single person she talked to if they'd met a tall, seventeen-year-old auburn-haired Joe who said he was from near Monterey, or maybe Pueblo San Jose.

Finally, there it was. Men's Emporium. This time, the shopkeeper, short, balding, smelling like sweat and moth balls, did not laugh as she opened her bags. His greedy eyes stretched into thin slits and he scowled at each item, turning it over and over, rubbing the fabric with callused thumb and forefinger.

"Give you twenty ounces for the whole lot," he said, continuing to stroke the merchandise.

After grunting a "no," she mentioned the prices she'd seen advertised at the general store over on Kearny.

He lined it all up, counted the pieces, turning each one again.

"This is solid fabric woven in Mexico, fine leather made here in Alta California. What are you getting off the ships?" Juanita extolled the quality of each item just like she'd watched her grandmother do.

"Fine, fifty ounces, but that's it. Got any more where this came from?"

"Yes. And I also have fine women's clothes. From the beautiful señoritas on the El Camino, from the wealthiest Californio ranchos. Fine china too. Know who'd want them? A good hotel maybe?"

"Not much call for feminine finery here. Not too many fancy ladies 'round. Head over to Washerwomen's Lagoon and ask. Lotta ladies in town work there. Well, besides in the cribs. And just 'cause you got good product, here's a copy of *The Daily Alta California*. Might see some ads to help you out. Come back with more men's apparel and I'll take it."

"Thank you, sir. And with my dust, I'll take a pocket scale and pouch. You have an extra one?"

While he rustled around behind the counter looking for a scale, she flipped open the newspaper, scanning the headlines and advertisements. One ad, "Photographer to the Miners," caught her eye, especially since it listed a woman's name.

"Maybe some of the ladies want their picture taken too," she mused. "Might want a nice dress for the daguerreotype."

He gave her a skeptical look. "Huh? None of those ladies 'round here. Some of the men sit before they go up to the diggings. It's expensive but you know, the novelty and all. Probably they got girls back in Boston or Ohio. Don't think they want any San Francisco ladies in those pictures!" he said, laughing at his own joke.

She was grateful to the gruff man who knew fine cloth and leather. She'd bring him the remaining men's apparel. Off to find Washerwoman's Lagoon. She needed to sell the dresses quickly. Fifty ounces of gold dust wouldn't go far, and she needed the new American silver too.

Juanita strolled the shoreline, passing ships turned into saloons and storehouses and hotels made from ship's masts, hoping she could get to Washerwoman's Lagoon without having to climb the hill to the west. A mail steamship was in the process of docking. Men crowded the wharf, grabbing at crates of letters, but the postmaster ordered his crew to carry overflowing boxes to pushcarts and horse-drawn wagons as guards with batons threatened the hordes if they touched an envelope.

"Two days. Give us two days to sort!" he shouted. "Y'all want mail from your sweethearts, letters from your mamas, then line up at the postal tent in two days. No line, no letters. Got it?"

Finally, Juanita reached a lagoon where several dozen women were scrubbing clothes at the swampy water's edge. Sheets and shirts, petticoats and blouses lay spread atop the border brush to dry. Most of the women were young, but a few had motherly postures. The poorer Californios wore colorful Mexican blouses and ribboned braids, while Natives were easy to spot with their jet-black hair and round faces. But the majority were white yanquis or the French girls favored by the entertainment halls.

As she approached, she heard hissing. A tall woman with tangled chestnut hair was walking toward Juanita and shouting in a strong Scottish brogue. "Go on! No men allowed. No dirty girls here. Just dirty clothes." The women collapsed in laughter.

Juanita gestured she understood, then walked backward several steps, searching for a way into this closed group. Off to the swamp's border, she spied a girl with shining red hair, alone. Juanita waited until the other women lost interest. Once they began to gossip and laugh again, she cautiously approached the girl.

"Miss? I've got some fine ladies dresses," she said, making her voice as deep as possible. "Know anyone who'd like to buy?"

The girl ignored her at first, then glanced over at the others. "Prove it," she said under her breath when she turned back. "I wanna see 'em. Wait over the hill 'til I'm done."

Juanita did as requested. After sitting an hour or more staring out at the ship-filled bay, Juanita felt someone approach. The redhead stood over her casting a shadow.

"Okay. Whatcha got?" she asked, hip cocked to one side to balance a pile of wet blouses and petticoats.

"Well, can you pay, miss?"

"Nah, not me. But my mistress can. I work for Miss Elizabeth Platt at the Parlour House Hotel, spelled with a 'U,' like in London—finest place in town. Them washer ladies don't like me 'cause I board there, too. Come see me tonight. You seem refined. That's what Miss Platt calls it. She don't just let anyone in. What's your name?"

"Juan." Juanita reached into her saddlebag and pulled out the silk petticoat and scarf. Good thing she'd thrown them in before leaving the Mission. The girl set her heavy washing down on the grass. She grabbed the underwear and felt the silk, caressed the fabric and eyed the lace border.

"Look, I've got some fine china and silver cutlery, too," Juanita said. "Would Miss Platt be interested?"

"Yes, sir. She might be. She's always sayin' she wants to bring in opera and singin' stars from Paris and London. We've parlor Sundays and she wants us lookin' elegant. She's gonna have dinner parties too. Takes too long to get quality from Boston, she says." She continued to feel the silk, rubbing it along her fair cheek, touching it to her freckled nose. "She don't usually have them silver coins the Custom House demands for merchandise off them ships so she's a good trader." She stopped suddenly. Thinking she'd said too much?

"Take the petticoat to your mistress and here's some gold dust for your trouble," Juanita said. "You tell her there's more coming when I meet her. If you get me in, I'll pay you another ounce."

The girl looked at the pouch and scoffed. "Mister, I can make more in one night just keepin' a miner company at the monte table. While he looks at me, nothin' else, you understand?"

Juanita relented and measured and added another pinch.

"Meet me three days from now, after I do the next washin',

and I'll let ya know if she's interested. Bring dresses and dishes too, or you won't get no further," the girl said. "Down at the square. Don' come to the lagoon. Them ladies don't like men around. Only place where girls can talk freely, get a break from the constant staring, the grabbing."

Juanita's curiosity got the best of her. "Where are they all from? I recognize a few Natives and Californios like myself, but the rest . . ." She clamped her mouth shut as she realized most men would never ask such a question.

Thankfully, the girl didn't seem to notice. "Some came with husbands who ran off for the gold. A few are church ladies who came to civilize the town. Couple a French girls used to be in my trade but got tired of workin' every night. So many drunks. Some men get violent when they can't, you know, perform. Some decided being a washerwoman for a hotel or boarding house was better. Them church ladies don't like my kind, but they let me have a spot at the lagoon."

Juanita nodded with a slight tip of her hat. "What's your name, Miss?"

"Lizzie to you, Mister Juan." She gathered up her wash and turned down the grassy hill, her waving tresses streaming behind her in the breeze, her dress stained down the right side from the dripping wet bundle.

Juanita's return to the Mission was easier with empty saddlebags. But she was drained from the long walk, the crush of humanity, and the overwhelming foreignness of a place she thought she knew. It was a much bigger, more complicated city than she'd expected. How long would it take to sell everything and get out of San Francisco? Three days just to meet a possible buyer? There were so many strangers here. She was from a world where everyone knew each other, at least by reputation if nothing else.

After checking on the animals, she crawled back into her Mission stall, nibbled her dried beef, fluffed the straw to check for snakes and promptly fell asleep. She dreamed she was sitting with her mother at the enormous redwood table her father had crafted for the family and their many guests. Her mother was young and beautiful and sparkling like sun on water—but then she turned old and haggard and began yelling at Juanita, calling her evil for pretending to be a man, threatening she'd burn in hell for lying to a priest, and for betraying Beatriz. Suddenly, the figure transformed into Agustín, loudly prodding, "Where's my money? Where's the translation? You're a traitor to all the Castro ancestors!"

Juanita woke, feeling nauseated. She brushed away her straw blanket and stood up to shake off the dream and step out to gaze at the night. A tiny sliver of moon twinkled in the black sky above her and the hobbled cows in the paddock, but the sight did nothing to calm her queasiness. How could she ever return to Beatriz's quickly with the silver and gold dust she'd promised?

The Parlour House Hotel

January 1850

Three days later, after presenting silks and a taffeta dress, she'd handed Lizzie another pouch of gold dust and finally had an appointment to meet the hotel's proprietress.

Lizzie stopped at a ramshackle pine door with "Boarding House/Hotel" painted on the cross beam. After Lizzie's coded knock, a large Black man answered and escorted them into a narrow alcove, pointing to a shallow basin in which Lizzie rinsed her shoes. As she soaked the mud off her boots, Juanita peered across the atrium and noted there was an entire building hidden behind the crude facade. Once he verified their shoes were clean, the butler or guard or whatever he was, led them through the more elaborate entrance.

A thick, red carpet spread into a parlor at the right, a dining room on the left, and a set of velvety stairs in front. The man examined their shoes once again then nodded and pointed for them to head upstairs. Lizzie waved for Juanita to follow, and she did, catching a glimpse of girls in cheap muslin dresses, with no petticoats underneath, lounging in the parlor. Some leafed through books. Others played cards. Several young women ate at the dining table. They all looked up, giggled or whispered, but then ignored the visitor.

At the top of the stairs, Lizzie motioned to sit on fabric-covered chairs at one end of a hallway. While they waited, Lizzie boasted that Miss Platt was building a fine hotel up another hill. "Above Broadway," she said, as if it were an important location. They heard a call and Lizzie ushered her into the boss' chambers.

The rooms were plush, filled with upholstered furniture and elegant fixtures, a stark contrast to the barren thoroughfare outside. Purple velvet chairs with knobbed arms were scattered throughout. A thick blue rug covered gleaming dark-wood flooring. Glass windows decorated with heavy drapes framed the rooftops visible below. A fire burned behind an iron grate. Candlelight waved in glass lanterns even though it was midday. This woman's private chamber was light and warm, so unlike the chill and tumult of San Francisco's cluttered streets.

A hint of nostalgia for the grand hacienda adobes of her childhood momentarily filled Juanita. But enough, she scolded herself. Back to business. This woman might have funds to purchase her silk dresses.

The madam was young, but of an indeterminate age. She wore a dark-green taffeta gown with a twill weave, which highlighted her black eyes and pale skin framed by long, curling black hair. She had pulled it back with combs and a velvety green ribbon, but it strained to release itself from the tie. Wisps danced around her smooth forehead, angled cheekbones and fine nose.

Magnetism flew off this woman like a mist. Juanita's grandmother had been a similar force, even though Alta California women usually relegated themselves to the background, deferring to the men.

Juanita strained to increase her height, thrusting back her shoulders without emphasizing her chest. She then hooked her thumb in the top of her pants. A manly pose. She cleared her throat to introduce herself, but the woman spoke first, using accented but passable Spanish.

"Madam Isabel Platt Avila, sir," she said, extending a hand. "I understand you have some fine linens and dresses, maybe even ladies' shoes and dinin' ware for me. How'd you come by these elegant clothes? Not easy to get here."

Lizzie's eyebrows went up at the Spanish, but when Juanita looked at her, Lizzie just shrugged. The madam quickly dismissed Lizzie with a wave. "Off you go."

Juanita removed her glove and shook the madam's hand as firmly as she possibly could, leaning in and moving her arm up and down as she'd observed men do.

"Juan Hanford, ma'am," she said in English. "Pleased to make your acquaintance. I have merchandise from the Alta California ranchos. Many need to raise funds to defend their land grants."

A small smile started to form at one corner of the madam's mouth—the future site of a wrinkle. She switched to English. "Ah. Is that so, Juan? How did you come by such finery? Y'all look like no more than a cowboy! I heard you met my Lizzie down at Washerwoman's Bay. Ain't she a sweet one with the gorgeous strawberry hair? Men love it. You like that too, Don Juan?"

Despite her loudness, there was an unexpected softness in her inflection, and a lilting accent different from those of the Englishmen, Boston whalers, and hide traders Juanita had met over the years. She drew out certain words. It took a moment, but Juanita listened intently and caught up. This black-haired, pale-skinned woman asked so many questions.

Juanita hadn't conversed extensively in her disguise except with the tipsy mission priest and Lizzie and she was very uncomfortable. She tried to keep her shoulders back, no hint at a female curve to her waist. She cleared her throat. She needed to move this along and make a sale.

"Well, ma'am. One of the ranchos down past Pueblo San Jose sent me to sell some of their clothes. You interested? Did you see the quality?" She decided to push a bit. "I can see you appreciate finery."

Miss Avila's face broke into a full smile and she let out a hearty laugh. Not a throat trill or upper chest guffaw, but a tremor which shook her whole body.

"Well, Mr. Juan, I can tell you I don't do business with anyone tryin' to fool me. But if y'all come clean, we might be able to talk trade."

"Excuse me, ma'am?"

"Come on. You sure ain't any Juan. Let's have it. What's your reason for comin' here in disguise? Didn't think I'd let a woman in the door? Thought you were too old?" She laughed heartily. "That's what I do. Take all types of girls and turn 'em into San Francisco's best entertainers. Might even have a place for you. Could be pretty if you wore one of those fancy petticoats, put some weight on. You're awful thin. Got troubles, Mr. Juan? Come on, what's your real name and reason for comin' to my establishment?"

Juanita gaped. The Pico cousin at the door and his stable boy hadn't noticed. Neither had Father Mateo. On the Mission Road and at the docks, where there were so many men of all shapes and sizes, colors and backgrounds, no one had noticed a slight Californio cowboy in a sarape and sombrero. What now?

The madam did not stop talking. "Look, Mr. Juan, or whoever you are. Everyone here has secrets. Did you know one of our city councilmen ran away from a murder charge in Ohio? And the hotel owner buildin' next to the Niantic ran off from Boston, abandoning a young wife and babies. Everyone's come here for a new beginning, or to escape a nasty past. You wouldn't believe where I've come from. But nothing from me until I know who y'all really are."

Juanita squirmed in her boots. What could she say now that wouldn't jeopardize the sale? She needed the gold dust to get mules and equipment to sell in the diggings.

"Decide quick or out you go," the madam said, her voice growing firmer.

Juanita sighed. She hadn't found any other customers for dresses or candlesticks in the grubby outpost. She removed her hat. Maybe a sale was still possible.

"I'm Juanita Castro de la Cruz. Third-generation Californio. Lived my whole life on my family's land grant rancho raising cattle and produce."

"Well, now, ain't that somethin'. I'm a Californio fan. Most of my stableboys are Californios or Sonorans. Damn, y'all know horses. You almost had me 'til the gloves came off. You gonna run around as a man, don't ever take them gloves off. It's my business to know men and women, Miss Castro!"

Juanita winced. She should have thought of that. She admitted she didn't really want to be a man and was sore from riding the male way even though it was easier to move around without long skirts. And once accustomed it seemed a more efficient way to ride.

"Well, just wear pantaloons under your skirt, and good boots. You skilled with a pistol? A machete, Miss Castro?"

"Yes, ma'am. Spent my whole childhood with the horses and stable boys. Figured I could pull it off."

"Maybe you're a horsewoman, but you're lousy at disguise. Keep your weapons close, always. Never hesitate to use them and you should be fine. Lookin' for work? You're a little old for me, but I've got all ages of customers. You got that silky brown skin and good hair. No gray in that bun, right? French girls are the most popular but lots like the *señoritas*. We fatten you up, put some color back in those lips and cheeks, and you'd be an elegant woman on the arm of a respected gentlemen. We don't just let anyone in here, Miss Castro. I'm sure Lizzie told y'all."

Juanita's head was spinning. Was she recruiting her to be a prostitute?

"Sit down," the madam said without stopping for an answer. "Tell me what y'all got and why you're sellin'." She paused slightly as Juanita sat in the armchair. "And call me Miss Avila. I love the Spanish two names—I switch for what suits me. For the Californios and Sonorans, I'm Isabel Avila. I come from the big farms in Tennessee with horses, tobacco, slaves, so I know what y'all built out here, with the Natives instead of slaves. But I wanted to be part of something different. At first, for the yanquis, I was Elizabeth Platt from out East. But now Isabel Avila suits me. Don't want my father comin' out here tryin' to bring me home!"

She laughed again, and not a feminine twitter. Juanita didn't find any of this very funny, but Miss Avila seemed to love to talk so she stayed silent. Might learn something.

"I married one of y'all's Dons for his name, his money, his connections, but he can't tolerate the city. So he's back south of Santa Barbara . . . well, almost all the way to San Diego. Some God forsaken place called Los Angeles. No one there but

Californios and Natives. He's my insurance. If all goes badly here, I'll head south to the rancho and Señor Avila. But it's too isolated down there for me—just a bunch of cows and sheep, vineyards, orchards. I like being where the action is. And, boy, is there action here. You gotta keep your head straight to stay caught up."

She finally stopped, brushed the curly wisps back from her forehead and stared at Juanita with those flashing black eyes. It felt like firelight sparked off this woman. She seemed sympathetic but could Juanita trust her? It was risky to be honest with anyone in times like these, but she needed funds.

So she told Miss Avila of her lineage. A grandfather in Spain's Portola expedition to claim Alta California. A grandmother who, as a child, walked from central Mexico with De Anza's settlers. The family had built a thriving rancho on land-granted tracts, which was eventually lost to debts just before the US invasion. She did not elaborate on the new owner or his treatment of her family. But Miss Avila seemed to sense something amiss. She cocked her head and gave her the black-eyed stare.

"I'm looking for someone and need to get to the gold diggings," Juanita admitted. "Thought it might be safer as a man, a muleteer. We Californios have no gold dust, no nuggets, just land, cattle, our homes. We've produced and traded for eighty years. I need pouches of dust, yanqui money, whatever works in San Francisco and up in the gold camps."

"Are all these dresses and things yours? If y'all lost the ranch where'd they come from?"

Nothing slipped past Miss Avila. Juanita explained how her sister and brother-in-law had to pay lawyers to prove ranch ownership to the Land Commission.

"So you takin' this money back to them?"

"I promised I'd return with their share. But I'm starting to wonder…everything's so expensive."

"Hmm, where you staying?"

"Somewhere safe, out near Mission Dolores. Don't worry about that."

"Look, Miss Castro, I'm the parlor madam. I'm not a thief planning to steal your merchandise. I run a quality operation and treat my girls and workers right. I don't have cribs or creep joints. Some places are like cattle pens, the girls abused, not paid, getting pregnant or sick with terrible diseases. My girls are refined—we have Sunday singing and piano concerts for the gentlemen. I keep them healthy and teach them manners, skills. Like I learned back home. Despite your lousy disguise, it's clear you're an educated woman, Miss Castro. But my girls, and my customers, have to follow my rules. Trading partners too." The black-eyed glare.

"I understand," Juanita said. "Let me bring back more to prove I've got quality. I have dresses, hats and gloves, silver cutlery and candlesticks, ladies' shoes . . . what are you interested in?"

"All of it. But I gotta see it. Everyone's a liar here. You bring me samples and we'll see about a deal."

"How do I know you'll give me a good price?"

"Who else is gonna buy your silks? The City Hotel? The El Dorado? I don't think so. Plus, you want me to keep your secret or not?"

Her charcoal eyes flashed, clearly waiting for a reply. The contrast between constant chatter and electrified silence was a style of negotiation Juanita had never experienced.

All right, she told herself. This woman is tough. So am I. Time to use the Castro de la Cruz El Camino bargaining power.

She heard her grandmother's voice admonishing her to get the best of the deal-making.

"I'll be back, Miss Avila," she said. "However, your man needs to let me in next time. No meeting Lizzie out at Washerwoman's Bay or Portsmouth Square. I expect nuggets and dust and all the US dollars possible for your purchases."

She strode out without a glance back, a handshake or a "Thank you for your time," Abuela Quina's spirit guiding her. She could almost feel her grandmother looking down from the heavens and relishing this new challenge.

Jaunita barely noticed the water-filled potholes on the long walk back to the Mission. She had to decide. From here on out, was she a man or a woman? After all, there were a few more women around than Beatriz had predicted, and Juanita's disguise was apparently a failure in any bright setting or one occupied by anyone with observational skills. It was uncomfortable to not be oneself, difficult to keep up the pretense with strange clothes and mannerisms.

Pretending to be a poor vaquero, rather than a respected Mexican *doña,* added complexity to the charade. Although she'd grown up riding across the hills with the Natives and cowboys, she was in fact a *ranchera,* the *jefa,* the boss, directing the staff. She'd so much rather be herself anyway, a mother looking for a lost son. Maybe that would tug at the heart strings of miners and prostitutes.

Back at the potrero, Juanita removed the hat she'd pushed down over her eyes ever since she'd left Beatriz's ranch, then stripped off the pants and man's shirt and threw a muslin dress over her head. No need to change shoes; she'd worn men's riding boots beneath her skirts since she was a teenager. She shook out her hair, surprised when it hit just above her shoulders rather than at mid back, and patted Canela, talking in her regular voice. Her hair was an odd length for a woman but she could use combs to wear it up until it grew out.

Canela nuzzled her, looking for a treat along her hips. No pockets anymore. She reached in a storage basket for a carrot and stretched her hand out for the mare to nibble. The horse sighed and crunched, content. Even Canela knew what was most natural. What had she been thinking?

Father Mateo looked startled when a woman walked into his kitchen. His wide-eyed expression clearly said he was wondering if he'd started his wine too early in the afternoon.

"Sorry, Father, a bit confusing, I know. I was Juan. But I'm really Juanita. Juanita Castro de la Cruz and Pedro Castro was my father. By the way, he was never a gambler. Our cattle got the plague and he went into debt trying to replace the herd. Just so you have the story straight."

Father Mateo coughed into his tumbler. His brow furrowed as he sat down hard at the simple table.

"Okay, good. You're sitting. I'll explain." She told him about her poor choice to use a disguise and getting caught, but gave no details on how her true identity was revealed. She then promised to keep working in the dairy but admonished him to say nothing to anyone. "I've got some business in the city but then I'll leave your sheds."

"Do you need to take confession, my dear?" the Padre asked. She declined as she headed to the stables to pack an impressive selection of women's clothing for Miss Avila.

Though the slog to the city was even more arduous in a dress, she was relieved to return to the Parlour House Hotel as herself.

The front door guard, Josiah, welcomed her and she climbed the stairs with a triumphant air. Maybe this would work.

Miss Avila pored over each dress and pair of shoes. She caressed the silk and worsted wool, admired the brocade trim, complimented the printed cotton patterns.

"I'm having an opening party for my new hotel soon and I want the girls in the finest dresses west of the Mississippi. I'll take it all."

The madam turned out to be a haggler just like Juanita's grandmother. She held her ground for fair prices but cut just under what the Men's Emporium gentleman said the going rate was for ladies' linens, velvet, taffeta, and silk off the Boston schooners. Finally, they agreed on the sale and Miss Avila disappeared behind a heavy door, returning with pouches of gold dust and nuggets, a bag of ten- and twenty-dollar Pioneer Gold Coins.

"I want at least some American Liberty silver coins."

"I have to save those for merchandise going through the customs house. Can you go to that brother-in-law in San Jose and bring me more dresses? I'd like another set of china and cutlery. Have any ladies' hats? Maybe then I can dig up some US silver for y'all."

"I still have more clothes stashed where I'm staying, some hats and china too."

"I'll buy every bit of merchandise you got," Miss Avila said after a moment, "but you need to give me something in return."

"What? Can't we just make a solid sale? A regular business transaction? Where else are you going to get such finery quickly, Miss Avila." She tried to hide her desperation, frustrated at this woman repeatedly changing the agreement.

"Not so fast. Who you really looking for, up at the gold

diggings? It's a dirty, hard place. For anyone. Gold's not easily scooped out of those rivers. Hangings up there, thieves on the road. The girls and I hear stories. You want to do business? You gotta come clean." With hands planted on her hips, the madam stared, unflinching, into Juanita's eyes. Her black eyes and pale countenance were impossible to resist.

Exasperated, Juanita hesitated. This tortured process had taken much longer than she'd anticipated. It was at least ten days since she'd left the Dominguez Ranch and she still hadn't sold all the contents of her mule packs. What options did she have? Must be how this woman operated, luring the desperate into her web then manipulating the circumstances to her benefit. Feeling trapped, Juanita reluctantly explained how she'd sent her young son away as gold fever started. She gave a description, that he spoke English and went by Joe. She did reveal he might be hiding his perfect Spanish.

"Ah, trying to pass. As a yanqui? As white. I know something about that from the South. Dangerous business, Miss Castro. Hope he knows it."

Juanita remained silent, grim-faced. Why'd she include that detail? Ugh, another mistake. Miss Avila continued right on.

"Let's make a deal. I'll put the word out to keep an eye out for your son. If he comes into one of my places, I'll hear it from my girls. But I want to know if there's a new vein discovered. Or perhaps some needed equipment? I want to invest in the mines, but I need eyes and ears up there. I don't trust any of the miners—they come and go like flies on rotting fruit." She finally stopped, took a breath and leveled the heavy stare, daring a response.

"I don't know anything about the mines. Haven't been there yet. Just trying to survive in the disappearing Alta California.

Don't see how I can help you. Don't know cities, or mining. Just ranches and horses. Can't you just buy my remaining clothes and housewares?"

Isabel threw her arms out wide. "That's it! Didn't you say you're staying by Mission Dolores? I want in on the racetrack planned out there. Old Leidesdorff had a race before my time and now there's some gentlemen who want to build a track. Find out who the investors are. Then I'll persuade them to let me in. I need names, the quiet, hidden ones especially. Tell them y'all got a silent investor. If you get me contacts to participate in the racetrack, I'll keep an eye out for your son and I'll take every item you've got. Can you do that, Miss Castro?"

Extortion, plain and simple. But what choice did she have? No one else would buy all of Beatriz's clothes and flatware. And navigating the crowded shops and bustling waterfront soliciting sales of women's clothing was not a strategic approach. Everyone was out for themselves, greedy for a get rich scheme. And there were so few women. It was all about survival now.

"Hmm, don't know. Let me see what I can find out from the Padre. There's a few Natives and Californios around the Mission," she said.

"You'll have to do better than a dying Mission. Come see me when you have investor names. You've got a fortnight." Perhaps noticing Juanita's skeptical, bewildered expression, she added, "Remember, Miss Castro, most everyone here is from somewhere else. There aren't many of you Californios, so use it to your advantage."

Then the madam waved a dismissive hand. Somehow knowing the conversation was over, Josiah opened the door right then and ushered Juanita out of the private chambers.

As she pushed through the crowds down the hill toward

the Mission Road, she mused that her very Catholic mother and grandmother would be shocked at this twist requiring negotiation with a scheming madam. How on earth would she uncover horse race investors?

Racetrack Investors

February 1850

This time, the nightmare included a rattlesnake in her father's seat at her parents' massive table. Sea captains and Dons with refined wives and luminous daughters crowded the dining room, but the snake rattled that Juanita must take all the gold-filled pouches and silver coins to Agustín—it was his money after all. The guests all nodded before evaporating into a wet, gloomy cloud.

The chill woke her to a dense fog drifting into the shed. She shook off the haze of sleep, checked on Canela, who stood unmoving, oblivious to the mist and bad dreams. Now, rolled into colorful *cobijas* nestled deep in the straw, Juanita pondered a narrative for potential horse race sponsors. She thought back to the conversation with Miss Avila and realized the madam could be right—perhaps there was power in her position.

She decided to present herself as what she really was . . . or, well, what she had once been. A wealthy Californio Doña with quality horses who knew ranching, the terrain, the local landowners, and who could source hearty stallions and speedy mares for races.

She dug through the remaining dresses and exquisite cloaks in her possession and set aside an outfit for this latest persona. Then she planned how she'd approach the gambling houses and hotels tomorrow night after Mission chores, armed with gossip she'd gleaned from the novice priest. Father Mateo would be confused by yet another incarnation of the worker sleeping in his milking sheds.

The next night, as she dressed for the escapade, she smiled—if Miss Avila saw her now, she might even welcome her as a potential recruit for the Parlour House Hotel. Beatriz's most fashionable shoes were perfect with their elegant heels and handsome leather. Her sister's finest combs hid her short hair behind their luminous mother-of-pearl veneer. She pulled strands loose to frame her thin cheeks and hide the worry lines spidering out from her eyes.

With a russet velvet cloak around her shoulders as the final touch, Juanita strode out of the potrero, stretching to her full height to resume her role as a wealthy landowner of the finest estate on the El Camino Real. Juanita decided to channel her businesswoman grandmother to spice the performance with just enough arrogance to be really convincing.

In the almost two weeks since she'd arrived dressed as a vaquero, the Mission's entertainment barrio had gained several new venues. Rumors of newcomers planning grand storefronts percolated through the streets and many original businesses spruced up their entrances and offerings to compete. A formidable wooden structure labeled "The Queen of Dolores" now outshone the scrawny, thrown-together saloons lining Mission Boulevard, one of which had burned down last week, ashes still piled on the empty lot.

The Queen of Dolores stood three stories high, taller

than any other façade. Constructed with finely milled pine, a heavy redwood door and framed glass parlor windows with curtains, it welcomed gamblers and bar patrons. No shafts of light spilled out between the slats, and the walls were thick enough to keep the bustle and energy contained within. It was the most dignified structure in the zone, which gave it an air of mystery and polish, unusual enough in this part of town that anyone walking by would be tempted to see what the Queen had to offer.

Juanita entered as if she were the establishment's owner, and whispered to the pistol-wearing guard, who then escorted her to a back room decorated like a European library. A sparkling chandelier lit up the patterned rug, while opulent furnishings and obligatory monte tables lined the back wall. Several gentlemen sat in overstuffed chairs sipping whiskey while a high-stakes game behind them was prompting the typical cursing in several languages.

"Mr. Wyatt? George Wyatt?" she asked.

A man tipped an imaginary hat, then waved a dismissive hand to the gentleman next to him and gestured for Juanita to sit. His actual hat, a black top hat, sat on a side table just behind the curve of his richly upholstered chair.

"A whiskey, señorita?" he asked impatiently, as if his upbringing forced a begrudging politeness. Even sitting, his perfect posture was evident, as was his abundance of confidence. His sandy brown hair was thinning and a bald spot shone through single strands at the crown. His silk shirt had gold cufflinks, which he lifted and turned in the uneven light more than seemed necessary for a simple greeting. His long nose, broad jaw, and cool air hinted at a patrician lineage, but the browned skin and creases above his brow belied the truth of time in the sun. Juanita assumed he'd been up at the gold diggings, struck it rich, and was here to parade his good fortune to Mission gamblers aspiring for the same.

"Mr. Wyatt. I am Juanita Castro de la Cruz. It's a pleasure. I understand this is your gambling hall and you're planning a racetrack and stables in the neighborhood. I have horses which can best any of the European and Australian stock you're importing. I'm a third-generation Alta Californian. We have the fastest horses anywhere."

As he looked straight at her with no curiosity, she recognized the signs of a man born into wealth whose arrogance just might match hers. This could be an entertaining challenge. For the first time since she'd galloped away from the rancho, she felt comfortable in her skin. She conjured all of Abuela's bravado.

"I'm from one of the many Castro land grant ranchos. I'm sure you've heard of us. We were here for four generations before any of you arrived in Alta California. In addition to horses, I have interested investors. Is there somewhere we can talk business?"

The gentleman kept his posture stiff but raised an eyebrow. "Excellent English. Not much of an accent." Did she detect a condescending tone? "Right here is fine."

Juanita launched into a description of her horses but then pummeled him with questions. How could she be confident in his partners' financial ability to build such a place? Did he own the land? Who would manage the track and betting? Who were his stockholders?

"A lot of men have dreams in this town," she said with authority, as if she were an experienced investor herself, "but few can deliver on their promises."

In turn, while he seemed intrigued, Mr. Wyatt had his own

list of detailed questions and demanded to see the horses and gain proof of their speed.

Finally, she came away with one name besides this gentleman's brother. There were other partners, the landowner was enthusiastic, he hinted, but he insisted on seeing the horses before revealing anything more. She promised to show him one, explaining the others were back on the ranchos. They agreed to meet at the *barrio*'s grassy fields, where she'd give him a horse race.

"Got any horses fast enough to challenge an Alta California mare, Mr. Wyatt? Let's hope so. I don't want to waste my time. I insist on the landowner and investor names before my horse starts the race. I need to know if this is a serious enterprise."

Then, Juanita nodded a farewell and abruptly walked out, much like she had the first time she met Miss Avila. She'd observed the influence of the yanqui style since the US intrusion. The cultural change had been quick, dramatic, none of the long pleasantries before completing a transaction required in her father's day. Aggressive, no-holds-barred dealing was now the California standard.

Canela had no inkling of her upcoming debut as a racehorse, just that she was getting extra brushing and more time to nibble her favorite grass each day. She grunted her appreciation with every carrot treat. Juanita decided to add a little Californio flair, braiding her mane and tail with the bright red and yellow ribbons she'd talked Miss Avila into lending her when she'd visited the Parlour House Hotel to explain the ruse and ensure the strength of their agreement.

"Oh, a horse race! Such fun, Miss Castro! Clever. You know I grew up on a horse farm? My father had famous racehorses!"

"What? I thought it was a tobacco plantation?"

"Well, yes, but we had racehorses too. My favorite horse almost won the Peyton Stakes. Biggest race in the whole world. You've heard of it, right? It was the most exciting thing that ever happened to me. Well, 'til I ran across the country and came out here! I, too, know horses. Yes, girls is a different business, but I've adapted!" She pushed back her wild tangles of hair. "Oh, I wish I could go watch. You've never mentioned my name, right?"

"Of course not," Juanita assured, irritated. "No one here is trustworthy. But we have an agreement, which you better honor. I need to sell my last things, get my mule train stocked and depart for those hills to find my son. I can't stand this place. The fog is freezing. Too many people. Everyone out for themselves." She glared. Miss Avila ignored her.

"Do they know you'll be riding? What if you don't win?"

"I just need to show a fast horse so they'll tell me the partners and you'll buy my dresses. Then I'll leave town quick since I don't have any other horses. And Canela is not for sale."

"Good. Then we'll get those racetrack investors to our party. The new hotel is almost finished. I need every cloak, petticoat, and hat for the grand opening. Even though 1850's barely begun, it will be the ball of the year."

The day of the horse race, Juanita returned to the men's pants she'd used as Juan and decided to forgo wearing her thin cotton shift over them. Why bother? It would just get tangled. She strapped on her hat, buckled up her chaps, slid on the riding boots and spurs and was off to the Mission fields.

The novice priest cautioned her to be careful with these men who were "sharks and liars, con artists," solidifying her suspicion that he drifted over to the gambling establishments every night. He always seemed to know the latest gossip: how the fire started, who had fought whom, which gambler had the biggest win. He offered to tag along to watch out for her, and she appreciated the caution—maybe Mr. Wyatt and his partners would be less likely to cheat and be freer with information if a priest attended the race.

Mr. Wyatt had sent a message that he would be bringing several horses. Juanita had sent back a reminder, no investor names, no race. There was silence in return.

Canela sauntered onto the field as if she knew she was the star of the day, her deep chestnut coat shining after days of brushing, the red and yellow ribbons splashing color with every switch of her tail. Meanwhile, Juanita had topped her own outfit with a colorful vest she'd quickly sewn from a sarape. She pictured her mother and sisters laughing at her crude sewing; she'd rejected every darning or needlepoint lesson required in childhood, instead spending her days in the stables and on horseback. Silently, she thanked her mother for allowing such rebellion. That upbringing had given her the confidence to try to pull off this feat, this charade. Yet more lies, but necessary to find Joaquin.

The duo trotted on to the impromptu racecourse Mr. Wyatt and his partners had constructed, a grassy field framed by scrub brush and sand dunes, and marked by tall, whittled pine poles pointing skyward at each corner. Juanita could see where these men planned to locate the formal racetrack. No one had revealed this before, so she was delighted with another tidbit she could share with Miss Avila.

Still, the nearby Precita Creek had made the course's edge damp with brown mush—an area to avoid with galloping horses. George Wyatt had a Sonoran rider on his mare and there was a Californio rider on the third horse, a strapping stallion. She'd met her match. They likely could ride with skill and poise. But did they know their horses?

The men reviewed the agreed-upon course. They would circle the field four times. The other riders looked at Juanita skeptically, as she clearly was a woman dressed in men's apparel, but neither said a word, likely assuming she would disappear after the first lap.

A small crowd gathered at the west side, having climbed up the sandy slope to get a better view, and Juanita spied the novice priest and several of the Mission dairy's Native workers. The priest gave an encouraging salute. But she still had no list of investor names. Mr. Wyatt had kept his distance during the race preparations.

As the other riders moved toward the start, Juanita, with Canela trailing behind, followed Mr. Wyatt off the course.

"See this fine horse, sir? I've got many more but no names, no race. We had a deal. I honor my commitments and I'm sure a gentleman such as yourself does too." She turned toward the creek to walk off the racecourse.

"All right, all right, here," and he handed her a piece of parchment scrawled with a list of names. She was pleased to see investment amounts included. Miss Avila would be delighted. Maybe she could finish their strange transaction, purchase mules and mining equipment and finally leave the clamor of San Francisco.

Taking a deep breath, she steered Canela to the starting line, then leaned over the ribboned mane, rubbing her neck, quietly telling her the plan in Spanish. They breathed in together, and understood, in a horse-and-master bond.

"It's a test, Canela. Proof you're the best. We'll show them. Together," she whispered.

The starter's arm raised up, pistol facing the heavens. Juanita sat in a crouch, calm, her thighs resting firmly on Canela's torso.

Crack! The starting gun fired. She dug her legs into the horse's flanks and click-clicked her into an immediate sprint. Juanita leaned further forward to push Canela faster and faster, encouraging her to focus on the front, not on the other horses. The speckled mare pulled ahead. Juanita synchronized her breath with Canela's.

"*Vamos*, Canela!" she called as they reached the mare's head, then took a slight lead. The black stallion was behind them both, but she could hear the *thud, thud* of his hooves approaching.

Faster, Canela, she wished as they completed the first lap. Three more.

The field was firm, but the damp toward the edges made Juanita even more determined to stay on the inside. They rounded the first pole again and almost hit it, causing her to pull the reins tight for a swift left. Going off the course meant immediate disqualification. She'd agreed to those rules. Where was the speckled mare? She didn't dare look.

Suddenly, the stallion clomped up from behind, now even with Canela. The rider was pushing the horse in closer, crunching them too close to the next pole. She had to get ahead or they'd hit the course marker. Was that his intent?

She yelled in anger at the careless rider then kicked harder. Canela jerked but responded. They moved ahead but were still too close to the upcoming pole. Juanita had no choice. Pulling right, they leaned into the black horse, Juanita pushing with all her weight and that of the horse's flank. As they bumped into the stallion's side, the rider jerked his head up in surprise. An angry, dark look clouded his eyes as the stallion was caught off balance and moved out. Juanita did not flinch. She kept Canela on course and rounded the pole. Where was the stallion now? Could she keep this pace up for another lap? Could Canela?

Juanita felt light as air. As if she and the horse were the same tissue, their sinews and muscles connected, working in unison as if one body. Her mind let go of the other riders and her focus sharpened to see only the field, the poles, Canela's mane. They galloped together so smoothly she felt transported back to the rancho, to riding the hills and fields of her family's land as fast as possible. She was seventeen again. It had been a different horse then, but now she and Canela flew together as if she were that girl, riding wildly, in love with the land, with a ranching life, with freedom.

Juanita rounded the final pole with a horse at her tail. She could not turn to see how close or which one it was. If she broke the union with Canela they would fall, crash to the ground in defeat, in life-threatening injury. She crouched even lower above the horse's neck, ribbons and mane almost in her mouth, gripped her legs tight and kicked.

"Vamos, Canela!"

They pounded through a thin strip of canvas Mr. Wyatt's workers held as a finish line, the black stallion just breaths behind, the gray speckled mare coming in third.

Juanita slowed Canela to a gallop, then a canter and then an easy trot, both breathing hard. Sweat poured down her spine, soaking her blouse and colorful vest. Once trotting, she rubbed the horse's gleaming neck, patted the ribboned mane,

"Good girl," she said softly. "We did it!"

Canela snorted in short breaths and slowed to a walk. Her heart still pumping, limbs tingling with adrenaline and breath still shallow from the exertion, Juanita surprised herself by realizing she felt complete joy—an emotion so foreign to her these past four years, ever since the war, Papá's death, losing the rancho, that it frightened her in its deliciousness. She let the warmth flow into the neglected corners of her heart, where happiness resided before grief, duty, loss, and pure survival had tried to extinguish it.

The rider of the stallion rode up beside her, cursing in Spanish and calling her foul names. "A woman riding, that's a sin! You should be ashamed. And clearly you don't know what you're doing. You were dangerous out there."

"Hey, you got too close. You almost pushed me into the pole!" she shouted back, throwing in a Spanish curse word. "I had no choice. Don't blame me for your mistake." Then, adrenaline pumping, she couldn't resist an insult, "Tough loss."

After dismounting, she walked Canela slowly around the track to cool down. She had to calm her beating heart if she wanted to use this win to her advantage.

"Still think California horses can't beat Spanish ones?" she said when she finally approached Mr. Wyatt. "Or Australian ones? Let's build a racetrack and we'll have some fine races here," she said with a slight smile of victory.

There was no silver-dollar prize like Miss Avila's father had hoped to win in Tennessee, but Juanita felt like she had just won the world's greatest race. Alta California raised quality—she had proven her point. Yes, she had done it under duress to obtain information for the madam, but it had been a satisfying win. Now to the purpose for this whole charade.

While she stalled Mr. Wyatt on horse sales, fabricating excuses for her delays on showing him more fine animals from ranchos south of San Francisco, she prepared to leave. Miss Avila bought every remaining Dominguez ranch item, but the gold dust, jagged nuggets and Pioneer coins did not stretch far. San Francisco's supplies of mules and mining equipment were limited, and in great demand, so if she could even locate pans and pickaxes prices were exorbitant.

Her coins and gold dust dwindled quickly as she spent days scouring the wharf and hills for mules, saddlebags, and packing boxes, hidden in makeshift stalls, tucked behind tents and roughshod structures. She often had to outbid a potential miner eager to ride out or another opportunist planning to sell up in the camps. She purchased five more mules, then visited every dry goods store to fill the pack boxes with flour and whisky, beans, candles, calico cloth, and even a small safe. She tucked ropes and spurs, bridles and leather reata between sacks of rice and barley. She stuffed her machete alongside the saddle and hid the pistol in her satchel.

She had nothing left, not one Liberty Coin or brimming pouch of gold dust to offer to her brother-in-law for his boots and horse tack, his wife's dresses and stylish shoes. Ever since arriving at the Mission, Juanita had been in a frenzy. To find buyers, to maneuver through an urban environment teeming with mobs of unruly men like she'd never experienced. To convince Miss Avila to buy her merchandise through an unlikely horse race. She felt foolish. She'd been naïve to promise to return to Beatriz with cash in a week.

Now, finally with a stocked mule train to support herself and a path to the gold diggings, she had nothing left to pay Beatriz and Agustín for the items she'd borrowed. Well, stolen. She needed every mule and bolt of calico to finance her trip. Finding Joaquin was her priority. *I'll save a portion from every transaction and pay them back fairly,* she told herself. Would this delay lead to more nightmares?

Juanita bade farewell to Father Mateo and the novice, thanking them for allowing her to stay in the stables, even when she turned out to be a woman. She had one final stop before leaving town. Unable to reveal her connection to the ball's hostess, Juanita had not attended the lavish hotel opening party nor had she seen Miss Avila since handing over the coveted list of racetrack investors.

Dressed in her traveling clothes of simple muslin dress over riding pants and men's work boots, she was almost turned away at the lavish entrance to the brand new Golden Nugget Hotel. Fortunately, Josiah recognized her and led her upstairs.

"Godspeed, Miss Castro. What a pair we turned out to be!" the madam said with belly-shaking laughter. "You headed south to your sister's ranch for more silks? Remember, I'm your best, oh, your only, customer," and continued laughing.

"No, can't go back there. I've nothing left to pay them. Everything I've got on those mules is for sale. I'm headed right up to the diggings."

Miss Avila's face darkened.

"Then, you won't be bringing me more of those quality dresses, those heavenly petticoats? Wait, then you stole from your own sister? My, my. I thought the Californios had better morals than all us Yankees and foreigners." She stopped suddenly. Was she concerned for Juanita? Then she shook her mass of swirling curls and changed the subject.

"Oh, Miss Castro, you shoulda seen the party. Up on our top floor overlooking Broadway and Kearny, a view of those ships in the harbor ... champagne and oysters ... all of San Francisco society was there. Well, can't really call it society in this pioneer town, now, can you?" The laugh again.

"Josiah had men bribin' him to get in the door, imagine that. The Wyatts and their colleagues showed up. One took a likin' to Lizzie." Her eyes sparkled as she seemed to relive the event, to imagine her importance among the elite and powerful. "They'll be regular customers now. I do have you to thank for that."

Irritated with Miss Avila's self-centered focus on her status, Juanita shifted uncomfortably in her riding boots. The madam finally remembered the reason for the call. She promised to keep an eye out for a tall, auburn-haired Joe who was good with horses, came from near Monterey, and had a secret ability to speak perfect Spanish. She would communicate any sightings to General Delivery in Stockton, Sacramento, Marysville. Juanita thanked Miss Avila. Her new colleague? Was she in partnership with a madam?

How the world had changed, she mused as she led her mule train down the Mission Road, noticing surveyors making plans for the planks they intended to install on the swampy trail. Here she was, someone who, just a month ago, had never lived anywhere but her rancho, setting off alone for the foothills of the high Sierra to search for her son. She'd also won a horse race, with a madam as a co-conspirator, turned into a muleteer, and become a thief. What strange choices the new California required.

As she reached the tail end of the great bay then headed northeast toward gold country, she glanced down the southern turnoff toward her sister's ranch and her own former home. Remorse, sadness, and guilt pulsed in her chest. She made a promise, out loud, so she would never forget.

"I vow to return to you someday, Beatriz, and repay you double what I took. Bless you for your dresses. You're helping me find Joaquin."

Up to the Diggings

February to April 1850

With San Francisco's bedlam finally at her back, Juanita followed the old Alta California trails which led north past Mission San Jose, then rode east toward the Livermore family's valley. She'd been there once before in those years her parents were trying to marry her off to a landed Alta California aristocrat. With old habits, she stopped to water the animals and hoped for some of the still-famous hospitality. It was the first place since leaving Beatriz's where she'd represent herself accurately.

The family was away for a taste of city life, the stable hands said, but they offered whatever she needed. So many visitors stopped at the Livermore ranch, the vaqueros boasted, a postal stop was coming soon. The men raised an eyebrow or two at Juanita's unusual garb, but hearing Spanish and determining she was a ranchera, they slipped into the Mexican tradition of solicitude and deference *peones* showed the upper classes. Juanita took advantage, peppering them with questions about the mining Bars, the trail conditions, and the Mudville and Sacramento stores where she could unload provisions. Yet these cowboys were like those at Juanita's former home. They knew little beyond the leagues of Livermore property. They could tell you about every delicious spring and pretty creek-side rest stop as they moved cattle from one field to another, but they knew nothing of the diggings beyond the rumors weary travelers passed on.

The familiarity of the Livermore ranch brought memories of Joaquin. All he ever wanted to do was ride, brush, or clean the horses. Even at nine or ten, he'd had such a way with them he could lead a wild stallion into the corral and break him into a cattle herder faster than the experienced cowboys. He had a calm, firm presence the animals understood and respected. She'd loved to stop at the fence and watch him. So focused. Such a gift. He'd trained Canela, she remembered with a smile.

Upon leaving, she continued through rolling hills and crossed the long wide valley, flat and grassy with dark, rich soil peeking through the underbrush. The fertile land her family had profited from along the coastal hills clearly extended inland, although here much of it was still occupied by Native groups, most whom had escaped the Mission priests generations before. Juanita had never been so far into the valley. She could see the Sierra Nevada mountains, now poking up from the great plain, their peaks capped with white snow.

Along the way, she met former miners stumbling back complaining of terrible illnesses, some with scurvy. Her grandmother had always insisted her sea captain customers purchase fruits and vegetables, lemons and oranges to keep their sailors healthy before sailing to Manila, Panama, or the Sandwich Islands. Hmm, maybe she could deliver fresh vegetables and fruit to the prospecting areas.

Whenever she encountered Natives fleeing deeper inland, she politely spoke with them in Spanish, which most could maneuver through. Some single Native men were headed to the diggings, but Native families wanted to get as far as possible from the white settlers flooding their homeland.

One day, she encountered Mexican *arrieros* with a pack train of eighty mules headed to San Francisco to restock. Based in Marysville, they serviced the Bidwell and Long Bars on the Feather River. A steamer, as well as small schooners and launches, sailed up the delta into Sacramento now, but only mules could transport food and equipment up rocky passes to the gold river camps. There was more demand than the muleteers could meet they said.

Juanita was impressed with their operation, and lobbed question after question about the Bars, convinced Joaquin would be there. They inspected her small mule train and packing boxes, shaking their heads and joking in Spanish about a woman on the trail. They grilled her on her stock and offered to buy most of it. No, she told them. She needed to survey Mudville and Sacramento to understand the sales opportunities for herself.

"Okay, ma'am," the leader said. "But you wanna sell whenever you got an interested buyer. Never know if the demand matches your needs and inventory."

Good advice, but she'd take her chances as she was just learning the trade. They invited her to visit their Marysville sheds, but they were rarely there, mostly on the trail selling, stocking, resupplying. It was not a sedentary life.

Juanita made mental notes in case of future expansion. If she wanted to grow, she'd need several arrieros helping guide a larger train. She would do it alone for now, trusting no one.

Day after day, she walked, rode on Canela or pushed stubborn mules. While she was often alone, she did encounter aspiring miners who were walking to the diggings due to a lack of funds to buy a steamship ticket. One group aiming to sail Back East from San Francisco with their gold earnings told her there was a ferry made of an old wagon at the San Joaquin River.

"A couple old coots sit there and charge two dollars per man and horse to get across. Those old badgers are making five hundred to a thousand dollars a day! They pull the ferry with a thick rope across the river. Charged for mules too. Maybe a dollar each. They even set up a saloon right at the ferry crossing." Too expensive. She stayed on the trail.

Since leaving San Francisco, she'd been free of nightmares involving rattlesnakes or dead relatives reminding her of her guilt. She figured the nightly peace was the result of finally moving toward Joaquin. She was out on the land where she was most comfortable, no complicated people, just the animals and her determination toward a fixed goal.

One night, sleeping under a star-filled sky, the embers of her fire glowing with their final hour of warmth, she woke to rustling grass and a boot heel *stomp*. Not moving, she listened hard to identify the sounds. Was it an intruder? When she heard steps near the sleeping mules, she grabbed her pistol. Why had she left her machete on the horse? She cursed herself as she crept from under the wool blanket. No time to put on shoes. She stepped lightly to keep the sycamore and cotton-wood leaves from betraying her.

Another boot *thud*.

The mules rustled nervously. With no moon and thick cloud cover, her eyes adjusted slowly to the blackness. *Snap*. She cracked a twig. Damn. She stopped and listened. More mules shifting and braying. *Thunk*. Was that a pack box open-ing? She needed to scare off whoever it was.

Juanita charged toward the mules, screaming in the loud-est Spanish she could muster and shooting her pistol in the air.

"Get the hell out of here, you thief!" she yelled, adding in every curse word she knew, hoping she'd guessed right and it was only one miscreant.

She heard a stumble and a yell. "What the hell?"

She shot again, aiming high above the animals. All awake now, they brayed and belched in distress. She saw a figure flee-ing and shot again over his head.

As she returned to calm the mules, and Canela neighing and struggling with her hobble, she heard the *pound, pound* of hooves racing away. He was gone. She searched around the camp for any others hidden among the trees. No one. Whew! That was close. She found an upturned packing box with its contents strewn about, but nothing seemed to be missing. Woke up in time, thank God. She'd search more in daylight.

From now on, everyone would sleep right next to the fire. They would all be one every night—no matter how little the animals liked the fire or how much she liked the quiet. She pulled Canela and the mules in closer, stoked the flames high and sat sentry. She reloaded the pistol and rested the gun and machete on her thighs. No more sleeping tonight.

Another night a group of coyotes swarmed in close and she was glad she had a flickering fire. She could only sleep a few hours each night if she wanted to safeguard the animals and supplies from man and nature.

Mudville had recently acquired an official name—Stockton—but as she rode into the town, she could see why the original name might stick. It wasn't much of an outpost save for the docks at the end of the slough—only a few canvas storefronts and wooden lodgings lined the soggy main street.

She found the mail tent and asked for letters from Miss Avila of San Francisco and if anyone had encountered a man matching Joaquin's description. Nothing. Still, the place was smaller and less chaotic than the city, which suited her.

She sold some supplies at the dry goods tent, pleased to be starting a collection of gold nuggets and yanqui American coins. She asked around about Marysville and Bidwell's Bar at the end of the California Trail. If Joaquin had sent letters from somewhere called a Bar, then there was a good chance he was there. Even so, she cursed how little she had to go on.

Several folks in Stockton told her Marysville was a miserable collection of tents, very far and hard to reach in rainy season. Better to stop first in Sacramento with its unending need for rations. Good place to buy and sell merchandise. In the saloon tent that night, one muleteer bragged he was making three thousand dollars a month. She was still getting used to the American dollar but calculated roughly what that would buy in the dry good stores and eating tents. She bought two more mules.

While checking at the postal stop again, she agreed to a contract with a man who needed to send a mule and boxes of mining equipment to his uncle in Sacramento. He'd pay half now and gave her a pouch of twenty-dollar US double eagles. The uncle would pay the other half upon delivery. The businesswoman in Juanita was skeptical, but she practically salivated at the American gold dollars. How would she find this man? The gentleman gave a detailed description of his uncle and the boarding house where he often stayed.

"If he ain't there, go to Brannan's Dry Goods. They'll know

where to find him. All the miners go there."

Against her better judgment, she decided to take the risk and loaded his boxes on her train. Her only insurance was mining tools and a mule. She trudged out of Mudville with a loaded-down, expanded mule train.

Sacramento City looked more like Monterey than any cluster of dwellings and businesses she'd seen in Alta California since greedy Argonauts flooded in for gold. Although the simple buildings were constructed of wood, rather than adobe, the streets lined with sycamores and cottonwoods were familiar. The *embarcadero* at the confluence of the Sacramento and American Rivers, however, was much less stable than Monterey's rocky cove. Built at shoreline level, the wharf was susceptible to constant flooding. Town leaders had installed a primitive levee system, which had held despite recent heavy rains. But so much wood looked dangerous to Juanita. Why on earth don't these *yanquis* use adobe, she wondered again as she led the mule train toward Brannan's General Store.

At one intersection, men with rifles stopped her.

"What's your business here?" the sentry asked sharply as he pointed his rifle at Canela's chest. His sun-wrinkled cheeks squeezed his black eyes to narrow slits as he turned to spit a long sluice of tobacco juice at the horse's hooves. Canela snorted and reared her head.

Juanita tipped her hat as she reined the horse to calm her. When the guard noticed her legs on either side of Canela, he pushed up his hat to get a better look. She wore a thin muslin skirt over her riding pants, but it was pushed up, almost to her hips, for maneuverability and control. "What the . . ." he started, but Juanita quickly jumped in.

"Bringing in supplies for Mr. Brannan's store. He's expecting my delivery," she lied. Amazing how easy it was now to invent stories on the spot. Perhaps she'd learned too much from the madam in San Francisco who was often flexible with the truth. She'd also observed how to use a woman's privilege of chatter when it was useful. "Not the welcome to Sacramento City I'd expected. Most miners are just stopping here on the way to the diggings, right? Why the weaponry?"

"None of your concern, ma'am. Got our Vigilance Committee to keep order. Some of them can't make it on the gold want to squat on our lands. Can't have that. You not planning to stay, right?" He approached as she held the reins tight. "Let's have a look at whatchya got," he said as he poked at the baskets and buckets on the mules.

Juanita decided that was enough.

"Nothing there for you, sir. I'm off to the dry goods and mail stop. Could you kindly point the way?" she said as she swirled Canela around and nudged the lead mule to start moving. The man gave her a surprised growl but stepped back to allow her through.

The general store was a wonder of crude pine-bough shelves overflowing with sacks of flour and beans and well-worn gold pans, picks and shirts and pants, all on top of one another with no apparent organizational system. Other shelves were empty. Behind the main counter were more sacks of rice and oats on the floor, with beige jugs of whisky lined in rows. Seeing no one in the store, Juanita called for Mr. Brannan, a clerk, anyone.

A boy of about fourteen with blond hair sticking up at all angles, blue eyes, and pale skin with limbs and elbows pointing out from every opening in his too-short overalls appeared through a curtain shielding the backroom. He tripped on a sack of flour as he entered but caught himself on the rickety counter, causing it to sway.

"Whoa! Can I help you? Mr. Brannan's in San Francisco for his paper. All the rest gone up to the diggings."

Juanita explained her mission to complete the contracted delivery. Did he know this man? Could he get him a message? And would Mr. Brannan be interested in purchasing any of Juanita's items? She wondered if this gangly boy had the authority, and most importantly the gold dust, to make a purchase. Doubting he'd be interested or able, she still showed her stash on the mules, quickly opening boxes and saddlebags.

"I'll take the safe. Mr. Brannan will anyway. And them blacksmith and farrier tools. Ain't got many tools lately."

Juanita was surprised when the boy returned from behind the curtain with nuggets and pouches of dust which she weighed on her hand scale. It seemed a fair price.

As she grilled the kid, she realized Joaquin had only been a year or so older when she'd sent him away. Seeing how young and green this boy was, she felt more guilty and distressed than ever. She'd sent her own son out into the world when he was not yet a man, still awkward, growing into his frame and confidence.

"Have you met a young man, Joe?" she tried. "Tall, auburn hair, might claim to be from south near San Jose, or Monterey. Not much older than you."

The boy looked at her quizzically. "Don't get most people's names, ma'am. We get so many through here I don't pay much mind. They all talk different languages. Old and young, from all over. They want to buy or sell, I help out. But I don't ask questions or get names."

At the mail tent, she asked once again for any information on Joaquin. The harried clerk shook his head, wiping sweat off his bald head with a handkerchief despite the cool air outside.

"Look, lady, there's probably a lot of Joe's. Got no idea. Ya need a full name to match a letter. Sorry."

"What about the Bars? Can you tell me which way to go to get up there into the diggings? This Joe may be in the Bars, and I've got supplies."

The postal employee looked at her curiously now, maybe even a little shocked. His mouth opened. Then closed. Then opened again.

"Well, which one? The ones on the Yuba River? There's a Barlow's Bar up there. Or on the American River? Up there you got Mormon Bar, Smith's Bar, Manhattan Bar, and several more, don' recall the names. On the Middle Fork there's Spanish Bar, Big Bar, Volcano Bar, and a few others. On the South Fork you'll find Coloma and Sutter's Mill what started all this mess. Then you got the Dry Diggin's in the south, understand? Why there's Murphy's Camp and Sonoran Camp and Hawkin's Bar down there. This place is full of Bars, ma'am. There's new ones gettin' named every day. Which one you want?"

Dismayed, she sat down hard in the single rickety chair in the postal tent, face in hands, and stared at the packed-dirt floor. Bars along every river and a dozen rivers up and down California's golden curve lining its Sierra Nevada spine. She had no idea which Bar she wanted.

To further add to her frustration, the miner never showed up to claim his mule or equipment and pay the other half of the thousand dollars. No word of him at the boarding house. No sign of him at the dry goods. Tobias, the skinny blond boy staffing the general store, nailed a notice to the store's message board which read:

MR. LEEDS OF STOCKTON—YOUR MULE'S IN
SAC CITY WITH MRS. CASTRO. ASK AT COUNTER.

While trying to locate the man, she stayed at the American River Boarding and Rooms, barren lodgings serving one hot meal, a room with a straw-filled mattress on the floor, a bowl and chamber pot, and a tiny square table barely large enough to hold the basin.

"Don't get many ladies in 'ere, so no mirror or chamber stand for washin' up. 'ot baths once a fortnight for extra," the stout English manager said, a strong accent breaking his words in two. They were missing beginnings and some ends, thought Juanita as she struggled to understand.

But it was clean with a solid door and a paddock for the mules which appeared reasonably safe. Still, the first night she checked on Canela and her mule train three times—she didn't want a desperate aspiring miner grabbing a mule to ride into the hills to prospect for gold strikes.

After several days, when Tobias reported, "No news, ma'am," yet again, she swore to change her business practices forever. Only buy and sell what she had and do it when money is on the table. No credit.

She was out the five hundred dollars, but at least she'd gained a mule for her fledgling train and could sell the mining tools. She'd be off in the morning, having decided to aim for the string of camps with names ending in "Bar" along the American River, closer in than Marysville and Yuba River diggings, giving her a greater likelihood of quickly encountering potential miner customers. Perhaps someone there had met Joaquin.

The climb up to the first Bar was rocky for the mules, dangerous for Canela, and slow going overall. Every day, one mule or another rebelled and stopped mid track. Canela whinnied at each sudden drop-off, protruding roots, or rock-clad path, with Juanita desperately trying to keep her from tripping or falling. A hobbled horse was no use in the steep, arid terrain; the land here was filled with little save enormous manzanita bushes, their bark sharp and red and hard as iron. No machete could pierce those bushes if they blocked the path, and so clambering over rocks and through streams around the brush was the only way to climb.

She forged on day after day, nibbling down her dried beef and noticing the oats and alfalfa for the animals were getting low. How much farther up the hillsides were these Bar towns?

Juanita was shocked when she finally arrived at her goal. It was nothing like she'd expected, but in reality she didn't really know what she'd pictured. Maybe she should have paid more attention to her sister's letter.

The diggings were miserable. Desolate, wet, muddy, and cold, with nothing but tents and shanties lining the frigid rivers flowing from Sierra snow melt. Miners tromped from a rushing creek rapid to a gleaming pool, scraping and digging, panning and swinging a pickaxe, day after day.

There were no towns. Each "Bar" was simply an encampment of men living in tents or sleeping out in the open, sometimes almost in the graveled riverbed. One tent had a washing station, and a woman doing the cleaning, but often the men washed their own stained clothes in the same rivers they mined. Another tent served hot biscuits and a gruel of oats or potatoes for breakfast. When there were no provisions, the cook switched to hardtack. Dried beef was the primary treat once a week. Butter and eggs, milk, fresh fruits and vegetables were rare. As soon as a cook came in on a mule train or with a new trader, he was overrun with miners paying fifteen or twenty dollars in gold dust for a breakfast with eggs, bacon, biscuits, gravy, and real coffee—a standard offering in cities Back East for fifty cents.

Men worked from sunup to dusk, and even into moonlit nights, digging jagged river bottoms, shaking out the pebbles, sand, and sludge as they searched for a glint of gold flakes. Or best of all, a nugget, a chunk so large it could be thrown in a pocket without fear of it sifting through tattered fabric. Maybe one as big as an acorn or an apple. Stories swirled of men finding baseball-sized nuggets then leaving the diggings for Sacramento or San Francisco and going home rich.

Now, not many knew any such man, but the tales circulated, prolifically, and the frantic activity continued. Men's boots were always wet, some succumbing to foot rot causing the skin to peel; this was particularly common in the rainy season, when the diggings changed from hot and dusty to sodden. Fewer mule trains made it up the steep trails in the soggy months, and the diggings grew thinner and more spare, hungrier. As the days shortened, it was impossible to last in the snow-fed rivers for a full day.

Still the gold shone, and men gathered it, either squandering it at the gambling tents surrounding every encampment or collecting it to spend on moving out of the diggings to more comfortable surroundings in Sacramento or Nevada City, Marysville or Stockton. Many returned to San Francisco, where thousands upon thousands sent millions in gold back to East Coast cities, where it was saved or lavishly spent by those not courageous, foolish, intrepid, or adventurous enough to venture West.

Juanita spent the spring of 1850 clambering up and down the rivers of gold country selling food, clothes and boots, hats and belts, pickaxes and shovels. At every single tent, makeshift hotel, boarding house or feeding stall, she'd ask about a Joe, auburn-headed, tall, seventeen, good with horses, and come from San Jose, Monterey area.

"Sounds like so many we get 'round here."

"Nope, don't know that one."

"His mother? Well, ain't that sweet. Will pass it along if I see the likes of your Joe."

"You're his mama? Maybe he don't wanna be found. Think of that?"

"Lady, we got thousands in here from all over the world. All kinds of colors and languages. We got rich men who are swinging a pick just like the slave who came with his master and escaped. California's got 'em all. Don't know about no Joe, though."

She heard everything except a "Yes." Never a "I met the guy. I worked with him last year." She grew despondent yet more determined.

Back in Sacramento, she refilled the pack train at Tobias' store. She bought more mules until she was at fifteen, which made her wonder if she could keep on going up and down the rivers by herself. So far Canela had not sprained a leg or taken a spill, but there were many close calls. She sewed her growing silver and gold dust supplies into her clothes, stuffed it into her saddle bags, and hid any nuggets in her boots and underwear until she ran out of places to hide the money. She needed a safe place for her cash and a way to invest her earnings. She decided she needed to save enough to pay Beatriz triple for what she'd taken and continue her business.

The life was hard; she was lonely for company beyond the drunk men who gambled all night and shoveled in the rivers all day. The doctors and farriers, blacksmiths and hotel owners who might have encouraged development of a community were stretched so thin they too were constantly on the move. In addition, the camps were growing increasingly segregated with the Sonorans gathering over their cookfires featuring beans and rice while the English and Scots stuck to their beer and pasties. The yanquis—or "Americans" as they were starting to be called— gathered at the gambling tables. She encountered almost no women, just as her sister had described.

That spring, the rain did not stop for weeks. Juanita could no longer stomach the long, steep journeys up to the uncivilized camps. Her nightmares had returned, with miners and coyotes and thieves taking the place of the rattlesnake chiding her for her sins. She longed to settle in one place, but was that even possible up here? Sacramento and San Francisco had no appeal. And what of Joaquin? Of her business? If she were to grow a full-sized mule train, she would need to take on assistants, but she was distrustful and reluctant to do so.

One night, up at Volcano and Big Bar area on the Middle Fork of the American River, Juanita strayed over to the Sonoran camp for some familiar Spanish around the firelight.

She and the mules knew this river well having traveled up and down it for the past month.

The Sonoran men still awake were mellowed by hours of drinking. They tipped their hats to welcome her to the merriment. She told them what supplies she had remaining in case anyone needed something before she left in the morning. They grunted, said little, passing their bottle of whisky for a pull.

She smiled but declined. "It's a long day tomorrow. I'm headed down to Sac City. Gotta restock. But this weather is so bad. I'm not coming back 'til summer. Trying to figure out where's next."

Several of the miners took interest and pelted her with questions. "You been to the Southern Mines yet? The dry diggin's down south? There's a Sonoran Camp down there. All them miners are Sonorans. Everyone talking what we can understand. You Sonoran, right, ma'am? Might like it there."

"No, I'm a Californio. Born and bred in Alta California—my grandparents came with the Spanish soldiers and padres eighty years ago."

"Whoa. No shit. Damn, that's a long time ago. You one of them ranchers? What ya doin' up here with us then?"

"Yeah, ain't you got a fancy ranch with thousands of cattle on them hills by the ocean?" another one asked.

She laughed with bitterness and reached for the whiskey jug. The man who had it smiled and handed it over. She took a sip and passed it on.

"*Sí*, I grew up on one of those ranchos but lost it to the yanquis. And my relatives might lose their ranches too. Ranching's a dirty business now. Look at the fights at Sutter's land outside Sacramento City. In San Francisco there's corrupt politicians stealing land. Probably gonna happen here too."

"Yep, that's right, señora," one man slurred. "What happens when you can't just scoop the gold outta the mud on your own? There's men buying up the hillsides and bringing in sluice boxes now to clean the rivers out faster."

Another chimed in with the latest gossip. "I hear they got quicksilver down by Pueblo San Jose that can break up the quartz and get more outta the rock. It's gonna be rich men mining now. We seen it in Sonora. Most of us worked the mines there. That's why this place's so crazy. Anybody can come up here, scoop up gold and run off rich. Ain't like that in the big silver mines in Mexico."

Several others chimed in.

"Yeah, señora, go on down to Sonora Camp and see what you can sell and buy there. Maybe find a nice Mexican husband. You kinda young still. This ain't no life for a lady."

The men laughed and continued to pass the jug, toasting her in the firelight. She took one more sip then asked her constant question.

"Any of you meet a tall auburn-haired young man going by Joe? Speaks good English but he knows Spanish too."

The group murmured and pondered, the whiskey thickening recollections by this point in the evening. Several shook their heads, but one man nodded.

"Why, sounds kinda familiar. Might've even been in Sonoran Camp," he said with a slight slur. "Was a kid who talked English with the yanquis, then some nights came to our end of the camp for the fire. That boy had perfect Spanish. Wasn't no Sonoran, though. Not sure where he came from. Some of the guys thought he was uppity. Maybe trying to pass as yanqui. Only saw him a few times."

Juanita sat up straight, her heartbeat rapid and her temples throbbing. Had this man met Joaquin? She asked more questions, but the man just grabbed the jug and shook his head, not remembering any further details about a campfire conversation.

Memories she'd tried to suppress flooded her mind, of the tortuous night she'd sent Joaquin away with nothing but a horse, the family bible, a pouch of Mexican silver, and an admonition to head to the gold diggings, speak only English, and become American. She certainly was not going to admit to these friendly Sonorans that she'd put Joaquin up to turning himself into a yanqui. But it was too coincidental a detail. She was sure the man had seen Joaquin.

For the first time since leaving San Francisco, a spring of hope welled inside her. Realizing no more information was forthcoming, she thanked the miners, and they called out farewells and good fortune for finding a husband amid hearty laughter.

Finally, a Joaquin sighting? Tomorrow, off to Sonora, the so-called queen of the southern mines.

Queen of the Southern Mines

April to June 1850

Water dripping off her hat, clothes soaked, and mules drenched, Juanita and the train slogged into Sonoran Camp on a chilly late-April day. Snow dusted the mountains above, but fortunately at this elevation it was just rain.

The main boulevard, not looking very royal, was a brown soupy path, and the canvas tents and pine-log cabins were black with mud spatter and mildew. However, a hospital building adorned the end of the street. Not even a three-year-old camp and they had a hospital? Impressive, she thought. How'd a bunch of miners raise the money—and agree to spend it on a hospital? Then again, she'd heard miners in the Northern Bars tell stories of men dying from scurvy here last winter. Must have prompted hospital construction. She shuddered to think of how cholera also could spread in such conditions.

As she wandered the town's few streets searching for dry lodgings, hoping for something more substantial than canvas walls and dirt floors, a sign with "La Bienvenida" in large red letters caught her eye. She hitched the animals and stepped inside, surprised to find her feet once again on terracotta

"

tiles. The smell of moist clay blended with a kitchen fire's smokey aroma.

"Adobe!" she exclaimed, causing the weathered, brown-skinned man behind the pine-board counter to look up, startled. A Mexican sombrero sat next to his logbook and he wore the loose muslin shirt and black wool pants common among the rancho vaqueros. His dark brown eyes matched his walnut-colored hair and his hands were gnarled and spotted. Feeling a warm familiarity she had not known for months, Juanita wondered what this man was doing here. She suspected he was more comfortable snaring wild horses than staffing a front desk.

He changed his posture immediately, stretching to his full height.

"Sorry, sir, I'm dripping all over your floor," she blurted before he could even issue a greeting.

"Señora," he said with surprised deference, dismissing the puddled floor with a wave of his hand. "How can I help you? Are those pack mules with you?"

"Yes, sir. I've been mule-training through the diggings for months. I'm ready to stay in one place for spring and just do local runs. Sonoran Camp sounded as good as any. Do you have a room I could rent for a while? Not sure how long I'll stay."

"By yourself you been driving the mules?" he said with a squint, causing wrinkles to form across his forehead.

"I just have fifteen. And my mare. Don't trust anyone else to drive a bigger train with me. Juanita Castro de la Cruz, sir. I recognize a fellow Californio. What rancho you from?"

"Francisco Gallegos Guzman at your service, ma'am. The Castros east of San Jose or by Monterey? Lotta Castros around. I worked Arroyo Seco rancho with the Yorbas. My family's been with the southern Yorbas for generations. I came up for the gold but didn't have any luck. My son helped me bring supplies from the rancho to build this place."

"Well, Mr. Gallegos, you and your son have done a fine job. These last few months, I've only been in tents with dirt floors and mules wandering in to raid the kitchen fires! This place feels like home."

That brought out a slight smile. "Sí, señora, adobe is best. Won't burn down, stays warm or cool, whatever you need. I've got a room on the second floor above the paddock. You can keep an eye on your mules."

Juanita instantly liked this practical owner, the type of man who had worked on her ranch. Despite being a muleteer renting a room now, their former status difference hung in the air as he was overly deferential to the former doña. Gold Rush California was chipping away at deeply embedded Mexican social stratification, but cultural norms die hard.

He moved out from behind his counter with a bowlegged swagger and she followed him up the squeaky stairs to a tiny room. He suggested she approach the main dry goods store with her wares. Mr. Gallegos understood a horsewoman would not like keeping too much merchandise on the animals, which could entice vagabonds or drunk gamblers to help themselves. She didn't know this community yet—who could be trusted and which places to avoid—so she appreciated the advice.

She left her saddlebag of personal items in the room and immediately led the animals through the storm to the general store. The owner bought all the food and clothes and boots, but she was left with several boxes of mining and farrier tools, blacksmith supplies. When the weather cleared, she'd work on selling those while exploring the camp. It looked large and spread out, much bigger than she'd pictured. The Sonorans in the northern diggings had not mentioned this was a bustling town.

She returned to La Bienvenida, thanked Mr. Gallegos, smelled a pot of beans boiling in the kitchen and collapsed in the little room. Next to the straw-filled mattress was a rickety nightstand just big enough to hold a flowered pitcher filled with water, and there was a chamber pot in the corner. In the diggings, this was luxury. She promptly fell into a dreamless sleep. No rattlesnakes or guilt-producing padres reminding her of her sins. For once.

At the morning breakfast, she found out Mr. Gallegos' secret. A wife! Señora Gallegos was a petite woman who embodied the strength of every Mexican mother she'd ever met. Not even five feet tall, she was lit with a fierce energy. She didn't say much, but her loving power over Mr. Gallegos shone in every gesture. She wore her long braids tied up in a crown, as if she were a little girl, and her silver earrings with brown topaz hung low on the lobes, looking as if the pierced hole would stretch and slice through at any moment. A rebozo tied around her back looked ready for a baby to slide in or for a bundle of firewood. Perhaps they had grandchildren.

The señora moved quickly but with a smooth glide, no jerking, as she cooked up beans and rice with a morsel of pork. Mr. Gallegos boasted about her contributions over steaming coffee in metal mugs. She had selected the pitchers for each room, the striped colorful sarapes on each mattress and the color and name of the lodgings.

Juanita found herself wishing this gray-haired woman had been in her childhood hacienda cooking and caring for her and her sisters all those years. Señora Gallegos felt like a grandmother most any child would adore, not the cold, efficient businesswoman of Abuela Quina. Though devoted to her grandmother, Juanita had not experienced a cozy, lap sitting childhood. Then she shook her head to dismiss such ridiculous thoughts. The exhaustion of traipsing up and down the flinty hillside trails had caught up with her.

The Gallegoses always ate dinner with their *huespedes*, currently two Irishmen, a Frenchman, and seven Sonorans who joked and laughed loudly in Spanish while the Irish shook their heads and shrugged, uncomprehending, while asking Juanita questions in English. The Frenchman just looked blank and ate more beans and tortillas. Juanita loved the mix of cultures and languages sharing a meal.

"Have you had a tall young man with auburn hair named Joe come through?" she asked Mr. Gallegos during a break in the conversation. "English-speaking."

"Hmm, don't remember anyone like that? Do you, *mi amor*?" Mr. Gallegos asked his wife. She said nothing but gazed over Juanita's head for a moment, apparently trying to remember. She shook her head. "Only English?" she asked. "No. Most here speak Spanish. And you know, Sonora has ten thousand miners. We only get a handful of them here at La Bienvenida."

Ten thousand men in this one camp? She'd imagined heading into yet another scrappy Bar with maybe a hundred men in total lining a riverbank. There'd only been about five thousand non-Native Mexicans on the ranchos and Missions in all of Alta California, which covered over a hundred thousand square miles. She still found the population explosion daunting and strange. Finding Joaquin in this crowd would not be easy.

Just then a new guest clomped down the stairs to join the crew around the table. A young man, maybe twenty, with walnut hair and dark brown eyes matching the host's. The same forehead wrinkled in surprise when he saw a woman at the table.

"Ah, Miss Juanita, this is our son, Jose Alonzo," Mr. Gallegos said, the pride evident in his tone. "He's here to help with a hotel we're adding on. He works at the Yorba rancho. He listened to me when I told him the gold for us in California is land. Gold flakes in the rivers are too hard to get."

The young man smiled at his father, kissed his mother's cheek, nodded to all the boarders who shouted greetings, and offered a hand to Juanita all in one smooth movement. Inherited grace from his mother was evident in every gesture. Surprised, Juanita choked back her food behind one wrist as she shook the young man's outstretched hand.

Was this what Joaquin would look like now? So grown up and confident and politely deferential to his parents? She longed to see her own young adult son. What was she doing here enjoying the terrible jokes and laughter of the Sonorans when she should be out looking for him?

She finished her dinner quickly, all the while watching Alonzo's interactions with the miners. They teased him for being soft, working on a ranch rather than prospecting. In response, he asked if any of them had been lucky with gold. A few said yes, but then mentioned they sent the gold back to family in Sonora—their parents and grandparents were very poor, barely able to farm the hard desert land of Northern Mexico. The Irish told Juanita in English they wanted to return home with their riches to help their parents who had suffered through the famine. So many hoping the gold would be the secret to riches and improved conditions for their suffering families.

She excused herself, then fled to her room and wrapped herself in the striped blanket. She was consumed with guilt for sending Joaquin away with no resources. What if he was one of the cholera or scurvy victims? She tortured herself through the night, picturing her boy desperately ill beneath a canvas overhang or sliding down a mountainside on his stallion. There were no bad dreams because she did not sleep. She breathed through the nightmare.

The next morning at breakfast she questioned Alonzo about his life. Maybe, she rationalized, she'd been all wrong and Joaquin had drifted back to a ranch and vaquero ways.

"Alonzo, did you ever meet a young Joe at the Yorbas? Or at any other ranchos? He's got the touch for the horses. Could break a wild one even as a boy." She didn't explain fully why she was looking for him for fear of revealing her terrible actions, but no need. So many locals had run off for the gold, everyone assumed the motives behind a missing young man.

"No, ma'am, doesn't sound familiar. The Yorbas are struggling now. Can't keep a full bunkhouse like they used to. No new, young ones around, though we sure could use such talent. Fewer vaqueros, but still plenty of horses."

Juanita spent the following weeks getting acquainted with brimming Sonora while making an even greater point to ask after her son. This camp was indeed filled with a true mix of people, not only Americans, English, Germans, French, Irish, and Italians, like in all the camps, but many Mexicans, Chileans, Peruvians, and Argentines. Juanita found the Latin American flair comforting.

As Juanita peeked into each tent and clapboard building, asking if anyone needed anvils, hoof picks or nippers, a center punch or tongs, she collected more dust and nuggets, but almost no American dollars. And she threw in a question at each stop, inquiring whether anyone knew her son. She scanned every crowd for the taller Joaquin she'd created in her mind, but there was no news or sign of him.

At night, miners ambled in and out of parlors with faro and monte tables, reminding her of the days in the Mission Dolores neighborhood. She strolled through the bars and gambling houses but found no one familiar there either. Only a few señoritas seemed to do business at the back of the gambling halls—there were no clear operating brothels like had sprouted up in San Francisco. Still, with thousands of men hiking up each day to Woods Creek and neighboring streams to prospect, she expected it wouldn't be long before one opened.

But Juanita had other business in mind. Sonora was so crowded she needed more time for her search. This place felt like a magnet for Latin American miners. Even if Joaquin wasn't here now, he could be drawn to Sonora's reputation, not only for its Mexican flair but also for recently uncovered pocket mines, holes stuffed with piles of enormous nuggets.

"Señor Gallegos, I'd like to stay here and just do the Stockton mule run for the town. Can I help you with the horses? Or clean rooms, work the desk at night? I'm no good in the kitchen, but I can do anything else. I know ranching. I can raise cows and chickens. I can start a garden." She stopped herself before she overdid it.

"Didn't have no luck prospectin', so don't have a lot of extra dollars. But you can stay and have our one meal a day if you work the desk some days and nights. You got seeds in them packs? You can plant out back, and you can get a cow and chickens if you buy 'em. We get some eggs and cheese, our breakfasts would be damn popular. And some vegetables. Like you and me ate growing up, right? Fresh, right from the ranch."

His eyes crinkled when he smiled. "All these men homesick for good home cookin'."

"Never learned my way around a kitchen," she said, "but I can get you all the fixings for good meals. How about a pig or two? I can go to the closest rancho. They need silver dollars or dust, since they mostly have Mexican silver if they even have cash. But señor, I know hospitality. You end up opening that hotel, I'll manage it for you. And I can do the accounts. I ran a rancho of over ten leagues with my father. I learned from my grandparents. Well, my grandmother really. My grandfather was a soldier for almost fifty years."

It was too much, she realized. But she felt such kinship with this kind, soft-spoken, competent couple. If she was going to halt the mule train work for a bit, figure out her next move, she felt this was the place. A Spanish-speaking community of fellow Mexicans and an entree into the hospitality business, which she was starting to feel might be a familiar move. Her family had welcomed guests in their grand hacienda for decades.

Was she betraying Joaquin if she stopped searching through the mines for now? Just through summer. Was she a bad mother if she needed a rest? For wanting a life in one place as she was accustomed to? A home, maybe a little hotel and boarding house like the Gallegoses had, filled with comfort and warmth? Was that so bad? Or was she just being nostalgic for her youth, foolishly wishing for the old Alta California which was gone and clearly not returning. But it did seem a promising location to find Joaquin.

At the end of June, she noticed an increasing number of literate, English-speaking miners reading *The Sonora Herald*. Mexican Alta California had no newspapers until just before the US war. Spanish and Mexican authorities sent formal edicts and government announcements to the customs house and the Mission to be read aloud and posted. The Dons primarily relied on these official proclamations and gossip for news.

In San Francisco and Sacramento, newspapers were vital for the diverse, growing populace of the new state. California was complicated now, no longer profiting solely from trade in cow hides and tallow, or even gold mining. New industries like agriculture and timber were sprouting up daily, and the growing towns demanded more and more goods and services. Daily and weekly newspapers informed residents of local and national news and advertised these businesses and community events.

Deciding she needed a new tactic in her search, Juanita went into the *Herald*'s cramped office and bought a personal ad. She struggled with what to write that would get attention. The editor looked over her shoulder.

"Gotta name, ma'am? Might help."

"No, sir. Just Joe. Probably using an American name but there's so many. From all different countries. Adams? Miller? But could be Strauss or Meier, or Lafitte or Doucet. Joe is all I've got."

LOOKING FOR TALL, AUBURN-HAIRED JOE, 17, COME TO THE DIGGINGS FROM NEAR MONTEREY. ANY INFORMATION CONTACT SEÑOR GALLEGOS AT LA BIENVENIDA.

Then she went to her boss at the boarding house to reveal a bit more of the truth of her story. She hoped he'd be sympathetic, especially since she'd decided to stay longer, assisting his hotel expansion while deepening her Sonora search.

Sonoran Troubles

July to September 1850

"Got this Goddamned tax on us miners. But just us foreign ones."

"Twenty dollars to 'em yanqui collectors? Every damn month?"

"That's crazy. Nobody's got extra. Anybody who finds a nugget or has pouches full of dust sends it home, or leaves the mines."

"Wasn't this Mexico before? They're trying to push us out of our own land!"

"I ain't payin'. I'm the one sloggin' through them rivers and diggin' up hillsides. They want gold they can dig it up themselves."

The miners were complaining each night at La Bienvenida's communal table over their stew and beans. But not about the food; the soups were heartier thanks to Juanita's garden and occasionally Mrs. Gallegos butchered one of the chickens. There were eggs at breakfast on Sundays, even bacon some days. Miners had taken to lining up outside the kitchen where Mrs. Gallegos sold extra milk and eggs, squash and tomatoes.

It was the Foreign Tax recently levied on non-American miners that got the complaints. Arguments broke out frequently and the once-friendly camp which had welcomed anyone with a pick and pan became competitive, contentious. The town's *alcalde* and his force circulated through the riverbeds and lodgings demanding payment and recording those in arrears.

Juanita had been so focused on helping build the new hotel she barely noticed the miners' complaints about the foreign tax until it reached a fever point. The Gallegoses began restricting guests to Sonorans to avoid nightly fights, which meant the lively conversations in many languages ceased. She missed the cross-cultural camaraderie of her first few months at the boarding house, but at least the new hotel, La Posada, would open soon and welcome all passersby at a slightly higher rate so landowners, mine owners, and wealthy East Coast businessmen looking to buy were the likely guests.

Juanita was itching to start a Sunday Salon like Madam Avila had in her hotels, thinking music and poetry and conversation between travelers and Sonora's growing gentry might be a draw. They were far from San Francisco city life, but why not bring a little of it here to the gold country hills? Mr. Gallegos told her it was a foolish idea and didn't see how salons would attract customers. They argued over the concept while building infrastructure for an adobe kitchen and central foundation for a two-story structure with a balcony over the entrance. Her boss had agreed to expand the garden and add more cows, pigs, and plenty of chickens between the hotel and the current La Bienvenida.

Still, as the tenor of the camp changed, Juanita and the Gallegoses grew concerned about the violent stories of shots fired in the saloons and Sonorans beat up in their tents at night. Was this a good time to open a fancy new hotel? Could the diversity of people here get along enough to enjoy music at a Sunday Salon? Maybe Mr. Gallegos was right and Juanita's idea was a fairy tale.

She was torn by her commitment to the hotel and her outrage at the treatment of the Sonoran miners. Mr. Gallegos told her not to be concerned about herself, for he would protect her. Besides, they had the most popular boarding house due to Mrs. Gallegos' cooking and weekend sales of milk and produce. Yet it all angered Juanita, whose frustration at the changes also fueled her curiosity. What would happen to the town? She'd had no response to her newspaper ad but what kind of a community would Joaquin find if he saw her personal announcement and walked into La Bienvenida now?

One night a Sonoran miner brought a stack of flyers to the boarding house table and made an impassioned speech for everyone to join a protest up the road at the biggest group of Mexican tents. He asked them to pass the flyers around and nail them to tree trunks up and down the trails.

FRENCHMEN, SONORANS, CHILEANS, PERUVIANS UNITE TO STOP THE AMERICANS STEALING FROM US. MEET IN SONORA NEXT SUNDAY TO DECIDE HOW TO STOP THESE UNFAIR TAXES LEVIED ONLY ON THE FOREIGN MINER. WE MUST UNITE AND PROVIDE SECURITY FOR OURSELVES AGAINST THOSE WHO CALL THEMSELVES CITIZENS OF THE UNITED STATES.

After the miner's speech, Alonzo said he sympathized, but everyone must be careful.

"The yanquis are forming vigilance committees. Even got volunteers collecting taxes for that town council they just elected. No one leave this building without a weapon."

On the Sunday of the planned demonstration, a curious Juanita dressed in her short-lived costume as a male muleteer, hair combed up under her hat, which she pulled low over her eyes. She switched her shoes to the boots she kept for their utility and grabbed gloves. She stopped in at the kitchen, stuck her fingers in the cold fire pit and rubbed ashes along her cheeks to complete the disguise.

Before leaving the boarding house, she checked on the mules and patted Canela's neck, who whinnied and nuzzled her pockets.

"I've got to see what's going on, Canela. Joaquin might be at the protest," she whispered, feeding the horse a feathery carrot top.

Instead of walking on the main street, she crept quietly up the hill in the shadow of the pines. At the top, a large crowd of Sonorans had gathered, foreign flags flying. A Frenchman gave a speech in accented English with some Spanish thrown in. A Sonoran spoke in Spanish, decrying the new tax and its unfair application. Not everyone was listening.

"Why ain't the Irish or English or them Sydney Ducks getting asked to pay? Them's foreigners too!" one shouted.

"It's too high. Twenty dollars a month is robbery. We ain't all digging up pocket mines."

As the arguments and grumbling continued, Juanita moved closer to the tense crowd while remaining hidden. More men piled in, streaming out of tents and down the hills. It looked like several thousand pushing and complaining. No one seemed sure what action they wanted.

"What would you all pay? What if it was a dollar or two?"

"No. We ain't payin'! Why should we? We dig up the nuggets and pan the dust."

"Has to be on all us miners. Not just the Mexicans, Peruvians, and Chilenos."

"Or them Chinese. The yanquis sure don't want no Chinese comin' in diggin'."

Suddenly, a crack rang out from down the main street. An angry mob of several hundred men roared in toward the protestors, pistols out. Men on horseback, waving rifles, followed. This new group yelled in a chorus of harsh English and raspy growls.

"Pay the tax or leave!"

"Go back and mine in Mexico. Got your own mines there."

"This is our home now. We won it fair and square."

"Only Americans can prospect here. Sonorans sure ain't Americans."

The yanqui vigilante mob swarmed the protestors, swinging and punching and waving pistols. Hats sailed off, fists flew. Instantly, it became a riot.

Above the melee, Juanita pressed her body against a tree trunk, trying to be invisible. Protestors ran toward the Stockton trail while others fled into the woods. She crouched down tight so no one could see her face. She heard horse hooves and whips, rifle shots and nearby pistol cracks. Sonorans and foreign miners who couldn't flee fast enough were getting beat up. She heard footsteps and winded breathing as men ran past seeking safety in the forest.

Juanita was ashamed of her cowardice. But with no machete or pistol she didn't have a choice. Why hadn't she brought a weapon? What a fool she was to expect the protest to stay peaceful.

Once the sun had set over the distant western hills and dark shadows covered her, she stood up gingerly, her muscles stiff from crouching for hours. After stretching her legs, she crept through the dark, staying high on the wooded hillside before dropping down into the camp. She slid in the kitchen door and tiptoed up the stairs to change, not wanting anyone to know she'd been at the protest and mob battle, especially dressed as a man.

A scream interrupted her sigh of relief upon making it to her room. The front door banged, pots clattered in the kitchen. The señora cried out, "No!" and began sobbing.

Juanita, still in men's clothing, bounded down the stairs to see a collapsed Jose Alonzo with blood pouring down his leg. His parents were at his sides, and the Native kitchen girl was tearing sheets for bandages.

"They shot my boy. Alonzo, hold on," Mrs. Gallegos sobbed.

Juanita had seen every phase of an animal's life and death in her ranching years but she'd never seen so much blood coming from a human. She grabbed the rags and began tying them around Alonzo's leg with Mr. Gallegos' help. The señora was too distraught to do anything. Alonzo moaned in pain, his torso rolling back and forth.

"The doctor's coming," the Native girl whispered, gulping to hold back tears while she ripped the sheets. Juanita wasn't sure what the strips were for now, but the distraught young woman ripped feverishly.

"Where's the damn doctor?" Señor Gallegos said as if he hadn't heard.

A young doctor rushed in, blond hair tangled, and cheeks so smooth Juanita doubted he could grow a beard. His blue eyes were bright with a desperate, overwhelmed look. He tore off his coat, rolled up his sleeves and pushed the blond tangle back from his forehead.

"'ospital's full. I'll sew him up 'ere," he said in English with a strong British accent. He felt for Alonzo's pulse at his wrist, then neck, and examined the bloody mess. "Bullet's still in there. Gotta git it or leg'll go bad." He gave hasty instructions to each of them for hot water and blankets, whiskey and reins. Juanita translated.

"Let's move 'im on a blanket, clean up this bloody floor," the doctor said when they had all returned from their assignments. "Git another blanket ready. Fill 'im with as much whiskey as you can, double up the reins and stick them in his mouth. 'urry it up."

Mrs. Gallegos sobbed next to Alonzo until the doctor glared at her,

"Ma'am, sitting there crying won't git the bullet out. I need basins a 'ot water. Git me soap."

As they each brought in the supplies, the doctor ordered, "Now you all gonna 'old 'im down. No one's leaving."

Juanita and the girl held his legs while the doctor removed the bandage strips, applied a metal tourniquet from his kit of knives and tools, then washed the leg. He grabbed a small bottle from his bag and swiped it under Alonzo's nose; he stopped moaning.

The doctor grabbed a knife, then made a quick slice above and below the bullet hole. When Alonzo's body jumped, they each pushed hard to hold him steady. The doctor handed Juanita the knife. Surprised, she took it while trying to hold the squirming man, watching as the doctor grabbed a set of forceps and dug around in the incision as Alonzo writhed in pain, screaming curses in Spanish.

"'old him tight," the doctor said. After what seemed like an eternity to Juanita, he said, "I got it," and held up a conical bullet. "Now let's sew 'im up," he said to no one in particular as he washed the leg again, carefully wiping the wound as much as he could, given the blood still flowing. He stitched the hole with a long needle and black catgut.

Juanita watched with nausea foaming in her stomach. Can't get sick now, she repeated to herself. Hold him tight. She had grown up dealing with cows struggling with difficult births, sheep with a broken leg, and lame horses that had to be shot, but somehow those incidents hadn't made her squeamish. They were a natural part of ranch life. But a man, a vibrant young man in his best working years, felled by violence made her feel ill. She swallowed to keep the bile down.

This was no accident. This was deliberate harm. She was not naïve or overly coddled, and she'd lived through the US Invasion, but Alta California's isolation had kept her distant from battlefield skirmishes. What a protected life they'd led there at Rancho Castro, she realized. Sure, they were not spared economic woes or natural tragedies, betrayal or cruelty. But viewing the violent horror one man could inflict on another out of fear and greed was distressing.

At last, the doctor tied off the stitches and pronounced it finished. He gave instructions for cleanup and subsequent care, then went to wash himself up in the kitchen.

"More of them up at the 'ospital," he murmured, tipping his hat in farewell as Mr. and Mrs. Gallegos profusely thanked him in Spanish while offering food, blankets, gold dust. He waved it all off. "Not taking any money for treating these poor boys who just wanna mine, whether they're Sonorans, Yankees or them Chinese."

Juanita followed the young doctor out the door to thank him in English.

"I'll come check on 'im in a week or so," he said. "Tell the parents they can pay me something then. Came out 'ere to mine myself, but no luck, so doctoring to make a living. Never thought I'd see this violence out in Gold Country. Was the wars I worried about when I pursued this profession. Keep that area clean so I don't have to come back and take the leg."

Alonzo was feverish for days. Juanita and his mother, with the maid's help, cleaned the wound and changed the muslin bandages multiple times a day.

The first morning Alonzo was conscious it was Juanita's turn to bring him breakfast and apply a fresh bandage. He looked at her with watery eyes, dark half-moons shading below to his cheeks.

"Miss Castro. Will I ever ride again? Can't have the Yorbas replacing me on the ranch. And our new hotel, my father can't finish it by himself. And who'll keep my parents safe?"

"Hush, Alonzo, rest now. You just focus on getting well. I'll stay here awhile longer to help. We've got some loyal boarders who'll watch out. Shhh, eat some eggs and beans."

For the next two months there were daily fights in the saloons. Sonorans raided the yanqui tents looking for victims and Anglo miners threatened any Mexicans who showed up along their river claims. If you left your tent or boarding house, you carried a pistol or machete. Everyone was armed, everyone looking for a fight.

With so much turbulence and Alonzo still lame, the Gallegoses abandoned the hotel project while everyone in camp hunkered down and kept to their own kind—or packed up and left town. Every lodger at the boarding house had a story of being attacked, threatened with a pistol, and told to leave. Several were injured with broken arms, bloodied noses, and bruised ribs. Chinese miners, assaulted the most brutally, were the first to flee, heading to San Francisco to do laundry, clean hotels, and open dry goods shops.

"I'm going back to Sonora, Mexico. My parents and grandparents are there, so I should help them anyway" became a familiar refrain.

By September, the boarding house was down to Juanita and two miners. Mr. Gallegos approached her one morning over steaming coffee.

"Your help while Alonzo recovers is appreciated, but you'll have to pay now. I'm sorry. You'll be safe here. The Vigilance Committee knows we're Californios. I'm hoping it will get better. This ruthlessness is bad for business. The alcalde is appealing to the state to drop the miner's tax."

Juanita was conflicted. She felt obligated to help the Gallegos family until Alonzo recovered fully; he was itching to get on his favorite horse, but the young doctor advised against riding until the wound stopped bubbling pus and draining liquid. But with this new chaos, shouldn't she leave town as well and continue her search?

The Sonora Herald ad had produced no results, although it had been printed in the edition right before the tensions began when all were distracted. Joaquin was out there somewhere, experiencing this along with every other Californio.

"Mr. Gallegos, thank you for your kindness. For letting me stay and find some peace here before the miners' tax troubles. Sonora is beautiful. I hope it can be safe and profitable for your family again. But it's time for me to return to my mule train. I must keep looking for my son. If he was ever here, he probably left town like everyone else. If anyone mentions seeing him, please let me know at the Sacramento mail stop."

He frowned but said nothing. Perhaps he understood, realizing he'd do the same if Alonzo were missing.

Juanita couldn't safely carry all the gold pouches and US silver and gold coins she'd collected. She asked Mr. Gallegos if he would keep a few of her pouches in his safe, and he agreed.

"When I'm nearby, I'll stop and visit you and Mrs. Gallegos," she said. "Your hotel will be grand someday."

As she rode out of Sonora, Juanita stopped at a large live oak where the forest met the edge of town and buried canvas bags full of gold dust pouches and sacks of US silver dollars, careful to leave no trace. She intended to return to Sonora to collect her savings when she finally had enough to pay her debt to Beatriz and beg forgiveness. When that would be was unclear.

News for a
Gold Country Muleteer

September 1850 to November 1852

Juanita left Sonora the way she had arrived, riding Canela and leading a fifteen-mule train. But gold country was changing. She wondered if the situation in the northern diggings was as bad as it had gotten in Sonora. The foreign miner tax applied to all the new state. Now, she felt unwelcome in her own homeland. She'd read the history of wars and defeats in piles of leather-bound tomes under Papá's tutelage, but to experience it firsthand was not academic. It was excruciating, disorienting. Now there was a new country in charge. Unusual rules and surprising cultural norms to interpret and adapt to.

The gold-seekers were changing too, no longer idealistic adventurers but greedy profiteers. The population explosion was leading to new social stratification and Americans seemed determined to ascend to the top rung, pushing foreigners out of the way. The opportunities to get rich quick brought out the worst in people she observed.

Once on the trail, Juanita returned to her former habits, inquiring at every rest stop, every mail delivery outpost, every dry goods store, and every miner-stuffed tent or rickety hotel if anyone had met a tall, auburn-haired Joe. She never heard a "Yes."

This trip, she was determined to reach the Yuba River Bars. In Stockton, she purchased popular miner items—flour and whiskey, candles and calico, boots and picks—and then added bullets to her offerings. She decided against pistols as they were heavy and bulky and she hadn't liked their recent impact on her short-lived stay in Sonora. She also added two small safes for towns developing near the camps. Or for a growing Sacramento business.

In all her inquiries, Juanita also asked about her sister, Josefa, and husband, Charles Hanford, the bakers, but no information was forthcoming there either. And she always checked the mail delivery tents for letters, still hoping Miss Avila hadn't forgotten her promise to keep an eye out for Joe at her establishments. Silence from San Francisco.

For over a year, Juanita traveled up and down the Sierra foothills, going from camp to camp, from pueblo to cluster of mining structures as she sold the contents of her packs. She added more mules, although stopped at eighteen so she didn't have to take on an assistant arriero. She still trusted no one and hid her growing wealth in her mule packs and clothing, even in her hats and boots. She never stopped anywhere for more than three nights.

The trails were now worn, thanks to the passage of long mule trains and Wells, Fargo & Co. couriers. Traveling up them was a hopeful sight, defined by eager miners who had flocked in after long journeys aboard ships, or months crossing plains and mountains, or surviving the snake- and dengue-filled jungles of Panama. Hiking down the mountain roads was the opposite; mostly she passed the frustrated and impoverished, the dejected who'd found nothing but handfuls of glitter dust mixed with dirt and sand. The times she saw someone running down the trail, she knew that was a fortunate man who was hiding nuggets to send Back East or spend as fast as possible.

Despite the crowded diggings, Juanita was so alone. She contemplated writing letters to Beatriz, but realized refusing to help defend their land and stealing dresses, silver and china was a betrayal difficult to forgive. Eventually, she decided to write Miss Avila.

After a year of leaving every mail stop empty-handed, she finally received a letter from San Francisco.

The Grand Palace Hotel, San Francisco
October 16, 1851

Dear Miss Castro,
I hope you are well. Life as a muleteer sounds extremely difficult. Come to San Francisco and we can find something civilized for you to do here. The city continues to bustle and grow. I now have four hotels and a boarding house and am planning more.
You, of all people, will be most interested to hear the Wyatt brothers proved useful in ways beyond the horse track investment. Lizzie overheard enough to uncover the brothers were selling and building on city lots they did not own. Their fortune had not come from the gold fields as we'd suspected but from fraudulent land dealings and

construction right here in the city. I've promised them discretion, as several Vigilance Committee members are also good customers. But in return, Mr. George Wyatt takes my advice and investment in whichever one of his projects intrigues me. It has been a fruitful arrangement ever since that crazy horse race of yours!

I am sorry I have nothing to report regarding your son.

Sincerely,
Isabel Avila

Juanita was dejected but also elated. Despite its lack of Joaquin news, her first ever letter in the diggings gave her a much-needed connection to someone, anyone, and she decided to write back. Mr. Brannan's *Daily Alta California* was flourishing, but it was very locally focused and those in the Central Valley were often weeks behind the news San Franciscans could grab off the Wells, Fargo & Co. coaches. Miners coveted the rare *New York Posts* and *Tribunes* that made it west. She knew Miss Avila heard all points of view, rumors and predictions in her salons. Her news, while often primarily gossip, would be most illuminating.

Hangtown, South Fork American River
November 30, 1851

Dear Miss Avila,
I received your letter of October 16 while visiting Sacramento for my regular trading at Brannan's Dry Goods. I had ceased being hopeful when entering a postal

stop, so I was elated to hear from you. Even though you have no word of Joaquin, I am desperate for news of any kind.

I continue on the trail despite the hardship winter brings. But the men need more than potatoes and onions, hard ham and salted mackerel. So I ride on. You'd be pleased to know that for Christmas festivities, I am adding oysters and champagne into my packs to supplement the ever-present claret and canned sardines of which every hardened miner has grown tired.

You also would be pleased with the profitability of my business, though I struggle with storing my earnings. I've run out of hiding places in my baskets and clothes! I recently invested in Sacramento by purchasing several lots but do not plan on becoming the land and hotel baroness you are! And Sacramento floods frequently, so the value is unclear.

Congratulations on the growth of your business. What new entertainment or social events have you hosted lately? How do you manage it all yourself? I recall you trust no one with sensitive information or your finances. I understand as I cannot build the mule train any bigger without an assistant arriero but refuse to take on a partner or employee.

I am often troubled, as I am sure you are, by what US news I can find (any Post and Tribune copies that make it to the dry diggings are usually six months old). I hope leaders in Boston, New York, and Washington can find some compromise as the country grows so divided over slave states and Manifest Destiny moving West.

What news do you hear of Tennessee and your father's

plantation? What do your many politician customers think about the slave state controversies? And this Napoleon character in France seems to be generating a lot of debate as well.

The diggings are in a commotion over the discovery of quartz mines, but equipment and know-how to extract the gold are in short supply. Quicksilver is necessary, apparently, and so, yet another provision required by the thirsty mining community.

In my humble opinion, Miss Avila, it's a good thing you did not invest in mining companies as they seem to come and go like the wind.

Thank you for continuing to keep an ear open for news of my son. I do not give up hope and ask after him at every encounter. Please send any San Francisco news to this lonely muleteer.

Sincerely,
Juanita Castro de la Cruz

And so, they began a correspondence. Isabel Avila kept Juanita informed of her San Francisco enterprises and latest political escapades, while Juanita reported on mining camp life. They exchanged tidbits of gossip and news of free state and slave state tensions.

Each mail stop brought a lightness in Juanita's step and a tingle in her hands. Would there be a letter to hear of the world beyond her solitary existence? Could news of Joaquin ever be a possibility? At one point she asked Miss Avila for a favor.

Sacramento General Delivery
January 28, 1852

Dear Miss Avila,
Best wishes for a Happy New Year! I'd like to ask a small
favor. Could you request a personal announcement for
me in The Daily Alta California? Mr. Robert B. Semple,
Editor, is the contact there. Wording to the effect of:

LOOKING FOR INFORMATION ON LOCATION OF A TALL,
AUBURN-HAIRED YOUNG MAN FROM THE MONTEREY AREA,
19 YEARS OLD. GOES BY JOE. SEND ANY INFORMATION TO
TOBIAS AT BRANNAN'S DRY GOODS, SACRAMENTO.

Thank you for your assistance in this matter.
Juanita Castro de la Cruz

Miss Avila's letters so pleased Juanita she decided to communicate with the only other people with whom she'd had positive contact—the Gallegoses. Since Alonzo was the only one literate in Spanish, she directed correspondence through him.

Sacramento General Delivery
March 20, 1852

Dear Alonzo and Mr. and Mrs. Gallegos,
I remember my time at your boarding house in Sonora
fondly and often wonder how you are faring. I continue to
trade along the trails throughout the diggings. While it is
a nomadic life, the muleteer business is a good one in these

*times given the thousands of men in the camps and small
towns needing food and supplies.*

*I do hope to return to Sonora sometime soon and
continue our lively conversations on the changing
nature of California. I was pleased—as I am sure you
were—when the state legislature dramatically reduced
the Foreign Miner Tax and applied the small one more
equitably.*

*I look forward to staying in your new hotel someday.
Alonzo, I do hope your wound has healed and you were
able to return to the vaquero life.*

Sincerely,
Juanita Castro de la Cruz

The Sonoran updates were discouraging. Alonzo wrote that
after the foreign tax uprising and violence, the population of
Sonora had dropped by half. Without customers, the Gallegoses could no longer maintain the boarding house.

The couple had returned to Rancho Arroyo Seco seeking
their former jobs. Señor Yorba was consumed with document-
ing his land grant ownership for the Land Commission hearings, so while he took the Gallegos parents in out of loyalty, he
could only trade rooms in an abandoned storage shed for their
work. They expanded his garden and orchards and livestock
as they'd done for the boarding house. The Sonora hotel plans
were nothing but a lost dream.

Other letters revealed more difficulties.

Rancho Arroyo Seco, Amador Valley
June 18, 1852

Dear Miss Castro,
I am writing without my parents' knowledge to give you the full details of their move from Sonora. An Englishman, James Braddock, was scheduled to buy the boarding house but he cheated my parents. After we left for Rancho Arroyo Seco, before the deal was fully signed, Braddock moved himself and his brother into the empty building. He refused to leave and got the new alcalde to declare the buildings and land his via a falsified deed. My parents were devastated but lacked the funds to hire a lawyer to fight this transgression. Fortunately, Señor Yorba will let us stay indefinitely, although now he is talking of selling the rancho.

Thank you for remembering my injury. I still limp and am not as strong as I used to be but can ride and assist with the cows at least.

Thank you also for your correspondence to my parents. They look forward to your kind and lively letters.

Sincerely,
Alonzo Gallegos Pacheco

She was so sad to hear the Gallegoses were struggling, and she hoped they'd used the few pouches of gold dust she'd left in their safe for basic expenses. Or maybe this Braddock had stolen that too. Everyone was out for themselves in this survival of the strongest landscape, which grew increasingly threatening.

Alone, always moving, disconnected, Juanita felt her only success was in her mule train business. She kept much of her cash in leather satchels, Canela's saddle and the mule packs, but that was getting more dangerous every day. She considered buying more land but needed to accumulate enough coins to give Beatriz and Agustín. She knew banks were now the way of the sophisticated, but hand over her hard-earned wealth to a stranger with a vault in a tall, stone building? Seemed risky.

Still, in the summer of 1852, Juanita decided to take a small portion and trust it to the newly established Bank of the Gold Miner in Sacramento. The young gentleman who'd opened the institution, a Mr. O. D. Hart from Massachusetts, had put overconfident ads in the newspapers spouting his prowess in the field. Juanita couldn't believe he'd secure her funds, but she figured this was part of the new California. And she couldn't keep burying gold and coins in empty lots—a squatter was likely to dig it up before she returned.

She visited young Tobias at the dry goods store every Sacramento delivery and pickup stop. He had grown into the position. Now he was confident in his bargaining and very clear on what he knew he could sell—and what would sit on the shelves. The scrawny young man still looked as if he'd just emerged from his cot in the back, uncombed hair sticking up at impossible angles and clothes too small for his ample height. He still stumbled over his unkempt warehouse strewn with flour sacks and mackerel tins, but he delivered, always disappearing behind his red calico curtain to come up with a tool or food item to satisfy the trail weary miner or mule driver.

Juanita developed a fondness for the boy, and considered hiring him to help steer the mules. She'd love a Mexican vaquero, but the successful—and seemingly honest—ones ran mule trains with fifty to seventy-five animals and were uninterested in her small operation. Yet she kept on alone, despite often having to refuse supplies Tobias knew were in demand up in the diggings. She had to build up her savings. Her guilt never waned.

"Miss Castro, ma'am, good to see you again," Tobias said, his mouth full, as she entered the general store, her arms loaded with empty saddlebags. She was stocking up before a late fall trip to the mining camps with final supplies for winter.

Juanita frowned at his rudeness. "Chew and swallow, then speak," she said, a motherly command in her tone. "And offer to help your customers if you aren't otherwise occupied."

He choked down his food and rushed over. "Sorry, ma'am. It's just the new bakery's sourdough is so delicious. Everyone's talking about it. There's lines out their door most mornings. Not solid like the bricks of bread the miners carry. Light. Got pockets of air, flavorful. Rumor is they got some French baker from the Boudin family in San Francisco. Wait, didn't you say you had a baker relative you were looking for? New place is on J Street, corner of Third. Hanford Pioneer, I think it's called."

While loading his arms with her pile of leather bags, Juanita almost dropped one. "What?" She'd thought he was jabbering to excuse himself for bad manners. "That's my brother-in-law's name! Where's it again?"

It was late morning when Juanita stepped through the door of the Hanford Pioneer Bakery and Confections, which had a sourdough loaf and rock candy stick painted above its adobe entrance. Empty trays lined wooden shelving, but the warm smell of fresh bread lingered. She called hello across the empty counter.

A slight, pale-skinned young woman emerged from the back with hair so light it was almost blond. Her pretty face had delicate lips, a button nose and large brown eyes, but was so thin it was clear she was sickly. The woman looked like a little bird, or a fawn wobbling alongside its mother after birth.

"Can I help you, sir?" she asked in Spanish. "Or . . . ma'am?"

Juanita's hand went to her mouth in surprise, feeling as if an apparition had appeared. In the four years since they'd seen each other, her sister had transformed. But then again, so had she. Juanita had forgotten she went everywhere basically dressed like a man, the worn skirt barely hiding men's trousers and riding boots underneath.

"Josefa, my darling. It's me, Juanita. You look just like Mamá. It took my breath away."

Startled, Josefa almost dropped her tray, then came around the display case. "Hermana? Is it really you? I thought I'd never see you again. No one knew where you were. You look like a man."

She recovered quickly with a long embrace, then ushered Juanita to a kitchen table close to a slow flame lingering in the large brick oven built into the wall. Juanita was surprised, as most Alta California ovens were *hornitos*, beehive-shaped ovens built outside with adobe bricks.

Josefa noticed the eyebrow raise and said, absently, "Charles likes the American-style oven. His family's bakery in England had a brick one. He's seen the *hornos* collapse if they aren't built right." Josefa brushed flour off the table with her hand. "I just knew you wore pants under your dresses when we were little. Me and Bea would argue about it. Now I see I was right," she said and giggled.

Juanita smiled at her sister and their memories. "I've been looking for you and Charles for years, ever since I left the rancho in '50."

The front door opened with a shudder and Josefa jumped up to greet a customer. Juanita heard her explain in simple, heavily accented English the bread was all sold. Only candies left today. She returned and offered Juanita a piece of black licorice.

"If you want the sourdough, you'll have to come in the morning," she said with a slight smile, then sat down heavily, breathing hard.

Juanita caressed her hands. "Tell me everything. What ails you? Did you make it to the diggings? How's Charles? This bakery? And, *mi amor*, I know you've lost babies. I'm so sorry." She said nothing about Joaquin. That could come later.

Josefa nodded, a shadow on her delicate features. She looked so much like their mother, Candelaria. Juanita and Beatriz were both dark-skinned with sturdy physiques, long legs, and shoulders and backs made for work. Both had thick black hair, wide eyebrows and red lips, like their father. Their youngest sister had inherited their light-skinned mother's countenance and, it appeared, also her weak constitution. Throughout their childhood, Candelaria was often ill, but, devout and duty bound, she had pushed herself to host travelers and grand entertainments at her husband's side with a graciousness that made the ranch famous. But it was always a struggle for fragile Candelaria. How had Josefa survived the mining camps?

The young woman rose. "Let me make some tea first."

Juanita offered to help but Josefa waved her off. Instead,

Juanita sat patiently, taking in the bakery kitchen's stocked worktables and the cauldrons heating water over a small fire for washing pans and trays. Josefa returned with an iron tea pot and blue-patterned china cups.

"We don't know why, but I can't get strong enough to take a baby to term. I'm sick often. Too weak now to start baking at three in the morning. And the doctors don't know what to do. Charles is so worried. He carries many burdens these days."

Juanita seemed to have done a poor job at protecting her youngest sister too. She'd been blessed with a strong physique and ingenuity to survive on skills needed in a male world, but not the ability to support her loved ones into adulthood.

"And the diggings . . . what a disaster," Josefa continued. "We were both ill, constantly. And Charles never found much in the rivers. He was obsessed, but passion doesn't bring you nuggets. He slogged in freezing streams day in and out. We tried a bakery in Marysville, but it was too early, in '49. We didn't have steady customers to make it through winter. Town's probably big enough now. They've got a mail stop."

She sipped her tea, then wrapped a black wool shawl around her shoulders. Juanita was warm in the steamy kitchen.

Josefa explained that after they'd moved to Sacramento to open a bakery, she'd suffered another miscarriage. Fortunately, they'd recently hired a baker from a popular San Francisco sourdough family. They were hoping he'd marry and stay in town. As word of their flavorful, fluffy loaves spread, they had developed loyal customers. They needed another oven but had to get through this winter before investing more.

"We both want children, Juanita, you know. They could help us someday. And it's too quiet, just us two. But I don't think God has that in mind for us. I pray on it daily and go to mass. A bigger town is better for church too. I went to mass at St. Rose of Lima on Seventh three times a week until it burned down. We've given a little so they can rebuild." She put down her tea, looking exhausted. "I need to rest now. Can you come back for supper? Charles will be here."

Juanita carefully hugged her frail sibling and led her into a small bedroom behind the brick oven.

"I'd love nothing more. Tell me when and I'll come help prepare."

Josefa grimaced and they managed a little laugh, both knowing cooking was a skill Juanita lacked. The familiarity warmed Juanita to her core.

"It is so good to see you. I want to help," she whispered into Josefa's soft hair in a long embrace.

"Ah, Juanita, what a surprise. Welcome to our simple 'ome and bakery." Charles, while cheery sounding, was gaunt with bony arms, haggard cheeks, and purple circles under his eyes. What a toll four years of failed dreams could take. Juanita remembered him as a muscular, broad-shouldered businessman with a bushy mustache and thick, wavy brown hair. Years before, his sparkling blue eyes and hearty laugh had charmed their mother and other family members as Josefa's future husband.

Now a depleted Charles leaned in for a polite peck on Juanita's cheek as he kept a protective arm on Josefa, worry lines creasing his forehead.

"Whatchya doing in Sacramento City? You leave the ranch too? You look thin. You wearing trousers? I 'ear the new ranch owners weren't pleasant bosses." His tone was not unfriendly, just distracted, heavy, as if his problems weighed down every word.

Charles Hanford was an English sailor who'd jumped ship at

some point in the Mexican era. No one really knew whether he rode in from the south or he'd refused to return to the sea right there in Monterey. By the time Juanita was searching for a suitable husband for Josefa, Charles had a bustling warehouse at the intersection of Alvarado and Calle Principal. He'd dreamed of adding a bakery and Josefa's primary responsibility as his young wife was to assist him in establishing the new business.

In 1848, however, when news of the gold strikes leaked out of the mining area, gold fever took hold of Charles. Obsessed with the opportunity to strike it rich quickly, he led his new wife up into the Sierra foothills with barely a farewell and no plan for contacting family.

"Sit, sit. Let's talk over supper. Steam beer?" Charles asked.

Juanita declined, but she did savor the soft rolls and the carrot-and-potato stew flavored with small chunks of beef. "Your bread is delicious. I've been looking for you for years but just heard about Hanford Bakery because of your sourdough. It's the talk of Sac City! I'm not in town often."

Juanita decided to wait to grill them with her many questions about Joaquin until everyone was relaxed and full. She explained about Candelaria's death almost three years ago, and starting her muleteer business after she'd fled the ranch. She did not confess to stealing from Beatriz and selling her belongings to a San Francisco madam. She stretched the truth about her time at the Mission, suggesting work there had helped her start the mule train.

Josefa didn't question how Juanita was surviving in the diggings. She listened, ate slowly, nodded occasionally. She seemed weak and involved in her own problems. Charles raised his wide eyebrows now and then but mostly rubbed his wife's neck or gestured for her to take another spoonful of stew.

"Have you heard from Beatriz?" Juanita asked. "She showed me a letter from you. Maybe from winter of '48 or '49." Despite her curiosity, she forced herself to be patient. Couldn't scare them off or overtax Josefa.

"Yes, Bea wrote about Mamá's passing. She said you'd stopped by but didn't say where you went. I wrote and asked for more details but never got a response. We've moved quite a bit. I hadn't realized how confused Mamá was." She paused for a long moment. "But I'm glad you left the horrible new owner, hermana. Selling the rancho was too much to bear. It was the only reason I agreed to leave Monterey and follow Charles up to the gold. I was heartbroken. What would Papá and Abuela Quina think about the land grant gone, no longer in the hands of Castros?"

Juanita, guilt and regret flowing, squirmed on the chair but said nothing. Food seemed to have given Josefa a bit more strength.

"Also, Bea said they were trying to prove ownership of the Dominguez ranch and were having financial problems because of it. Another ranch lost to the old families. Tragic."

Could Juanita use some of her savings to ease their situation? Since seeing the brick oven and hearing about their success, she was determined to aid her sister in some manner. Josefa clearly was too sickly to work. Maybe give them funds to add another oven? Or raise the French baker's salary so he'd stay. What if they had borrowed money to build the Pioneer Bakery? Could she help repay a loan? Any contribution would delay her ability to take significant funds to Beatriz, but here was her ill baby sister right in front of her. She put Beatriz out of her mind for the moment.

"Well, good of you to stop by," Charles said. "I've gotta git ta sleep 'cause I get up at two and Josefa needs to rest. You have a safe place to stay? Sorry, we've no extra beds."

"I stay over at American River Boarding. But I'd like to see you again. I have some questions about the time you saw Joaquin? Josefa wrote to Bea about it." Her voice dropped low. "I'm looking for him. That's why I'm muleteering . . . well, besides needing to make a living. I've been searching for almost three years. I'm desperate for some news."

"'mm, I see. Come by early then." Charles got up from the table, gathering the stew bowls. "You can 'elp with loaf sales. Then stay for breakfast. Was a long time ago. Lot's 'appened since. I'll try to remember."

Relief. Finally, some Joaquin news. How would she sleep until then?

By five in the morning, a line had formed out the steamy bakery's door into the muddy street. Juanita collected silver coins, dust, Cal Fracs, and Pioneer Coins in exchange for sourdough loaves, rolls, and a few candies. Many bought two loaves, which she knew they'd nibble on throughout the day. Miners in the diggings had to saw slices off their rock-hard loaves. This soft, tasty sourdough was a revelation. Maybe Charles and Josefa could finally have some stability baking for the hungry throngs of Sacramento City's growing population.

All the loaves were gone by eight. Josefa had not emerged from their bedroom.

"Charles," Juanita started, careful to keep her tone calm. She didn't want to plead but felt she had to break through the distractions of his own problems. Hoping for some family loyalty and compassion, she decided to start with the ultimate betrayal, wanting to garner some sympathy.

"Right after Mamá died, I found out Mrs. Brennan, the

ranch owner's wife, had received letters from the gold diggings. For me. But she destroyed them. Joaquin must have written, but I never knew."

When her voice cracked with emotion, Charles' attention seemed to focus.

"I left immediately to search for him," she continued. "Thought maybe I'd find him in a tent on a sandbar. I didn't understand the scale of the northern to southern mining area. Clearly, I was naïve. But Beatriz told me you encountered him in the camps early on."

She stopped and waited with a penetrating look, staring into his cornflower-blue eyes. He nodded.

"I saw that boy in a sick tent a doctor set up to wait out rain, and snow. Was cold, damp. Rivers so icy you couldn't prospect long. Everyone sick. Some didn't make it that winter." He paused, clearly processing a painful memory. "Mighta been when Josefa lost the first one."

Juanita reached over and squeezed his hand. "I'm so sorry about the babies. I hope she can get stronger now you're more settled."

He took his hand out from under hers and swallowed more coffee. She waited and, mercifully, he continued. "Think it might 'ave been up on the American River, one of the Bars on the forks up there. Can't remember. We moved around a lot, tough to survive. We're staying put now. No going back to Monterey. 'ere's the opportunity, Miss Juanita. I gotta get my wife well, get a stable income, so we can 'ave a family."

Juanita shifted in her chair, then sipped her coffee. "Yes, I understand. Do you remember anything else?"

"Well, let's see. I remember your boy was sick too, slumped over, waiting like everyone, but I recognized 'im. My own nephew up there in the diggings. I never knew you all well, but I recognized that boy. Always remember that gift with the 'orses. Was something to see, 'im breaking a wild one. I sat down and told 'im who I was. 'e seemed surprised, sat up, said went by Joe now. Changed 'is name. You know that?"

Juanita swallowed hard. "Did he say a last name?" Charles shook his head. If she wanted the details, she'd have to be honest with her brother-in-law. So, she confessed.

"After you left, he kept getting taller, his hair more reddish. The stable boys were gossiping he looked like the new owner. I knew his wife was crazy and ambitious, so I had to act quick. Mamá was confused, refused to leave. I couldn't get us thrown out with nothing. I sent Joaquin away, told him to become Joe, American, speak only English and go up to the diggings for the gold. Just gave him a horse, some silver, and the family bible. I regret it now, every day, Charles, but at the time I saw no other option."

He look startled.

"A bible? That reminds me. Said something strange, kinda surly, after he told me never heard from 'ome. Seemed sad, lonely, but kinda 'ard too, but remember we was all sick, and the diggings is no easy living. I offered a place in our tent. But wouldn't have it. Gonna make it on 'is own. I remember it 'cause I thought some family might be a comfort. 'e was still young."

"What did he say about the bible?"

"Oh, right. Said something like, 'Why would she give me the family bible? Said it would protect me, but it's just a book. Not gonna stop a bullet. Or help me dig up a pocket mine, now, is it?' Course, I couldn't answer the boy. Seemed sour but also determined."

Juanita felt as if a hot knife had stabbed her. She put her hand to her sternum, trying to calm her thumping heart. Surly? Angry? And yet, of course, what did she expect? He must have been mystified by the middle-of-the-night send-off with scant information. And then never receiving any letters back. She hadn't thought about him being lonely or sad when she'd made her desperate decision. Of course, he felt abandoned and angry. She had to find her boy, show him she'd sent him away out of love. To protect all of them.

"You know, Juanita," Charles seemed to have warmed up, a slight smile forming. "I remember thinking, even in the cold, and being so ill, that boy reminded me of you. Stubborn, single-minded, focused on a certain path. I think the doctor called then. Said 'adn't struck it rich yet and maybe didn't have the talent for it, like with 'orses. Said if another winter of sickness, might leave all together, maybe to Mexico. Wanted to make something of 'is self before seeing family."

"Anything else? Did he ask about me or any of us?"

"No. Remember, we was all real sick. Was a bad influenza in winter '48 to '49. For me, it was nothing but a miserable slog. Maybe we're breaking our bad luck streak now 'ere with this Frenchman's bread recipe and wild yeast starter. Mostly about luck, Miss Juanita."

He patted her hand, pushed his chair back, and went to check on Josefa in the bedroom. She heard them murmuring. Charles had nothing more for her.

Sorrow filled her every pore. At least she'd learned Joaquin had been determined to make his way in mining. Who knew if he had any success or died of the influenza?

She thanked Charles and Josefa for their generous hospitality and the information on Joaquin, then departed, but not before whispering to Josefa she wanted to assist them. They should decide how to use the funds, whether it was a new oven, the baker, another helper, or paying off any debts. She told Josefa about the sack of gold dollars and pouches of dust she'd hidden under their bed. She knew proud Charles would be reluctant to accept her charity.

She rationalized wealthy Beatriz and Agustín had started with more on their large, successful rancho. Sickly Josefa could really benefit from some of her savings at this very moment. Her debt to Beatriz would have to wait.

As she rode out down J Street with the mules trailing behind, she thought of her grandfather's bible. In giving it to Joaquin, she'd been trying to communicate an attitude of protection, love, of respect for tradition. The foundational strength of family. Perhaps, he hadn't been with her enough years to convey the message completely. From her point of view now, sending him away with an old bible seemed foolish. As apparently it had felt to young Joaquin.

With a load of winter supplies in her mule train, she decided to do one more run up the Middle Fork of the American. She had to leave immediately as it was getting late in the season. She hadn't been up to those camps in some time and there should be new miners to ask about Joaquin. Plus, if she emptied out this load, then re-stocked in Sacramento once more for the valley towns, she'd have enough to deliver to Beatriz and Agustín and apologize, finally.

While she was camped in Spanish Bar, a competitor arriero approached her as he rode in from the entry trail.

"Juanita Castro? Got a letter for you from San Francisco. Tobias at the Sac City dry goods was insistent I bring it up to the camps. Was headed up this way to bring holiday extras to the guys who stick it out the whole winter. Here you go, ma'am." He tipped his hat and rode off leaving Juanita mystified.

San Francisco
October 30, 1852

Dear Miss Castro,
I trust this letter finds you well in the diggings. We've heard a rumor of a young, tall, auburn-haired Joe visiting rooms at one of my boarding houses. Rumor was he was raised on a big rancho near Monterey and had special skills with the horses. Dear Lizzie, bless her heart, remembered your request and passed the information on.

I tried to track him down but had no luck. Probably just another unrelated rumor as more men float in, pouring off the ships sickened with dengue from the Panama crossing or weak from months at sea around the Horn. Those that drag in off the wagons after crossing the plains and mountains are depleted from losing half their colleagues to cholera (as happened to my dear brother), Indian attacks, desert heat or the freeze of the Rocky and Sierra Mountains.

We are inundated with men not only seeking their fortunes but some comfort in an alien land after a terrible journey.

I don't know if there is anything at all to this rumor, but I felt I should inform you of its existence. Come see me in the city and we can discuss this further.

Sincerely,
Isabel Avila

Shocked at being handed a rare letter in a remote mining camp, then reading of a promising lead, Juanita knew she had to get out of the mountains. Quick. But her train was full with overly stuffed packs so she couldn't drive the mules fast to the city to investigate the rumor immediately. High in the Bars, she was forced to deliver as many supplies as possible to the most remote Middle Fork camps before turning west.

Could the madam have located her son as she'd predicted she might? Charles' memory of his encounter in the early prospecting days fueled her urgency to find Joaquin before he died of illness, or fled the country out of frustration, or loneliness. Perhaps, once down on the valley floor, she could purchase items in Sacramento which were in scarce supply in the city—like a reverse delivery—to keep filling her satchels with gold and silver coins. Then after finding Joaquin, she'd bring him along to Beatriz and Agustín's ranch to pay her debt and reunite the family.

Juanita's mind was brimming with plans as she hustled in and out of the supply tents at each Bar camp without stopping, anticipating a longed for reunion with her son and a break from cold, mountain living. Her hopes were so high she was even looking forward to seeing San Francisco's rumored dramatic growth and changes since her stay almost three years before.

Disaster on the Middle Fork

November 1852

Juanita stirred under her pile of woolen blankets as the soft *plat, plat* of snowflakes landed on the tarp over her head. More snow? She sat up and pulled on her boots, glad she slept fully clothed. Visibility was nil. The usual peppery pine smell had dissipated. An absence of scent. It just smelled winter cold.

After folding up the canvas, she wrapped it around the pine poles she'd cut and stripped to create a shelter for herself and one or two of the most fatigued mules. She quickly checked packs and straps, bridles and lead ropes. She'd just finished up in Spanish Camp, Volcano, and Big Bars on the Middle Fork of the American and would now aim west. Even though it was still dark, this latest snowfall made it clear it was time to move down out of the mountains. She still had a few loaded packs but she wanted to get to the city fast.

She stepped into the stirrup and swung her leg over Canela. She was weary of the wintry and constant damp and regularly pulling mules out of snow drifts. Early snow had started in October and continued for weeks. She'd noticed a larger than usual exodus of miners leaving the gold fields at their backs as the cold pushed them down the mountain away from prospecting. Maybe the merchants in Smith's Bar or Morman's Bar lower on the trail could use some items before winter halted the supply trains.

Juanita led the mules slowly on the narrow path, craggy cliffs on one side, the river far below on the other. Giant snow drifts coated the rocky terrain, creating white walls at least twice her height on the mountain side of the track. The trail was treacherous, covered with not only fallen rock from slides but also patches of ice under piles of the feathery, overnight snowfall. Green needle clusters poked through the white on weighed-down pine branches.

Flakes fell softly, and Juanita frequently dismounted Canela to check on the mules and keep all eighteen moving steadily. Slow going. She'd waited too long to leave. She scolded herself for the error. Why hadn't she driven the train west the minute she'd received Miss Avila's letter?

She mounted the horse again just as she heard a *crack*, *shush*, and a loud roaring. Suddenly, she saw only white. A moving snow wall blinded her, then pushed her and the horse over as the hillside above loosened. Snow rushed onto the path in front and behind her, enclosing around all the animals, knocking them over, pushing them down, down the cliff toward the river.

She gripped Canela's reins and mane tightly. They rolled and tumbled off the trail into a snowbank, Canela squealing and whinnying in terror. The horse struggled to right herself. Juanita jumped away to not be dragged down by the animal's fight but continued rolling, hitting rocks and packed ice beneath the powder. She finally hit a tree trunk and stopped.

Picking herself up, she shook off the white entombing her

and assessed she had no broken bones, just bruises and cuts. Her head hurt but she had to move quickly. She pushed the snow away from her legs and stomped up the hill to her horse. Canela was struggling to stand up, knee deep in the bank. Juanita dug around each leg rapidly to free her.

"It's okay, girl," she repeated. "We're going to get out of here. Easy now." After she released the horse's legs, she led Canela slowly, coaxing the terrorized animal to firmer ground. The avalanche had finally stopped moving and there was an eerie silence, with only the river's rushing sound rising from below.

The mules. Where were the mules? She had to calm Canela before searching for them. She smashed her boots hard to form a stable landing. Finally, when she felt the footing was secure, she tethered the horse to a barely visible tree branch. Continuing to use the soft, coaxing tone Canela liked, Juanita searched through her clothes and her satchel, miraculously still over her shoulder. No treats for the horse, words were her only tool to quiet the beast.

She had to go dig out the mules.

"I'll be right back. Hold on, girl. I'm right here," she repeated as she walked back up the trail, then stepped off into the white vastness where they'd gone over. She listened for animal cries as she whipped her arms through snow piled in front, to her sides, surrounding her. No packs or debris. No turning ears or honking calls. Only Canela whinnying above her and the roar of the Middle Fork's rapids below.

The enormous slide hadn't stopped until it reached the water's edge. How far down could she hike, tossing snow, calling for the mules, without sinking under herself? Her gloves were soaked through, her boots grew heavier and heavier, and she began to shake as her teeth clattered together, chattering.

The river was still a long way down the slope. She would never be able to get any animal back up to the trail at this distance, even if she found one. It was pure white below her, all around and above, and the snow continued to drop steadily, softly, adding a whispery touch onto the existing mounds. She had to retreat or she'd freeze to death right here.

Fingers numb, feet soaked, snowflakes coating her eyelashes and cheeks, Juanita reluctantly trudged up the hill to Canela. The mules and the pack train were buried completely. It had happened so quickly. And so completely. She was shocked there was no sign or sound from any of the animals. All eighteen gone? Just in a flash?

A mountaineer had to use fear to make good decisions. Time for her to do that now. She'd heard tales of snow drifts as high as three men or small mountains. Of men suffocating within a snow slide and never reappearing on the trail. Tough, strong miners gone in a moment, as if they'd never existed. Snow and cold were not weather to trifle with, her mule leading years had taught her. Such a contrast to her youth in the green valleys and soft rolling hills east of Monterey Bay.

She pushed such gloomy thoughts from her mind as she climbed, almost on all fours. She and Canela had to get out of here fast or they'd be the next victims. Keep moving, don't stop for anything, she told herself. Her heart raced, but she could not feel her feet or fingers. Her breath was heavy and short as she forced herself to pick up one leg, move forward, then the next foot. Snowfall continued to blind her.

"Canela, where are you? Canela?" she called. She realized she hadn't heard the horse since she'd turned around. Got to keep moving. She was so tired. Maybe just stop and rest right here. No. Can't stop.

"Keep moving. If you stop, you're dead, Juanita," she said out loud. "Canela!" Was the ground a bit harder beneath her? She heard a snort and a soft whine. "Canela!" she called and moved toward the sound. Finally. She could see the horse on her knees, mid-collapse.

"Okay, Canela. Get up. We gotta get out of here," she yelled, using the energy from this victory to propel her forward. She pulled the horse hard to get her moving. Can't let her fall or I'll never get her up. Taking a deep breath, she used all the energy she could muster. "Canela, up, now!" The horse seemed inspired by Juanita to make a final effort and she stood, her knobby legs shaking.

Slowly, Juanita led the horse down the mountain path toward the encampments below. Maybe Manhattan Bar would have shelter with a hot fire. But it was pitch dark. Still an hour or two to daylight. Keep moving. Snow was still falling—maybe a little lighter now, or was that her imagination? The next settlement looked abandoned. Torn canvas, tent frames partially standing amid the snow drifts. No light anywhere. She couldn't stop to explore up the ravine. Gotta keep moving to lower elevations. Next camp.

At Mormon's Bar, there were still tents and structures in place. She smelled smoke and looked for the source. Was someone keeping a fire going all night? Through the dark and snowfall, she squinted to see a two-room shack with four walls, raised floor and iron stove pipe. A covered stall for horses out back. One visible candle flickering a feeble light.

She was so cold and was shaking so hard she couldn't feel her fingers or feet, her legs or arms. There was no choice but to interrupt their sleep. Juanita stepped up to the wooden door— not just a canvas drape—and knocked. A newborn's squeaky cry pierced the dark. A man propped the door open a crack with a pistol.

"Who's there? What you want at this hour?"

"Sorry, sir, to bother you but my horse and I are just about frozen. Got caught in an avalanche. Could we warm up here? I'll leave early."

"Goodness, it's the lady muleteer. Mae, get up! I'll warm up the horse in the stall. You get this lady some dry clothes and hot tea. No bother, ma'am. My wife's feeding the baby. Lucky she had the candle lit for you to see. Where's the mules?"

Juanita was so grateful and so cold she couldn't say a word. She just handed him Canela's reins and shook her head. Nodding silently, he went outside.

A small, tow-headed girl of about ten appeared and, after rubbing her eyes, handed Juanita a blanket and guided her to the potbellied stove. She cranked the door open and threw split pine logs on the glowing red cinders. The crackle of the pine catching fire was the best sound Juanita had ever heard. And the smell. The smoke escaping through the stove's door was so welcoming it almost brought tears to her eyes.

Mae expertly cranked the stove door to seal it shut, then hauled a cauldron of water from beside the stove and set it on the flat cooking surface. After disappearing into the back room, she returned with a thin cotton dress, thick wool socks and a wide swath of burlap. Without a word, the girl grabbed her hand and led her to a corner draped with a piece of calico serving as a makeshift curtain. They had to step over four, maybe five, children, some sleeping, others watching her every move. A boy, perhaps a year younger than Mae, stood up from the swirl of blankets. He rubbed his mussed blond hair.

"I'll go help Papa," he whispered to his sister.

Juanita pulled the calico closed to create a tiny changing room. She pulled off her pants and socks, yanked the soaked dress up over her head. Then she scrubbed the burlap rapidly over her skin before quickly donning the dry dress, which smelled faintly of barley. Her feet were still completely numb, and her fingers beginning to tingle. She was not going to put on socks just yet.

As she emerged, the previously reticent Mae began to chatter a steady stream of advice. "Now, ma'am, this is gonna sting like nothin' else. Get here by the fire but be ready for the tinglin' to turn bad. You had the frostbite before? Well, I have, and it ain't fun gettin' your fingers or toes back. Let's see if we can save 'em. Lot of folks around here lose a few each winter. But none of this lot yet." She waved toward the cluster of blond, pale-skinned children, now all awake, wide eyes watching her every move.

These were the quietest children Juanita had ever seen. Maybe getting woken up in the middle of the night by a frozen stranger had shocked them into silence. Or this small Mae led the group with authority. The oldest of six or seven children often took charge, she remembered from her childhood among aunts and uncles with enormous families. So long ago and so far away now.

Mae was right. As she held the steaming cup of tea with stinging fingers, Juanita's feet began to feel as if she had put them into the roaring fire. She squirmed on the hard pine chair and started to push away.

"No, don't you move. You stay put right by that fire. Here. Some whiskey in your tea might help. You'll feel like you're right in that stove burnin' like the logs, but you gotta stay put. Keep drinkin'."

Young Mae came around and massaged Juanita's shoulders with a strong grip, then moved down her arms. After taking the mug and setting it on the stovetop, she rubbed Juanita's hands tenderly but firmly.

"I think your hands are gonna be fine. It's the feet we gotta worry about. Ya gotta be real careful with the frozen skin or you can pull it right off. How they feelin'?"

"Like the smithy chiseled his metal from the forge on my feet, instead of his anvil." Juanita grimaced and moaned but did not cry out. An audience of tiny children, and their mother trying to calm a newborn in the next room, kept any theatrics under control.

"Yep. That's it, ma'am. Ya got the feelin' just right. I almost lost some toes last winter but we saved 'em."

"My horse?" Juanita asked, trying to distract herself by thinking about Canela. Would she make it if she had the same kind of damage from being immersed in the snowbank?

"My papa and brother know just what to do. Don't you worry. What's the name? A mare or stallion? No, you can't stand up. Can't put no weight on them toes. Just keep your feet close to the fire."

Mae kept on chatting and asking questions while Juanita stretched and tossed in pain as her feet unfroze. Her fingers slowly calmed, but her feet—how could she walk these mountain trails, lead mules over passes and into river valleys and canyons if she lost toes or a foot? The agony of picturing being lame, and the pain, were overwhelming. Just let Canela make it, she prayed. And dear God, let me keep my feet.

Juanita was not a regular with prayers. She'd rejected her parents' strict adherence to Catholic doctrine, her grandmother's deep beliefs in the church's right to take Alta California for the Spanish crown and bring religion to the Natives, who did not seem particularly interested. Nor did they thrive under Mission rule. Yet, she also was a product of her very Catholic Spanish and Mexican culture. Praying was part of everyday life. Mass and confession were rituals embedded in regular living. The priest was a highly regarded member of every community. Her grandmother had built a chapel on the rancho and prayed there every day of her ranching life. Juanita had always been respectful in such settings but had never fully absorbed prayer as much as her elders would've liked.

Now, however, in a time of pain, both physical and emotional, and with a loss so immense, prayer seemed to flow. As if it were a muscle her body instinctively knew to use in the worst of times. How had she gotten to this place of such aloneness that she and her horse had almost died swallowed up by a hillside of snow?

Not one person would have known she was gone, she realized as her feet burned as if in flames. Unacceptable. What crazy path had led to this dark moment? Could it be she'd been punishing herself for the mistakes she'd made and could not forgive? Had she absorbed her grandmother's beliefs after all, that she had to suffer hardships as penance for her sins? Juanita's mind swirled in confusion with the pain, the deepening realization of her aloneness, with her regrets.

She shook her head to clear her thoughts. Self-inflicted guilt and pain was a fool's errand. What was the point? Juanita disappearing in an avalanche would not bring her son to her, would not bring her parents back or return her to the good graces of her sister. She had to face her faults and make amends on her own. Accept that she needed others. The constant aloneness and extreme self-reliance were irrational and had almost gotten her and her beloved horse killed. And she'd lost her livelihood. The mule train, with all her savings stored in the packs, was gone.

Mae seemed to sense Juanita's despair, because she began to whisper in her ear as she poured more scalding tea and whiskey—mostly whiskey it tasted like—into her mug and raised it to her lips. She massaged her neck and arms and then her hands again.

"Ma'am. You the mule driver, like my papa said? Well, you must have seen an awful lot up here in the diggin's. Met some crazy characters. Ma and Papa always talkin' about how this gold drawn in the adventurers and risktakers and fortune-seekers from every corner of the globe. You ever tried pannin' yourself? Now it's too late to scoop it out like they did at first, Papa says. I never saw one of them gold nuggets size of apples. You? Maybe walnut-sized? That must be somethin'."

Mae went on for what seemed an eternity with Juanita's feet burning as if in an inferno. She tried to be polite but mostly shook or nodded her head in reply. Once Mae retrieved her mother from the now sleeping baby, the two of them decided it was time to work on her feet. Juanita could see Mae's confident authority came right from this woman. While pale and tired-looking, thin, with mousy brown hair but a large bosom with milk stains on the bodice, this mother was no nonsense. Juanita tried to thank the woman but she shushed her.

"Just have camphor liniment, but no good for frostnip. We'll make a paste of flour and water and bicarbonate. We're gonna coat your feet with it, try to save your skin. And toes. It might work," the mother said.

After a while, the pain lessened so Juanita, exhausted and woozy from the whiskey, drifted off to sleep with her legs stuck straight out in front of the fire, white paste covering up to her knees.

She woke to the newborn's squeal in a house quiet with everyone asleep. From the sound of things, the snowfall had finally stopped. The sun was pushing itself meagerly through the tarp-covered window. The pile of children, now including Mae and her brother, stirred to resettle itself but all stayed asleep.

Who was this family of white-haired children here in the Bars in winter? While tiny, especially for a family of eight or nine, this shack was far better equipped than most prospectors' tents. Who would bring a whole family and raise them here? Clearly, they'd been here a while, since the capable Mae had mentioned her own frostbite experience. She winced in discomfort but followed instructions and did not move. She drifted back to sleep.

Her dreams were filled with hammers and blacksmithing tongs waving before a blazing fire. Then her grandmother's face appeared in the smoke. With sparks flying from her eyes, she pronounced, "You fool. You're a rancher. What are you doing scaling frozen peaks and traveling alone with mules? Have you forgotten the family? What of our legacy?" Then her burning hand reached out to claw and scratch Juanita's face and body.

She woke with a jolt to a circle of small faces with pink cheeks and matching white hair sticking up as if they were fluffy dandelion tops waiting for the wind to blow wisps to all points. No one said a word, but they were taking in her red arms and paste-covered legs.

"You gonna lose your toes, ma'am?" the tallest one, a boy, asked.

A girl who mirrored her big sister Mae elbowed him in the side. "That's not polite."

"How long you gotta keep that stuff on your legs?" asked a much smaller girl.

"Hush, y'all. Let her rest. Get yourselves cleaned up for breakfast," Mae said as she came in all business-like, swirling her dress around and shooing them toward the washbasins on a ledge below the window covered with heavy tarp. She saw one blond head peek outside.

"Look, Mae, Ma, it's stopped snowing. Sun's out." And they all crowded to the window pushing the tarp until their mother tied the canvas up to bring in some light. Their little mouths fogged up the thin glass. How on earth had they gotten a glass window all the way up here, she couldn't help but wonder, admiring this family's industriousness.

As if he could hear her thoughts, the man came over and held out his hand.

"Jacob Clark, ma'am. Looks like your arms and legs might be okay. Your mare's gonna be fine. Needs some food and rest. Why don't you stay with us 'til you get back on your feet? Literally."

A chorus of "Yes, stay," echoed through the small cabin. And then they quacked all at once like ducklings.

"Do you know any stories?"

"You really run mules, ma'am?"

"Mae'll get you fixed up."

"What happened to you and your mare, ma'am?"

Mrs. Clark immediately shushed the little gang, admonishing there'd be no flapjacks for anyone without a clean face. Commotion ensued, water and shared towels flew, and then the whole crew was suddenly sitting at the table with their hands folded in their laps.

Juanita was incredulous. The long redwood table of her

youth had been loud and boisterous, sisters, cousins, aunts, uncles, everyone talking at once. Yes, they did fall silent at mother's insistence on a prayer or a history lesson from father. But after those moments, controlled chaos reigned. Here, Mr. Clark led the family in prayer and asked the Lord to watch over their guests in the house and stable. Mrs. Clark and all the children mumbled assent and then she and Mae served up pancakes.

"And in honor of our guest, you all can have a bit of butter and a few drops of maple syrup."

The children squealed with delight, bright smiles all around.

"Just remember to conserve, as we've a long winter ahead. Whew, what a start it's been. Oh, and thank your mother," Mr. Clark reminded them, and the children quickly produced appreciative phrases then dug into their treat-covered pancakes. When the baby cried in the background, Mae took over as her mother disappeared. Juanita and her sisters and cousins had never been quite so well-behaved, yet it all felt comfortingly familiar. She figured to survive all the seasons out here in the Bars, you'd have to raise disciplined children.

Finally, she felt energetic enough to talk.

"Mr. Clark, I am indebted to you, sir. Thank you so much for taking me in from the dark and storm. And for caring for my frozen limbs. I might be able to keep all my toes, and if I do, it will be because of you and your wonderful family. How is that you're raising such delightful children up here on the American River?"

He rubbed his hand through his dark blond hair and she absently pictured him as a tow-headed boy just like one of his sons. "Well, ma'am, we left New York City on the *Brooklyn* with Samuel Brannan and a group of Saints in '46. Come 'round the

Horn. Been in California over six years now. Was a carpenter up in the New York woods, but we had to move west. Eventually, had to leave there too and follow Mr. Brannan on that ship. Our kind not wanted much of anywhere."

He leaned closer to her and whispered while the children were occupied with pouring more maple syrup. "You know they killed our prophet, ma'am."

She nodded slightly, as she wanted to convey sympathy but, in reality, knew little of their religion. Except she had thought they didn't drink. Then again, whiskey on hand in the diggings was just a practicality.

To be polite she said, "Ah yes, I trade with Mr. Brannan's store in Sacramento. Young Tobias there is a relative of his, I believe."

Mrs. Clark returned and joined the conversation. "You think this place is rough in winter? The Ohio prairie, with nothing but grass, is worse. We had to dig ourselves caves and live underground to survive out there! No way to raise children, like wolves in a den. Mr. Brannan's California plan sounded like an opportunity for us. Whew, the Atlantic crossing, that was a terrible journey. Took six months 'round the Horn. Babies . . . little ones . . . lucky we survived."

Mr. Clark explained they'd been part of the failed New Hope settlement near Sacramento. Once the gold fever hit, Mr. Brannan had fronted them supplies to open a dry goods store in Mormon's Bar for mining camps along the American River's forks. They'd been able to pay back their debt in less than a year. Mr. Clark recognized Juanita as one of his muleteer suppliers. She thought back to stocking the Middle Fork camps and remembered a canvas structure, then an improved wooden cabin as his store grew in sales and reputation.

"What happened to the mule train, ma'am?" he asked gently.

From what little he'd told her, it was clear this man had restarted many times. He would understand the depth of her loss. Making no mention of her search for Joaquin, she explained her attempt to get a final delivery up to the highest encampments before heavy winter set in and how she'd misjudged the early storms. What a mistake. Now she'd lost her whole train, all the packed provisions and most of her savings with it. Wide-eyed, the children listened in silence.

"In the spring thaw, you'll find a lot more up there than just mule bones, Mr. Clark," she said. "Don't tell anyone else and whatever you find is yours. Least I can do. You've saved my life. Someday, I would like to have a home of my own like yours. With kindness to strangers, good manners and morals, too. I'm thinking of a hotel and boarding house, with a little ranch and gardens, maybe in the southern mines. Will take me a while after this loss. I'll have to work in San Francisco in order to purchase new mules. But once I get a train and pack equipment, I can get running again."

There it was. She'd just made a plan by telling him her story.

"What 'bout those wagons and coaches that are startin' to come closer to the diggin's now? I bet this summer we'll have more of them deliverin'. Trail still rough, though, so mules your best bet, you're right about that."

Mr. Clark was forward thinking. Mules wouldn't be the only way to transport in the future. They'd build wider, smoother roads into the hills and wagons and stagecoaches would stock up at the wharves of Stockton and Sacramento. But not yet. Still time for mule transport to be a thriving business. But how could she start all over again?

She needed to raise a sizable quantity of gold dust, US silver, and the fifty-dollar gold slugs. Those were quickly becoming the standard. She had nothing but a small amount of cash hopefully still in the ground in Sonora. The Gallegoses probably spent the dust in their safe in their distress. The few pouches of gold she'd deposited in the new bank in Sacramento would not help; she had not trusted the cocky Mr. O.D. Hart enough to give him much of her savings. The land in Sacramento was her final insurance, but she didn't want to sell. And would there be buyers anyway with leaky levees nearby? She'd have to see how this rough winter went.

She could not go back to Beatriz and Agustín and beg their forgiveness, saying, "Well, I had your money, but now I'm destitute because I lost my mule train in an avalanche." Her brother-in-law would probably say she deserved it. And she'd sworn to herself she'd return with triple the value of what she took. She needed to raise funds again to repay her sister before she returned to the Dominguez Rancho. She also didn't want to burden Josefa and Charles. The Mission Dolores priest, if he was still around, would probably be open to her working there, but not for any payment, just a temporary, free room. Right now, she had nothing, and no resources to draw on.

A San Francisco hotel was her only option. She'd go ask Miss Avila for a job. Not as the primary attraction, but as support staff, in the stables or cleaning or shopping for supplies, maybe accounting. The few letters between them had been cordial and newsy, if not overly friendly, but Miss Avila was her only potential ally. While it irked her to have to humble herself before the madam, she had nowhere else to turn.

And even before obtaining a paying position, top priority, was to find Joaquin. As soon as she got to the city, she'd go immediately to the boarding house at the former Parlour House Hotel to see if he was still in residence. She was anxious to get started but she could barely move. She'd have to heal with the Clarks for a few days. And get Canela stronger too.

As she rested, between chats with the inquisitive littlest ones and cards games with the older kids, she pondered possibilities for her future. What if she could make a name for herself, like her parents and grandparents had in the El Camino Real days? Create a haven where haggard, exhausted travelers looked forward to stopping. After raising starter funds in San Francisco, she'd rebuild the mule train and her savings, then return to Sonora to dig up the buried coins, buy land and build a hotel there. Eventually, she'd make it a little ranchito with gardens, and some horses to train and sell. When she found Joaquin, he would love it if her establishment included ranching work and horse training. She was convinced he wouldn't like city living either.

The Clark and Gallegos families gave her a thread of hope that even in this gold-obsessed California, this bedlam of gambling and drinking and lawlessness, there were moral people honoring home and hard work in the service of others. To find such community, you also had to rely on folks besides yourself.

One afternoon sitting at the Clarks' kitchen table, young Mae asked her, "Ma'am, excuse my forwardness, but where's your family? They know you out here on the American River with this early winter? Bet they'll be happy to have you back home."

She had no response. Her obsession with being independent, never reliant on anyone, had almost caused her to ride off a mountainside to a tragic end. With not a soul knowing her whereabouts. Time to make some changes.

Over the next week, Mrs. Clark kept Juanita warm and fed, with simple jars of canned fruits and more biscuits than she'd ever eaten in her life. Mae cleaned and sewed her torn pants and dress. The boys and Mr. Clark checked on Canela and even gave her a little extra hay, despite the need to preserve their stash for the long winter. Mae carefully bathed Juanita's damaged feet, creating more poultices for the ugly, red and oozing blisters which emerged, until all but two toes seemed to be full of color and working normally. The smallest ones on her right foot remained an odd, shiny gray. They felt numb and looked dead. As she packed up Canela to leave, the whole family offered opinions.

"Might need to be amputated," the oldest boy told her.

While Mae whacked his shoulder, they all chimed in telling her to go see a doctor.

"But best if you don't let him cut," Mrs. Clark said, baby on her hip. "Find a way to save them. Otherwise, you'll never walk the same. Will always limp."

Juanita gulped, waved to the children and their parents, mounted Canela and rode down the mountain trail toward Sacramento, Bars of the Middle Fork of the American River at her back, Joaquin, she hoped, ahead of her in San Francisco.

Chambermaid

December 1852 to April 1853

Juanita did not stop at the Hanford Pioneer Bakery as she could not worry her sister with bad news. She avoided Tobias and Brannan's Dry Goods since she had nothing to sell and no ability to purchase, not to mention she was reluctant to tell her mortifying tale to anyone. The teenager would be curious and concerned about the loss of a reliable trading partner.

It was strange to ride unencumbered by the mules and with a half-numb foot. She'd deal with the deadened toes in the city. Mr. Clark was right there were stagecoaches leaving Sacramento now, providing service to Nevada City and Stockton. Other gold towns would likely be next. What would happen to the muleteers?

Almost three years after first arriving, Juanita and Canela *clip-clopp*ed into the Mission Dolores neighborhood. And what a change. The Pioneer Racetrack was complete and signs of races were visible with grand horse stalls, flying flags, and colorful bunting decorating the stands. They must work hard on course maintenance because the swampy edge of the field she and Canela had raced around was gone. A true race on a formal track would be quite the event, at least compared to Juanita's foray into the sport. Chuckling at the memory, she patted Canela's neck, feeling fortunate the accident had not crippled her beloved mare.

Canela was not as fearless as before, however; the horse shied at unusual noises and scared easily at strangers. She likely would no longer trust her rider with such high speed, stress, and foreign horses. But Juanita was grateful she still had her stable companion with enough stamina for long rides over California's uneven terrain.

The Mission neighborhood streets had multiplied, and new buildings, pine sap still oozing through roughhewn milling, had sprouted up on each corner. The ever-present white-gray tents and awnings of the earliest Gold Rush years were disappearing.

And yet the Mission adobe itself was more decrepit. When Father Mateo opened the door, she noticed his nose had grown more bulbous and purple, and his cheeks streaked by red veins. He surprised her with a warm greeting.

"Can't forget a woman Californio who won a horse race and left here with a train of mules! Not much surprises me anymore in these gold times, but that was unusual," he noted, laughing as he ushered her in to the Mission's chilly, mildewed sanctuary. Juanita wrinkled her nose and noted the peeling paint, broken floor tiles and splintered pews. Brown water stains streaked the plastered adobe walls.

The novice had left for a more fruitful parish back in Spain, but the Padre's workforce had grown with the increased demand for milk, butter, and vegetables, and the gardens were flourishing. Juanita wondered how Father Mateo managed until she met the Mission's foreman, an experienced hand from a land grant out near the Livermore's rancho.

I need someone like this to oversee bigger operations when I have a hotel and boarding house, she thought. She and her father had done most everything themselves at Rancho Castro. Maybe that had led to their problems.

Father Mateo gave her a cold cell to sleep in and told her she could stay as long as needed. When she explained her current distress and need to earn cash, he shook his head at her misfortune.

"You are lucky to be alive, my child. God watched over you. But I can only exchange the bed for your labor. No silver coins or gold dust here," he said, indicating the decaying sanctuary. She did not tell him she intended to earn cash at a brothel. Father Mateo was not naïve, just beaten down by the lack of structure in an abandoned church and the disarray of a rapidly changing pueblo.

Riding out early the next morning, Juanita was captivated by the new pine-plank road leading into the city. Workers carried vegetables, flour, whiskey, and milled lumber both directions on small wagons, no longer only on backs and shoulders. Once on Market Street, she found a gentleman with a shed boarding horses and paid half the fee, promising double if Canela was safe when she returned.

Not sure where to find the madam amidst the gleaming new hotels and monte halls, she headed to Washerwoman's Lagoon only to find it completely full of Chinese men. She asked several about Isabel Avila and the Parlour House Hotel, but all shook their heads or shrugged. Not one spoke English or Spanish.

Back on the streets, however, it was clear there were more women in town. Many appeared to be prostitutes, shopping for food or dipping into a faro or monte hall before the festivities intensified for the evening. She stopped a few to ask about Isabel Avila but no one wanted to talk to a strange woman barely wearing a dress over men's trousers and work boots.

She tried the Men's Emporium, then Mr. Brannan's *Daily Alta California* offices. But neither place was forthcoming, everyone saying they didn't know a Miss Isabel Avila. "A hotel owner? Parlor what? No such place. No one here with that name."

"And we know everyone," a reporter bragged.

She decided she'd just have to search the old haunts herself. As she walked up the hill to the former Parlour House Hotel, she saw a tall redhead strolling down the hill. What luck!

"Lizzie!" she called as she approached. "How are you? Remember me?"

"Of course! Mr. Juan with the petticoats! Couldn't forget that!" Lizzie laughed, fine lines stretching out from the corners of her eyes and a small furrow deepening between her eyebrows. The lifestyle could age you. But Lizzie also appeared confident, less saucy, but more formidable. Must be learning from her boss. Her dress was simple but made of a fine linen, not the tattered muslin she'd worn when they first met at Washerwoman's Lagoon.

"I was headed down to the new hotel by the water but come over and see Madam Platt. She's living up at the Nugget while the new apartments above the Grand Palace Hotel are furnished. Lots changed since you were here, Mr. Juan," she said with a wink. "You barely look like a woman now either. You'll have to clean up to get into her chambers, you know." Juanita got lost through the new names and places.

Lizzie was right. It was an elaborate process to get approval from the large Kanaka security guard with jet-black hair flowing to his shoulders. He had her clean up with fresh rose water and Turkish towels in a powder room inside the entry hallway. Then she removed her riding boots and trousers from under her dress.

"Much better, ma'am," the Kanaka doorman said, and grinned. "Lizzie vouches you really know Madam Platt, but I couldn't let you in looking like a vagrant right off the trail. Here's some slippers." Juanita put on the thin shoes, grateful he hadn't offered a pinched boot which would be a struggle to get her foot into with the two useless toes.

As before, Juanita opened the door to reveal a world of opulence. But now, it displayed true wealth, not ersatz elegance. Imported English furniture, lush, genuine velvet drapes, a true Persian carpet. The chandeliers were crystal. Artwork from French masters hung on the walls. It was luxurious and warm, a fire crackling in the fireplace, a grand piano in the corner. Quite beautiful.

Turning from her spot at the window, the madam greeted her in a polite, but businesslike manner. She appeared considerably older than her true age, and a tad bit thicker at the waist, restraining her mass of black hair in two mother of pearl combs, and wearing a velvet dress with long sleeves and starched white lace collar. Dark kohl framed her jet-black eyes. Her lips were bright red with a gleaming substance. The wild curls were still trying to escape, betrayed by wisps below the French knot and framing her forehead and eyes. A crystal earring dangled from one hand. Perhaps the madam was preparing for a trip to her new hotel on the wharf.

"Thank you for seeing me without an appointment. You are Madam Elizabeth Platt now? I couldn't find anyone who knew Isabel Avila or the Parlour House."

"Sorry to say, but I needed to be a Platt again to gain respect. It's all Americans in charge now. The Avila name has lost its usefulness! 'Round here I'm still Isabel."

"Yes, I know, Miss Platt." The name came out with a hard, unintended tone. She'd been around too many hardened men trying to survive in freezing, gravel-filled rivers. She needed to rediscover her hacienda hostess manners for city life. She cleared her throat.

"I left Sonora after the foreign tax fights and constant attacks on anyone not from Boston, not a yanqui. A Californio family I stayed with suffered, their son shot, their boarding house stolen via corrupt yanquis. I'm well aware of who's in charge now."

"Indeed," the madam interrupted, giving a raised eyebrow at Juanita's rudeness. "Well, I did honor our agreement and look for anyone fitting your son's description. Plenty of redheads, but short or ugly. Then the recent rumor I wrote you about. We'll have to see if the gentleman in question is still around."

Juanita nodded, unsure what to say and uncomfortable with the tension in the room, she couldn't help but add,

"I'd really like to see for myself. Could I visit those boarding rooms? Oh, and were you able to place the ad in the newspaper? We never got any word in Sacramento."

"Advertisement? Oh dear. I forgot. No. But who would read such a thing anyway?"

Juanita simmered in frustration. This Madam Platt, or whoever she was, was so self-absorbed. The silence continued. She'd been inside so infrequently in the past three years, and never in such elegant surroundings, it was a bit hard to breathe.

Finally, the madam, herself, inhaled then seemed to relax her formality. More softly she said, "I am sorry about your Sonoran friends. You do need to watch your back and trust no one. Don't worry, I'll get Lizzie to take you over to the bordello to see if he's there." Then, patting the velvet chair next to her sofa, she said, "Now, tell me all of your adventures in the diggin's! Never been but sure would like to see it once. Do sit for a moment."

Juanita sank into the softness but remembered to sit up straight and be polite. She had to comply since she had no idea where Joaquin might have visited, plus she needed work.

"The diggings are horrible, really. Rough, dangerous, either muddy and cold or dry and dusty..." Juanita recounted her three years leading the mule train through Stockton and Sacramento, up the rivers to the gold camps and the Sonoran hiatus and incident. Then finally, the mountain accident. "I've lost my mules—all eighteen of them—my supplies, my gold, and US coins."

"You're lucky to have survived. The mules weren't carrying it all, right? Oh, were they?" Her face must have revealed the truth but Juanita hesitated, debating sharing her assets with this hard-driving businesswoman. But she'd already lost every- thing and needed help. Might as well be honest. Madam Platt certainly was not going to squat on her Sacramento plots or dig up her coins in Sonora. She was already a very wealthy woman.

Juanita explained her current need for cash, having nothing but two small water-logged lots in Sacramento and Canela to her name. And the tiny amount she had experi- menting with bank deposits. Then she asked about the race- track, wanting to subtly remind the madam she'd helped sig- nificantly with the project. At mention of the racecourse, the madam seemed to light up and return to the chatty young woman Juanita remembered.

"Oh yes, quite successful entertainment. Good investment

too. Great fun to go to the races, as if we were in the south. Makes me almost miss Tennessee, but then, no, thank God I'm not there with this slave state madness. Hope my father's seeing some sense and freeing his slaves. But no …. And if there's a war? What then?" For a second, a frown marred her lips, but then she brightened again. "Fortunately, we're far from that controversy and way too busy out here getting rich. Thank God California's a free state. Any other stories? Your shenanigans and taste for adventure appeal to me, Miss Castro, as it's not unlike my own, just in different industries."

At the woman's hearty laugh, Juanita relaxed. She'd forgotten how much the madam talked.

"And let's call each other by our names. There's not many who I can be frank with, and you seem trustworthy—though I haven't forgotten you stole from your own family so don't think you can do that to me."

Juanita finally admitted she was there to ask for a job. The madam raised her eyebrows, smirked, and looked Juanita over, eyes scanning her frame from forehead to boots, assessing her shabby appearance.

"You're too old to be one of my girls! But you can stay and work in the kitchen feeding them and the workers."

"So sorry, Miss Avila, uh, Miss Isabel, the one thing I cannot do. I can wash pots or clean. I never learned to cook. The price of a luxurious upbringing. I can do accounting."

"Ha. I never learned to cook either—something else in common. Well, no one touches my books but me. That's my livelihood and my power here. Though you seem to be an honest soul, Miss Juanita, we don't really know each other well, do we?" Her eyes sparkled in challenge. No wonder she was a powerhouse in town.

"Look, I just want something for a few months. I can't wait to get out of the city. I can't stand so many people, the noise and filth, the stench and mud, the drunks and gamblers."

"Hold on now—those are my customers you're talking about!"

Juanita started to mumble an apology, kicking herself for her continued rude gaffs. The gold trail and muleteer life had wrung all the Spanish and Mexican hospitality out of her. But Isabel laughed and barely seemed to notice.

"I can find a place for you. But only out of loyalty from your help with the racetrack and those clothes you sold me when I needed to become high class. I am not a charity operation, you know, taking on an extra employee."

Juanita's chest grew tight. She really needed a job. How else could she earn silver dollars, golden Liberty coins? She swallowed her pride and poured out flattery, if not quite begging.

"Of course. But Miss Platt, Isabel, I really want to settle in one place and run a hotel and boarding house like yours. I can learn so much working here. I want to grow vegetables and offer a comfortable stop for tired travelers. Sort of a return to a small rancho. These United States are different, but I think I can use skills from those days."

"You want to start a brothel?" She laughed and laughed. "Just so long as you don't do it here in the city. Don't worry, I understand. We'll get you working in the kitchen and laundry. Lizzie will get you some old dresses. You'll have to tell her a little of your story, but she'll keep it to herself. Wait, didn't you meet her at Washerwoman's Bay? She'll love you're now doing her washing!!"

Another hearty belly laugh filled the chamber.

Lizzie escorted Juanita to one of Isabel's collection of private rooms tucked upstairs and behind a hotel. "Hope it's your son, Mr. Juan," she said. "You sure been looking a long time." Juanita hid in the brothel's kitchen to look over the gentleman when he arrived for his appointment. He was in his late thirties, much too old.

She sat in the kitchen, dejected, while the cook made her a pot of strong, hot tea. Was it an unrealistic fantasy to try to locate Joaquin? There were now more than two hundred thousand souls in California. Finding him was hopeless. Yet, how could she ever give up?

The hours Juanita spent cleaning brothel and hotel rooms, kitchens and inner courtyards gave her time to ponder the future. Isabel was stingy, so it took longer than she'd anticipated to raise the gold dust needed to buy mules healthy enough to survive the trails. And the numbness in her foot made cleaning a difficult chore. Would it ever return to normal? She never visited a doctor, not wanting to spend precious funds on anything but animals, pack train supplies, and mining equipment. She wrapped any blisters, which occasionally formed, in muslin bandages. She forced herself to walk normally, without a limp.

Changes in San Francisco occurred almost daily. The Wells coach company constructed a bank building of stone and brick rivaling any edifice in New York. Wells, Fargo & Company promised a fine vault to hold everyone's gold—certainly a better option than throwing rattlesnakes in drawers or hidden safes under floorboards. The abandoned ships in the harbor still housed a few vagrants, but many were now scrap used to build homes and dormitories, eating halls and faro parlors.

Throughout the long days, Juanita also took the opportunity

to observe how Isabel conducted her businesses. The former Parlour House, now called the Pacific Hotel, was a full-service hotel and a boarding house, with quiet brothel services late in the evenings for those who requested them. However, Isabel also offered traditional hotels, no prostitutes allowed, with elegant dining rooms and French linen sheets for all travelers, including the growing number of wives coming to town.

Occasionally, the proprietress summoned Juanita to the private chambers she maintained in each location. "Y'all a safe person for me to talk with, Juanita. I need a smart ear. I'm convinced you have no intention of competing with me," Isabel said.

"Just trying to save enough to re-start my mule packing business. And to learn from you, so my little hotel and ranchito will have a good reputation which might appeal to Joaquin." Isabel raised her eyebrows but just smiled and nodded.

Often the madam would launch into her latest client problem or competitor threat. "What do you think I should do about one of my girls wanting to go out on her own? To compete with me. I fear Lizzie might. She's a smart one, so I try to give her responsibilities."

Or, "I think my cheese, milk, and butter supplier out by the Mission is cheating me. I heard of another hotel getting better prices. Can you find out?"

Or, "I've got the Vigilance Committee members in my pocket, but now they're sending for their wives. This religious group of ladies is giving me a headache. They're harassing my girls. Some even protested in front of the Grand Palace—which is well regarded as a hotel, not a brothel. But they know my reputation." Sometimes Juanita offered advice but often the madam just wanted a safe place to express frustrations or talk through strategy.

After several months, Juanita finally had earned enough to run a mule train. She'd supplemented the maid work by delivering greens and dairy items to the city's dining halls for Father Mateo. Hotels valued the Mission's regular deliveries since keeping ice boxes and pantries stocked for crowded dining rooms was a challenge.

When she was ready to leave town with a full set of mules and packed satchels, Juanita sent a message requesting to meet with Isabel. She wanted to thank the madam and also remind her she'd need a new staff housekeeper. Lizzie presented her with a written response on personalized stationery, a thick white notecard encircled with gold trim.

Madam Elizabeth Platt invites
Miss Juanita Castro
to her new apartment
Top floor of The Grand Palace Hotel
2:00 p.m., Tuesday next

Irritated and amused at the ostentatious summons, Juanita busied herself shopping at the Men's Emporium for sturdy boots. She made a special trip to see inside the brand new Wells, Fargo & Company building next door to the Union Saloon on Montgomery Street. Juanita was glad she didn't have any extra savings, as she'd be tempted to deposit in the impressive new brick building.

It's lofty, ornate ceiling, marble floor and counters, gilded enclosures for private banker consultations, and shimmering chandeliers gave the impression of solidity and uninterrupted wealth. A fortress to build confidence. Juanita's skepticism remained. How would they ever guarantee people could get their money back? Or were deposits only for Wells, Fargo & Co. coaches to carry across the plains to Eastern cities? Banks still mystified her.

On the Tuesday of her meeting with Isabel, Juanita passed through the columns making the hotel look like some sort of Greek temple. Josiah was there to greet her in a gleaming black suit and tie, shiny shoes, and a starched white shirt. He looked like he'd stepped out of a Parisian fashion magazine, not like he was the doorman at a gold-era hotel in roughhewn San Francisco.

The Grand Palace Hotel had a large atrium filled with trees and flowers in enormous clay pots and a glass dome overhead. Josiah motioned for Juanita to peek in the glamorous room to admire the white tablecloth seating, fine silverware, and delicate goblets sparkling at every place setting. A string quartet played in the corner. When Juanita let out a slight gasp, Josiah murmured a pleased assent.

It was clear Madam Isabel Platt Avila was determined to put San Francisco in league with the finest cities she'd been forced to read about when bored and restless during the long, hot days on the Tennessee tobacco plantation.

"Elegant, isn't it, Miss Castro?"

She nodded, surprised he remembered her name. She couldn't help but be impressed by the higher levels of luxury Isabel brought to each new establishment. Her private apartments in this hotel were more opulent than ever, the plush carpets leaving almost no polished floorboards visible. Extravagant furniture sat beneath gold-framed European artwork.

Isabel emerged, jewelry glittering from her throat and ears. Today it was cobalt-blue earrings, a gold chain necklace with a diamond encrusted medallion, and a serpent-shaped bracelet made from diamond, gold, and opal. Taken aback, Juanita did not restrain her reaction,

"It really is a palace. You trying to be Queen Victoria?"

At first she glared, then Isabel burst out laughing. "Leave it to you, simple Señora Castro, to question my attire. Most people are impressed. Which is the point after all. And sure, why not? The Queen of San Francisco." She smiled. "I hear you're leaving. Where will I get such a reliable maid? Do tell me your plans."

Juanita admitted she was impressed with the courtyard dining room and all Isabel had built. She hoped to have even a fraction of the size and opulence in her small community some-day. "No plans for pioneer girls in my hotel, but I will steal your ideas for salons with music and less risqué entertainment."

"Best of luck, dear Juanita. You're one tough Californio. I look forward to hearing your progress. Please write—and I will continue to ask the girls to keep an eye out for your son."

Entering Sacramento, Juanita rode up from the wharf to check on her lots to make sure no squatters had moved in. The land was untouched, but there were neighbors now building to the north. Concerned they might casually forget the property line and stretch into her land, she sought out Tobias for conversa-tion and an arrangement. He still lived in the back of the Dry Goods store. Still no other adults in sight.

He stumbled out from the storeroom as she strolled through the merchandise spilling off the shelves. No evidence of an organizational system, yet the disheveled boy, now a young man, always seemed to be able to locate any item his customers sought. Currently, he was dragging sacks of barley from behind the counter.

"Glad you got two like I asked," said the pleased customer, a man with dirty boots and worn trousers.

Tobias carefully logged the items and amounts in his ledger. "Got a fortnight before you owe me, Mr. Cochran. Don't forget now. My uncle don't take to no freeloaders. Think you were late last month."

The man grumbled as he dragged the burlap sacks to his wagon.

Once the store was empty, Juanita approached.

"Nice to see you again, ma'am," he said, sweeping his long bangs away from his face.

She smiled slightly in return. Reticent to show weakness to anyone, she did not mention the avalanche or months as a maid to purchase a new team, and he didn't ask any questions.

"Tobias. I've got a proposal for you. If I build a small house on my lots, would you oversee construction, then live there? Rent-free. But it's my land. Not giving it to you. You'd just be a caretaker in exchange. And check on my sister over at the bakery now and then."

Tobias liked the idea since he had been wanting to find a wife—hard to do when he slept at the back of a store on a cot—and said his uncle would be fine as long as he still oversaw the place and it wasn't robbed at night. He knew how to make it work.

"Know a Native who'd be happy to sleep here if I give him the shotgun. Need more help during the day too. Sac City is growing, Miss Castro. And I love the sourdough at Pioneer Bakery. No problem stopping in there."

Juanita paid an American lawyer to draw up an agreement.

Tobias signed it and they each kept copies. She was wary of land contracts and determined to do it legally under US laws. Then she gave Tobias a budget for planks and milled wood and drew out a basic design.

"I want a floor, no dirt under your feet. Don't go too cheap. You want a wife and baby in there some day, don't you?"

He reddened and nodded.

"Go over to the Sonoran tents and see if you can find someone who imports tile and knows how to lay it. Make a nice Mexican floor so that baby can crawl around all day and not get sick or dirty."

"Yes, ma'am, Miss Castro," he mumbled, pushing his bangs back. "Need a girl first, ma'am."

"There's more women coming to town. Good, strong, Catholic girls out at the ranchos too. Handsome, smart man such as yourself, you'll have no trouble finding someone."

Tobias blushed and stared down at the drawings. "Uncle would want me to marry a Mormon girl," he murmured, then seemed to remember his manners. "Thank you, ma'am. Never had such kindness before. Much appreciated."

"Well, you make me miss my son, about the same age as you. Now stand up straight and don't mumble. You're a businessman. A builder and caretaker too."

She patted him on the shoulder as they returned to work. A warmness expanded in her chest. Memories of the Gallegoses and the bond they had with their adult son came to mind. It wasn't just envy filling her, but heartache at the absence of family closeness. The tug of nurturing was missing everywhere in her life.

After they finished the plans, she restocked her supply boxes, making sure not to overload them. She stashed her growing pile of silver dollars and gold slugs in her clothes, shoes and several satchels—she'd never keep her savings on the mules again.

Her final stop was to the outwardly formidable-looking Bank of the Gold Miner preening with a brown brick exterior and a covered planked walkway. Once inside, the redwood counter, teller windows, and banker desks were considerably less elaborate than Wells, Fargo & Company's San Francisco marble edifice built to impress. Reasonably respectable for fledgling Sacramento, but would the redwood deter a pistol-wearing bandit? Bank and stagecoach robberies occurred more often now, highlighted on many a *Daily Alta California* front page.

Juanita approached the young man working behind knobbed wooden slats looking like table legs. He wore a starched, white shirt with sleeves rolled almost to his elbows. A large scale with two golden measuring plates hanging from gold chains sat behind glass next to his teller window.

"I'd like to withdraw my deposit. Here's my account."

"Yes, ma'am. All of it? Here's your earned interest amount," and he pushed a sheet with a scrawled number through the opening below the grill. "Don't you want to leave some coins with us? Can earn more interest." Just as she was about to decline, though impressed her deposit had grown, a tall gentleman in a shiny top hat and black suit strode in from behind the teller, then pushed through the swinging half door to face her and put out his hand.

"Mr. O.D. Hart, ma'am. Pleased to meet one of our finest customers. Your trust in us is appreciated. As a token of our gratitude, for continuing to place your faith in Bank of the Gold Miner, we're offering a fine Birmingham fountain pen. With a small ink well included, of course."

Juanita was so surprised she almost dropped the parchment and her satchel but quickly recovered to shake his hand. A fountain pen? Really? She'd not expected lavish gifts and just wanted her money but the earned interest, and the startling fact the Bank of the Gold Miner had not stolen her Liberty coins, also surprised her. She'd trained herself since her teenage years to resist charm and persuasive personalities but this man delivering on his promises caught her attention.

"Nice to meet you, sir. Juanita Castro," she nodded thanks as he handed her the pen set. She turned back to the teller,

"I'll leave it all with you."

Perhaps this banking escapade would work in California after all. She'd watch Mr. O.D. Hart's enterprise carefully as she invested in her own new business.

La Hacienda Hotel

April 1853 to March 1861

As Canela and Juanita clopped into Sonora, a packed mule train behind them, nostalgia swept over her. Was she naïve to be hopeful Sonora had retained some charm after the tragic violence toward anyone without US citizenship or light skin?

She stopped at Southern Mines Supply to unload as much as the owner would purchase. A potbellied stove roaring in the corner warmed the store. The pungent smell of tobacco, coffee, and whiskey melded with the crackling pine logs, creating a welcoming aroma. She was impressed the owner had installed thick, milled boards to create a solid floor which didn't turn muddy in winter. Crudely sewn red calico curtains kept out cold mountain air and protected the shop's wares from prying eyes.

The owner was grateful to refill his empty shelves, buying up a huge portion of her inventory. "The lady muleteer," he said. "You back or just passing through? The Gallegoses are gone, you know. James Braddock runs it now." He frowned when she nodded. "Not the same place it was," he said, and she detected a hint of unpleasantness.

She then stopped at the former La Bienvenida—now named Miners Lodgings in large black letters—pretending she was a muleteer trying to make a sale, unaware of the owner's fraudulent takeover.

A large man with sun-burned arms and neck, a dark beard, and brown hair pushed through the curtain when he heard the bell. A Native woman was washing pots behind him in the kitchen. Was it the girl who worked here before?

"Whatd'ya want? Don't take no ladies 'ere. Miners only," he said gruffly.

Juanita introduced herself, explained what she had to sell.

He waved a hand dismissively. "Don't need none of it. Git on your way. And don't come back neither. I buy at the dry goods. Don't buy nothing from no Mexicans. No tramps neither. All loyal Americans 'ere."

"Understood, Mr. Braddock. But aren't you from England? I'm the true Californian, third generation here. Glad you like my home so much. And the Natives who do all your work." The bell protested when she slammed the door behind her, ringing repeatedly. Was he the exception or the new face of Sonora?

She paid a Native boy to watch the train, then explored for a suitable place to stay, peeking in boarding houses and the few hotels, finally finding one for the night. Then, before the sun disappeared fully, she led Canela southwest of town to the empty field and wide, gnarled oak where she'd buried her riches. Sneaking glances over her shoulder, she placed Canela between herself and the town, dropped to her knees and dug furiously with a small pick and trowel. At first, there was nothing but dirt and spiky, brown oak leaves. Where were her pouches? Had she forgotten the spot? What a fool she'd been to bury any of her funds. She tried a different patch and then another. Then returned to the first one and dug deeper.

Finally, she struck something firm. Thank God. It was here. She uncovered the canvas bags of silver US dollars and small sacks of gold dust, fabric deteriorating but intact. She burrowed a wider circle around the tree trunk to make sure she'd uncovered all her savings, then scooped up her treasure and stuffed it in the pouch at her waist and the leather satchel over her shoulder. She would still have to do the mule route from Stockton to Sonora and neighboring southern camps to grow her reserves, but she had enough to buy land and start construction.

Before riding Canela back to the heart of town, in the sun's final purple glow behind the mountains, Juanita looked at the live oak, the grassy field, and made a decision. This was it. She'd find the owner and buy several acres right here. Here was a small plateau perfect for a solid foundation under the hotel, an orchard and row crops. She patted Canela, gave her a carrot top from her pocket and said, "This is it, girl. We'll start over right here."

Juanita took her funds to the new town alcalde, Jeramiah Cooper, an American man from Boston who'd bought lots between Woods and Sonora Creeks now boasting new treasure. Sonora had become famous for its pocket mines, and everyone had a story about being next to someone who uncovered huge rocks of glorious metal in a cavernous hole.

Mr. Cooper formed the El Dorado Sonora Mining Company to compete with the Bonanza Mine and was paying miners weekly rates to dig and work sluice boxes. If they found nuggets or any caches of gold, he owned the gold but gave generous bonuses to the discoverer and a smaller bonus to the rest of his crew. Men had enlisted with him for steady pay while maintaining a chance at a get rich quick discovery.

The El Dorado Sonora Mining owner also was trying out new techniques, using hoses to spray water at the quartz rock—hydraulic mining—and even attempts at lode mining, or breaking the granite. These methods took large equipment and a steady supply of quicksilver, so it was a significant investment. Companies were the new miners.

This Jeremiah Cooper also headed the Vigilance Committee. Rumors were that guns were no longer allowed in Sonora's saloons, but customers strapped them to their ankles while bartenders ignored the ridiculous rule. She wondered how Cooper and his Vigilance Committee handled rule violators.

Mr. Cooper was not much more friendly than the Miners Lodgings owner, but with actual American gold slugs, twenty-dollar silver coins, and gold dust pouches in her hands, he couldn't refuse Juanita permission to buy the land along Sonora's entrance road. He located the owner, a former soldier who'd had some success at Dragoon's Gulch and drew up a contract. She insisted on a map and property line descriptions, all signed by multiple witnesses. After observing her sister's land experience and hearing the Gallegos family story, she was not going to be intimidated or chased out.

"Don Jeremiah," she said using the polite Spanish salutation to show respect, "I will run a boarding house and hotel to make this town proud, but I will not be cheated or disrespected. My grandfather came here as a Spanish soldier almost a hundred years ago. I'm an American citizen by the Treaty of Guadalupe. I expect to be treated as such. I'll be fair and welcoming to everyone, including you and your colleagues. But you need to know—all will be welcome. Best business practice and how I run things."

"Not everyone 'round here takes kindly to a lady muleteer," he said after a beat.

"That's their problem, not mine. I'll create the finest hotel in town, where your friends will want to attend my Sunday salons. You'll see."

Juanita took her deed and swung out, her shoulders back in a defiant posture, with Mr. Cooper shaking his head.

Over the next several months, Juanita worked tirelessly. She purchased timber and had it milled in Columbia by a lumberjack who dreamed of his own sawmill. She contracted a mill employee to make furniture she covered with plush fabrics off the Stockton steamboats. She purchased nails and tools, screws and washers from her preferred general store customer, Mr. Frazier at Southern Mines Supply. And she kept the mule train operating, learning his favorite items and delivering them regularly. He was relieved to avoid monthly supply trips himself. Frazier's, as everyone called the store, was soon a town favorite with well stocked shelves from Juanita's regular mule runs.

As the hydraulic mine camps grew, Juanita extended her mule train reach and visited more little towns. She spread money around the Sonora area in those first few months, combating any grumbling about her unusual ways. She generated plenty of gossip. A muleteer with no husband, barely wearing women's clothes, riding a man's saddle, and building a hotel alone. Juanita ignored it all. Eventually most Sonorans tipped their hats politely when they saw her on the town's new planked walkways and saved the head-shaking for after she passed by.

After months, using her mother's design sense and her father's skill for gregarious hospitality, Juanita's finally opened her simple but comfortable boarding house. A welcoming environment with good food was an improvement over the Miners Lodgings down the street, with its flea-infested straw mats and watery stew. Curious passersby peeked in and word spread among the Bonanza and El Dorado mines and within a few weeks she had a full table of hungry miners at each boarding house meal. She wrote to Josefa asking for Hanford Pioneer Bakery recipes but never got a response. Must remember to have Tobias check on the bakers, she told herself. Determined to someday build a hotel and include fields of produce and orchards, she called it La Hacienda Hotel and Boarding House.

Juanita dreamed her hotel expansion would offer a taste of extravagance, with raised beds featuring feather quilts and thick cotton mattresses, velvet curtains, plush carpets, and artwork on the walls. Isabel's comfortable, elegant interiors inspired her, though her resources were smaller and her taste less extravagant. But for Sonora, a central town on the diggings trail, La Hacienda Hotel would be a luxurious respite.

Just as Father Mateo had grumbled in the early gold fever years, it was difficult to find a maid, cook, handyman, or stableboy who'd stay for more than a few weeks. The migrant men, often disgruntled they could no longer get rich yanking apple-sized nuggets from the rivers remained transient, still hopeful for a gold strike. She looked for Natives, but many had disappeared from ranches and towns thanks to state leaders like the first governor, Peter Burnett, who had actively targeted them for extermination. Many had no means of making a good living, generationally dependent on their Spanish, then Mexican owners. Her grandparents and parents had never paid their Native servants at Rancho Castro. The more she learned about the southern US slave states and slave-trading empires, the more determined she became to pay all her employees, Native or not. Even Mexico had officially outlawed slavery years ago, in 1829. She honored that tradition without hesitation.

As Juanita hunched in the dark outside the kitchen entrance to the Miners Lodgings a month after opening the boarding house, she shivered and pulled her wool shawl around her shoulders. Had she come too early? Finally, the Native girl she'd seen in the kitchen stepped out, loosening her long, straight, black hair from its knot to fall well below her shoulders.

Juanita cleared her throat, not wanting to scare her. The young woman turned sharply and scowled. She pulled a thin cloak up over her head.

"What do you want?' she said in Spanish.

"Pardon me for stopping you so late, but didn't you work for the Gallegoses?" she asked very quietly. "I think we both held Alonzo down when the doctor cut the bullet out of his leg."

The girl nodded slowly, still guarded. "What do you want?"

"I want you to come work for me in my new hotel, La Hacienda. Well, it's a just boarding house right now, but I'm building a hotel next door. Like Mr. Gallegos dreamed, remember?"

The woman looked over her shoulder back at Miners Lodgings, nervous.

"Come work for me," Juanita tried again. "I'll pay you and you'll have a room of your own. Much better place than here. You'll be able to save, have your own money."

"How much would you charge for the room? I've no way to pay."

Juanita realized generations of servitude made it hard to comprehend compensation could include a room. She explained quietly in the dark.

"I'll pay you each Sunday when you get a half day off, and

the room is included. You don't pay me one coin." The girl's eyes opened wide. She hesitated then nodded. They agreed she would tell Mr. Braddock in the morning she was leaving the Miners Lodgings.

The next day, the Native young woman, Ines, arrived with a scrubbed face, bright white apron covering her frayed dress, and thin shoes polished so black they gleamed in the sunlight. She seemed worried. "He'll be furious. He might come after me.

"You let me worry about Braddock," Juanita assured her. "I've got pistols and a shotgun and I'm not afraid to use them. Come see your room and the kitchen."

"Miss Juanita, you know the militia doesn't like us Indians. If they come to the hotel…"

"Don't you worry. We're going to make such a nice place they won't even notice who's working here."

She calmed Ines' fears as best she could, mostly by putting her right to work and listening as she slowly revealed her story. Ines, who didn't know her last name, was born to the Sheep Ranch Miwok Rancheria, a village of Natives who clung together for community and protection. Ines knew cleaning, kitchen prep, and cooking for boarders because she'd grown up with her mother as a Yorba Rancho servant. When her mother died of scarlet fever, Mr. and Mrs. Gallegos had brought her along to Sonora for their new rooming house venture. Ines knew no other Natives and couldn't return to the rancheria of her birth. She had no idea if it still existed. Work was all she knew.

Her first employee a success, Juanita tried former miners for the animals and gardens but, while some were helpful on hotel construction, they did not return for daily work like digging ditches, planting seeds, or feeding Canela and the mules. She needed a vaquero.

She wrote to the Gallegoses and asked if Alonzo would leave Yorba Rancho and come work for her. But he was loyal to his parents, and too lame, he said, to help her. Plus, he could tend to animals but never seemed to get a plant to grow. Juanita had hoped having Ines there might be an enticement, but Alonzo seemed stuck at the rancho for now.

Slowly, over the months and into years, the boarding house filled with locals, most working at the Bonanza or El Dorado mines. By January 1855, Juanita completed the hotel, which hosted mine owners, curious investors from out East, merchants expanding successful mining camp dry goods stores and lumber and agricultural industry barons.

Right from La Hacienda Hotel's opening day, she borrowed Isabel's ideas and furnished a lovely parlor alongside a small bar. In addition to Sunday musical performances, on Saturdays she opened the parlor and bar for live newspaper readings but was strict about no gambling and no prostitution. La Hacienda developed a reputation for comfort and for welcoming everyone, no matter wealth or station. Ines' dishes made with fresh ingredients from the gardens, pigs, and chickens added to the allure, as tasty, nutritious food was always in short supply through the over three hundred miles of mining district. While the hotel did build a positive reputation as Juanita had desired, no tall, auburn-haired gentleman going by Joe ever stopped in for a room.

Any time Juanita offered a new entertainment, such as music on the tiny harpsichord she'd lugged back from

Sacramento by mule, Mr. Braddock spread rumors she was really running a brothel, her prices were exorbitant, and she'd obtained her land fraudulently. Juanita had made an enemy for life when she'd stolen the capable Ines, and paying her Native staff well had only made it worse. Soon, Mr. Braddock complained to the town's leaders, the Vigilance Committee, and even the new sheriff, unhappy his fiercest competition came from a woman successful without a man guiding her.

One summer's day, the sheriff approached her. "Miss Juanita, why don't you marry a yanqui to protect yourself? I can't keep the militia away from your workers, but I might be able to prevent them from harassing you if you married an American gentleman."

She laughed off this idea. "Who am I going to marry? I'm not young anymore, Sheriff."

"I'm serious, Miss Juanita. Look, we all like your Sunday entertainments. And no one would argue the Hacienda Hotel and your Saturday News Readings aren't the finest in town. But you're alone. You've just got those Natives there. I'm sure there are plenty of fine gentlemen who would be fortunate to take you for a wife."

Juanita ignored such warnings, but kept an eye out for her staff, listening carefully to the gossip of her hotel customers. As she'd learned from watching Isabel, information was power. As the business grew, she also took another lesson from Isabel and invested. She bought additional lots in Sacramento and was comfortable with the distance because Tobias managed them. Searching for local investment, she purchased land thick with pines and logging forest in the Sierra foothills above the town.

Occasionally, she faced the fact she finally had sufficient savings to pay Beatriz back for the clothes and supplies she'd taken from the Dominguez household. But her days were filled from before sunrise to well after dark managing her multiple businesses, so she rarely took a moment to stop, think through the journey, and serious apology required, so she let her promise founder. Josefa and Charles continued their successful bakery but never had children. Juanita couldn't possibly help with their deepest sadness, so she stayed distant, rarely stopping by for a personal visit.

She recognized she needed to be at La Hacienda regularly to help Ines provide excellent service. She could no longer successfully run a mule train, a boarding house, timber forests, and a hotel all at once. After years on the trail, she finally searched for a trustworthy vaquero and found a Mexican with Native blood, just like Ines, from one of the few remaining rancherias.

Jacinto was a Maidu from the Feather River area who had worked ranchos before gold fever. He'd found mining unappealing, primarily since he wasn't wanted by the immigrants pouring in. He'd tried city living but found it as distasteful as Juanita had. He loved land, animals and growing things just as much as she did, which she found endearing.

After months training him at the hotel, she felt she could trust him with the mule train, the supplies and quantity of silver dollars it generated. Jacinto became the La Hacienda muleteer, taking on Juanita's routes and adding more. He said he liked the independence and, as far as she could tell, he never stole from her.

While Juanita finally had some stability, the fresh, new state and the rapidly growing US were in turmoil due to a constantly changing economy, slave state wrangling, and exploding new technologies.

The telegraph reached Stockton by 1853, poles going up in her favorite pastures. What an amazing development. Send a letter in the air? How could that be possible? After a few years of overhearing it really worked, Juanita decided to send a message herself, but to whom? She couldn't write to Beatriz—she'd severed that relationship. She didn't want to bother Josefa, who continued to be weak and sickly. She could write to Tobias in Sacramento, but she saw him every few months and theirs was a working relationship. And while she would love to telegraph Joaquin, she still had no idea where he was.

So she wrote to the only person she could think of.

To: Madam Platt,
The Grand Palace Hotel, San Francisco

Hope all is well STOP La Hacienda Hotel is
growing STOP Come visit STOP

From: Juanita Castro,
La Hacienda Boarding House and Hotel, Sonora

To: Juanita Castro,
La Hacienda Boarding House and Hotel, Sonora

Congratulations STOP Too busy to leave SF STOP
Best of luck STOP

From: Isabel Avila Platt
The Grand Palace Hotel, San Francisco

Would this new technology stop people from corresponding? Much less satisfying than an actual letter, she felt. She'd learned nothing about Isabel or San Francisco. She'd stick to the postal stops and more newsy letters.

By the mid 1850s, convenience and rapid communication appealed to fast moving California and telegraph offices became community hubs in the fortunate towns which had them. She saw a new opportunity to reach out for Joaquin and asked Tobias to place a poster in every telegraph office between Sacramento and Sonora. This time she added more personal information, though she was still reluctant, guilt-ridden, and ashamed to include she was a mother searching for a lost son.

LOOKING FOR A TALL, AUBURN-HAIRED MAN ORIGINALLY FROM MONTEREY AREA, GOOD WITH HORSES, EARLY 20S. GOES BY JOE. SEND INFORMATION TO JUANITA CASTRO OF LA HACIENDA HOTEL AND BOARDING HOUSE, SONORA.

Sonora and California somehow survived the tailing off of the gold rush by 1855 and the panic of 1857. As war rhetoric heated up with issues like the Dred Scott case and the question of slavery in the territories, the debates grew hot in the hotel parlor. Juanita managed to keep the peace with her no weapon rule and limited saloon hours to after supper three days a week.

At the same time, slave plantation debates and central plains homesteading frenzy seemed so distant from mining town California it was as if they were in a novel or history book. Local politics and violence absorbed most customers' attention. The new state capitol in Sacramento, and taxes and politicians there, led to plenty of grumbling at Saturday News Readings. Mining town violence was mostly drunk, bravado-filled men gambling, stealing weapons or gold dust, or approaching another man's wife.

A woman had been hanged up in Hangtown for killing a man. That got Juanita's attention, as she wondered how many miners had killed someone yet never been hanged. Or attacked and raped women with no consequences. She kept her head down in Sonoran debates, stayed away from Braddock, and focused on offering the best lodging and most enticing, respectable entertainment in Sierra foothill towns.

Throughout the 1850s, Juanita continued to place ads in newspapers and post bills in telegraph offices in her search for Joaquin. She finally wrote a letter to her sister, Beatriz, asking for forgiveness, saying she'd like to come visit and bring gifts. Only silence back from Rancho Dominguez. She never received any news of Joaquin. Josefa seemed distracted by a planned bakery expansion in Sacramento and so rarely communicated. Through it all, Juanita remained alone.

In early spring of 1861, war talk was at a fever pitch and even in far off California the tension was palpable. Eastern conflict and economic turmoil were on every mind and pressing into every wallet. Struggling miners who still hadn't given up the dream were fleeing Sonora for the Comstock Lode silver rush over in Utah Territory. So many headed to Virginia City on the eastern side of the Sierra Nevada, the gold diggings started to feel empty and neglected. Juanita had just lost yet another handyman.

Jacinto was away with a large mule train. She now had fifty mules, so Jacinto had recruited an assistant, Manuel, to help run long packs. He pitched Juanita on taking their hearty

Mexican mules up to the silver rush in Nevada Territory, and she'd finally relented. It was far, but reduced business in the gold mines made opportunities in the silver boom attractive.

That left Ines and the young Rosalía, who Juanita had plucked out of a Stockton saloon rumored to be a recruiting site for the bordellos. She'd offered the girl a position at the hotel with Ines training her. Rosalía fit right in, grateful for a steady paying job, a clean bed and fewer grabby men.

Today, Juanita was in the orchard, as she called it, even though it was mostly a large garden with fledgling fruit and nut trees. She was harvesting lettuce, onions, cabbage, potatoes, carrots, and turnips for upcoming Saturday and Sunday suppers.

Despite the weakening winter daylight, a shadow cast over her. She heard a throat clear.

"Excuse me, ma'am?"

She twisted to look up, her hand shading her squinting eyes. "Can I help you, sir?" she asked as she rose, stumbling slightly. The numb half of her foot sometimes made sudden standing awkward, less smooth a transition than she'd like.

The man was tall, thin and muscular, with dark brown skin and cropped black hair. He had deep-set black eyes with tiny crinkles at the edges, a rounded forehead, an angular jaw and narrowing chin, and a wide nose that balanced his prominent cheekbones. He looked to be about the same age as she was. No longer a young man, but not old either.

Her first reaction was he was Kanaka. Then she quickly realized he was an American Black man. He wore the clothes and boots of a horseman.

"Wonderin' if y'all have a room at the boardin' house, ma'am? Couldn't find anyone at the entry desk. Didn't mean to interrupt your work."

His deep voice was hoarse, as if he'd been yelling for some time. His accent had a slow softness which stretched the words long then dropped off into a quiet politeness. She recognized a drawl like Isabel's.

"Looks like y'all could use some help. I could work the orchard while I stay here a spell, ma'am. I see your stalls. I'm good with horses." He gave her a bright smile which lit up his eyes and hinted at a dimple in one cheek.

Juanita was charmed, not only by his lilting accent and politeness, but because he called her garden an orchard; she imagined he could see her vision. Had he heard she'd just lost the hired man?

"Juanita Castro, sir. And you are? Come on and we'll get you signed in. Not sure what happened to Ines. Sorry about an empty front desk."

"Silas Holloway, ma'am."

She wiped her hands on her skirt, shoved an armload of carrots with fluffy green tops into his large hands and hustled toward the lodge with her basket overflowing with lettuce and turnips.

"Welcome to the Hacienda Hotel, Mr. Holloway. We'll have to talk about putting you to work, but you might have come at just the right time."

"I can't pay for a hotel room, ma'am. Just here for the boardin' house."

"Yes, I understand, it's just La Hacienda Hotel and Boarding House is a long name so everyone calls it the hotel. Don't worry. The smallest, cheapest room is available. Or do you want to share with others?"

"No, ma'am. I'd like a private room, if possible. Not everyone wants to share with a Southern man, you understand."

"The Hacienda is proud to welcome all, as long as they pay."

She smiled at him. "Where you're from, what you did before or where you're headed are no concern of ours. You're welcome because you made it to Sonora, a little out-of-the-way place, but a sweet one."

Juanita was conscious to not ask prying questions, like why was he all the way out here in Sonora? A few Black men could be found in most every camp and mining town, but not in large numbers. Yet, there was a school in Sacramento now for Black children, and there were some important leaders in San Francisco, like Mammy Pleasant taking on the streetcars for not letting Black people ride. Ridiculous, in Juanita's view. Why not take everyone's money just the same? And respect people for their hard work and morals? But war fever and heated debates at her salons made it clear not everyone shared her sentiments.

She was happy to welcome him into the boarding house, but her lifelong curiosity was brimming like a steaming tea kettle about to burst into a whistle. Why on earth had a southern, Black man ridden into Sonora looking for work?

At supper that night, Juanita decided to join the communal table to learn more about the new boarder. She often took a break from constant hospitality by eating alone in her rooms, but when the boarding house crowd was especially intriguing, she joined in for company and spirited conversation. So far, she was pleased to have kept the slave state debates polite by feeding everyone delicious dishes. La Hacienda Hotel's meals, which included fresh dairy, vegetables, and fruit, provided a conversation topic all could agree upon. She'd found it lessened the tension over weightier subjects.

Mr. Holloway did not disappoint, commenting generously on the side greens and the hot apple pie dolloped with a frothy cream. "Who's the cook? You, Mrs. Castro?"

Juanita laughed, shaking her head. "Oh no, no. One thing I never learned is to cook. I can do most everything else, but not at the stove. That's Ines. I grow things, and Ines here makes them for your plate."

Enjoying the camaraderie of the mixed group, some who spoke little English, Juanita raised her glass and called for a toast to Ines and her cooking. The gentlemen around the table echoed the sentiment and cheered, coaxing a shy smile out from under Ines' tucked head and long hair. More cheering ensued when Ines produced a bottle of brandy and tiny glasses.

Juanita surveyed the scene with contentment, feeling like a mother whose children were all getting along for once. She remembered the Gallegoses' early gold rush tables and was thrilled when she could recapture a sense of shared humanity.

Mr. Holloway was enjoying the moment, seemingly more relaxed than when he'd first arrived. Maybe Ines' hearty food would fill in his angular shoulders and thin frame. He might be a nice addition to the group. Although the sadness behind his eyes betrayed past difficulty, there was a quiet, confident ease about him she liked. She'd try him out as a ranch hand for a few weeks.

"Mr. Holloway, you can start work at daylight tomorrow, if you're still inclined," she said, leaning toward him to speak under the noise of the boisterous men. "By the way, it's not Mrs. Castro. There's no Mister. You can call me Miss Juanita, as they all do," she stretched out her arm gesturing toward the rowdy crowd around the table.

He revealed those bright teeth when he smiled. "Silas, ma'am, freedman from Charleston, South Carolina." And he stretched out his hand to shake in agreement.

Well, that's an unexpected description, she thought as she shook his hand. What did that mean?

A Steady Hand

April to November 1861

Coming to depend on Silas' productivity after just a month, Juanita realized how much they'd missed having a steady ranch hand. No wonder her father always treated his vaqueros well, though of course they weren't paid. But, she rationalized, Don Pedro had been generous in accommodations, good food, access to horses, and two days off a month to visit relatives on other ranchos. He'd even built a family bunkhouse once some of the men married and had children. At least she'd improved on Papá's management style, not only providing boarding but also a salary—she refused to participate in a forced labor economy.

Silas was competent in almost every area a budding ranch and lodging house could desire. He was able in the stalls with the mules, Canela, the three cows, two pigs and a coop crowded with chickens. The vegetable gardens were hoed and weeded in the lean, rainy time, and flourished through the harvest months. He'd pruned and tended the mini orchard, with the citrus trees likely to bear fruit next summer. He could repair a broken shingle and flapping shutter and was determined to learn any new technology, such as how to repair glass or how to bring water directly into the kitchen from the well via pipes.

Throughout months at the lodgings, Silas' skills allowed her to expand. She added hotel rooms and two outhouses behind the buildings with a covered walkway from the kitchen door. The outhouses were a favored innovation, but best for Ines and Rosalía who no longer had to empty chamber pots.

Saturday News Readings grew raucous, as most every news story led to hearty debate over the Confederacy and secession. Silas acted as an enforcer of peace and decorum and encouraged her to add more entertainment outlets for Sonora's hard-working residents. She would never run a brothel like Isabel, her morals and strict Catholic upbringing too ingrained to even consider it. But she did open the bar after dinner every day of the week and offered gambling, via the most popular card games, every other Sunday.

Her rules were strict—anyone drunk was ejected and no one was ever allowed to carry a debt. If you couldn't pay on the spot, you were removed and not allowed back for a month or two. Everyone must put coins or gold in for a game, buy drinks and cigarettes with cash. No credit.

"Leave your guns and knives back at your lodgings, gentle-men, or you don't get in." Silas worked the door, while Ines and Rosalía served drinks and Juanita monitored her dealers. She had learned a lot watching Isabel's practices over her months as a maid. If you kept strict standards, you could develop a busi-ness most customers appreciated. A drunk had to be thrown out now and then. A knife confiscated at the table, a leering gentleman ejected for overly flirting with Ines as she poured, or grabbing Rosalía as she served the tables. The saloon was popular and Sunday nights brought in plenty of cash.

As word spread down to valley towns and up to the

mining camps, Juanita thought she'd have to build a bigger saloon or limit the numbers so no one stood too long waiting to get into the monte or faro game, drank too much, and got antsy to play. Maybe now she could finally add a small horse training stable, which she'd dreamed might attract Joaquin. But they were so busy it was hard to imagine adding a whole new business operation.

Alonzo seemed to stop by Sonora more often, possibly to visit Ines, but no one was sure. Silas suggested he help at the door Saturdays and Sundays. Juanita loved the idea, and Alonzo became a regular addition to the team.

Juanita found herself relying on Silas regularly, but even more than his quiet competence, she valued his steadfastness. He was the first hired man who stayed around for three seasons. He was quiet and respectful, always with a bible or book in his hand. With no hint of him leaving soon he became a valued member of the Hacienda team. He'd joined Ines and Rosalía, Jacinto, Manual, and the animals to round out a little homestead.

Was this what Juanita had secretly dreamed about during those years on the trail through the diggings? She remembered the camaraderie of the Gallegos boarders and the cohesive caring of the tow-headed Clark family. It felt to her as if her Hacienda team had transformed from an odd collection of lost souls to a family of sorts.

After months working closely together, regularly discussing hotel business but with little time for the personal, Juanita no longer could control her burning questions about his roots.

"You mean there are Black freedmen who own Black people as slaves?" Juanita was incredulous, mystified by the

Charleston Silas described. After months of Silas working the mule sheds and produce fields, the two had settled into a habit of drinking steaming coffee in the boarding house kitchen for a quick break. She'd finally worked up the courage to ask about the description he'd given her the early March day when he'd first arrived.

"That doesn't make sense," she persisted that morning over coffee. "I can't imagine any Natives here forcing other Natives to work for them as slaves. Well, now I think about it, there were never any Natives rich enough to have their own homes which needed servants…" Juanita trailed off.

Silas shifted in his chair, his lips closed in a soft, pained frown as she digested his background and tried to make sense of it.

"It's a strange world, indeed," he said. "Never made sense to me neither. Slavery is in the culture, the very roots, of South Carolina, so profound every man there has absorbed it in such totality that it corrupts. But not one slave ever stops thinkin' about freedom."

Then, a sadness covered him so completely he almost disappeared, like a cloud had consumed him and drained his spirit. She felt him slide away into a memory, a distant world. What was his life as a freedman in the South like? Had he always had his independence? She was dying to ask but dared not.

For a moment, there was not one sound in the kitchen, not one breath of wind outside, not one animal braying. It was as if they'd fallen into a dark well and were closed off in the abyss.

No longer able to tolerate the pain on his face, Juanita reached across the table, almost knocking over the coffee mug, to lay her hand on top of his. He started, then appeared to return to the present moment. Slowly, he moved his hand to enlace his fingers between hers. Neither of them moved. The stillness in the room was thick, profound. Intimate.

Juanita, who had not had anyone touch her beyond a handshake in over a decade, was startled by the vulnerability consuming her. And the longing she felt to know more, to see into Silas' soul. Suddenly, it was more than just her curious nature propelling her into dangerous, uncomfortable territory.

She pulled her hand away, sliding her chair back a bit from the table.

"I'm so sorry, Silas, for my intrusion into personal things. But I'm curious about the American South. About this slavery everyone is arguing about. And now a war. And you?" she said, moving to clear the coffee mugs, reaching for a rag to wipe the table. She needed to reestablish herself as the matron of the manor. "How was your Southern life as a freedman? I'd like to hear about it. Some day."

As she rinsed the mugs, her back to him, she could feel his discomfort, embarrassment. He was the hired man, after all, and holding hands with the boss was most unusual and inappropriate. Folding the dishtowel, she glanced over to see him watching her with a questioning look.

"Juanita, I appreciate your interest in my past," he said. "But maybe we should get to work and talk later."

"Yes, right, of course," she said, all business, then left to ensure everything was ready for the Saturday News Reading later that afternoon.

As Juanita strode away from the kitchen, she was irritated with herself for losing her composure. This man was her employee, and yes, he was now a valued part of the Hacienda team, but enough personal conversations. And touching his hand out of sympathy? What had she been thinking? Or was it something more? She was furious she'd let her guard down and allowed emotions to overtake her.

They did not talk for several days. Juanita avoided the late-night whiskey they had started to share after the Sunday gambling nights. Then Jacinto returned from a mule train trip and handed her a letter.

The Grand Palace Hotel, San Francisco
November 4, 1861

My dear Juanita,
I hope this letter finds you well. I am writing to let you know of a recent rumor we heard. A tall, auburn-haired gentleman in the Monterey area is searching for his mother. His name is Joe and he claims his origins to be "an orphan from Ohio." I have no proof of this man's existence or any exact location, but as this struck a chord with me, I wanted to let you know.

Come visit me. I have so few I can talk to openly—of business and all other matters. Isn't war terrible? How sad my former part of the country is at war with your part, which is now my forever home. Tragic. I'm so glad to be out here far from death and betrayal. I have trouble getting accurate news of my father. I hope to God he's freed his many slaves and not taken up arms with the Confederacy. Thanks to God also my brother and I left when we did, although, sadly, the trip brought his untimely demise.

Your friend,
Isabel

P.S. I don't think I've ever called you a friend openly, but I do consider you so. I hope this does not offend you and you feel the same.

Juanita was stunned, letting the paper fall through her fingers after reading it several times. She stared into nothingness. Her face felt hot. Searching for his mother? Orphan from Ohio? It was just too much of a coincidence.

As a boy, Joaquin had heard Rancho Castro's new owners had moved from a failed homestead in Ohio. Years earlier, when she, at nineteen, she'd fallen hard for the itinerate woodworker, Malachy Brennan, he'd told Abuela Quina he was an "orphan from Ohio." Or maybe it was Ireland? Or was it his parents who'd fled the famine? He'd had so many fantastical tales, who knew what was true.

Still, she had to leave immediately. To discover if there was truth to this rumor. Maybe Joaquin was right there in Monterey, close to the home where she'd raised him. And it was time, she'd waited too long, it was time to visit Beatriz and, finally, make long overdue amends.

She packed up eight mules to keep the trip light and practical. If she traveled as a muleteer, she could check in on favored customers and suppliers and pick up items for the hotel. Pack mules were so prevalent, so necessary for every single person's survival, that the trains were mostly ignored, unless you were a general store owner anxiously awaiting supplies to fill your shelves. It still felt like the safest way to travel alone.

However, when she asked him to watch over the hotel, Silas did not agree.

"I'll go with you—it's not safe."

"I'll be fine. I've traveled by myself for over ten years. I don't need anyone, a man, to protect me," she said.

"But alone on the road? Why you goin'? Let me go. There's bandits and thieves—"

"I realize you don't know this, but I managed traveling through the early gold camps filled with men. I've macheted rattlesnakes and run off thieves. Even survived an avalanche. I've got my pistol, shotgun, the same machete. You speak the best English, so you need to be here." She turned her back to finish loading the mule boxes, her shoulders set tight.

"An avalanche? What? Juanita! It's not safe out there. Grizzlies . . . And this weather is awful. This is a mistake," he said, struggling to complete a full sentence, his raspy voice cracking more than usual.

"A little rain never hurt any cowhand I've ever known," she said curtly, ending the discussion.

She departed for Stockton without another word. In some ways, it was easier to leave when they were angry with each other. As she bounced gently in the saddle, rain streaming down into the eyes of the horse and mules, she regretted she hadn't mentioned the foreign tax mob riot—she'd survived that too. And she'd even tried to pass as a man but that hadn't gone so well. She smiled slightly at the memory of Isabel catching her in the poorly disguised deceit.

What a turn her life had taken since she'd left the rancho. And now, might she get some of her old life back if she found Joaquin, and atoned for her terrible behavior toward her sister?

Silas

November 1861

After Miss Juanita rode away on Canela leading a short mule train, Silas fired questions at Jacinto. Why'd she leave so suddenly? What was in that letter? But the muleteer had no idea whose correspondence had made her snap into such desperate action. Jacinto squinted up at Silas, his hand shielding his eyes from the sun.

"Don't know, man, I just give her what the postmaster hands me. But she seemed kinda mad at you when she rode off, huh? Whatdya do?"

He'd held hands with her at morning coffee, is what he'd done. Why hadn't he just stood up and left the kitchen when she put her hand on his? He knew better. And now she'd run off with no explanation.

"Nothin'," he lied. "I just said she shouldn't go alone over to Monterey or San Francisco. I'd go along for protection. It's dangerous on the road."

"Well, clearly, you still gettin' to know Miss Juanita. She's one stubborn boss lady. Took me months to get her to trust me with the train. She ran them mules up and down the diggin's by herself for years. She's got the independent streak, for sure. Probably thinkin' she needed you workin' here more." Jacinto chuckled as he strode off.

Silas shook his head and tried, unsuccessfully, to clear his mind by doing his regular chores. As he tossed breakfast scraps to the pigs, he pictured their kitchen table interchange. Juanita's kind curiosity, and questions about Charleston, pierced his hardened exterior so he'd been transported back to a past he worked hard to erase from his thoughts. It was painful and he was touched she appeared to feel his agonizing wounds. She seemed so compassionate, caressing his hand, a caring sadness in her brown eyes. He couldn't help but return her touch.

Oh, this woman, she was going to be trouble. She was compelling, intriguingly feisty and tenacious, yet there was a softness buried under her toughness. He'd sensed it the first moment he arrived at La Hacienda.

Every single morning since he'd left the South, the moment he stirred awake, he reminded himself to embody the free man he'd become, the man he'd molded himself into. Discard any slave mentality, any habitual practices of servitude, he told himself, like the grandmothers taught him. Mostly, he was successful. Copying bible passages and writing in his book every day. Obtaining work he wanted to do. Protecting and managing his earnings. Finding good souls, whoever and wherever they might be, and creating a peaceful life. Always on his terms, which included never revealing his past and never forming close bonds with anyone. Juanita's warm fingertips had threatened all that. Yet had awakened a yearning as well.

Then she'd been so cold, so rude, this morning when she put him in charge of La Hacienda and rode off. What was in the letter? He realized he was hurt and the feeling was unsettling.

Maybe Juanita was uncomfortable they were friendly. Perhaps the status difference concerned her, as it should him. He knew relations between slaves and masters never went well. Sure, sometimes nannies and plantation children genuinely cared for one another. And every now and then a house slave and family member developed secret, shared intimacies. But it never led to positive outcomes. However, I'm not a slave here, Silas reminded himself. Gotta maintain a free man mentality.

Juanita was a formidable woman. Smart in business and tolerating no nonsense from men, treating her employees fairly, but hiding sorrow, loss. He could feel the pain she hid underneath, which occasionally seeped out as if it were sweat from her pores. Clearly, their backgrounds were completely different, but a common suffering was there. He realized, suddenly, he'd like to be a comfort to her.

The surprising realization took him back to a harvest afternoon a month or so ago with the sun setting over the western hills and a chill in the fall breeze. The two of them were in the zucchini and pumpkin rows scouring the drying stalks to cut the last squash from the vines. All the others were mucking the mule stalls or in the kitchen.

The fading sunlight narrowed through a distant oak's branches and caressed Juanita's black hair, causing it to shine. Sweat beads dripped off her chin and she wiped across her brow absently with a gloved hand. The garden was so quiet Silas felt as if he were in a church pew in that pondering silence, that anticipation just before the preacher's sermon. When no one moved for fear the minister's words would reach deep and let God see into your soul. In the tranquil crop rows, Silas moved from fear to elation.

This woman moved him deeply. She was stunning in her fierceness, her capability. Her confidence and features made it clear she'd been striking in her youth. In that moment, she seemed at one with the earth where she hunched. A desire to embrace her, to soothe her, to reveal his secrets overwhelmed him.

"Juanita," he said, without thinking, his voice cracking with longing. He'd never called her anything but "Miss Juanita."

Startled, she looked over at him, a questioning furrow between her eyes, and wiped her drenched chin and nose with her work glove.

"Oh, just goin' in with the squash," he said. "Isn't it a beautiful sunset?" he added quickly. She nodded, looking mystified, and kept on gathering pumpkins.

The next day, he'd invited her to share a coffee with him at the usual mid-morning break. Then, the morning conversation became a habit and, sometimes, he even could coax her to share a whiskey after the gambling nights.

Silas shook his head and heaved his shoulders now to rid his mind of the memories and release the ache in his chest. In a confused haze over a situation he'd never encountered, he returned to the comforting habit of work. He did what the boss ordered, fed the cows and pigs, hoed garden rows, surveyed mules for injuries, attended to building repairs.

Before arriving at La Hacienda, Silas had been on the road for over a year, never staying long in one place. He trusted no one. Kept moving west. Don't ever look back, he told himself. Keep your head down, work hard, collect the pay, then depart. Finally, in early March 1861, he reached his goal, California.

Once in Sacramento, he found a ramshackle boarding house which welcomed all migrants, no matter their color or country of origin. He asked around the supper table for local tips and received a chorus of advice on ranches to try, mining camps to avoid, stores which would welcome his business.

"Over at Brannan's Dry Goods you can usually find whatchya need. Gotta board posting for those hiring."

The day Silas entered the general store, it was busy with lines of customers. A skinny blond man and a serious-faced Native retrieved sacks and jugs, bottles and boxes from behind the counter. They moved back and forth, helping men haul crates out to their wagons and pack tools into saddlebags. It was noisy and chaotic, so Silas surveyed the store's cluttered shelves and read posted announcements while he waited. Most men ignored him but a few frowned in his direction as they hauled sacks out the door.

One handbill advertised the need for an experienced farmhand who could also do hotel and boarding house maintenance. He'd never heard of Sonora, just knew gold country now added silver extraction, timber, and agriculture to its enterprises. Once the business calmed, he approached the young man who seemed to be in charge.

"Y'all sure busy here. Silas Holloway, sir. I'm looking for steady work and noticed a post bill for a hotel. Think they still need a hired hand?"

"Yes, sir, Mr. Holloway. Pleased to meet you. Tobias Hunter. Miss Juanita, well Mrs. Castro I guess, she runs a good operation. She's ambitious, hardworking, that lady. She's got a boarding house, hotel, gardens, and animals. A mule train too. If you could stay through spring, I know she'd be real glad."

"You think she'd be willin' to take on a Southern man?"

"Huh? Oh, yes, sir. She just cares about hard work and honesty, and that you're good natured."

He thanked the dry goods store clerk and headed immediately for Sonora's La Hacienda Hotel.

Silas had only planned to stay a month but now, after three seasons, heading into winter, he realized he did not want to leave. For a mining town, Sonora was pleasant, set in a pretty valley with pine-covered hills leading up to snow-topped mountains. The air was fresh, the land was rich. He liked every single one of the staff members, which for him was unusual.

In the frontier town stables, silver mining camps, and construction sites he'd worked since leaving the South, he'd often had to tolerate an unpleasant co-worker to reach pay day. Sometimes, he felt a sour scowl behind his back or detected mumbled curses, many not welcoming to a Black man. He slept with his knife at his side. The secession divide often led to bitterness. Men struggling to reach their goals could turn mean-spirited.

There weren't many Black men in California, but he'd met a share. Some former slaves who'd escaped the South. Others who'd been forced to do the prospecting by a white master then run off once in gold country. A few Mexican or Northerner migrants who'd been fortunate to avoid slavery all together. And while white Californians could be particularly harsh on the Chinese, and many Mexicans were chased out years earlier, in Sonora he observed a delicate balance between the diverse set of inhabitants.

Work hard, don't steal, don't cheat at the tables, use your weapon judiciously, and don't even look at another man's woman. If you could manage those rules, then most let you be. Compared to what Silas was used to, it was almost friendly.

He felt so fortunate to no longer be in the Carolinas. As much as he tried to block out his past, he heard the debates every week in the Hacienda salons and news readings. Slavery, the confederacy, plantations, and the future of America were on every tongue. He could not imagine emancipation, as slavery was so entrenched, so embedded in the soul of the South. And now his former home was at war. He'd known the Southern establishment would fight bitterly to hold tight to their property and peculiar institution. Thank God he'd gotten out.

The feeling of a team at the Hacienda Hotel was a revelation. Another positive—Juanita's high expectations and respect for anyone who worked hard had created that unity. He knew all too well it was easy to be cruel. Consistent decency was the challenge.

And now? An unexpected complication. This Juanita was disarming. He was charmed and interested. He liked their comfortable chats, and, maybe for the first time in his life, he had a friend. Or was she just being polite? Being a kind boss? Or was she, too, as self-reliant and lonely as he was, and desiring companionship? He could tell she was curious about his past circumstances, but she didn't pry; she was allowing him to set the pace. He respected that.

If they were to become friends, if he were to stay and truly be a part of La Hacienda, if he truly cared for her, then he would have to be honest. Silas had little experience with relationships based on respect and caring, but he knew to his core if he wanted to develop one with this woman, who just might want to do the same, he would have to tell her the truth.

I'll do it when she returns, he promised himself.

Searching Monterey to San Francisco

November to December 1861

Despite endless rain, Juanita decided to search for Joaquin throughout her former home on the way to visit Isabel in San Francisco. She hadn't been in the area since burying her mother and fleeing the ranch. Guilt at stealing from her sister, which she'd buried for years, now smothered her. She could ignore her responsibility to repay her debt no longer. She had to visit the Dominguez ranch before anything else.

Although the archbishop had successfully recovered many mission lands from the US government and brought them back into the fold of the Catholic Church, the Carmel Mission remained decrepit with a non-existent parish. The building was a shell of its historic past. The roof had fallen in, and wild turkeys, boars, and grazing cows wandered through adobe debris.

Never devout, Juanita still respected the church's role in her upbringing—to see her family's church in ruins was depressing. Where were the Catholics to rebuild a Monterey congregation?

This Mission, inhabited only by ghosts, was even worse off than San Francisco's. There was no one to question about Joaquin.

While not deserted, Monterey had hardly grown. The town was so familiar it pulled at her heart. Sure, it was no longer Mexico, morphing into an English-speaking enclave, but the changes were less stark than in dense, bustling San Francisco and expanding San Jose.

Diagonal streets crisscrossed the straight ones, and lining the rocky roads all the way down the hill to the sea were adobe and wood-frame homes, eating establishments and boarding houses. Planked sidewalks were few and far between, installed in front of only the most successful businesses. A man called David Jacks seemed to own most everything, and a Chinese fisherman's village now balanced on the bay's rocky outcroppings. Wealthy shipping company owners, a few successful miners and prosperous ranchers had built large Victorians, while Sonorans loaded ships at the docks, served in saloons or herded cattle on the Salinas Valley range. The Chinese were relegated to fishing and harvesting otter pelts. It still felt small, familiar, and influenced by its years as the Mexican capital, yet also evidenced a mix of the cultures dominating new California.

She moved north, stopping briefly at Mission San Juan Bautista's pueblo, remarkably unchanged save for an American business or two. The tiny parish continued to offer mass to the devout every Sunday, having somehow survived Mexican secularization, the US Invasion, and conversion to California statehood.

But she found no sign of Joaquin in any of her former haunts. No matter how she framed her questions, no one had seen or heard of the man.

"A Joe? Joe who? We got a Beer Joe, a Smithy Joe, oh, and

Dry Goods Joe on the main road."

"From Ohio?"

"Could be anybody."

"So many change their names when comin' West."

"Sorry, lady. Need more details," store clerks and postmasters reminded her gently, as if she were a newcomer herself. Yet another transplant searching for errant family members who'd disappeared while seeking a fortune. No one offered to ask around, help in any way. The nation's collapse into war against itself brought more distrust and skepticism as the secessionist and unionist fight spread. Discouraged, she headed north to San Jose to leave the mule train with a favorite calico merchant, then rode Canela toward her sister's ranch.

Galloping up the road to their hacienda, Juanita was swamped by memories of eleven years before, when she'd fled her home expecting her sister to help her create a new life. This time she approached in the dark and knew she was not welcome.

As she reached the large adobe, she slowed Canela to a quiet walk, then tied the horse to a hitching rail and tiptoed below each window, peering in. No sign of Beatriz or Agustín, but she spotted a Native servant washing dishes after the evening meal. In the library, a light-haired gentleman with bright white skin and a bushy mustache sat in front of the fireplace, smoking a cigar. Definitely not Agustín. Had they sold the property?

She stepped quietly through the back buildings, still the structures of an elaborate working ranch: housing sheds for workers, a blacksmith forge, milking stalls, and covered horse stables alongside a tack house. She spied through gaps in the pine boards and saw stacked beds filled by ranch hands talking, smoking, playing cards or sleeping.

Creeping on, she found a small shack behind the dormitories, perhaps for the house servants. Peeking in the window, she saw Beatriz washing dishes in an oval silver basin, a young boy of about fifteen drying plates and cutlery by her side. No sign of Agustín.

She moved to the front door and tapped lightly, then straightened her shoulders, tied her thick hair into a braid, smoothed her skirt. A young boy of maybe thirteen opened the door and stared at her, mouth agape.

"Who are you? You look just like . . ."

"Who is it, Chepe?" Beatriz called from the back. She stepped into the crowded living space with a dish towel in her hands. "Oh," she said, a hand flying to her mouth, the towel falling to the floor. "Oh, Juanita. You're here."

She approached slowly, put her hands on Juanita's shoulders and gazed into her face. Then she pulled her closer and whispered into her hair, "Good thing Agustín is in San Francisco. He thinks you're a thief," a dry, emotionless tone noticeable.

Juanita pulled back, nodding. "I'm so sorry, Bea," she mouthed as Beatriz turned to her astonished sons and a little girl with the thick, lustrous black hair characteristic of all the Castro women.

"This is your Tia Juanita, children. Be polite," she said, and each one approached Juanita with a cheek-to-cheek touch and air kiss, announcing their names: Francisco, Jose, and Candelaria.

"But everyone calls me Lia," the little one squeaked. "You look like Mamá. How come we never met you before?"

Juanita smiled as Beatriz shooed them off to bed then gestured for her to sit down on the small sofa. "We haven't lost everything, but we had to sell much of it, and the big house, to pay lawyers. Agustín's very bitter. It's better when he's away. He thinks you stole from us. Not how you treat family, he says."

Beatriz's voice was cold, harsh. It was a lot to forgive, even eleven years later.

"Bea. I'm sorry. I needed it to get started. You had so much back then. I sold your things to get my own mule train. You helped me survive up in gold country." She squeezed Beatriz's hand in apology.

Stone-faced, her sister did not respond. But she didn't pull her hand away either.

"It took me years but now I've got two trains, a hotel, and a boarding house. A little orchard and rows of produce. Up in the southern diggings. I own my own land, all with clear titles. Our land troubles taught me the importance of legal paper. And, Bea, I would not have come unless I could repay you and Agustín."

"Oh? Might be good. But Agustín is so proud. He wouldn't want to take anything from you." She looked down at their joined hands. "But we need it. If we want a working ranch, we can't sell any more land."

"Your claim never got settled?"

"No. Still at the Land Commission. Still reviewing what maps and land agreements we could find. Homesteaders kept pouring in, so we sold the big house to keep up the fight. Lawyers, translators are expensive," she said pointedly. "Where will we go if we lose the rest of the rancho?"

"Let me help you now," Juanita said. "I have a lawyer in Sacramento."

"Hmm, we might be interested. Some lawyers are crooks and they're all expensive. And Joaquin? Josefa? Did you find them?"

"Josefa and Charles have a popular bakery in Sacramento. But Josefa is often sick. Just like Mamá. Never could have children. No luck with Joaquin. I've been searching all these years. But I just heard a new rumor. You haven't heard of a tall Joe from Ohio around here, have you? The rumor was he was searching for his mother."

The tightness around Bea's mouth relaxed, slightly. "No. But then I don't leave much. Busy trying to keep the family together and the pigs and cows healthy. Keep the garden producing. And the vines. We make wine. Remember the priests used to buy it." She looked thin, and so dejected. "You've got to go. Agustín will be back soon."

Juanita could see dread in her eyes. "I'm leaving now. Take this. Please forgive me. I want to make up for my thievery." She handed Beatriz a large canvas bag filled with pouches of gold slugs and silver dollars. "This is worth more than at least triple what I took. Your beautiful clothes, hats, shoes, your china, and undergarments even, helped me survive. Thank you, Bea."

She gave a brusque hug and disappeared into the fading light to collect Canela.

Whole blocks of San Francisco's sodden streets were lined with planked walkways, while brick and stone edifices rose above her, sometimes up to four stories. Canvas tents, once ubiquitous, were now an oddity. The city had a permanent air, hinting at its desire to become substantial, as significant as East Coast and European cities. And Isabel was always part of the gossip. This time she knew to ask for Madam Platt, owner of the Grand Palace Hotel.

As she asked directions, she chatted with shopkeepers and newsboys on the corners, and according to the rumors, the Grand Palace Hotel was no longer the finest in the city. But never to be outdone by the men, in 1857, Isabel had constructed the six-story Diamond Crown Hotel atop California Street's hill, anticipating newly wealthy railroad and silver barons would build magnificent mansions there. The gossips whispered all of society coveted invitations to Madam Platt's exclusive soirees throughout her hotels, usually after opera and dramatic performances in the budding theatre district. Juanita was curious to see Isabel's latest extravagance.

The Grand Palace Hotel doorman, wearing a starched navy uniform with gold epaulets, informed her Isabel had moved once again.

"She lives up at the Crown now, ma'am. You'll have to climb the hill," he said with a slight smile, as if he were glad she had to do it, not him. Once again, Juanita paid to leave Canela in a presumably safe stable and hiked slowly up the hills of San Francisco. Some of the more well-off banks, foundries, steam breweries, and hydraulic mining equipment fabricators had put in stone or plank walkways, but mostly it was up through the slop.

The carriages she passed bore mine owners, bankers, and stock speculators, wealthy wheat and cattle barons, flour mill owners and sugar beet kings, dressed in pressed black suits with striped trousers, cravats, and shining top hats. Meanwhile, miners, clerks, beer brewers, stableboys, and metal workers maneuvered on foot between the horses and buggies in simple bowler hats, wool pants, and scuffed work boots. At Market and Montgomery Streets, she pushed through a crowd gathering to support the Union troops. Men yelled for one indivisible country, the union and nothing but the union.

Catching her breath and brushing dirt off her boots at the top of the hill, Juanita entered the grand lobby of the Diamond Crown Hotel. She stared in awe at the opulence dripping from every corner. Golden wall sconces with fine tapered candles—clearly changed regularly so no gray soot discolored the warm white tallow—accented thick painted-plaster walls. Gleaming chandeliers with shimmering crystals dangled over every open space. Persian carpets and fine wooden furniture polished to gleaming decorated every room. Nothing was out of place, not one frayed drape or cracked bench betrayed anything other than luxury and quality. Isabel's wealth shone in every golden stitch of upholstery and polished marble tile, in every mahogany staircase and mirrored hallway dotted with bountiful bouquets of colorful flowers. Where did she get fresh flowers in rainy November?

Juanita was escorted into a private study by yet another elegantly dressed butler. Isabel sat at a writing desk, half dressed for the evening's events. Her hair, jewelry, rouged cheeks, and reddened lips perfect. But she was still in a petticoat, which let Juanita see she had grown slightly plumper, but in a soft way which emphasized her voluptuous bosom, wide hips, and sensuous neck, accented by a silver emerald necklace. Silver bracelets wrapped up her wrists, and a silver barrette strained to hold her curling mane away from her still striking face. The blazing dark eyes were as bright as ever under their thick brows.

"Ah, Juanita. Good to see you again. The era of silver is dawnin', so I've to change my accents. Gold is almost passé. Imagine that!" And she belly-laughed, reminding Juanita of the chaotic early days in upstart San Francisco. "How long's it been since we've seen each other? Seven, eight years? You look the same. Thinner, perhaps. Workin' too hard? How do you never get gray? Sure hope I keep my color at your age! Tell me all before I have to get dressed for the evenin'. Do you need my help, yet again? Love the telegrams. Isn't it delightful we can communicate through the air? Can't get away to visit. Sorry. You like my new hotel?"

Ah, Isabel. Always talking, always focused on her own accomplishments. She'd forgotten her latest correspondence.

"You sent me a letter . . ."

"Oh, right. A tall, reddish-haired Joe. I can't remember the source of the rumor, but it did make me think of you. And now here you are. How delightful."

Juanita sighed, irritated. "Do you think you could ask around again? I came all this way because you mentioned searching for his mother, an orphan from Ohio. That's new, Isabel. My son's father was rumored to be an orphan from Ohio when he came to the ranch after jumping ship in Monterey. Seems an unlikely coincidence. Don't you think?"

"My friend. We are friends, right? I feel you understand me somehow, because we met in those early years. Anyway," she threw her hands apart, up toward the ceiling, "everyone here is from somewhere else, with buried secrets, hidden pasts. We've got more scoundrels pretendin' to be gentlemen in San Francisco than probably anywhere. I'll have the man who does investigative work for me see what he can find. And I'll put it out to the girls again. Sometimes they get those lonely men talkin', you know."

Frustrated, disappointed, Juanita sat on the side sofa while Isabel called for a servant to bring her four different dresses. Had she fled La Hacienda and questions about her interactions with Silas only for this frivolous woman and her wardrobe obsession? At least, she had apologized to Beatriz, paid her back, and offered her legal assistance. Even if she'd uncover no news of Joaquin, redeeming herself with Bea was a relief and lightened the shame.

"Help me pick the right one for tonight while we chat. Just in from Paris. It's a Christmas party. You like this cream silk? Ain't the light pink just divine? Have you heard of these Singer sewin' machines? I just got one and am going to get some girls to learn. I'll make my own dresses. Bring the cloth in from Paris, Italy. Anyway, tell me everythin'."

Juanita complied, describing La Hacienda Hotel and her plans for the future. She spoke of her employees, how lucky she had been. She briefly mentioned paying her sister back for the items Isabel had purchased to launch Juanita's mule train. Isabel nodded absently while stepping into another dress.

"Wait. Who's this Silas? I can tell you're interested." Isabel stopped admiring herself in the tall floor mirror to stare at Juanita.

"What? No, he's just been a big help around the hotel, with the animals and produce. We have an orchard now."

"Ah, no. Don't be coy. Bet you know him better than just talkin' about milkin' cows or seeds or whatever you Godforsaken country folk talk about!" When she shook her head, the great crown of hair flew behind the barrette.

"Once in a while, we enjoy a whiskey after the monte nights."

"Ah, a whiskey, huh?" Isabel murmured as she adjusted the neckline of the current dress. This one was a brilliant emerald green and the effect was striking against her white skin, curling black hair, and those flashing eyes.

"He helps keep the gambling tables calm. Jacinto is often away with the mule train. We talk business. Sometimes about the war and politics and what came up at Saturday's news reading. I did tell you about those, right? It's very popular."

"I don't care about the news readin's! Tell me about the man. I can read people, Juanita. Remember? That's my gift. Why I thrive in this cutthroat business. I've got sophisticated competition, and enemies, now. Ah Toy is bringing in ships filled with Chinese girls. That's what some of the men want, so I've got to be quick on my feet, read the signs, keep my customers satisfied. Now, which dress do you like? Which one goes best with the silver? Want to highlight the metal *de jour*."

Juanita rolled her eyes. Now Isabel was speaking French? Juanita feigned interest as the maid helped her step in and out of the other elaborate gowns. Once the dresser left, Isabel returned to the earlier topic.

"But tell me about this man. Is he good lookin'? Is he from that tiny town you like so much? Still can't figure out why. Do flee the God forsaken place and come live in one of my apartments. I've got them in all the hotels. I need a smart companion. Who I trust."

Juanita ignored the suggestion she move. "Yes, he's handsome," she said, surprised to find herself beginning to flush. "He's a great worker, but also kind. A gentleman. Which is rare in gold country. He's a freedman from out your way. From South Carolina. Charleston."

"What? You met a freedman from Charleston in that minin' town? What's he hidin' from? Well, the South, of course. I understand. I am too. And now this war. It's horrible. Did y'all ever imagine war in our own country? In my former state?"

"Yes, Isabel. I went through my country's revolution, Bear Flag Revolt, the US Invasion. Mexicans know war," she said, her tone bordering on parental.

"I know. I don't mean to be ignorant or disrespectful. Remember, I married a Californio. Even though I haven't seen him in years. Never bothered to get a divorce." Her voice trailed off. Was it regret?

"What about you?" Juanita decided to turn the situation around. "Don't you have someone you can talk openly with after a long day? Maybe your Californio husband can come live with you here?"

"Yes, and no. I've someone at the moment, but my relationships are superficial. He's a business investor so we discuss what's necessary to keep my business successful. You know, I never fully trust anyone with my books, investment decisions. I'm on my own here."

"Do you get lonely?"

"Sometimes. But I'm so busy with my girls and events of the season. Romance is too messy. How do I know someone isn't just after my money? Plus, I get bored easily. I enjoy havin' the bachelor of the moment in my bed, on my arm for a ball or my salons. I like them a bit younger—it keeps me challenged and youthful."

"What about children? Did you ever want babies?" Juanita knew asking a madam such a question could be considered rude, but weren't they friends now?

"Children? I have my girls. They take up what little maternal energy I have, which isn't much. Growing up with slave nannies constantly coming and going and a father who paid me little attention, I never learned about parentin'."

"What about your mother?"

"Never had one. She died when I was born. Or, so they told me. But you know, I've thought about it a lot since leavin' the plantation. It's entirely possible my mother was not Black

Irish as my father liked to say. She could have been one of the slave girls. I look like my father but I didn't get his blue eyes or light hair. Descended from Vikings, he'd tell me and my brother. Hmph, Vikings? More likely Black slaves. Never got to ask him myself. Almost never saw him. He kept us busy with tutors, then horseback ridin'. Did I ever tell you about the horse racin'?"

It was a rhetorical question. But as Isabel adjusted her hair and jewelry, fluffing the dress and strategically arranging the lining around her opulent chest, the pause lasted long enough for Juanita to respond.

"I'm sorry about your mother," Juanita said, trying to imagine a childhood devoid of the constant noise and companionship she experienced being surrounded by generations of family. Knowing you were included in a loving set of traditions and expectations was foundational. How had Isabel figured out what she wanted, what values were important?

Isabel raised a hand and waved it as if to say it was nothing, though she drifted off in a memory, staring in the mirror for a moment. Then she continued with her story as if she'd never revealed anything personal.

"We were expected to know all about breedin', jockeys, race stakes. Spent hours cleaning the stalls and ridin' but were never allowed to attend races. But that race, we finally got to go—the biggest horse race ever, The Peyton Stakes. He had three horses in it. It was the most excitin' thing that ever happened to me. I was only twelve. People came from all over. That horse race showed me there was more out there than my father's world, the world I was drownin' in. My father was furious none of his horses won. But he knew the winnin' owner. They were all in the Jockey Club together. What a time . . ."

She called to the maid to bring several other necklaces. She fiddled with the jewelry, then dismissed the maid.

"We are friends, right?"

Surprised, Juanita struggled to get out an appropriate response. "Well, yes, of course, I . . ."

"Y'all got to focus on your own life, my friend. Make one with this farmhand you call a gentleman. I'm happy with a steady stream of consorts, but my impression is you wouldn't be. You want stability. Companionship. You were still with your parents and siblings and cousins when you were my age, right? I know you miss a big family, and want your son, too, of course. But the search seems fruitless. He surely has his own life now. Did you ever think he might not want to be found?"

Shock rocked her. Isabel's brutal honesty could be so cutting. Yet hadn't Charles told her Joaquin wanted to make something of himself before interacting with family?

"But what about the rumors of someone searching for his mother?" she argued. "A Joe—that's the name I told him to use—tall with red brown hair. Orphan from Ohio. It's too coincidental. You don't believe in coincidences, do you?"

"Yes. I do. There are so many folks here, so many searchin' for all over California. Probably the rumor got twisted up anyway. Go home, Juanita, and make a life with this freedman from South Carolina. See what I mean? Who would ever think a freedman from Charleston would end up in a little town in gold country?"

Kidnapped

December 1861

On a rainy, late December night, with creeks running high and storm clouds thundering, the Hacienda's monte and faro tables were busier than ever. The month's incessant wet had everyone on edge; the floods drowning Sacramento were not far away. In addition to bad weather, the full civil war in the East with battles in Missouri and Bull Run, Virginia, made everyone jumpy.

Every man present had connections in Boston or Virginia, in Tennessee, New York, or the Carolinas. Even the most lone cowboy hung on every scrap of news and shared letters from business associates, wives, and brothers with opinions on Mr. Lincoln's election, the Confederacy, the Union Army, Fort Sumter, and slave owners. Fights broke out more quickly than usual, especially when gambling and drink were involved.

Juanita, too, was in an unsettled state, uncertainty roiling in her gut, making her queasy. On the ride back from San Francisco, she'd tormented herself with endless questions. Wouldn't Joaquin want his original family in his life? What were her true feelings for Silas, beyond appreciating he was a great worker? Should she listen to Isabel and pursue, at least, a friendship with him? Who takes advice from a madam, anyway? But Juanita had accepted she was more than a madam to her; she was a friend.

These profoundly personal questions involved emotions she usually avoided. She'd felt unmoored ever since losing the family's ranching business and all her relatives after four generations of prosperity. To survive her losses, she'd pushed aside any lasting human connections. Now, she felt the tug of a close relationship with another. Maybe Isabel was right. She should appreciate what was in front of her—a dedicated, caring hotel family which reminded her of Rancho Castro just enough to be comforting. And Silas? He was a beguiling mystery, and she did enjoy his company. Maybe she'd relax her self-protectiveness, just a little, to see what would unfold.

That stormy night, both Alonzo and Ines worked the saloon while Manuel monitored the line out front and Jacinto and Silas oversaw the door, patting down each man for weapons. Juanita moved between tables, swirling her skirt, peering over dealers' shoulders, putting a hand on an arm here and there, keeping control over the bustling room like a school matron in a one-room schoolhouse of only boys.

Once the evening's betting subsided, the men staggered out, winners bragging, losers cursing, tin-glass lamps dimmed with a kerosene smell fogging the room. Juanita and Silas sat at a saloon table as rain drummed on the roof.

"Isabel, my friend in San Francisco, sent this bottle of Kentucky whiskey for me to share with you. She likes that we have a drink after the faro nights. It's from slave country, I know, but she's a southerner. World's best whiskey made there. Says she's working with the importer to start distilling here. In San

Francisco. California whiskey. One we could sip with pride." She laughed and toasted him.

He smiled, glanced in the glass, hesitated, but downed a large swallow.

"Why'd you leave so suddenly?" he asked. "Surely not just to visit an old friend."

She hesitated, still fearful of sharing the private. "Thanks for keeping an eye on the hotel. I appreciate knowing I can leave and the Hacienda's fine. Glad to be back though. I don't like cities."

"Of course. We're a good team here." He took another sip of the amber liquid. "How was San Francisco? Hope you got whatever you left for in such a hurry."

Shy, she said nothing, feeling a warm blush arise as she realized she wanted to confide in him. He certainly was persistent.

"I've never been there," he continued. "Not much of a city man myself. Sounds too crowded and violent. Hear everyone is a crook, out for themselves, tryin' to get rich on the gold, the silver, whatever they can grab. I'm more comfortable out in the country, in the pine forests."

Then, through her quiet resistance, something inside stirred, broke open. Was it his gentle tone? Isabel's advice? More heartache around Joaquin's absence and the remaining rift with Beatriz? What did she have but her life in the hills at the Hacienda, her staff and this kind man? Perhaps there could be more with him.

He continued. "Trip not go well? You seem sad."

"I went looking for my son. I got word of a rumor he might be near Monterey or San Jose, maybe in San Francisco." She looked directly into his eyes, as if challenging him to also be open, sincere.

His thick, black eyebrows spiked almost to his hairline. "You have a son?"

Juanita couldn't move; it was as if the despair and the whiskey had paralyzed her.

"What happened to him? I've never heard about your rancho. I hope someday you'll tell me about your family." He paused, put the glass down, and poured them both another shot. "I'd like to know all about you, Juanita." She shivered slightly, emotion prickling her skin. She could feel the heat between them.

Maybe it was the whiskey talking, or his soft, drawling kindness, which covered her like a blanket and opened her numbed heart, but against all her instincts, she told her story. About her father passing away, leaving the ranch awash in debt, forcing her to sell to a calculating stranger. She told him about working for the new owner because of her sick mother, her son and sisters. How they had nowhere else to go, no cash or belongings left. How she felt forced to send Joaquin away at fifteen to protect her family. She did not mention the boy's father.

Juanita figured she'd already revealed far more than necessary. She'd hardly discussed the details of Malachy with anyone, no reason to start now. But this man did inspire her to be more trusting, more candid than she'd been with anyone.

Silas didn't press further. He must have sensed she couldn't give him more. Not tonight. Not with the open wound of Joaquin's absence raw from yet another fruitless search.

A wind picked up outside and rattled the windows. Rain pelted the panes.

"I've no family. Never had any," Silas said. His gravelly voice so quiet Juanita had to lean closer. "My mother was sold when I was a baby. I've no memory of her. There were several older slave women who made sure I got enough food, didn't get trampled by the overseer in the rice swamps. They taught me to look out for myself."

Quietly, imperceptibly, Juanita moved her chair closer, her leg almost touching his. The torture of a slave past was unbearable. To not have a mother was unimaginable. She was filled with a desire to embrace him and wished she could make such painful experiences disappear.

"I pretty quickly noticed my skin was lighter than most. When I got older, I learned how many slave women were raped by owners. Realized my father was likely the master, or some relative. It's possible my mother also had a white father. That's always made me sad for her, and so ashamed. Best for me to be alone. But those women who taught me to survive also encouraged me to think of freedom. Some think if a slave dreams of freedom, he'll make himself crazy. But the grandmothers said different. 'Always look for ways to escape or buy yourself. Think, plan, keep quiet, act.'"

Juanita didn't move, trying to picture his early life. She was not naïve, and she had suspected something difficult, but it was so horrific.

"Once I was about eleven, I was rented out to other plantations on Sundays and got paid a little. I hid my silver and bought my freedom. My master was a hard man who didn't want to sell me, but he took my money. I went to Charleston for a while."

He stopped to take a breath, took a sip of the whiskey. Juanita exhaled softly. His goodness astounded her. How could one survive such pain and cruelty at the hands of his fellow man? Would she have been able to overcome such a terrible childhood and youth? She wasn't sure. The foundation set by her early family life gave her strength, a goal. Silas had to escape an inhumane existence—alone—and then create a completely new reality.

She moved slightly and pressed her thigh against his leg. He jumped a bit, as if startled, then she felt the pressure of his leg into hers. Setting her whiskey down, she placed her hand over his on the table, determined not to pull away as she had in the kitchen weeks ago. Neither one moved.

He continued. "I left the South because there's nothin' there for Black folk. Black people are disposable, their lives worth less than a mule's or a goat's. I needed to start fresh. I heard about the gold rush, so I just jumped to come out West."

He put his glass down and took her other hand in his. Before she could say something, he spoke again. "I like it here. With you. Your staff. I like the peace in the mountains, the forest and creeks. Open land. I'm not one for cities. Too many unknowns. Here, y'all can see people coming from far off." He squeezed her hands firmly then raised one to touch her cheek so gently his rough, workman's hand felt like a piece of muslin caressing her skin. "So it seems we've both built somethin' from nothin'. New lives here. And to me, to me, Juanita, it seems like we both wanna stop wanderin', stop searchin'."

It was very quiet for a moment. The wind ceased. The rain slowed to a light *tap, tap.*

He turned to face her and brushed her hair away from the other cheek, then, holding her face in both hands, leaned in to kiss her. Juanita, sad, warmed by the whiskey and the intimacy of the moment, bent forward. She felt a tingle rising to her cheeks, then flooding her entire body. Maybe even a sensation in the numb foot.

Suddenly, there was a shout from the hallway. A crash and swearing. A thump against a wall. More yells and cursing. Sounded like a drunk had come into the hotel and was headed toward the bar.

With a reluctant expression, Silas stood up quickly, gave her shoulder a squeeze and hurried out. Always keeping the hotel secure for the guests. The commotion continued, more shouts. She heard Jacinto and Manuel. They'd help take care of the problem.

She couldn't focus, her chest pounding, her cheeks flushed, her limbs languid. Ardor filled her veins. The shoulder he'd squeezed burned; the memory of the whole evening, starting from when she'd opened the whiskey bottle, spun in her head. Thirty years after Malachy broke her heart, did she still have any sensuality within her? Her mind wandered to imagine Silas squeezing not just her shoulder, but her entire body, her arms and back, her breasts and hips. She pushed the thought away. Passionate affairs led to nothing but heartache and despair.

Though commotion outside continued, she put the whiskey behind the bar and climbed the stairs to her private room. Alonzo and Jacinto would help Silas send the drunk away or put him in the stables to sleep it off, Manuel watching over him. She needed to be alone.

Next morning, groggy from lying awake most of the night, nervous and disoriented, she decided to avoid him. She needed to think and always cleared her head best when alone on the trail. She'd do the supply run to Stockton herself. She told Jacinto to prepare the mules and packs and tell Silas she'd be back soon with supplies. He should oversee the Hacienda in her absence.

As she rode to Stockton with a small mule train, she pondered the night's events. She was conflicted. Shouldn't she be looking for Joaquin? An affair seemed so selfish. Yet, she was curious, interested, perhaps a little excited.

She argued with herself, how it had been thirteen years since she'd sent Joaquin away—he, a grown man at twenty-eight, surely had his own life, as Isabel had pointed out. Probably a wife and children. But they should have a grandmother. Her grandparents were so important in her growing years.

Her heart was a twist of emotions. Get the run completed and ask around again for Joaquin in Stockton while purchasing supplies, she told herself. There was time to think over this complication with Silas.

A week later, after being away for longer than a usual run due to bad weather and because she'd checked in at every postal stop to ask about Joaquin, she finally slogged back toward Sonora. She needed to consult the team on flood plans, and what to do with the animals. All this water would wash the hydraulic mining debris down into town. They needed to prepare in case the river overflowed its banks.

As the road curved toward Sonora, she could just see the outline of the Hacienda . . . and Jacinto, galloping toward her at full pace, something clearly wrong.

"Silas' been kidnapped, Miss Juanita."

"What? What happened?"

"Remember the fight the night before you left? That drunk was furious. We threw him in with the mules to sleep. Went looking for a fight with Silas in the morning, so Silas ran him off."

"Yes. But what's that got to do—?"

Jacinto didn't let her finish. "A few nights later, a fugitive slave catcher snuck in, surprised us in the bunkhouse and grabbed Silas. We was sound asleep. Beat him somethin' bad and dragged him off. There was two of them, ma'am. With pistols. Manuel and me chased but couldn't find 'em out in the woods. In the dark. Raining something fierce. Didn't know which way they went."

"Oh my goodness. We gotta go look for him! In Stockton or Sacramento." Confused, her heart drummed hard with concern, and yet more loss. How could he be gone? She'd finally accepted she was looking forward to seeing him, to continuing their conversation.

"We already searched all night, next day. Couple boarders even joined in. No sign anywhere. He's probably on a boat or on the Overland Trail by now. Plus, a few days later the miner came back to gloat. He told us he'd seen Silas' likeness on a wanted poster for fugitive slaves, with a big reward. The catchers do this for a livin', ma'am. They get out of California quick once they got some to return. But we got that miner good. Don't you worry. He ain't comin' back to Sonora."

Juanita was glad to hear it. But Silas kidnapped? It was terrible he'd been taken. If he couldn't escape and survived the journey, surely he'd be conscripted to fight on one side or the other. This war in the East was a death sentence. They'd all heard the descriptions, seen drawings, and even photographs, of fields strewn with bodies. Heard tales of horrific bullet wounds gone bad, limbs amputated. The terror of Alonzo's surgery in the Gallegoses kitchen rushed into her head. What would happen to Silas now?

And wasn't it her fault? If she'd not been a coward and run

off after Silas almost kissed her, then maybe she could have calmed the drunk the next morning. Or somehow prevented the slave catchers from breaking into the boarding house. Or convinced them Silas was a freedman. His own man. Must be a case of mistaken identity. He wasn't someone to trap and return to the South like an escaped prisoner.

Or was he really a slave? She cursed herself. Another lying man? Malachy had misrepresented himself when he'd come to her family's ranch. Now Silas? Oh, come on, Juanita, you know it doesn't matter she told herself. He was free here and belongs in California. They had to get him back. How on earth could she help him?

Flood and Fire

December 1861 to July 1862

Drenched, with her thick hair plastered to her cheeks, work boots squishing with every step, her muslin dress heavy, Juanita stumbled through the office door of Mr. Thomas Ralston, Esquire. Parts of Sacramento had flooded, but Mr. Ralston's minuscule storefront was on a side street which, while resembling a river of gray-brown rock, was better off than most.

"Mr. Ralston, sir, my foreman was kidnapped."

Her attorney looked up from where he and his assistant were conversing across his walnut desk.

"By a fugitive slave catcher," she continued breathlessly. "It's mistaken identity. He's a freedman. I need him working. At my hotel. Is there any way to find him?"

"Miss Castro. Nice to see you again," Mr. Ralston said, rising and sticking his hand out for a shake then gesturing for her to sit. When she didn't, he waved away the clerk, then sat back down behind the formidable desk.

The formal Thomas Ralston, Esquire, in perfectly pressed pants, shining brown leather shoes, pomaded hair parted straight down the middle, gave no sign of irritation, looking like he'd stepped out of the tailor's shop on a sunny morning.

"California is a free state but we have a fugitive slave law in effect," he said. "Slavecatchers are operating legally here. Do you know where he was a slave? You might want to start looking there. But, ma'am, if he were, there is nothing you can do. Legally speaking."

"But he's a freedman. From Charleston. How can they catch someone free and transport him against his will? That's kidnapping. That's illegal here, isn't it?" She twisted her hands together.

"Well, yes, it is. But it depends. Maybe he really was a slave. And, ma'am—there is a war going on. South Carolina is right in the middle of it. I do not expect you would have any luck finding your foreman in the Carolinas right now. Perhaps, when the war ends. But when that will be is unclear at this time. Is there anything else I can help you with, Miss Castro? Did you buy more land? You'll be pleased to know your sister and brother-in-law finished their loan payments last month on the new, larger bakery."

"I'm well aware of the war in the East, Mr. Ralston. Don't you realize how dangerous it could be out there for a kidnapped freedman?"

Juanita stomped out, drenched and disgusted with this new country of hers. Not even a hundred years old and already in a war against itself. How could innocent people be kidnapped with no recourse? Attorney Ralston was no help at all.

She hugged the street's border to avoid the thickest mud from swallowing up her boots, stopping by the postal cabin to check for letters and repeat her tired refrain of asking about her son. But now she had Silas to add. And she was hoping for some word of the Hanford Pioneer Bakery and how it had fared in the deluge given she'd heard they'd moved to a new location.

"You sure missin' a lot o' folks," the postmaster said. Despite the rain, he was a cheery man. Bald, with round cheeks, soft arms, and the protruding stomach to match. "You always in here askin' about a tall son but now you lost a hired hand? And a sister too? Seem to lose a lot o' people, ma'am. Bad luck, I'd say. Lemme see if I got any letters."

She waited, dripping all over his crude pine floor.

"Here," he said, holding up an envelope. "We got sumpin' for a Charles and Josefa Hanford but it lists a neighborhood's flooded out." He shook his head, as if to say how could one person have such bad news. "You might try out at them tents for those that got flooded."

Juanita slogged through the street, leaving Canela tied by the lawyer's office to avoid her getting lodged or panicked in the muck. She approached the group of tents cautiously, sensing the despair surrounding the soggy field. Although it reminded her of the mining encampments, these inhabitants were not filled with hope or dreams of golden riches. Straggly haired children clutched older siblings' hands or held dirty cotton dolls. Hassled mothers tried to cook a meal over smoky fires. Men gathered, complained, schemed on next steps. Haggard, gray faces everywhere, and not a one particularly friendly to Juanita's questions.

"Hanford the baker?" one finally said. "Think the shop and his ovens might have got swept away. Not sure though."

Juanita searched for hours, combing the accessible areas of flooded Sacramento. Looking for Josefa soaked up some of the energy she wished she could use to search for Silas. But she couldn't travel thousands of miles to South Carolina, and certainly not in the middle of a bloody war.

Floods, wars, missing persons, this place was a disaster.

Finally at a loss for where else to look, she gathered Canela and took the highest road possible back to Sonora. Every creek was roaring, whole trees and boulders torn up along the banks, and still the rain did not stop. She pushed the aging horse hard. How would she save the animals from harm, the gardens and orchard from flooding?

She couldn't rely on her father or grandmothers' knowledge this time. The rancho had never flooded. Wet winters sometimes. Drought other years. Storms hit with big winds and sometimes lightning strikes ignited the forest into flames. But never a flood which filled the pastures and fields, ripping out crops, trees, vines, sent cattle on surging waters to the ocean. How on earth could they save her hotel, her investment, her livelihood if the rivers overflowed and the rain did not cease?

Maybe it wouldn't flood so much in Sonora—Wood's Creek was much smaller than the American and Sacramento Rivers in downtown Sac City. Maybe Jacinto and Ines would have some ideas.

The rain continued so heavy in a pitch-black sky Juanita was essentially blind as she rode up the Sonora entry road. She'd pulled her hat down low and wrapped her scarf over her neck and mouth and nose. At first, she didn't notice the altered outline of the Hacienda. When she did, she cried out, jumping down off Canela.

"What? What happened?" No one was around to hear.

La Hacienda Hotel was a shell of its former self. Blackened beams lay strewn across a soaked pile of ash—perhaps a back wall remained, but it was hard to be certain in this deluge of water and night. A half-burned hotel sign lay in the mud at the former front door, the kitchen's fireplace stones singed black. Dazed, she stumbled through the destruction, kicking a plate here, a candlestick there. She picked up a melted silver spoon, crumpled as if it were made of soft cloth. It had been a hot fire.

Did Braddock do this? Finally gone crazy with jealous, competitive rage? Did she have other enemies she didn't even know about? Could Ines or Manuel have been careless with kitchen fires or tapers? Where was everyone? Her workers, her boarders . . .

It was all gone, save three small rooms toward the back. The boarding house was completely destroyed, her lodgers homeless now. She and her staff could stay in the remaining rooms but there was no way to generate income. How on earth would she rebuild? And she'd been worried about flooding.

Stepping through ash behind the former kitchen, she saw the little orchard and winter row crops looking drowned but still holding firm in the soupy soil. Anger welled in her, all the loss was just too much. Silas, her sister, now La Hacienda too. Raising her head, she released a scream, water filling her mouth and nose, pouring down off the back of her hat. It was a scream like she'd never let out before. And, somehow, it was a release. She screamed once, twice. Then stopped. Climbing out of the scorched hotel, she grabbed Canela's dragging reins and went looking for her staff.

They hadn't abandoned her after all. Jacinto and Manuel, Ines and Rosalía were at the orchard's highest point constructing a makeshift dam between the swing of the creek and Juanita's land. The men lifted huge river stones out of a wagon, strain on their faces. Ines and Rosalia shoveled dirt. Rosalia's lips were set in a grim frown, Ines wiped rain from her eyes.

"We couldn't save the hotel, but maybe we can save the orchard, Miss Juanita," Ines said, then broke down in tears.

"It was terrible. Started in the kitchen. Don't know how. Were asleep. Lucky to get out," she blubbered, not making a lot of sense.

Juanita held her shoulders hard, forcing her to look into her eyes. "It wasn't your fault. I'm just glad you're safe. The boarders all right?"

"Yes, Miss Juanita. No one got hurt, thank God. Animals okay. But we couldn't save it. Wasn't raining that one night. Might have saved more if had been raining like this."

"You think it was Braddock?" She had to voice her suspicions.

"Maybe. But no, ma'am. I don't. I think it was a boarder up drinking. Forgot to put out the fire. Probably a taper too. We found some bottles in the kitchen."

Juanita nodded. She gave her a quick hug. Thanked them all for their work, their good thinking to get everyone out safe. What next?

There was plenty of time to ponder the future as they finished building the fledgling dam. Then, as they turned the three remaining rooms into quarters for Juanita, a room for the men, and one for Ines and Rosalía. And even more time as the rivers poured down and flooded parts of the town, cows, goats, and pigs washed away as even small streams gushed over their banks.

Sonorans forgot their differences over the next few months and pitched in to save whatever buildings, livestock, and supplies they could. The little town was fortunate to be higher up than many. They worked and worked, with little news of others.

The telegraph poles that hadn't been destroyed by rockslides bobbed and floated past.

It was a while before Sonora got the news. The entire Central Valley was flooded. Hundreds of miles of it. Sacramento was floating away. Many ranchos which had survived the Land Commission now lost their cows to a Noah-sized flood. Thousands of souls were swept out to sea, from small children to the strongest of men. For at least a week, the great bay's entrance to the Pacific had no tide change and freshwater fish were prevalent in the normally salty San Francisco Bay. The Sierras had unleashed a thousand-year flood on the new state of California, changing its trajectory yet again.

But the undaunted rebuild. And so the Americans—despite their color or backgrounds, race and religion, whether they were pioneers or former slaves, confederate sympathizers or abolitionists, immigrants or Native Californians—who'd warned the newcomers for years the great Central Valley could flood into a giant lake—dug in and dug out.

Like most of California, Juanita and her crew spent the winter and spring of 1862 shoring up what they could of their homesteads. San Francisco's Benevolence Society sent hams and clothes, shoes and cash on the weekly Sacramento steamer. Men and women hauled away broken furniture and loose telegraph poles and brought freshly milled lumber to rebuild the towns and ranches.

But Juanita had decided enough was enough. She would never build with wood again. She'd grown up in a land adept at avoiding America's constant fire problem by building with adobe. She would rebuild with adobe, slate and bricks. The only problem was the art of adobe construction was fading into the past. She needed a creative, hardworking brick mason to build her a new hotel with a tavern, a boarding house, and accommodations for herself and her team. Still, how on earth would she pay for it? Or find a brick maker? Or obtain brick? With no steady income from the lodgings, and the gardens and orchards mostly washed away, her hospitality and produce businesses would take years to recover.

Thankfully, the pine forest above had survived mostly unscathed. Juanita had no problem selling her lumber to ravenous, reconstructing Californians. Demand was insatiable, so she logged more timber than usual that spring and summer, sending Jacinto and Manuel to sell it to the highest bidders. Feeling for poor, damaged Sacramento, she even directed a few mule trains filled with timber up there.

In the meantime, she decided she needed to make her own bricks. She and Jacinto discovered the county next door had a plentiful supply of fire clay. She took her timber profits and bought up the most clay-filled land she could find, keeping Mr. Thomas Ralston, Esquire, content by legally forming the Calaveras County Clay Company.

Tobias, who'd barely survived the winter with his wife and young children, happily accepted her offer to leave flooded Sacramento for higher ground in Calaveras County, where he would oversee clay mining and brick manufacturing. But she still needed a pressing machine and brickworks, and kilns to bake the bricks.

Every Sunday night, huddled in her tiny room with no company other than her thoughts, wishing she was sharing a glass of whisky with Silas, she forced herself to not go mad wondering about his whereabouts or if he were even alive. Instead, ever practical, she pushed her thoughts to clay, bricks, masonry, hotel construction. Couldn't she make her own brickworks in the Sierra foothills? Could she build a formidable hotel? She needed help or restarting would take years. She needed city resources and expertise.

Time to, once again, turn to San Francisco.

Ruins of La Hacienda Hotel, Sonora
May 6, 1862

Dear Isabel,

I trust you have heard what a terrible winter it has been for us in Central California. I hope you have weathered a more successful season than most of the state.

Forgive my bluntness, but I need your assistance. Please put down your bracelets and look away from your latest fashionable opera dress and read my entreaty. You know me well enough to know I would never request anything if it were not urgent.

I and my business have suffered terribly. We did have flooding here, though not as disastrous as in Sacramento and lower elevations of the Central Valley. But the Hacienda Hotel and Boarding House burned down amid this calamitous winter.

I'm determined to rebuild, but I will never do it again with timber and wood frame. While you may recall I purchased tracts of pine and cedar for the lumber mills, I refuse to use it in my own construction. I will rebuild with brick and stone, adobe and slate, strictly separating kitchen and cooking, as my parents and grandparents did in those Californio years. I never once heard of a Don's home burning. I recall San Francisco burning five or six times during the early gold fever years.

I've used my logging proceeds to purchase land in the neighboring county, one with rich clay deposits. Tobias and his young family have agreed to move south to oversee clay extraction at my Calaveras County Clay Company.

However, in order to begin operations, I need equipment—excavation tools, a kiln, drying sheds. I am also keen on obtaining the new steam-moulding machine from England.

For this, I need a loan. Without my hotel, it will take years to amass enough capital. I am hoping you can also lend me a skilled mason for a few months to oversee the brick making and hotel construction. You are the queen of building in San Francisco.

I know this is a large request, but I have nowhere else to turn. Little Sonora has become my home and I'd like to rebuild better than ever. If my son is indeed "searching for his mother" as we once heard, he will hopefully hear of my reputation and come find me.

I can repay you quickly once the hotel and boarding house are operating. I have high logging profits due to the construction frenzy, and I have sufficient clay deposits to sell to other brick makers even as I fabricate bricks for my rebuilding efforts. We will continue the mule trains.

I trust you will treat me fairly. I would never ask if the need were not great.

Thank you for considering this. I look forward to a rapid response.

Your friend,
Juanita

The Diamond Crown Hotel, San Francisco
May 24, 1862

Dear Juanita,
Of course, we know of the shocking flooding in Sacramento,
and beyond. We weren't immune here in the city. I was on
the Benevolence Committee—well, you know, behind the
scenes, but leading a group that donated huge amounts to
send food to Sacramento. We did our part.

I must admit your rude tone did not incline me to
read past your insults. However, we have known each
other many years, and I find you intriguing, so I was
curious to uncover what exploits would precipitate such
a dastardly introduction. You know, many would have
taken taper to the parchment at your first paragraphs.

Now, Juanita, my turn to be blunt. This is a strange
friendship. Although I deal with ways of the heart and loins,
I rarely speak openly with women. I have my girls, I have
employees and customers, but that's different than friends.

Everyone here is about transactions and negotiations,
seeing what you can get for cheap. And I understand—it's
often out of survival. But to thrive in San Francisco you
must constantly be on alert for the cheats. Maybe your
past was different, but now it is all about the dollar.

A friend is a rare commodity in golden, now silver,
California. I do believe our honesty and trust does define us
as friends. Even though they say it's dangerous to go into
business with friends, I will help you.

I can loan you the funds you seek, but I am expensive.
I have to charge you 15% interest. I have also persuaded a
skilled mason to move to your Godforsaken country town

for six months. No more. He is a city man who enjoys the comforts I provide here. And I need him for my next building project, a fine home, the mansion I have long envisioned and deserve, atop California Street, where I've purchased several superior lots.

Your loan grew very expensive with this mason, but to start a new business in an industry you know nothing about you need an expert. I sense you are in a hurry and want to start in dry season.

My man will wait while you draft a reply and deliver it to me immediately.

However, I have a question you must answer in your response. Whatever happened to the foreman you had there? The handsome one. He seemed like someone you could trust.

I await your reply.

Your friend,
Isabel

Ruins of La Hacienda Hotel, Sonora
May 24, 1862

Dear Isabel,
Thank you so much for your shockingly quick reply, for looking past the rudeness in my letter and agreeing to assist me with a loan and a mason, and for having your man deliver a letter directly to me and having him wait while I respond. Goodness, what a lot of thank you's.

I do appreciate your friendship and agree that, despite our many differences, we are fortunate to have found a kindred soul. My mother and grandmother would have been shocked by our growing trust, and honesty, over the years. They would never have seen past the madam occupation. The times have taught us differently.

Sadly, Silas was kidnapped last December by a slavecatcher. I believe it was a case of mistaken identity as he'd told me he was a freedman. But whatever his status, his fate in the Southern states is surely not good in the least, especially amidst war.

Thank you, dear friend. I will build a hotel and rooming house to make you proud,

Juanita

The Diamond Crown Hotel, San Francisco
June 29, 1862

Dear Juanita,
I trust by now you and your attorney have reviewed all documentation and received the funds to start your project. I look forward to having my mason back by the new year, and to begin receiving loan payments in January as well.

I am sorry about your foreman's disappearance. Though you claimed he was just an employee, I could tell you cared for him. I certainly hope you were sleeping with him at the very least. Hasn't it been a long time? Though that might shock some, you've learned my occupation leads me to unfettered honesty.

Whether this poor man was an escapee or freedman, I trust you won't forget him. Not likely, as your persistence in searching for your son demonstrates. Perhaps when this horrible war finally ends, you can look for him in Charleston. That's a hard place, with nasty plantation owners fighting to keep their rice and indigo. Such men have long memories.

My father would send slavecatchers to retrieve anyone who escaped. He'd torture other slaves to uncover the whereabouts of escapees. Once caught, he'd whip them in front of everyone. I'm sure even in wartime, he'd send out a slavecatcher.

Those nannies who raised me—he'd let them be beaten, or worse, by the overseers, then just sell them off if there were problems. And there were plenty. A maid or nanny was always pregnant, but you never knew whose child it was. Clearly, he didn't want a bunch of mixed-race babies showing up on his farm.

You see why I had to get out. I hope your man can stay safe. I envy you if you found a friend and lover in your lost handyman. If this war ever ends, maybe he'll come back West to your new hotel.

I've always admired your fortitude and determination, Juanita. We both have the gumption to survive in this wild, unpredictable time and place.

Your friend,
Isabel

Juanita's mind spun with images of motherless little Isabel. Of Silas getting whipped for escaping. Of pregnant maids being punished and sold. What kind of hell was this place Silas was forced back to? Enough. Stop the negative picture show, she told herself, shaking her head as if she could dislodge the ghastly images. It was time to put her survivor energy into rebuilding.

Letters at the Hotel Phoenix

July 1862 to May 1869

Throughout the war years, Juanita focused on her businesses. The minute a roof covered her boarding rooms she rented them out. The mason built an expanded boarding house and impressive hotel and trained locals in brick technology.

She called the new complex the Hotel Phoenix, Sonora, envisioning a replica in another town. And within two years, she established the Hotel Phoenix, Stockton. She still thought about adding wild horse training as a possible enticement for the horse-loving son she missed, but her days were stuffed with the myriad details of six businesses and revolving employees. Horses continued to be simply a means of transportation.

Juanita restarted the music salons and offered weekly card games. She built a larger restaurant and saloon inside each hotel. Her mother and grandmother would have been horrified, but it was the new reality. Travelers and workers wanted comfort and delicious food while also craving distractions from hard wartime living and the distance from their loved ones.

At the time, Juanita had thought Isabel naming her hotel the Diamond Crown was ridiculous. But she decided to call her

Sonora tavern the Paragon. Nothing else. She could just imagine Isabel's belly laugh as she teased her.

"Of all the saloons in all the west, in all the world, this one is the paragon? The very best?"

"Why yes, Madam Platt," Juanita pictured herself responding, *"it is indeed and aren't you lucky you found us. Welcome!"*

She missed Isabel and their repartee. Yes, the madam was manipulative and obsessively focused on displaying her wealth, but she was good for a laugh and open conversation. And it was true, Juanita admitted as she sent the mason back to city living, Isabel had been a good friend. The loans were a godsend. She paid them off within a year of opening the first hotel.

As the years passed, Juanita updated her posted announcements in the telegraph offices looking for Joaquin and sometimes bought newspaper ads. She refrained from bringing up Silas, as no one in California would know his whereabouts in the South, and, in reality, she didn't know his actual status. She tried to forget him but found it difficult.

Josefa and Charles Hanford were eventually confirmed lost to the flood of 1862, which drowned over four thousand souls. At least, she hoped they'd found happiness with the popularity of their bakery. She had no response to letters to Beatriz asking about the success of their legal battle to protect the ranch, but she continued to send bags of coins to her sister each year.

Still, the red brick Hotel Phoenix and its staff provided a stable domicile. Would she ever be able to fill the tavern with family? Or have her own formidable redwood table spilling over with relatives? Not likely any time soon.

Then one day, the Sonora postmaster surprised her with a letter. She opened the envelope that night in her candlelit room.

General Mail Delivery, Charleston, South Carolina
September 18, 1864

Dear Juanita,
I remember our times together fondly and pray you have not forgotten me. I've never truly had a home and felt most at peace when with you at La Hacienda Hotel. I also pray daily this frightful war will end soon. I'm working on the South Carolina Railroad but hope someday to return to California.

I'm sorry I left so suddenly. Remember the drunk that night? He was angry at being put in the stables to sleep it off and thought he recognized me from a poster. He contacted a fugitive slave trapper who attacked and kidnapped me and brought me to Charleston.

I hope the hotel is doing well and Jacinto is helping since I've been gone. The war has created so much disruption here in the South. You cannot imagine how the tranquility of Sonora's pines and mountain views have served as a talisman I hold precious in my darkest days. You, dear Juanita, are the jewel in that talisman.

I believe a life together would be possible for us. Quiet and peaceful. Running the hotel and rooms, adding more gardens and animals. I remember you bought land in the hills. Were you able to sell the lumber? Did you build anything up there for yourself?

I wonder constantly how your days are, if you ever located your son, how your heart is in the loneliness of having no close family. I hope to change that someday, dear Juanita.

I apologize for my boldness, but the disruption

and chaos of war has made me lose any reluctance for forthright honesty.

Yours sincerely,
Silas

Juanita read and reread the letter, so shocked it was as if she were frozen to the chair. Why weren't there more details of what happened to him? Where had he been all this time since the kidnapping almost three years ago. Forthright honesty? Yet, of course, she was pleased to read he was working a railroad job and not on a plantation.

After folding the stationery gingerly and sliding it into the envelope, she decided she would not reply. She placed the letter in the side table drawer. What was the point? He would never get out of the South, especially during a war, and such a bloody, gruesome one.

And yet her hands shook while she washed her face and slipped on her nightgown. Then Juanita sat on the bed and opened the drawer and stared at the letter. He wanted to make a life together? While this was very forward and surprising, it was quite nice to be desired by somebody. To have a good, kind man wanting a relationship pricked at her callused heart. She read it again before blowing out the candles and trying to sleep.

Every night, after she finished the day's work stripping beds, washing linens, weeding the garden, or clearing mule manure—she never had found a reliable Silas replacement who would stay on longer than a few months—she would dig the letter out from its hiding place, lean on a pillow against the headboard, a cup of steaming tea next to her, and reread the letter. It was quite eloquent, though brief.

One night she responded. Then she tore it up but started again the next night. Finally, she made the decision to write a polite, newsy response but not delve into personal feelings.

Hotel Phoenix, Sonora
January 5, 1865

Dear Silas,
I received your letter dated September 18 (months later due to war disruption I assume) with great surprise. I am glad you are well and have employment with the railroad. It is astonishing the growth and changes occurring everywhere. There is now a train from Sacramento to Folsom, no horses or stagecoach needed. They say there will be a train across the entire country someday. I cannot fathom the changes this will bring to our land.

Thank God the war seems to be coming to an end and the slaves emancipated. I hope some sense of normalcy will return soon. While I grew up in another nation, I do feel strongly the United States should remain together as one entity.

Sadly, we lost La Hacienda Hotel to a fire and only a few rooms were spared. I rebuilt with loans from my friend Isabel in San Francisco. I refuse to ever build with wood again. (I must admit after losing you while I was out of town and then the boarding house under the same conditions, I am quite reluctant to ever leave Sonora!)

I bought land over in Calaveras filled with fire clay and have a brick-making operation there. I sell in the Valley and to the towns along the Sierra Nevada range. Now the Hotel Phoenixes in Sonora and

Stockton are adobe. Rosalía, who proved to be quite the businesswoman, runs the Stockton hotel with Manuel. I've had to cut the mule train back and now Jacinto mostly carries the harvested pine logs down the mountain to our eager customers.

You asked about my family. The time I visited my sister near San Jose right before you were kidnapped, I gave her some funds to assist with her attempt to keep her ranch. I do not know the outcome of their legal fight. Tragically, my other sister and her husband, the bakers in Sacramento, drowned in the Great Flood of '62.

Silas, while I am touched at your offer of a life together, I think we should each remain as we are, in the homes we know, pursuing our own paths. Focusing on our personal needs or family right now seems a fool's errand. We are no longer young and have our own established lives. Your honesty leads me to respond in kind.

Best of luck,
Juanita

Juanita drafted the letter several times but finally sent it from the Stockton post when she checked on the second hotel. Rosalía and Manuel were good business partners there, but nothing more. She had secretly hoped they would marry once running the new Phoenix together, but it wasn't to be. He had married one of the maids within a few months of the hotel's opening. Perhaps Rosalía had learned too much from her boss' example and would make a life on her own.

No letters addressed to her were ever at the general delivery checks, so she assumed she had silenced Silas' offer with her realistic response. Good to have taken care of that nonsense, she thought absently.

Then, a year later, another letter arrived.

Virginia Central Railroad, Richmond, Virginia
January 21, 1866

Dear Juanita,
While I was saddened by the business like tone of your reply and rejection of my offer, I am heartened you responded at all. Perhaps there is a chance you will change your mind in the future. Please note the new address above for any future correspondence.

You are right, we are not getting any younger, and this is why I propose we join forces and enjoy our twilight years together. You cannot deny we make a good partnership.

I am so sorry for the difficult loss of your beloved Hacienda. But I have no doubt this new Phoenix Hotel is just as grand and hospitable. Do you still live in Sonora? I like to imagine where you are and what you are doing. I only have the Hacienda images to sustain me.

I also am deeply disturbed by how much tragedy continues to haunt you. I am truly saddened by the loss of your sister and brother-in-law in the huge floods a few years ago.

I continue on at the railroad but now am in Virginia. It is very difficult work. Most of the workers are former slaves and the company owners treat the workers much like the overseers did on the plantations. While I too am pleased the war is finally over, I was terribly saddened when Mr. Lincoln was shot. I fear conditions have changed little in my part of the country. I am exploring new opportunities.

I carry you in my heart and hope you will reconsider my suggestion for sharing a life together in California.

Yours,
Silas

Hotel Phoenix, Sonora
May 3, 1866

Dear Silas,
I am glad you continue to have a job, but fear for your safety in this type of work. I trust your situation in Virginia is superior to the frenzy here. I've seen the Chinese outside of Sacramento building the rails going over the mountains. I cannot imagine the difficulty of such a life, as we hear stories of workers falling to their deaths off the cliffs or being worked to starvation by the railroad barons.

Having traversed those same mountains with pack mules in the depths of winter, through wet springs and hot summers, and even an avalanche, I cannot imagine clearing rock and laying track across the same expanse. It is quite the endeavor, although I imagine the new explosives help. I am sure there are many former gold miners wishing they'd had dynamite back then!

Yes, I continue much as in the years when you were here. I live in an apartment above the hotel rooms, with the boarding house next door. I still am partial to taking my meals in the kitchen with Ines and sometimes with the boarders, if they seem interesting, as you did when you arrived.

I still work in the gardens and tend to the animals and rooms. I occasionally travel to Stockton and Sacramento to check on my business interests, although, as I mentioned, leaving Sonora makes me nervous. The fear of losing something valued while gone does not leave me.

While not unexpected, but still sad, we did lose Canela last month. That horse and I went through so much together in her twenty plus years. She has been the most stable thing in my life since I stole her and fled the rancho seventeen years ago. Someday, I must tell you about a horse race she and I were in. You will laugh at that story.

Fondly,
Juanita

John Jones Tailor Shop, Chicago, Illinois
January 29, 1867

Dear Juanita,
I am grateful I received your letter of May 3 and hope I didn't miss any others as I have moved again. Happily, this time, I can report I am now a Pullman Porter, gratefully working inside the train cars instead of laying track. Have

you heard of them? We are like waiters or hotel porters, tending to the needs of mostly wealthy white men who now travel by train and want comfort as they travel.

I appreciate how much I learned about hospitality from you and La Hacienda. I think the hotel work helped me get the job and keep it. So far! Finally, a steady income. It is not much but we get tips from the customers, which helps a lot. We work all the time and have to travel 11,000 miles a month in order to receive our pay.

The days are long, and the sleep short. But I am thrilled to not be digging ditches, carrying rails, and hammering creosote-soaked ties, so I don't mind. I'm also not sad to be far from Charleston and Richmond. It is a mess there, and I fear the slave states may never recover from having lost the war. I don't know what will happen to my people there. I had to get out. I know I am more fortunate than so many still in the South.

As Pullman Porters, we have elegant, crisp uniforms—I dare to imagine that if you saw me, you would think me handsome. I had never worn a uniform or formal hat or shiny shoes before. Now that is all I wear. You would hardly recognize me.

I am based in Chicago, where I found a shared bunkroom with others who left the South. I have kind neighbors, but all carry difficult stories and job situations, many focused on trying to locate relatives they lost during slave days and the disruption of the war. As I am rarely there, it is not a home, so I'm happy to spend most of my time in my Pullman car. I have no family to miss.

There is only you who I think of with fond memories. While you continue to reject my proposal, I am heartened by your comment that I was something you valued when I was kidnapped from Sonora. Also, a horse race? I can't wait to hear. And, by the way, I never heard about the avalanche. Southern boy that I am, I can hardly imagine such a scenario.

I, too, am sad Canela passed. She was a good horse and a good companion to you. I hope you can find a new steed, but also perhaps I can someday be that stable presence in your life. While Canela was steadfast and true, I believe you would find I am also.

Please write me again in Chicago. You have no idea how your letters, although few in number and often business like in tone, sustain me. I finally am saving a bit of money and plan to someday take the train as a passenger and come see you in California. I would love to hear those stories in person.

I remain forever yours,
Silas

Hotel Phoenix, Sonora
October 18, 1867

Dear Silas,
I am pleased to hear of your improved employment and living situation. I hope you will meet a nice woman there in Chicago and settle down. I am so far away in California, in my own independent life.

I fear you are holding on to some distant memory of

me and unrealistic expectation of what could be. I do not want to mislead you in any way. I am happy to continue as friends and correspondents, but please do not imagine me as anything other than that.

All is well here in Sonora. We have settled into a steady pace of regular customers at the hotels and in our timber and clay businesses. I've hired Tobias—remember the young man from Sacramento who oversaw my lots there?—to be a manager of all these enterprises. He is urging me to form a holding company, and I am considering that.

I am always leery of lawyers and yet also painfully aware of how important legal documents can be in the US. I suppose should anything happen to me, my businesses would best go to my sister, who would probably divide the spoils with her husband and children. Then at least I would feel I have provided for my family in some significant manner.

Sadly, I continue to have no news of my son. Despite my steady questions, which I am quite sure grow tiresome to all.

Sincerely,
Juanita

P.S. I imagine you look very fine in your Pullman Porter uniform.

John Jones Tailor Shop, Chicago
January 16, 1868

My dearest Juanita,
I have sensed your tendency to push me away in your letters. Your tone seems stiff and formal most times, but then occasionally I am encouraged by a sweet phrase.

I have always felt there was a respect between us. I have clung to the deep feelings I have had for you over these many years. Your letters have given me some hope, perhaps foolishly I admit, that we could be life companions rather than just business colleagues. I have no other family. Never have. The time I had with you in Sonora at the hotel was the closest I ever felt to what I imagine having family is like.

Please accept my boldness here with an open heart. I can tell you fear losing your independence, but perhaps you fear sharing difficult memories as well. I understand. I've been fending for myself always, never trusting anyone. I believe you know something about that.

But, as one who respects you deeply, I believe we can find a path through the loneliness together. A support brace if you will, for a most meaningful life—one filled with love, partnership, and a goodness the evil in this world can never touch.

I continue on the rails and guard my savings in hopes of visiting you some day.

Yours always,
Silas

Juanita dropped the letter, overwhelmed by the eloquence and the strange sentiments swirling inside of her like a whirlwind of leaves swept up by a gust. Maybe he was right. But no, they hadn't seen each other in so long. What could they share now? And they had aged. Who were they to imagine romance? Wasn't it a foolish dream?

She loved her Sonora businesses and community, but she could not fool herself that it was a true home. It was a room above a hotel, a place to rest. Could Silas help fill that emptiness? She remembered their late-night conversations after cleaning the saloon or the morning coffees when they could sneak in a quiet break. His caress on her cheek. The memories warmed her. But her independence was fierce, and fears entrenched. If she cared for yet another who'd she'd eventually lose, or never really had, could she survive the heartbreak?

Hotel Phoenix, Sonora
February 21, 1868

Dear Silas,

I received your letter of January 16. While deeply moved by your eloquence, I cannot picture significant changes to my current life.

While brave on the back of a horse or with a rifle against a hungry coyote, I must admit I am not well versed in the ways of the heart. I've been alone for so long I cannot even fathom sharing my most personal thoughts and honest opinions with another. I fear I would not know how to be the loving companion you describe, and clearly desire.

Your kindness and persistence are touching. But do

let's correspond about our daily lives and not that of the internal. I fear I no longer truly know what it means to be family with anyone.

Sincerely,
Juanita

John Jones Tailor Shop, Chicago
March 30, 1869

Dear Juanita,
I know it's been a very long time since I've written. Please accept my apologies for the delay. But there is good reason, as you will see.

Enclosed please find a ticket for the brand-new intercontinental railroad, which I hope you will use to come visit me in Chicago. I cannot get away from my job for long, but if you come to Chicago, I can show you a glamorous city and we can discuss all that has occurred in the past eight years since I was taken from Sonora.

Take the Central Pacific to Omaha and then catch the train to Chicago. Go to Quinn Chapel AME Church or to the tailor John Jones' shop and someone will get you a place to stay while I finish my shift on the train. There are good people in these neighborhoods who will welcome you.

I agree it has been a long time since we've seen each other, so let's get reacquainted. I will not pressure you in any way, but you should know my feelings and determination have not ceased. I believe we can share a loving life together. In person, we can discuss this in more detail and see how we both feel.

However, if we have any hope of a future together, I must be completely honest as I have not been so in the past. I sense there are things you have not shared with me as well. In hopes of winning your love, and convincing you to come to Chicago, I must now be truthful.

I was a slave in South Carolina. I was never a freedman as I told you. My name is not Holloway, that of a respected freedman family, but Ward, from a notorious slaveholding man. I escaped one of Mr. Ward's plantations and went West, desperate to find the freedom I'd dreamed of for years.

It was a long and arduous journey across the Overland and California Trails. God must have been watching over me as I did not succumb to cholera or get massacred by Indians. All of which I observed. God clearly brought me to you in Sonora.

A slavecatcher caught me that night at La Hacienda and returned me to Mr. Ward, who was none too pleased, especially in the middle of a war which threatened his livelihood. Eventually, I was transferred to railroad work with other slaves. I've learned since that the transfer was when Mr. Ward learned of the Emancipation Proclamation, but he did not tell his slaves about Mr. Lincoln's declaration. I continued in the railroad work through the war, then left for Chicago. There is nothing but destruction and anger in the South and sharecropping is the only option there for someone like me.

I am truly sorry I did not trust you enough to tell

you the truth, but perhaps you will understand I could trust no one.

Please take the ticket to Chicago. It is for two months from now, so you have time to think over my invitation and make arrangements for the hotel and businesses.

We can get reacquainted here. You can ride the train and see my work all around you. I beseech you to consider my invitation most seriously.

Yours forever,
Silas

Every Silas letter had included some surprise, but this one shocked Juanita to her bones. A train ticket? Visit Chicago? He'd never been a freedman, always a slave? It was overwhelming to absorb the truth, and the gift. Over the next few days, she read the letter again and again. Somehow, this correspondence made her feel as if Silas were present, as if he were across from her in the saloon after a gambling night, confessing over a glass of whiskey. She sensed him reaching out through the parchment, touching her heart.

Phoenix Hotel, Sonora
April 19, 1869

Dear Silas,
Your letter caught me by surprise. I am both touched beyond words while also being a little upset with you for lying to me. And yet, I understand. I have absolutely no comprehension of the slave existence and am tremendously sad that such a horrendous wrong was your lot in life.

I'm so pleased you've been able to get out from under that yoke and find a profession to make your own living. That must be a great source of pride for you. Though I am sure it still can be difficult. And lonely.

I must admit I look back on my years on the rancho and am mortified to face the fact our Native servants were indeed slaves. They were not paid. They had nowhere else to go. They had no skills which would translate into any other profession. Indeed, in those Mexican years and in my grandparents' Spanish era, once they'd been captured by the priests for conversion their ability to live independently, as they had before the Spanish arrival, was extinguished. Many, many died in the Mission years, and have continued to suffer since.

As a child, I overheard a few stories of Native bands coming to steal horses or taking over and burning Missions. I think that happened in Santa Barbara. Many retreated to the hills and deep into the forests. I know our population growth in California has taken an even greater toll. I also believe my family has a deeper connection to its Native slave past than any would admit.

Anyway, I digress. This is just to say I am profoundly moved by your confession. I cannot even begin to feel your pain and suffering. And I wish very deeply you are fortunate to find some personal peace and financial benefit in your position as a Pullman Porter.

While it takes my breath away and causes me to blush at you professing that we might find success as a loving couple, I am quite nervous about such a prospect. As you have guessed, I, too, was not completely honest in our many late-night chats over a sip of whiskey or a quick coffee together (much as I did enjoy those moments).

What I did not tell you is I sent my son away because he was starting to look like the patron. After my father died, our ranch was overloaded with debts from a terrible cattle disease which ruined us, and I was forced to sell. The only buyer who could meet the terms was my former lover, who had been a worker on the ranch years before. Once he owned the place, he made my mother, sisters, son and me his servants.

As a lovestruck teenager, I thought we were devoted to each other. But he left, and afterwards I discovered I was pregnant. He never knew. I was devastated, especially when my parents almost disowned me. I bore the baby alone, far from home, while they fabricated a story turning me into a widow.

After they accepted me back, I worked to stay in their good graces, helping with the ranch and raising my son. Eventually, however, all was lost to me. Ever since, I've focused on avoiding such pain and betrayal again. Now you know.

I am feeling nervous and unsure, but I believe I will get on the Chicago train and come visit you. You are right it would be prudent to continue our friendship in person.

I have never left California. I am a horsewoman through and through, as you well know. I cannot imagine traveling thousands of miles on a mechanical beast of steam and smoke which does not neigh or beg for alfalfa and carrot-top treats. And Chicago . . . well, I prefer the countryside. Chicago seems even larger and busier than San Francisco.

But with you there, perhaps we can find a quiet

space and continue those conversations. I have so many questions—like how did you learn to write so well? And the train ticket as a gift. It is too much. I will repay you when I get to Chicago.

Fondly,
Juanita

She received the quickest reply ever from Silas, which pleased her enormously.

John Jones Tailor Shop, Chicago
May 1, 1869

Dearest Juanita,
I am happier than I have ever been in my life, except when I was talking into the night with you at La Hacienda. I will do everything to have as much time free as possible so we can talk over our lives as we walk the streets of Chicago.

I know it has been a long time, but I trust we will find deep inside we are the same people as when we worked together at the hotel.

Thank you for being honest with me. I always suspected something as painful must have happened to you, but I could not imagine it. You deserve the very best and I sincerely hope to provide it for you.

Yours forever,
Silas

P.S. The ticket is a gift I am so happy to be able to give. I will not accept anything for it except the joy of having you visit me.

None of her employees could believe she would go so far, and on a train. Those noisy bellowing piles of steel that plowed through Sacramento? Tobias was incredulous.

"You're going where? For how long? How will you get there? The train? Oh my."

She drafted a letter to Isabel before leaving.

Hotel Phoenix, Sonora
May 5, 1869

Dear Isabel,
I trust you are well and the Diamond Crown is thriving. How is the construction of your California Street home coming along?

In a few weeks, I will take the new transcontinental train from Sacramento to Omaha, then on to Chicago. I have not yet shared this with you, but Silas and I have been exchanging letters for several years. As you suspected, he has expressed feelings for me and wants to return to California to make a life together.

First, I ignored such talk, then told him I was not interested. Yet every time I think of him, I remember him quite fondly. I also catch myself reading and rereading his letters. He is quite eloquent. He is a Pullman Porter now on the trains out of Chicago.

He revealed some shocking truths about his life, and I told him some of my secrets, the foundation of which you too may have suspected. I will explain all next time I see you in person.

He is a good man with a big heart and is very handy to have around a hotel and boarding house. I decided to accept the ticket he sent me. Yes, he sent me a full ticket as a gift! I am nervous about traveling on anything but a horse, yet I'll take a coach to Sacramento and then a huge lump of smoke and metal to Chicago. It is amazing I will go some two thousand miles in a very short time.

I wanted you to know in case I don't make it there and back. The time I lost the mules in the avalanche, I realized not one person knew where I was and not one soul would have missed me if I'd gone down the slope with the pack train.

I have provided my business holdings to my sister if anything happens to me, with generous payouts to my loyal employees. My will is with the lawyer Thomas Ralston, Esq. on K Street in Sacramento. Tobias knows where copies of all my legal documents are hidden, if ever needed. The contact location for Silas in Chicago is John Jones' Tailor Shop. (I realize I do not know what last name he is using, but I expect it is Holloway).

I hope to see you again soon in San Francisco and tell you grand tales of train rides and Chicago adventures. Or better yet, you could get out of the chaotic city and come visit me in the peace of Sonora. While not as grand as your establishments, the Phoenix Hotel is comfortable and homey and you will see your influence everywhere.

Your friend,
Juanita

P.S. I fear I am being a terrible mother by not taking the time to travel to search for Joaquin. He most definitely is not in Chicago.

P.P.S. I thought I might come see you to get your advice on whether I should accept Silas' ticket gift or not, but I realized there was absolutely no doubt you would tell me to go! And to give up the search for Joaquin. In reality, I basically have.

Juanita secured a leatherbound trunk and stuffed it with clothes she thought one might need in a modern city. Then she sent Jacinto to the Wells office to arrange transport, and, for the first time in her life, took a stagecoach to Sacramento. To meet a train. What had become of this place? Of Alta California? Of her green, ranchland-covered home? Of the horse-trod trails, of the vaquero and rancher? Modern technology and an enormous influx of people had taken over.

With apprehension, and yet a bit of excitement, she hoisted herself into the stagecoach, Jacinto holding her elbow. The interior smelled strongly of cigarette smoke and sweat, and the worn leather seat was hard and unforgiving at every bump of the trail. The curtains had once been a plush red, but were now thin, the velvet crush rubbed off to a flat sheen. With every bounce, the curtains swayed, allowing dust into the carriage.

After only a few miles, dust covered every surface, filling her nose and coating her hair. She pulled a scarf out of her travel carryall—a more feminine overnight bag, as Ines had insisted she act like a lady going to visit a friend rather than a muleteer. She wrapped the scarf over her hair and across her face, then pulled it up over her nose, covering her eyes at the worst dust clouds.

Still, despite the dust, she pushed aside the curtains to see the view, feeling her dormant curiosity awaken. It was a freeing, and unusual, feeling to ride without a care for steering the horse or checking for potholes or watching for a specific turnoff. It was astonishing to simply observe the forest and mountains go by. As nervous as she was, she felt an exhilaration she had not experienced in years. She felt lighter, maybe a little younger.

But was this a mistake? Dreadful, unexpected things always happened whenever she left Sonora.

Train to Chicago

May 1869

In Sacramento, the driver dropped her at the Pacific Railroad Company after depositing her trunk at the hotel, so she could stroll to stretch her legs and explore the planked walkway down K Street past the Lady Adams building. She peeked in the shops and windows as she headed for the makeshift church at the end of the street.

According to the *Sacramento Bee*, Bishop O'Connell was available in the small structure next to the burned rubble of Saint Rose of Lima to provide comfort to local Catholics and take confession. She remembered her sister, Josefa, had been a devoted parishioner in the little sanctuary throughout its many difficulties.

Yet as she sat quietly in the tiny makeshift church next door to St. Rose, which had been damaged by the flood and burned many times, Juanita decided she could not take confession. She hadn't been since she was forced to mass by her parents as a young teen. What was she thinking? There were too many sins. She'd probably overwhelm the priest.

She rested in the back pew while other parishioners took

turns. The line thinned, then all departed, and at last she was alone in the cool dark. When Father O'Connell finally emerged from the confessional, she gave him a minute then approached him quietly.

"Oh, do you need to take confession, my dear?" he asked, surprised to see anyone left in the shadows. His strong Irish accent was a little hard to understand.

"No, Father. Thank you. I'm just wondering if we could pray together for a moment. Could you bless me as I am about to take a long journey on the new train all the way to Chicago? I've never left Alta California. I just arrived from Sonora in a stagecoach. First time in my life not traveling on horseback. It's a strange new world, Father, and I would appreciate your blessing."

"Ah, yes." A slight smile crossed his lips as he led her to the front pew. "I remember well the nerves when I was sent here to the mines from Dublin, the only home I'd ever known. What's your name?"

After she gave it, he took her hand, gave it a soft squeeze and said, "Let's pray together. Lord Jesus, please watch over Miss Juanita on her railroad journey to Chicago. And we pray for a safe return to California."

They knelt their heads, hands clasped, for several minutes. His large, plump hand enveloped Juanita's sinewed palm. She was astonished at the father's casual demeanor. Perhaps a career on the frontier lessened a priest's formality.

With great appreciation, she exhaled to find a moment of tranquility, her many sins temporarily forgotten, and the courage to travel by train to Chicago, and Silas, strengthened.

She decided to stroll through the growing town before stopping at the hotel for the night. Her new boots clomped on the planked sidewalk as she peered into an eating establishment here, a saloon there, a general store and a haberdashery. Apparently, the men of Sacramento had grown wealthy enough to need silk suits and neckties. What a change from the wool and thick cotton pants of the early miners.

A woman's name over the next shop caught her eye, one where "Daguerreotypes by a Lady, Margaret Anna McCallan" was printed in black letters encircled with gold above the large window. Juanita, curious about a woman photographer who owned her own studio, stopped to look at the display. A lush red velvet curtain framed the window box. At the front, several easels held large pictures, advertising the photographer's work.

One daguerreotype featured Governor Leland Stanford and his opulently dressed wife at his election to governorship. Based on the elegant backdrop, she figured it must have been taken inside his mansion. The former governor, now senator, was rumored to be planning another one near Isabel on San Francisco's California Street hill. One picture showed a little girl dressed in layers of petticoats with a doll in her hand. One showed a teenage boy wearing coattails and a top hat.

Toward the back of the window, propped on a chair, was a large image featuring four suited men in upholstered chairs, cigars in their fingertips, in a luxurious office. She recognized Governor Stanford again. Oh, these were the Big Four of the Central Pacific Railroad, she realized, thinking maybe she knew which one was Huntington.

Set in the background of the image was a large round table covered with drawings and maps, diagrams and engineering schematics, even a three-dimensional model of mountains. Three men in work boots and trousers, sleeves rolled up, one with a cap, gazed at the plans. One was pointing at a dark line. Presumably these railroad construction engineers were determining a route across the Sierra. The photographer had arranged the men so they appeared to gaze with appreciation at the four wealthy funders in the foreground. One engineer's face was plainly visible.

As Juanita stared at the daguerreotype, the skin on her arms puckered. It was Joaquin. She was sure of it. He was taller than the others, with longish locks escaping his working man's hat, eyebrows bushy, his pointed chin sporting a goatee. A set of bangs flopped to one side below the cap's brim.

She let out an unintelligible sound. It was as if she were seeing her lover, Malachy, again. But this man's eyes were not twinkling with mischief. They were serious. Sad, even.

She pushed open the door and a bell sounded.

"Anyone here? Hello?"

A sales assistant came through black curtains, then wiped his hands with a cloth smelling strongly of developing fluid. Juanita hurled questions at the clerk but he knew little about the display photos. She convinced the hesitant man to look at the back of the picture, but it was blank. The other pictures had labels and dates on them.

"Sorry, ma'am. I don't know much except Mrs. Stanford commissioned a series. Not sure when. Years ago. We can ask Miss McCallan—this is all her work. She's in San Francisco. Won't be back 'til tomorrow afternoon."

"Oh, but I'm supposed to leave on the train first thing tomorrow morning! For Chicago. Not sure when I'll be back."

"Well, you can speak with her when you return." He disappeared through the black curtain shielding the studio workspace.

Juanita stepped out the tingling shop door in a daze, then

stood completely still and stared at the daguerreotype again. When was this taken? Maybe early 1860s? They were just celebrating railroad completion now, so it was years ago they'd engineered routes over the mountains. Though the transcontinental had been built rapidly during the war years.

If this were, say, 1862, Joaquin would have been twenty-nine, which looked about right. While he appeared serious about the work, his striking eyes hinted at a charm behind the formality. Had Joaquin worked on the railroad? Was he some sort of engineer, or had they put him in the photograph for his good looks?

Finally, here was proof he had remained in California, but she'd been looking in mining areas all this time. Had he failed in the gold and then moved to another profession? Where would he have learned skills to architect railroad tracks over mountain passes?

She stood frozen to the spot for so long, staring at the picture, trying to work through a storm of raging emotions and what ifs, that the bell timbered again.

"You all right, ma'am?" The shop clerk poked his head out.

She nodded, embarrassed. "Oh, yes." She took a deep breath, smoothed out her dress and walked back to the hotel.

Once settled in her room, she sat on the bed staring out the window. Should she get on the train tomorrow as she'd promised Silas? She really did want to experience the train over the Sierra and see Chicago. Her homebody nature had not completely dimmed her strong curiosity. And what was Silas like now?

Yet, maybe the photographer had clues to locating Joaquin. She needed to find out. But if she didn't get on the train for Chicago, would she ever see Silas again? He'd be heartbroken. Plus, it was a terrible thing to do to the man, who was a good person who loved her. Oh dear. What to do?

In the morning, Juanita walked to the station while the hotel porter dropped off her trunk. She sat on the hard, wooden bench with her carpet bag on her lap and her pocket purse around her wrist. A whistle sounded loudly, and the train roared in with all its power and screeching brakes, steam billowing out from the undercarriage, the earth rumbling beneath her. Hot air spewed off the tracks and she had to grab her hat.

"Sacramento City!" Conductors in shiny black uniforms jumped to the platform and helped ladies disembark. Parents passed children to outstretched arms while passengers continuing the journey stared out the windows above the bustling station. As the excited crowd thinned, fresh travelers climbed the steps, hauling luggage, while conductors punched tickets and yelled for everyone to get boarding.

Juanita glanced down at her own ticket, *Chicago* in bold letters. She looked back at the feverish crowd as it dispersed, couples kissing, families hugging in greetings and farewells.

Suddenly, she knew—Chicago was too far away. The train was so foreign. She'd walked or ridden a horse everywhere her entire life. If she got up into that metal fiery beast, wouldn't it be giving up on her own son? Neglecting to follow the best lead yet. And there was too much uncertainty with Silas. What was she thinking coming here? Taking this ticket? She hadn't seen the man in eight years.

"All aboard!" the conductor yelled down the track. "You coming, ma'am? Train's leaving." He removed his cap and swung it gallantly in her direction.

An image of Silas in his Pullman Porter uniform flashed

thorough her mind, although she knew his position was a different one. She looked at the ticket again. And then up at the conductor. She shook her head and did not move.

He shrugged his epauletted shoulders, placed his hat firmly back on his head, grabbed the railing and swung up the steps, waving the depart signal to the engineer up front. He hung on the outside while the massive metal machine gathered speed along the platform and out from the station, then he stepped inside, train whistle blaring.

In a stupor, Juanita found a porter and carriage to return to the hotel, where she booked the room for another night. She sat down at the wobbly, knotted pine desk and penned a letter.

Sacramento
May 30, 1869

Dear Silas,
I am sorry I won't be on the train when you expect me
to arrive in Chicago. I am in Sacramento, but I decided
against taking your generous gift.
Yesterday afternoon, I walked by a portrait studio
with a window display. One daguerreotype featured the
Central Pacific Railroad barons with three engineers at a
table covered with drawings and maps, staged as if they
were planning the rail route. One of them is Joaquin. He
looks exactly like his father.
Yes, it was taken perhaps seven or eight years
ago, but if he is still in California, I cannot leave. The
photographer was not at the studio, but I can speak with
her late this afternoon for information. I am hoping to
finally have a firm clue to pursue.

At the railway station, I felt as if I were in another land. Such changes I've seen here. At the moment, I'm having difficulty accepting them all. And California is the only home I've ever known, so I really should not be leaving it—abandoning my businesses and staff and son more than I already have. I sat on the bench as the conductor called for boarding and just could not get up and onto the railcar.

Despite your kindness, I must find out all I can about Joaquin and what became of him. I would never forgive myself if I didn't try. I've not been working hard enough at it these past years.

I hope you will forgive me for this sudden change of heart. I regret the hurt and surprise this will cause you. I do hope to come to Chicago someday, and please know you are always welcome at the Phoenix Hotel in Sonora.

Sincerely,
Juanita

While waiting for the photographer to return to her studio, Juanita walked to the Sacramento General Delivery office and sent the letter. Heavy-hearted, imagining Silas' disappointment, she was also rewarded with a letter from Isabel. At first surprised, she then remembered she'd written Isabel about her trip. She stuffed the letter in her pocket purse to read after visiting the daguerreotype studio.

The clerk looked at her askance as she entered, perhaps remembering her staring at the railroad builders' portrait. The pungent smell of processing chemicals stung her nose.

"I'll get Miss McCallan," he said, disappearing behind the black curtain.

The photographer appeared and offered a firm handshake and businesslike nod. "How can I help you, ma'am?"

She was about Juanita's age but with a full head of gray hair wrapped up in an elaborate bun. She had brown eyebrows and sea-green eyes set in skin so translucent you could see the purple vein pulsing at her collarbone. She was striking, not only in countenance but in her perfect posture. As Juanita asked her questions, she could not help but wonder what color the photographer's hair had been before turning gray.

"The governor's wife commissioned a series after the Associates formed the Central Pacific Rail Company," the photographer said. "They were raising funds and scouting a route. That's Theodore Judah right there," she said, pointing to the man holding up the map. "You know, he's really the architect of it all. Scouted in the mountains for a year, mostly alone, or with his wife who did paintings of the ridges and passes. He got President Lincoln to sign the Railroad Act. Thought it might unify the country, but the war was already a bloody year in by then."

"When was it taken?" Juanita asked, trying not to sound too desperate.

"I think this was, maybe, early '62 we did this seating? Mrs. Stanford wanted to commemorate the occasion. She said it was historic—a railroad tying together America. Probably right. We'll see now, won't we?" She waved at the seated men in fine suits.

"They're out there celebrating right now after joining the rails. East and West. Quite amazing. Sadly," Miss McCallan continued, "Mr. Judah died in a Panama crossing in '63. Had a disagreement with those robber barons right there," she gestured angrily, tossing her hand toward the seated men, as if they were responsible for his death. "So sad. Was on his way to raise money from Cornelius Vanderbilt after they ditched him. Cut him out." She paused, as if in both memory and respect for the dead.

Juanita let Miss McCallan wander around in her memories. Might reveal something useful.

"I did quite a few poses," Miss McCallan said, looking at the photo anew. "This one was not selected for the final installation in the governor's mansion. That's why I've got it. She chose another one for their private quarters. I hear they've kept another image for the castle they're building in San Francisco."

"Who are these other two men in the photo?" Juanita could no longer resist asking. "Did they work for Mr. Judah? Or for one of the Associates?"

"I'm so sorry, ma'am. Mrs. Castro, is it? I have no idea who the other two are. I just did what Mrs. Stanford wanted for the sitting."

Juanita persisted but the photographer knew nothing more.

"Perhaps some of their staff would know," she said.

Awash in frustration, Juanita barely remembered to be polite, but she did thank her and offer to pay for her time.

"No need. I understand. So sorry I couldn't help." The photographer held her farewell handshake a little longer than expected. "Lot of lost people in those war years."

Despite little to pursue, Juanita felt somewhat hopeful. I'll go to Mrs. Stanford and ask her right now, she told herself. And then to Mr. Judah's company. If there still was one.

She'd need to look more presentable, however, if she was going to go knocking on the former governor's door. Juanita hid behind a shed in a barren lot, stripped off the men's pants beneath her long skirt, folded them and hid them under a bush. She couldn't do anything about her shoes, but at least she looked more like a respectable woman, pulling her skirt down to hide the scuffed boots. She rearranged her hair in its comb, then patted it smooth.

After asking directions on the street, she made her way to the Stanford mansion at 8th and N streets. She stared up at the enormous towers, layers of windows facing the street, and dual staircases curving to meet before a formidable mahogany door, and she gulped. It was an impressive mansion.

Hold your head high, Juanita Castro, she admonished herself. Remember your roots. Wealthy people who viewed themselves as important wanted to interact with other important people. She'd only get past the imposing door if she portrayed herself as an equal. She aligned her posture, copying Miss McCallan's, and knocked hard. Silence. She knocked again. Louder.

Finally, the door opened a crack to reveal a young woman in starched white uniform and black apron, frowning, an eyebrow raised. No greeting.

"I am Juanita Castro de la Cruz, third generation Californio, hotel and logging company owner. Is Mrs. Stanford home? I need to ask some questions about a series of daguerreotypes she commissioned in 1862 from Miss McCallan, the lady who does daguerreotypes. It's important."

The young woman sniffed, looked Juanita up and down and shook her head.

"She's just had a baby, ma'am. She's not to be disturbed."

"Isn't the baby about a year now? I saw his picture in the *Bee*. It's questions about my son who's been missing for almost fifteen years. He was in the photographs she commissioned. I'm sure Mrs. Stanford would understand, especially now, finally having her own son."

The maid's scowl deepened, a furrow formed between her eyebrows, she sighed, then held up her hand and closed the door with a resounding shove. Juanita waited, hoping the performance meant she'd return, even if she was none too happy about it.

After a long delay, the enormous black door opened a crack.

"As I told you, Mrs. Stanford has a baby and is not entertaining visitors, of any kind. Ask the photographer your questions."

The door slammed shut before Juanita could respond.

She spent the rest of the afternoon walking up and down the lettered streets asking about Mr. Judah's office, railway engineering companies, and the Central Pacific Railroad. She met with a lot of excitement but no information—wasn't it fantastic the East and West tracks had just met in Utah territory? Just eight days to cross the country they said. Mr. Judah died over six years ago, and Mrs. Judah moved Back East after his tragic death others reported. But no one knew anything about a series of photographs or Mr. Judah's contemporaries. Why worry about the beginning of the railroad when you should be celebrating the completion, they admonished.

Back at the hotel, she again sat alone, looking out over the Wholesale Grocer's in the Lady Adams building, frustrated, confused, and at a loss for where to turn next.

She fished Isabel's letter out of her purse pouch.

Platt Mansion, California Street Hill, San Francisco
May 18, 1869

Dear Juanita,
I received your letter of May 7 with great joy for my
longtime friend. Of course, you are right. I definitely think

you should get on the train and go to Chicago to meet the Pullman Porter. How romantic. I'm sure he looks very dapper in his uniform.

As you'll remember, I rarely leave San Francisco since my businesses cannot be left unattended, but I was on one of those Pullman sleeping cars recently and the service and elegance were splendid. And you know, I have high expectations for luxury and high-quality service.

To your other question, my new home on California Hill is exquisite. I am hoping none of these railroad "Associates,"—or "robber barons" as everyone calls them— build theirs to be any larger or more elaborate. I have my pride and reputation to preserve. Please do come visit when you return from Chicago.

Juanita, love is a rare treasure. A gift from God, even though I don't really believe in God. A gift many never experience. It sure sounds like this gentleman loves you. A train ticket from Sacramento to Chicago is not inexpensive, and I am sure the Pullman Porters are not receiving enormous wages. It is quite the gift.

Yes, it has been many years since you saw each other, but why not go visit and see if you still find enjoyment in each other's company? You can return whenever you want if it doesn't suit you to stay or to join forces with him.

This train now crossing the entire country in one week is amazing. It took me months to cross the horrid Oregon and California trails. My brother and thousands of others died on the way, as did so many walking through the jungles of Panama or at sea for months around the Horn. A rail car will be, not only quicker, but so much safer.

Train travel will change America forever. Maybe it

can help heal the wounds of the ghastly war. What a thing to see in our lifetime.

That's why you must go, dear friend. For the novelty. For the future. To see the world's changes.

Yes, maybe you'll find a loving and suitable companion, or maybe not—after seven or eight years it is quite risky. But for the adventure of it, for the romance, for the novelty, and for the possibilities, you must go.

Your friend,
Isabel

Persistence

May to June 1869

Silas squirmed on the bench as the last passengers accepted the conductor's white gloved hand and disembarked at the train station. He'd paced the platform several times already, hopping up the steps of each car to glance inside, standing back to peer through windows from afar.

Maybe she'd fallen asleep. Could she be confused about the stop? But surely not. Chicago was quite recognizable. True, it was confusing with so many stations. Had she disembarked at another one? Or had she gotten confused in Omaha and boarded another train? He waited until the last passenger hurried off the platform, then searched through the building, looking into the faces of weary travelers slumped over their trunks or nestled against a companion's shoulder.

Once convinced she was not in the La Salle Street Station, he walked to Canal Street to see if she'd gotten off there. He'd walk across the entire city if necessary. Or maybe she'd arrived early! He headed to the John Jones Tailor Shop to see if anyone had seen his guest. No Juanita anywhere.

As tired as his legs were, the disappointment and hurt

penetrated deeper; his insides were depleted. He'd been looking forward to Juanita visiting Chicago for months. He'd arranged to have one day free from the Pullmans at great difficulty. The boss had balked, and he feared he might be let go over the request.

Was it his confession that changed her mind? She didn't seem to be rejecting him in her responding letter, the one where she'd written of her own difficult past. She seemed to be a person of her word. A characteristic he admired. Maybe he'd pushed too hard.

As he roamed the streets, Silas decided he would not give up. No longer young, he was desperate to have a family. To feel bonds with others which were comforting, trust building, enduring. Family was yet another facet of human existence slavery had disrupted and disallowed, and Silas was determined to break all chains of his past life. He loved Juanita. His sinews and bones and muscles knew she was for him. He was convinced they could create something together. A soulful cohesion.

Climbing into his cot in the dark, exhausted after walking miles and miles through the city, writing in his book as was his daily habit, Silas decided he would keep working the trains. Assuming he'd not sacrificed his Pullman position, he'd save money and go out to California. Try one final time to win Juanita's devotion. In person. Looking into her eyes. And if that wasn't successful? Then he'd adjust the plan and find somewhere else to settle. There were many beautiful places in California where he could likely find work and make a home.

One thing I know how to do, he reminded himself, is dream and plan and work for a far-off goal. Patience and perseverance were Silas' strongest, most honed skills. He'd endured plantation life for years while planning for a successful escape. He'd saved enough of his pay to buy Juanita a ticket on the new transcontinental train. Now he'd save to get himself to California.

The following day, Silas' supervisor let him back into the Pullman car, grumbling about how he'd lost customers due to his absence. He'd have to make it up with an additional three thousand miles before his next payday. Silas bit his tongue to avoid blurting an impolite retort, then nodded and walked to the kitchen car to pick up the coffee tray for his guests.

During the next month, he numbed his sadness with constant motion. One day a fellow porter who knew more of his story than most tried to recruit him for the Pinkerton Detectives.

"Gotta be home more to find me a wife, you know," his colleague said with a laugh. "Those Pinkertons hire women, even freed Black folks. No one notices if a woman or Negro is in the background. Good natural disguise when investigating."

But after asking around, Silas realized he wasn't interested in the possibly violent work, as the Pinkertons often infiltrated unions and criminal gangs. He'd had enough of duplicity and violence in South Carolina. No, he'd stick to the Pullmans and focus on increasing his tips with exceptional service.

After traveling fourteen thousand miles, he finally got his pay and a short rest in his Chicago bunkhouse. When he visited his regular haunts, he found a letter waiting for him at the tailor shop. Relieved to hear from her, he ripped open the envelope right in front of the tailor's customers.

"Sorry," he mumbled, then stepped out into the street. She hadn't gotten lost but had indeed been scared off from coming East. But was the daguerreotype in the window just an excuse?

Silas rushed to his quarters and buried himself in rereading her letters, one after another. Clearly, she'd been hesitant since her first reply in early 1865. His heart had sealed over from the pain at her not showing up with nonstop work, exhaustion, and focus on pushing her out of his mind. This letter at least gave an explanation, but it ripped a new wound in his scarred insides.

Should he write her back? He had nothing to say, really. "Action not words," was his motto. Not going to change now. He folded the letters together and slipped them into his pillowcase, hung his Pullman uniform carefully on a hanger and brushed the fine wool, then shined his shoes for the early morning shift.

Return to Sonora

June 1869 to September 1870

Juanita did not immediately respond to Isabel's letter. The madam would consider her a fool for not using the ticket she'd received due to a seven-year-old photograph. Isabel would scold her it was wishful, magical thinking. Was it even Joaquin? Or maybe he was a handsome stand-in for a real railroad architect. Juanita had gained no clue to aid her search and instead lost the opportunity to investigate her feelings toward Silas. If she wrote Isabel, she'd be forced to admit all this to her friend.

A month after skipping the train, she checked the general delivery mail stops in Sonora, Stockton and Sacramento, but there were no letters from Silas. Was he angry, betrayed, heartbroken? Had he given up on her? Who could blame him? She sure didn't. Isabel would say she'd broken the poor man's heart, that she didn't deserve the love he offered. Which was probably true.

And Joaquin? Mystified to see him pictured as a railroad builder in the early 1860s, she realized her invented stories of him as a miner or horse trainer were likely false. How had he learned the engineering trade? Railroad work was dangerous. Could he have been a casualty? Probably not as a building engineer. The Chinese were bearing the brunt of the perilous explosion and digging work. Railroading could have taken him to Utah or into the mountains. Where would he be now that construction was complete?

The census takers reported California had five hundred and sixty thousand people living in the twenty-year-old state. How could she ever find a Joe, with no last name, who possibly worked on railroad planning, among this sea of people?

In the following months, she barely interacted with the Phoenix staff. She dined alone, not wanting to subject anyone to her foul mood. The staff kept their distance, respecting her solemnity, tiptoeing when she was near. She could see they hoped it would change, but she didn't have the energy to swallow her pride or muster pretend cheerfulness.

Work was Juanita's treatment plan. She pushed herself to exhaustion, helping Ines wash sheets and Jacinto brush mules and clean hooves. She pruned the almond, cherry, and apple trees and weeded between the rows of lettuce and watermelon. Constant labor was her only refuge.

She did decide one more attempt to gain information about the photograph was prudent and sent Mrs. Stanford a letter. However, a disappointing response from Sacramento added to her frustration and melancholy.

Office of Mrs. Leland Stanford, Sacramento
August 18, 1869

Dear Mrs. Castro,
Mrs. Stanford received your letter but is unable to provide
any information to be of assistance. Mr. Judah passed

*away the year after the daguerreotype series, in 1863.
We know nothing about his employees or co-workers, or
anyone else in the background of the daguerreotype.*

*Regards,
Bridget McLaughlin
Assistant Secretary to Mrs. Stanford*

With Juanita's attention focused in one direction, her businesses thrived. The two hotels boomed with reputations for cleanliness, delicious food, and unique entertainment. The timber land produced sweetly pungent pine, fir, and cedar, which was popular with the growing population seeking inexpensive building materials. Calaveras County Clay Company not only provided for her brick enterprise but had sufficient reserves to sell clay to distant brick makers who were not her direct competitors.

She was not as rich as Isabel, and had much simpler tastes, but her grandmother and father would have been proud at how she'd returned the family to prosperity. But what family? And to enjoy with whom? She contemplated writing letters to Beatriz but then rejected the idea when she reminded herself the Dominguez family wanted no interaction. She continued to send money once a year.

After more than a decade of commitment to Sonora, Juanita was finally accepted by the townspeople, despite Braddock's best intentions to malign her reputation. Thanks to her insistence on paying the same salary to whites, Chilenos, Natives, Sonorans and even the Chinese, Braddock constantly criticized her to his Vigilance Committee colleagues. He argued an unmarried woman was a danger to the town, especially due to the lowlife ne'er-do-wells she let work, and board, in her establishments.

When questioned, Juanita explained her standards: If you worked hard and were honest, the Phoenix might hire you, even if you gambled or drank. But she did not tolerate violence in her taverns or betting beyond the weekly sanctioned games. And there was never any credit—she was not the general store after all. If you were determined to bet, you had to buy in and pay your debts on the spot.

Since her hotel and saloon provided a much-needed outlet for lumberjacks and miners, bricklayers and ranch hands to relax and expend their energy, the mayor and sheriff accepted Juanita despite her Californio roots and unusual practices.

"Too bad you're a woman, Juanita, or we'd ask you to run for town council," the mayor said. And the sheriff, the same one who years before suggested she marry a white man to protect herself, admitted she'd done just fine on her own. "Hell, if anything happens to the missus, I might ask you to marry me!" he joked loudly one Saturday night in the Paragon.

A wealthy timber owner did try to court her, showing up at gambling sessions, Saturday News Readings and dining at the Paragon three nights a week. Ines teased her, but Juanita was cynical.

"He just wants to join my pine forest acreage with his to become the lumber king of the Southern Sierra. I'm too old for romance," she said, putting an end to town speculation on her love life.

Little by little, Braddock's criticisms fell on fewer ears as he had his own problems with revolving staff, dirty accommodations and bad food. Many of his customers came by Ines' kitchen door on Sundays to purchase fresh vegetables, eggs, and milk—a practice she'd copied from Mrs. Gallegos of La Bienvenida days. This just made Braddock angrier, but

Juanita ignored him and told her staff to stay far away from the Miners Lodgings.

Then, one afternoon in late summer of 1870, as the heat dissipated, dry static prickling the air, Juanita was in the garden picking through the last pumpkins and summer squash. Pulling up dying vines and brown leaves, searching for yellow crooknecks under the decaying branches, she tossed a hidden treasure into her basket, then yanked the spent brush out of the ground and threw it into a pile. She was wiping the sweat above her lip with the back of her hand when she heard the familiar *clop, clop* of a horse approaching.

The rider was coming from the west, so she shaded her face with an outstretched arm as she stood. Blinking away the sun, she could just make out a gentleman rider on an older horse, his black hair speckled with flecks of gray and wrinkles springing from his eyes. But Silas was still tall and slim, strong, confident in the saddle.

She dropped the squash vines in her hand and just stared.

After reining in his horse, he swung his leg over and dropped to the ground, leaving the reins to drag as he approached her.

"You're here. At the Phoenix," he said, as if he were surprised he'd found her at her own hotel.

She regained her voice as she moved toward the boarding house.

"Silas, it's good to see you. Come on in. I'll get you some water. Where've you come from?" She did not offer a hand and was on the move too quickly for an embrace. He gathered up the horse properly, then had to follow quickly to keep up with her.

Once in her kitchen, where boarding house staff were preparing dinner fixings, she found a glass and filled it from the tap.

"You remember Silas, right?" she casually said to Ines and her team, sounding as if he'd just been away for a season. The ones who knew him greeted him with hugs and cheers.

"Jacinto. Come quick. Look who's showed up!"

"We were so upset when you were kidnapped. How'd you get away?"

"Didn't Miss Juanita say you work on the trains now? So exciting."

"You live in Chicago, right?"

Just like that, Juanita was saved from an awkward reunion by the chattiness of all who remembered him fondly. Silas smiled and hugged the ladies, patted the backs of the men and asked about wives and children.

All the while, he glanced at Juanita over the crowd, a questioning in his dark eyes, a gentle smile showing bright teeth and creases in his cheeks. Warmth sailed across the room, hooking her, as if with a fishing line, and began reeling her in. Juanita felt the energy but avoided his gaze, busying herself with meal preparation while the staff showered him with welcoming affection.

After some time, Silas' deep, hoarse voice said, "Now, I'm sure y'all have got to get supper ready for the guests. I've caused enough interruption."

He tilted his head toward the door. Realizing she could not avoid him forever, she followed him outside.

"Is there somewhere we could talk?" he asked.

Still unsure of her voice, of her body, she nodded and pointed toward the hotel. She couldn't take him to her own rooms, too intimate. But boarders and hotel guests would be filling the parlor for an aperitif or smoke or to read the news by the fire.

All bustle and business, Juanita escorted him to the Paragon, where she sat at the end of the bar and signaled for him to take the corner seat.

"Quietest place this time of day," she explained, seeing his raised eyebrows. "We don't open 'til after supper. Don't want anyone in here drinking too long." She pointed to the bartender washing glasses in preparation for the Friday night crowd. "He won't bother us." He might have looked up when they walked in, but he ignored them now, understanding whatever the boss was up to was not his business.

Silas patted the counter with admiration as he stepped up and onto the stool. The toasted-brown Douglas Fir bar was long, decorated with whitish knots and jags of reddish cedar in unusual patterns.

Juanita perched on her Ponderosa stool, not fully sitting, as if she were to leave at any moment. Silas glanced around at the tables and admired the collection of liquors. Blue and green, amber and clear bottles sparkled in the afternoon sunlight. He was taking it all in.

Infuriating, Juanita thought. He's the one who shows up here unannounced after no communication for years and I'm supposed to start the conversation?

"Where's the monte room? Still got Sunday night tables?" Finally, he was looking directly at her. She could feel the emotion pouring off his body, though he was so quiet.

"Miguel, don't forget the snifters," she called to the bartender. "Tonight's crowd will want those."

"Juanita. Look at me," Silas said. "There isn't a better place for this conversation?"

"No, Silas. This is it. We're busy here. You came in with no warning. Look, I'm sorry I didn't get on the train, but I've got work here that needs my attention."

"Really? Looks like everyone knows what to do. Must have had good training."

He suddenly put his callused hand over hers. She flinched but did not move, still half on the bar stool. The warmth of his skin surprised her, and she felt the sensation rise through her arm into her shoulder. She exhaled slowly, feeling like she'd been holding her breath since the moment she recognized him looking down at her in the zucchini and crooknecks.

"I only came here when I had enough money to get a steed to ride in on. I wouldn't have come without some way to leave, in case you weren't interested in me staying for a while. I can head out this minute if you want. And never come back. Never write again."

Juanita moved fully onto the stool and finally tilted her head up to look into his eyes. She shook her head slightly. "No. I don't want that. Did you Pullman Porter out to Sacramento?"

"What? Uh, no, I had to ride in the Negroes Only train car. Won't sell me a ticket for the cars I've been working on the past three years."

Juanita grimaced at that but couldn't find her true voice. What could she say to this man who was a stranger and yet not? She was mortified she'd treated him so badly by not showing up on the ticket he'd given as a gift, but he seemed generous and forgiving despite her poor behavior.

As if he could read her mind, Silas said, "Workin' on your feet on them trains sure keeps you strong. Tired but strong. Hefting the luggage, fetchin' and more fetchin'. But never dull. Not one day like the rest. I've met governors and wealthy men, ladies in finery and people escapin' somethin', for sure. Some treated me like I was still on the plantation, but others were kind, gave me large tips. It's an excitin' life for someone with my background."

Oh, this man. So eloquent, so serious and reflective. Don't think I've ever met anyone as persistent, Juanita thought, but this is unexpected.

He continued. "But I love the mountains and forests, the rivers, and how you can thrive on your own here, with nature, and be free. I loved the meadows and streams of South Carolina, too, but it was filled with ugliness and hate, meanness, destruction. This place is a fresh start for someone like me. I'd like to work at the Phoenix again. If y'all have me. I had to know if you ever found your son. I know it's been years since the slave-catcher grabbed me, and I know we're not so young . . ."

He stopped and took a breath. His shaking hand had left hers and she absently noted it was colder without its warmth. She rubbed her upper arms.

"Sure. You can watch the door at monte tonight with Jacinto. I can't pay you what you probably made on the Pullmans, but you can sleep in the bunk room. There's an extra spot or two now summer's over. You can join them at supper. Perhaps we can talk more another time. I've got to get ready for the evening crowd."

She slid off the stool, patted his arm resting on the polished Douglas Fir, and moved quickly down the bar where she said to Miguel, "Be ready for a rush tonight," and disappeared through the back door.

Silas did not move, lost in thought as he stared at the shining bottles reflected in the bar's mirror. Not exactly the dramatic welcome he'd fantasized about all these years.

She looked tired and wiry, the sinews of her arms visible. Probably were in her legs, too, but he shouldn't think about those. Her hair was still a captivating crown, lush dark strands hanging down her back, eyes bursting with feistiness. Despite the cold reception, he was sure he detected a hint of roundness in her cheeks, and warmth in her pink, cracked lips. There was a softness under the frosty exterior. There had to be. Or was he just hoping? Was he a fool? Probably. But he stayed.

He decided it was best to work the hotel complex and figure out what would make her comfortable. How could he return to the relaxed, revealing conversations after Sunday night's gambling? Be so helpful she'd appreciate him again.

That night, swallowing his hurt, he joined the boarding house supper, then he moved his worldly belongings into the bunk room and searched for a hiding place for his Pullman Porter greenbacks and silver notes. The other boarding house renters and seasonal workers were much more welcoming than Juanita, and he was relieved to not be directed to sleep in separate quarters as would have happened in Virginia or the Carolinas. The seasonal crew was a mix of colors, languages, and religions. No one seemed to notice his skin tone or at least had no complaints, as long as he did his job, didn't cheat at cards, or steal from his bunkmates.

He kept the bulky stash of his life savings on his person until he discovered the perfect vault under a loose board in a cupboard behind the bar. It was shielded by what seemed to be rarely used champagne glasses. The Paragon might claim to be the best, but it must not cater to the bubbly crowd.

Over the next few weeks, he helped clear the fields and prep them for the coming cold season and winter planting. Juanita clearly avoided him, always working on another part of the property or checking on distant brick, pine tree, or Stockton businesses. Any free moment he had, she was far away.

As much as he desired a romance, a true partnership with her, he accepted it might be more complicated than he imagined. His mistakes before had cost him eight years away from this quiet valley surrounded by forested hills. Eight years he could have been with Juanita. Maybe they would have gotten married. Was it even legal in California? Sure, they were past childbearing years, even back then, but they could have enjoyed each other, grown the businesses together. If she would have wanted such a relationship. He wasn't so sure.

Of course, she seemed to be just fine on her own, he noted. Quite capable, this woman. She was a force.

Feeling like she was either ignoring or testing him, he strategized he'd rebuild their friendship around the business. Forget the personal and focus on hotel topics. He slid in next to her before the crowds arrived for Saturday News one afternoon.

"A tavern with regular hours," he said. "Never thought I'd see you operate a steady saloon. I like how you keep it tight, controlled." When she didn't reply, he continued. "And weekly gambling. Customers like it!" He winked at her. She gave him a shy smile,

"They do, indeed," she said, "and it's lucrative."

He laughed, "Ah, yes, the real reason." And Juanita apparently could not resist. She gave him a slight smile. He just knew all these years he'd really missed their camaraderie and easy connection. Could he get it back?

He coaxed her to sit with him briefly after the news reading guests departed and he broached the subject again. She accepted the small glass of claret he offered. She was slightly chattier but the matter-of-fact tone remained in her voice.

"The bar and gambling help maintain our reputation as the most popular place in town," she said, "besides the brothels and Chinatown opium dens, but not everyone wants those. Card games only on Sundays keeps it quieter. I could fill it every night with faro and monte, poker and roulette, but then it gets unruly, fights start, regulars start to think it's their bar, not mine. You can encourage secret criminals right under your nose. I'm the boss. No one else."

He loved she'd shared more than one sentence. Business topics it was, then. "You certainly are. No disputing that."

"That's what happened to the Miners Lodgings," she continued. "Braddock let the card games take over. Loan sharks moved in to feed the desperate gamblers and soon it was theirs." Before he said another word, she lightly, briefly touched her fingers on his arm. "Silas. I've been meaning to tell you. Well . . . I'm glad you came back."

He nodded, smiling slightly, a rushing in his ears. He feared she could hear his heart pumping. Could she finally feel what he felt?

"You've been such a big help. For Jacinto, with the mules and timber. With the saloon when we get busy. The field clearing went much faster this year . . . and your presence at Sunday gambling keeps everyone calm. Thank you."

She gave him a full smile, finally. Her lips looked softer, not so chapped. She raised her glass toward him. "To the Phoenix," she said.

Silas was crushed. He was still just a worker, a business assistant. But he couldn't show despair. He toasted her in return and then had to get out of there.

"My pleasure. 'Night," he mumbled as he tossed back the last of the claret.

He did not go to the bunk room but stepped into the darkness to walk alone under the patchy cloud covering, stars peeking through here and there. This was a new kind of torture. But he couldn't bring himself to leave.

The Lovers

October 1870 to September 1871

Slowly, Juanita felt herself beginning to thaw, as if she were an ice-covered pond softening as winter's dark days lessened and spring's warmth reappeared. She found herself looking for Silas while she did her chores, or hoping he'd stop by the tavern after it closed, staying later than usual to help Miguel wipe tables and scrub the bar. The bartender would try to chase her out and she'd protest, saying she should help, but really wishing Silas would stop in for a shared glass.

When he did appear, Juanita understood Silas was boring his way into her closed-off life, digging in to reach her heart. She had not written Isabel in months, perhaps because she could hear a sisterly admonition in her head. *Juanita, you fool. This man is head over heels in love with you. And you like him. He's strong, handsome, and devoted. And he's such a good worker around the hotel. Why y'all so frosty? He's gonna ride off and it'll be too late if you keep up this cold heartedness!*

Isabel was, so often, right.

Silas was in the barn one chilly October afternoon shoveling hay into the mule stalls when Juanita came in, pushing a wheelbarrow full of dried corn cobs, the last of fall's field clearing. She reached for a burlap sack and began stuffing it with winter feed for the pigs and cows. She hadn't seen him in the far stall, he didn't think, but he could wait no longer. He brushed the hay off his shirtsleeves, inhaled for confidence, and decided to act on raw emotion, on the longing and care he had for this remarkable woman.

"Juanita?"

She looked over her shoulder and dropped a sack onto the wheelbarrow. He approached softly and put his hands gently on her hips and slowly turned her around to fully face him, then leaned in and kissed her with tenderness, his fear of rejection so fierce it kept his desire at arm's length.

Her lips were warm, perspiration softening them, and she responded with an ardor he'd only dreamed about. He deepened the kiss, tightening his embrace so her entire body was pressed into his, her thinness enclosed in his muscular arms. He desperately wanted to protect her, hold her forever and never stop the deliciousness and heat filling every cell of his being.

When he broke away to breathe, to look into her eyes, she did not let go, nor did she look away. He kissed her again, then pulled her head under his chin and rocked her ever so slightly.

"I've been waiting years to do that. I fell for you when I first got here. Not only were you beautiful, independent, and smart, but I saw what a successful businesswoman you were without slaves, without cruelty to your workers."

He kissed the top of her head, astounded she was letting him continue and did not push him away.

"When you secretly paid the Miwok maids and stood up

for the Sonorans who didn't speak English, then you really had my heart. You're so determined, so fierce in your convictions." Maybe he should stop there but he felt as if a dam had burst inside and all the emotions he'd held so tight, so close, for so long, were rushing out in a torrent. "Some might call it 'cold.'" He felt her flinch but he kept right on, tightening his embrace. "But I know you're far from cruel or cold. It's a survival technique. When you have no one, don't know who to trust, then you rely on only yourself. It's lonely but it's a way to cope."

He paused but she did not say a word, just held on to him. Here was the opportunity he'd been longing for. "I love that we both care for the land and growing food and livestock. Before the Phoenix, I saw hospitality as foreign, evil even. Every time men drank with the master on the porch or visited for elaborate dinners, someone would be sold or beaten. With you, I saw there's a place for hospitality. If done with kindness. With generosity."

He lightened his embrace to kiss her again and look directly at her. "I admired your education, speaking two languages, even trying the Native ones. I couldn't tell you I was barely literate, copying texts every single day trying to teach myself to read. I wanted you to see me as a freedman like the Holloways I admired in Charleston. I wanted to be something different. That's why I lied to you."

"Silas." She put her finger to his lips. "Stop talking. Way more words than if you'd been here these past eight years." She smiled, her shoulders relaxed, her chin softened, tilting down. "We have time," she said.

Silas' breath caught, his pulse beat in his ears and chest. She was so beautiful as she finally seemed to let his love, his admiration and desire wash over her.

Reaching up, she cradled his cheeks.

"Follow me," she said.

Juanita decided they must keep their romance a secret, for she was still unsure about the whole escapade after decades completely alone. Besides, her experience limited to Malachy, hidden romance was all she knew.

However, it wasn't easy in a boarding house and hotel filled with constantly moving guests and staff. She'd glare at Silas when he was too intimate or casual in front of Ines or Jacinto. Other times, she'd launch an inviting, desirous glance in that lull between the afternoon aperitif and supper hour. Then they'd sneak up to her rooms or find an empty stall in the barn.

At their age, it all seemed ridiculous. But then she'd feel like a teenage girl again, waiting anxiously for alone time with her lover. She constantly strained to hear his boots on the kitchen steps, coming from orchard pruning or afternoon milking.

Silas often had dust on his shirt collar or straw in his salt-and-pepper hair, or tiny cuts from brambles on his wrists. He'd always nod a greeting to anyone preparing the boarding house meal and go right to the wash basin, carefully scrubbing his large hands and forearms. Usually there was something on his clothes he missed and Ines or Rosalía, or even Manuel, would point to it and he'd smile shyly in embarrassment and dust off his shirtsleeves or shoulder. Juanita would watch this across the room, longing to be the one to clean him up, to touch his arms, to give him a gentle kiss of greeting as the outdoor chores ended and afternoon light turned soft and dimmed toward evening.

He honored her desire to keep their relationship secret. And this sweetness for her rather ridiculous stipulations made her adore him further. But she couldn't quite bring herself to run across the kitchen, embrace him openly and announce to everyone they were sleeping together whenever a private moment was possible. What would the staff think?

She'd been solitary for so long, how could anyone imagine her enjoying a lover and companion? *She* barely could. She was nervous to reveal any vulnerability; ever since she gave birth alone in a decrepit Mission cell thirty-six years before, exiled there by her own parents, she'd believed her sole path to survival was to never rely on anyone else.

But Silas' patience outlasted her reluctance. With quiet persistence, he pushed through her fortress-like exterior. His passion never seemed to wane. He said he'd cared for her for so long he was a bottomless well of desire and love. If alone, he'd surprise her from behind and wrap his long arms around her waist and whisper into the hair over her ear. Or ever so lightly, secretly, touch the back of her neck or caress her dangling fingers when they were overseeing the monte tables. Or he'd arrange a bouquet of sweet pea flowers in the china water pitcher in her room, delighting her at the end of a long day.

One evening, after long hours of fieldwork to prepare for winter, her frostbitten toes acted up. The aching rub had worsened into painful blisters throughout the day. When she removed her boots, her foot was swollen with pus oozing out of blisters and stinging with open wounds rubbed raw, flaps of skin dangling. After she heated water on the wood stove top and gathered light muslin bandages, she sat at the kitchen table to clean and wrap the wounds.

Arriving to wash his hands, Silas was startled to see her with an injury. Juanita had never mentioned the shiny, gray dead half of her right foot, hoping Silas wouldn't notice the ugliness when they were in bed together.

"What happened? Did you cut your foot? Here, let me help." Taking the cloth, he hunched at her feet and began to wash the damaged foot. He looked up at her, beseechingly. "What..."

She gazed into his affectionate brown eyes, felt his gentle touch and suddenly saw how far she'd come since the mountain pass accident which she'd miraculously survived, but so alone. She leaned forward to caress his scratchy cheek.

"Remember I mentioned an avalanche?..." and she told him the story. His eyebrows raised high at the severity of the incident, mouth open in awe hearing how she rebuilt during the rough, early years after losing her livelihood. He bandaged the cleaned foot and stood up, pulling her with him and embraced her, tenderly.

"Juanita, I want to take care of you. We'll get this foot healed, maybe see a doctor. And I want to hear all the stories."

A few days later, with her foot recovered, at least for the moment, Juanita had a change of heart. *I'm fifty-seven years old. I adore this man and want him in my life,* she thought. *Why should I hide the truth?*

"Are you sure?" he asked when she invited him to move his belongings out of the bunkhouse into her apartment. He was putting his clothes on after a late afternoon rendezvous, looking back at her as she untangled herself from the sheets.

"Why? You don't want to?"

He laughed. "I can't think of anything I'd rather do than move in with you. But I don't want to rush this. Rush you, if you need more time."

"We've waited long enough, don't you think? I'm partly terrified but also excited. I did not think I would ever have a lover again. And I'm interested in exploring this with someone who I don't think will betray me, lie, or abandon me." She pulled him back to the bed and let the sheet drop, unbuttoning the shirt he'd just put on.

"Never," he said, as he kissed her deeply. "How could I ever consider leaving anyone who wants to make love twice in one afternoon?" He stopped talking, fully engaged in the kiss, extricating himself from his shirt, laying her back on the bed, and wrapped himself around her.

Later, before dinner, he moved his small stash of clothes and boots into her bedroom armoire.

The next morning, Juanita approached Ines after breakfast. Wind whipped wildly at the doors, rattling their hinges, and rain pelted the windows with a *tap, tap*. They were lacing all the thick curtains to reduce the whine of the storm.

"Ines. I have something to tell you."

Ines looked at her boss and nodded. "I know, ma'am," she said. "Everyone knows. It's great, you and Mr. Silas. We're so glad he's back. He helps a lot. He helped Jacinto turn a breeched foal last week. Plus, he seems to make you happy. That's good for all of us."

Juanita blushed, taken aback by Ines' admission and honesty.

"But we've tried to . . ." Juanita stopped, realizing how foolish she sounded. And felt. She was the boss lady, but she'd been sneaking around like a teenager hiding from her parents. Ridiculous.

Ines smiled and, uncharacteristically, gave her a quick hug. "I'm happy for you, ma'am."

Silas wanted to marry Juanita. Desperately. Even though he'd seen countless couples torn apart and families tortured by separation, the promise, the respectability, the faith demonstrated in the institution captivated him. He'd had intimate relations with various women in South Carolina, Virginia, and Chicago who were appealing for an evening of rare relaxation, to pass the time. But no one he wanted to wake up with every morning, no one with whom he sought to share dreams or stories, fears or mistakes. No one who he wanted to sleep with again and again. Could he find some peace and be the ultimate free man if he had a wife who he loved dearly and who loved him?

But he was hesitant to ask, both because it was against California state law for him to marry a white woman, as Juanita was considered, and because, despite her strong Catholic roots, Juanita was vocally critical of marriage. She'd seen her grandparents unhappy in a union forced upon them by the Catholic church. She'd seen thousands of married miners seeking fortunes, many who were not faithful to wives back home. She never blamed them, nor the prostitutes, as she understood the business from observing Isabel's operation over years. But why would anyone set themselves up in an outdated arrangement which often led to betrayal, suspicion, or complacency? Silas never argued but he took in every word. Perhaps it was good she didn't believe in Catholic marriage, for no church would ever marry them.

He wanted to convince her to do their own version of marriage, with a little ceremony even. He became obsessed with ways to win her favor so she wouldn't reject a proposal. After almost a year of living in the hotel apartment together, she'd still never said she loved him. What if he could find her son? Or could he help her reunite with her sister? He and Juanita would never have children, but maybe they could have a large table filled with loved ones surrounding it like in her youth.

In Stockton shopping for summer provisions, Silas stopped at the Western Union office and sent a telegram to Chicago to his former colleague. Maybe the Pinkertons, famous for locating fugitives and uncovering plots, could find Juanita's son.

To: Jonas Winters,
care of Quinn Chapel AME Church, Chicago

Seeking advice on locating a lost relative in California STOP Could you help STOP Write me at Sonora, California General Delivery STOP Please keep confidential STOP All advice much appreciated STOP

From: Silas Holloway, former Pullman Porter
Stockton Telegraph Office

Silas then led the mule train to Sacramento for further purchases and sales. Before heading home, he visited the Daguerreotypes by a Lady studio. He stared at the window display, then entered through the jingling door.

"I'm interested in the Big Four daguerreotype in the window," he told the photographer. "Is it possible to make a *carte de visites* or cabinet cards from it? You may remember the woman who asked about it some years back. She's a friend. I'd like to give her one."

"The railroad barons picture is an ambrotype, but no matter. Hmm, yes, I remember your friend. She had many questions I couldn't answer."

The clerk interrupted, "The lady stared at it so long out front, I thought she might pass out on the walkway."

The woman shook her silvered head at him for interrupting. "Come back tomorrow and we'll have them ready for you."

Several weeks later, Silas was pleasantly surprised when his Pullman Porter colleague telegrammed he was still at the Pinkerton Agency and would do what he could with all available information. It might take many months as he'd have to do it on his own time after his official responsibilities were finished.

Silas wrote the Pinkerton with relevant details he knew of Juanita's life and her search. He included a retainer in greenbacks and one of the cabinet card photographs. Then signed off the letter with gratitude.

Thank you for agreeing to this contract, Jonas. I am deeply grateful. I wish to make this woman my wife but she is reluctant to marry at our age. I hope helping her find her long lost son will bring her some peace.

It's occurred to me he might have used the Brennan surname at some point. He detested his birth father, but a good Irish name is so common it certainly goes unnoticed, especially if he was trying to hide his Mexican roots.

She does not know I am hiring you. I look forward to hearing anything you discover.

Sincerely,
Silas Holloway

Family

September 1871 to September 1873

In the heat of late September, under a blazing, blue sky, one year after arriving at the Phoenix Hotel, Silas arranged a private dinner for Juanita. He handed Miguel a silver coin to finish his evening prep early. He asked Ines to cook a Spanish tortilla stuffed with their own zucchini, basil, tomatoes, and yellow squash. The Yorba's famous salty, white cheese was the perfect complement, as were sizzling corn tortillas and Ines' spicy bean soup.

He set a tavern table with the crispest napkins and best gleaming cutlery he could scrounge from the cupboards. No sitting at the bar tonight. He centered a bouquet of pink tinted zinnias, orange dahlias, and purple pansies in a glass on the table.

Earlier in late winter, Juanita insisted they plant rows of flowers to display in the Phoenix and sell to neighbors. A petal rainbow now colored the field next to the apple trees and vegetable garden. Silas had questioned the value at the time, but the flowers proved to be very popular with the women in town, the hotels, and even with rooming house owners, who put at least one arrangement at their entrance desks. Miners Lodgings was the only boarding house which was not a flower customer, highlighting their increasingly shabby offerings.

Juanita was touched but clearly mystified. After the meal, Ines brought out coffee and pieces of a walnut cake she made for special occasions, then left quietly through the kitchen door behind the bar.

"Thank you, Silas. This is sweet to have dinner at a table with proper cutlery, like we are the guests." She toasted him with the coffee mug and tasted the cake. "Delicious. I'll have to put this on the menu more often."

"Juanita. Stop thinking business for a moment. I want to celebrate it's one year since I returned and you accepted me working at the Phoenix."

"Oh, that's the occasion. Yes, it is, isn't it. I'm glad you're here. We make a great team, don't we?"

"Well, yes. But, uh, it's more than that. I love you and want the best for you always. I believe you know I want to marry you. I know it's complicated. Doesn't have to be in the church. Might not be legal. Whenever you are ready, I am." She started to speak, but he continued before she could turn him down abruptly. "I know you're reluctant, which is fine. But I have a gift for you. And a request."

She looked at him, her eyes questioning.

"Thank you for being open to me returning, for letting me stay here. And for taking me into your bed, eventually." He laughed and winked at her.

As she blushed and looked down at the cake, he pulled a small bundle out from his lap. She unwrapped the soft leather cloth and pulled out the framed sepia-toned print glued to the cabinet card.

"Oh," she whispered and almost dropped the picture. "How did you?" Tears welled up in her eyes. "Thank you. This is lovely. But a painful reminder too." A bolt of light from the sun's western descent hit the windows across the street and shone bright through the tavern glass.

"I'd hoped it'd give you some comfort. There's something else."

She took her eyes off the photograph, brushing her cheek with the back of her hand, as if to prevent any tear from escaping. Juanita was not a teary woman.

"Let's reach out to your sister," he said. "Invite her to Sonora for a few days, a week maybe. They can bring their children. It's clear you don't need anyone to survive, but wouldn't it be nice to have some family here? I love you, Juanita. And I think maybe reaching out to your sister would make you happy. It's selfish on my part, you see, as I'd like to know everything about you. Meeting your sister is important."

She looked at the picture and then at him, placed the frame gently on the table, took his hand in both of hers.

"Thank you, Silas. For the daguerreotype, for returning to Sonora, for not giving up on me." The silence between them swelled and she caressed his hand. "I do love you, you know."

He gazed at their joined hands and then into the depths of her brown eyes, softer and more lovely than he'd ever seen them.

"Let me think about my sister," she said. "But you are right. It would be nice for her to see Sonora. For my family to meet you."

After the romantic dinner, Juanita sent Silas off to their room saying she wanted to help clean up. But they both knew she needed time alone. After the table was cleared and Ines off to bed, she sat and stared at the carte de poste. Where was Joaquin now? Where had life taken him? The emptiness and anguish had dulled somewhat, of course, after so many years, but it never left her.

She would work to make a family life with Silas, do as he asked to reach out to her sister, as a way to honor Joaquin, the Castro family, and the life she'd lost. This picture would remind her not to forget, but also to appreciate what she did have. Silas' gesture touched her profoundly.

Over the next month, prodded by Silas, Juanita sent several invitations to her sister. Finally, Beatriz agreed to visit with her young adult children and grandbabies at the Christmas holiday. Not surprisingly, Agustín claimed he could not leave the ranch.

She was so nervous when the coach pulled up, but Beatriz stepped down with open arms and embraced Juanita without hesitation. Perhaps, she'd finally let go of the bitterness of their ranch difficulties and Juanita's betrayal.

"Thank you, dear sister," she whispered. "Your gifts and your lawyer have helped us save the remainder of the ranch." Juanita nodded at Beatriz and welcomed her niece and nephews who were now grown, the eldest with two babies of his own.

"Come in, come in," she urged the family, hoisting carpet bags over her shoulder while Jacinto and Silas carried their trunks into a set of hotel rooms reserved for the relatives. The young ones immediately gravitated to the enormous pine from Juanita's timber forest filling the parlor, decorated with fluttering tapers and sugar candies, wrapped presents under the boughs.

While Ines prepared supper for the large group, Silas and Jacinto gave the young adults a tour of the complex. Juanita and Beatriz walked together through the row crops and orchard trees.

"It's beautiful, Juanita. You've done a wonderful job at creating a special place. I can feel a hint of the rancho." Juanita nodded and squeezed her sister's arm in appreciation. "Even though Agustín would never acknowledge it, the greenbacks you send us every year are a huge help to keep the ranch operating."

"I'm so glad. Beatriz, I must tell you, Silas is not a hired hand. He's my partner. Well, like a husband, you know." Beatriz pulled away and turned to stare. Juanita continued quickly, "I know father would never have approved but he is a good man, a huge help here. He's my family now. I've been alone for so long, which was fine, but we have a connection I can't explain. I hope you and the children can accept him."

Beatriz nodded, but said nothing and they continued strolling. She recounted the latest news from her ranch and that she and Agustín were best when they stayed far away from each other. "Most important, Francisco will inherit the small remainder of the ranch. It's still in the family."

Since her sister was devout, Juanita led the group to Christmas Eve midnight mass at the Catholic church. They enjoyed Ines' cooking together and cinnamon spiced Mexican hot chocolate and oranges delivered from the Pico Ranch's orchards south of Los Angeles.

Juanita considered the visit a success, especially when they agreed to make it an annual tradition to share Christmas at the Phoenix. She felt as if a hole inside her had filled slightly. But when Silas prompted her to send letters to her many aunts and uncles, after all, her father had ten siblings, she shook her head. For now, Beatriz and Silas were the family in her life.

Even though Isabel sent repeated invitations, insisting on an introduction to Silas, encouraging them to stay at her finest hotel overlooking the Bay or visit her mansion atop California Hill, the couple never left Sonora. But the women kept in touch via letters, Isabel hinting at complications in her business operations and Juanita updating on Sonora highlights, which Isabel always said were boring. But Silas did *not* seem boring. And were they ever going to get married? Juanita always ignored the question.

Alonzo surprised them by finally asking Juanita and Silas' permission to propose to Ines. How could they have missed the secret love affair right under their noses? Maybe they'd been lost in the swirl of their own.

They hosted a May wedding in the blossoming apple orchard with Señor and Señora Gallegos in attendance, followed by a delicious dinner in the tavern. Silas and Juanita sadly accepted the newlyweds' decision to move to Rancho Yorba to care for the aging couple. Ines and Alonzo promised to ride over to help with one gambling Sunday a month. They kept to the commitment, delighting Silas, making him feel as if he had grown children visiting. He openly asked about grandchildren until Juanita shushed him, explaining babies were more complicated than many men realized.

Privately, Silas was frustrated at receiving only disappointing telegrams from his Pinkerton detective friend. Mr. Winters explained he rarely had a moment to investigate as he often was embedded in a union committee or a band of bank robbers and could not break his disguise.

Then, in the summer of 1873, Silas received word of a lead in New Almaden. A Joe Brennan, rumored to be from Ohio, had a family south of San Jose in the quicksilver mining district. He was tall and the right age.

Taking Juanita's hand, Silas ushered her into the most elegant, comfortable room at the Phoenix: the library with its enormous, river-stone fireplace. Hotel guests were still in the dining room so it was empty. Pine logs crackled in a yellow-orange blaze, warming the room from the fall chill. He closed and locked the double redwood doors, which always stood open to welcome visitors. Although it was just after the dinner hour, he poured a small tumbler of whiskey for each of them from the bottle on the bar cart.

"What is this, Silas? A special occasion? You look very serious." Juanita tilted her head to level him with an inquisitive brow raised. He tilted his glass to her, then explained.

"Mi amor," he said, his raspy voice catching more than usual. "This Pinkerton Detective I know from the Pullmans, I hired him and he found someone in New Almaden, the quicksilver mine town, who matches all descriptors you have ever mentioned of your son."

Juanita almost dropped the whisky tumbler. Regaining control, she set it on the side table, but he saw the tremble in her lips.

"He goes by Joe Brennan."

Juanita lifted her head. "Brennan? Why would he ever use that name? He hated that family, the patron. They treated us so badly, especially my mother. And Joaquin was very protective of his grandmother." She twisted her hands in confusion. "I don't understand."

He squeezed her arm. "I know it's a shock after all this time."

"Why didn't you tell me about this detective?" she suddenly said, in a raised voice filled with anger, hurt. "I never wanted secrets between us. You know that."

"I'm sorry, but I didn't want to raise false hopes. I didn't expect any results, but I had to try. I know how important your son is to you. Means he is to me too."

"It could be one of the horrid teenagers from the owner's family all grown up and living near his father's ranch," she said. "Could be a mistake." She shook her head repeatedly. "Brennan?"

"Yes, true, but don't you think we should pay this family a visit? Maybe they know your son." He paused, holding both of her hands, trying to get her to focus on him. He cleared his throat. "Changing given names can be useful. I know something about having an identity forced on you. I hated Master Ward for stamping his name on me without my permission. I dreamed of being a freedman, so I took a famous name to create the identity I craved. And didn't your friend, Isabel, switch names with changing politics to maintain respect, the highest status possible?"

Juanita was squeezing his hand so hard it felt she was crushing it. Maybe he was getting through to her, past the astonishment. Would she overlook what she likely considered betrayal? The candles grew bright as the dark deepened outside. The fire cracked and spit embers onto the hearth.

"Crisis, loss, can lead to the need for a new identity. You

tried to disguise yourself as a man at first when you left the ranch, right?"

Juanita nodded. "I never asked about a Joe Brennan. The name was odious to us."

"An Irish surname was clever in the gold years—so many Irishmen here. Especially if he feared people would question his Mexican background. You told him to be Joe and become American, right?"

"Yes, and the regret of doing so nearly broke me. My father, my grandparents were so proud to be Castros. Your name and your reputation were everything."

"Then, Juanita, maybe he did exactly what you instructed. But took his blood father's surname out of anger, defiance, claiming it, as if he could get back the land his family lost. I understand such bitterness. And the motivation to do whatever it takes to survive. I know you do, too."

The Crash

September 1873

Unsure, nervous, but feeling she had to follow this lead, Juanita agreed to seek out the New Almaden family. To give her time to get used to the idea, anticipating yet another disappointment, she suggested they visit San Francisco and Isabel first. After so many years, it would be nice to see her in person. She finally could meet Silas.

On a steaming September morning, Silas hitched up the horses, unable to convince Juanita to take the stagecoach.

"This is who I am, and if I'm going to meet my son, or his family, or whoever this detective thinks he's found, I need to be grounded. I'm a horsewoman. Stage coaches fly too fast. I get nauseated looking out at the scenery. And stifled if I stay closed in. I need to see where I'm going and feel every bounce in the saddle."

Silas knew enough not to argue. He loaded their bags with favorite trail provisions and encouraged her to pack the most elegant dress she had for dinner at Isabel's hotel or a night out in the city. Juanita rolled her eyes, but did include her best dress, despite it being worn and so old she was sure it was many seasons out of fashion and not up to Isabel's standards.

It had been over ten years since she'd visited San Francisco. There was the ferry ride across the bay and this new cable rail company pulling folks up the hills. She couldn't wait to see the mini-railroad and avoid a climb to her friend's neighborhood. What would Isabel be up to, now she also was no longer young? Juanita was quite sure she'd conceal any signs of aging and keep up the competition to be the best madam, the best hotelier, and the fanciest mansion owner in the city. And what would Isabel advise on this latest hope of finding Joaquin? Who were these Pinkerton Detectives Silas had secretly contacted?

She'd been furious, and hurt, that he'd hidden his efforts. But after getting used to the idea, she realized the anguish it would have caused her these past two years. He'd likely been right to keep her unsuspecting, and not overly hopeful. But she was a bundle of nerve endings, her stomach in knots, unable to eat. Should she even go to this family's home? They were complete strangers. Had she been crazy all these years to hope for a reunion? Surely, she was a foolish dreamer. Isabel would undoubtedly have opinionated advice.

Though the city intimated her, she was looking forward to Isabel's forthright openness. Could it really be over twenty years since they first met? She in that terrible disguise. Ah, Isabel, always one to catch duplicity while fabricating her own reality. But she also had a talent for reading people. She had been right about Silas, after all.

Now, as instructed in Isabel's most recent letter, Juanita stood alone facing the massive mahogany door inlaid with swirls of unpolished oyster shells creating a sheen of translucent pink, white, and green mother of pearl. Juanita wondered absently if Isabel's unique taste for seashells and ocean colors appeared gaudy to the neighbors and gentlemen callers. No matter, she would never bend to any society matron rules.

The butler introduced himself as Thornton—no "mister," no first name, just Thornton. He was distinguished-looking in a starched white shirt and pressed black suit. His black shoes were so finely stitched Juanita knew they were not from San Francisco's rough tanneries. No, an Italian or French shoemaker had sewn the butler's leather footwear with devoted slowness.

Thornton called to a young boy peeling potatoes behind a curtain to open the back door and escort Silas through the kitchen to meet them in the front hallway. He shook Silas' hand with a little bow then gestured for them to follow him up the green carpeted stairs.

Juanita reached back and gave Silas' hand a squeeze as she chatted with the butler about her last visit to an Isabel property.

"I haven't been to San Francisco in over ten years, sir, and never to this home."

"Well, you are in for a treat. This is the most beautiful one, ma'am. Madam Platt never stops building," he said.

She nodded as she took in the wide landing, which led off to a long hallway filled with doors and marble tables adorned with large bouquets of sunflowers and dahlias. Paintings of French peasants at work in the fields, French countryside landscapes and Italian villas in muted tones hung in thick, gilt frames. Not a religious image among them.

Thornton knocked, then opened a double set of doors into a sitting room.

"Please wait here. Madam Platt will be with you shortly."

He took a little bow and disappeared, leaving Juanita and

Silas to gaze about the room. The formality was intimidating, especially for ranchers who mostly worked outside while their hotel guests enjoyed the parlor and dining room. Their boots suddenly seemed too muddy, their hems too frayed with tell-tale threads escaping the stitching, their hair uncombed from the journey.

Silas absently swept his pants and jacket sleeves with the back of his hand. Juanita smoothed the top of her head, then swiftly reswept her long mane up in the one mother-of-pearl comb she owned, hoping to look less unkempt. As if they hadn't just ridden one hundred and fifty miles on horseback and finished the trip off with a windy ferry ride from Oakland. Yet another first for Juanita, who'd never been on a boat other than as a child out on Monterey Bay with her grandmother trading cow hides for home furnishings on the Boston ships.

At least they weren't sweat soaked from a climb up the California Street hill, having ridden the new Clay Street Hill Railroad cars despite her unease with modern means of conveyance.

"Maybe you never got on the train to Chicago, but at least you've ridden to the top of San Francisco on a trolley," Silas had teased.

She'd wanted to swat his knee but was too terrified to take a hand off the wooden handrails.

He laughed. "A woman with no fears afraid of a tiny train?" and raised his hands as if to say, "Look, it's not so scary."

Now in the stuffy, richly decorated sitting room, the cable car ride seemed less frightening than being a small-town hotel owner in a rarified city mansion. They probably shouldn't have come. She was not made for the city.

Suddenly, with a loud whoosh, another set of double doors sprang open and there was Isabel in all her glory, decked out in more finery than ever. Diamond drop earrings sparkled at her ears, while twisting bracelets encircled her wrists and rings dotted at least three fingers on each hand. Her dress, a shiny forest-green taffeta, cut across her opulent bosom, then dropped to a plush velvet below the tightly cinched bodice. Then, just before hitting the floor, the taffeta appeared again with translucent pearls sewn in an undulating pattern, as if pearly waves were splashing around the bottom of the hoop skirt.

To tame the unruly mane, she wore a headband stitched with matching pearls, pushing back her curling black hair. Her pale white skin and flashing dark eyes still made an impact, though Juanita did detect a powdery substance covering her face and a rouged circle on each cheek. Isabel appeared ready to attend an evening opera at Milan's La Scala, not greet an old friend from a ranch hotel in the Sierra foothills.

"Juanita, my dahhlin'," she said and approached for an embrace and a kiss.

Juanita, surprised by the sudden, loud entrance, stumbled as she stood up and almost fell into Isabel's outstretched arms. Isabel firmly righted her, kissing each cheek in the French fashion.

"And finally, finally, you must be Silas. The Pullman Porter. You are even more handsome than I imagined, sir. It is a pleasure to meet you," Isabel said as she embraced him just as warmly and kissed both cheeks while he tried to make a little bow. "Oh, no, Silas. No formalities here. I welcome all in my establishments. Surely Juanita has explained that. I am sorry to send you to the kitchen door, but my neighbors are not as, shall we say, advanced as I am. And I've got some trouble with the tongs right now so I'm being extra careful. Please accept my apologies and know I'm delighted y'all are here."

She smiled, then leaned closer as if she were speaking privately, "I'm thrilled you finally got Juanita to see some sense. She should have gotten on the train and had the adventure of her life in Chicago. She is very lucky you are so persistent."

Juanita reddened, forgetting how much Isabel's unfiltered honesty was directed at everyone, even friends. But curious about city gossip, she did not interrupt, allowing Silas an introduction to the whirlwind of sensory input Isabel created. What was a tong? And was she really not letting Black men into her parlor house? Juanita found that hard to imagine as Isabel did not discriminate against anyone when it meant she could make a greenback. Maybe it was the two of them together that would disturb the neighbors.

Chatting nonstop, Isabel invited them to lunch with her in the dining room where Thornton served French-style mushroom soup, English-style ham sandwiches, and Italian cookies and marzipan for dessert. All complemented with coffee and French cognac, which Juanita and Silas declined, only used to a few sips of whiskey after weekend entertainments at the hotel. How could Isabel drink in the middle of the day and function for the rest of it, Juanita wondered. She also noted the lack of any Mexican or Californian fare. The madam appeared to be willing Europe into her mansions, hotels, and brothels, so San Francisco's connected clientele would feel as though they were on the popular tour of the continent.

She regaled them with story after story, frequently adding a phrase of "I haven't mentioned this to anyone," or "Don't tell a soul when you're out on the town," or "No one really knows this yet but..." She talked of politicians she'd gotten deposed when they wanted to block her home construction. Of the church ladies who'd tried to close her parlor house at the waterfront. Of hypocritical Vigilance Committee members. She admitted her views on those gentlemen were ferocious, since they usually were secret clients of the most expensive girls at her most lavish parties.

"Their hypocrisy astounds me, makes me furious. I understand the church ladies. At least they're consistent. But these men spoutin' off how brothels are ruinin' the city before a vote, then sendin' me notes requestin' entry to my balls and entertainments the same day? It disgusts me. Then the Chinese tongs bringin' in the girls so young. That I can't tolerate either." She took a quick breath. "Look, I'm fine with a sixteen-year-old girl making her own choices. I sure did, leavin' home young, goin' into business for myself. I've always treated my girls well. Keep them healthy, clean. But an eleven-year-old, that's immoral. The little ones are children, not women. So, I've become vocal on the topic with the same Public Safety Committee which claims they want to shut me down. I'm makin' progress."

Juanita and Silas said nothing. There was no room for a reply.

"But I stuck my nose in a bit too far, perhaps," she said after a beat. "I had some of the girls kidnapped and sent them to the church ladies to clean up and raise. No one liked that, but the church ladies did their duty, as I knew they would. Now I'm workin' on the politics of it. Probably no more kidnappin', though I can't stand it if I'm out walkin' and see one of those little girls with an old Chinese man. It disgusts me and I can't look the other way. Remember, Juanita, those racetrack fellas? One of the investors is a representative in Washington now, so I've been pushin' him to do something about these Chinese girls.

They've got to stop the ships bringin' them in by the hundreds."

Juanita, having regained her Isabel sea legs, responded with honest opinions and hard questions. Kidnapping children? Risking her success for political issues? Were those good ideas? The nonstop talking continued. Though mostly it was an Isabel monologue.

Silas sat still and silent through the meal, taking in the opulent decor, the delicious if strange food, the hostess' flamboyance. These two, who couldn't be more opposite in style, background, humility, age, and morals were longtime friends? It was disconcerting.

As he listened, Silas realized he'd had no expectations for this visit other than for Juanita to see an old friend with whom she shared an abundant correspondence. He'd pictured Isabel as a simple working woman, who ended up staying and opening a hotel after coming into profit during the gold years. Because Juanita had never mentioned Isabel's position in San Francisco society, he hadn't imagined such a force of personality and passions. This woman was someone he'd expect Juanita to despise or at least scoff at.

Now he understood why Isabel had never visited Sonora. She was clearly smart enough to realize any enterprise Juanita assembled would be no match for the lavishness of her entire life. Observing their mutual respect, he suspected Isabel didn't want to embarrass or belittle her friend.

Unsettling and strange, this friendship, but then again, his own relationship with Juanita was unexpected. A former slave and a former Mexican land grant owner of thousands of acres, partners in love and business? Who could have predicted either? Ah, California.

Before they departed, Silas decided to insert himself into the conversation to demonstrate his sudden appreciation for their unusual friendship.

"I heard there was a horse race some time back," he said during a rare Isabel pause. "Tell me the story."

And after the two women glanced at each other and burst out laughing, they were off.

"Yes, it's a good story, Silas." Isabel immediately grabbed the opening. "Did she tell you how she came dressed as a man trying to sell me slips and pantaloons?" Isabel's loud belly laugh shook the table as she collapsed with the memory.

Juanita nodded with an embarrassed smile and the two of them, switching back and forth as they described the individual parts each played in the escapade, told Silas the story of Canela's horse race.

Late that night, secreted into the premiere suite of the Diamond Crown Hotel atop "The Hill of Palaces," as it was being called, Juanita and Silas lay in an enormous bed, she in the crook of his arm. Tall windows, like enormous eyes, peered at the city below, gazing over its twists of fortune and excess, poverty, heroism, and failure.

"Whew!" he said and blew out a full breath. "What a meandering route life can take. I never, even in my wildest dreams, imagined I would one day be in the most elegant suite at the top of San Francisco with the woman I love in my arms. How on earth did this happen to me, Silas Ward, slave from a South Carolina rice plantation?"

She wrapped a leg over his and draped her arm over his

chest. "You did it. You escaped. Traveled across the entire country. You became Silas Holloway. You had faith. You saved. You never gave up, you were persistent and creative. You're a survivor." She propped herself up to look into his eyes. "Me becoming friends with a San Francisco madam is an accident of history. I lost my first life but did end up with a whole other one. I'm glad you're in it."

They kissed deeply, arousing a passion in each of them. They made love in the massive bed with sheets so soft it felt as if they were encased in a rabbit fur cocoon.

As they lay depleted and relaxed, Juanita made a decision.

"Let's go to New Almaden and see this family the detective discovered. I've been so afraid. Afraid to face disappointment, another false lead. But Isabel gives me courage. So self-absorbed, always out for herself, her reputation, her beauty, her businesses, but she's also principled in her own way. I think maybe that's why we became friends. She's been telling and showing me for twenty years to follow my heart with courage and conviction. Let's go see what the Pinkerton found."

Reluctantly, they left the Diamond Crown in the morning, noting ideas to add a taste of luxury for travelers resting in the Hotel Phoenix, Sonora. They had declined Isabel's evening invitation to a masked ball the night before, opting instead to dine quietly in their room with the magnificent view, but they'd agreed to walk the few blocks over from Clay Street to California and Mason and join her for breakfast.

As the Black doorman ushered them to the Diamond Crown exit, Silas and Juanita were startled by cries. The street was a chaotic jumble of young men yelling and older men racing down the hill toward the bank district. Horses wandered loose.

Hatless ladies in aprons streamed into the streets to check on the fuss. Newspaper boys on corners along Sacramento Street shouted, waved papers, collected a few coins, then called the day's headlines again.

"Cooke and Company, the government's financier, collapses!"

"Banks across the US shut their doors!"

"Wall Street bank failures don't stop!"

"Will the market close?"

"Railroad companies are next."

Juanita and Silas were caught in a mob in an unexpected crisis. They knew a panic had hit European countries earlier in the year, but now here? Silas fished coins out of his pocket to purchase a paper from a boy no more than ten, then stuffed it under his arm as they walked quickly over to Isabel's.

Thornton led them upstairs where a nightgown-clad woman with unkempt hair was at Isabel's dining table. Who was this with red-rimmed eyes and a gash along one swollen cheek, sewn together with angry black gut stitching? White strips of gauze ran perpendicular across the wound, leaking pink liquid at the edges. A bowl of chipped ice and a cotton towel sat at her side.

"Who . . . ?" Juanita stammered as she realized it was Isabel in no state she'd ever seen. Never once had Isabel not been fully polished.

"The tongs . . ." She took a sip of water and looked at the *Daily Alta California* in front of her. "What's going on?" she said, looking directly at them, as if her appearance was perfectly normal.

Juanita sat next to her and held her hand. "Cooke and Company is folding. Banks failing," she explained. "Wall Street's in an uproar. It's the war, the railroad debt . . . But none of that matters right now. Are you all right? What happened?"

"Oh, not good either. Hmm, railroad debts might hit my customers. But I'll be fine. I keep my investments in many places for this exact reason." Her regal countenance was sloping, diminished, her eyes unfocused. The doctor must have given her a strong sedative.

"Isabel. Eat your eggs," Juanita ordered as if she were her mother. Isabel nodded, sipped more water and took a forkful. "Who did this to you?"

"Hurts to chew," she said. After struggling through a few more bites, she put the fork down, decisively. "It was the tongs. After Ralston's masquerade ball, everyone goin' for their carriages. Sent a Chinese gang, set off firecrackers, horses going crazy. Carriages tippin' over. Was mayhem. Clever. Couldn't have planned it better myself. A kid came at me with a piece of glass. You should see my dress. It's all ripped. Don't know if they wanted me dead or just scared. I've got to find out about the others." She gripped the table and called hoarsely, "Thornton,"

"What are you talking about? Did you kidnap more Chinese girls?"

"No kidnappin'. It's bigger than a few girls. Congressman Page is trying to get Washington to prohibit Chinese women shipped in as prostitutes. They know I encouraged this, that I support him. He was at the party." She drank more water. "Keep those powders away from me. They cloud my head. I've gotta think straight."

Juanita was reluctant to leave for New Almaden with Isabel wounded and facing threats. But the madam insisted they investigate the Pinkerton discovery, assuring them her guards would protect her. "I was naïve to think the tongs wouldn't attack a ball and go for me physically. Limitin' the importation of young girls strikes a nerve, clearly. Could have serious pocketbook impact for the tongs."

"Let me help you, Isabel. I can send Tobias to manage your businesses while you recover. He's honest."

Isabel looked into Juanita's eyes, struggling to focus. "Would that Mormon boy want to run brothels? I think not. I've got to reemerge quickly, as if nothing happened. If I'm weak, they'll try to take my business. They chased Ah Toy out. And she's even Chinese. The tongs don't like a strong woman in this industry. I need a clear head. Maybe the doctor's workin' for them."

"Isabel, what kind of friendship is this if I never offer anything? You've given me so much—loans, jobs, buying my stolen goods, fronting me in horse races."

She smiled slightly, then winced at the pull on the stitched gash along her cheek. She shook her head and sighed and responded more softly than Juanita had ever heard her speak.

"Ah, Juanita, you are a true friend. Only person with whom I'm truly honest. You never make demands or look for a handout. Never reveal my secrets or gossip about my business. While we are very different, y'all never judged me. What's really golden in this watch-your-back town is a real friend. Someone trustworthy. But no pioneer can truly go it alone. You've got yourself a good man, there. Make the poor man happy and marry him. I'll help figure out a way. Maybe not legally, but that's never stopped me." She winked and laughed again. "I sacrificed companionship for wealth, fame, power. Don't you do that too. No one is too old for love."

Juanita put her arms around the depleted woman and promised more than a letter describing the results of the New Almaden visit. "We'll come right back here to check on you.

Maybe Silas' Pinkerton detective friend can be of service with the tongs? And I'm telegramming Ines to come immediately to be your nursemaid. She is loyal to me and will dutifully help my friend. There'll be no gossip, she'll interact only with your most trusted staff. She'll help you get strong quickly."

Isabel leaned her good cheek against Juanita's shoulder, her usually wild hair limp, her complexion pallid. The vulnerability was striking, and Juanita embraced her tightly.

Discoveries

September 1873

After sending a telegram to summon Ines, then traveling south for two days, Juanita and Silas cantered on to the New Almaden home described by the Pinkerton detective.

Black mourning bunting stretched across the porch's white slat railing on either side of the splintered steps of a simple house. The mercury mine's smokestacks rose up the hillside overlooking the village. A faded gray paint coated the wood siding and the porch floorboards were worn, scooped, and scuffed by the feet of scampering children and boot-clad visitors. A line of clay flowerpots adorned the porch, geraniums wilting in several, dead stalks and leaves in others. Thick curtains blocked any view of the interior.

The house was silent as they stepped up to the porch. No children in the scrub brush or neighing horses tethered out front nibbling the weeds. No pots clanking or family members calling to each other. No sign of a wagon or buggy.

Juanita looked at Silas with a questioning eye. It appeared they were grieving a recent loss. It was an intrusion. He read her look, squeezed her shoulder and motioned to the front door. She hesitated a moment, reminding herself of all she'd rehearsed. What to say to someone who might be your son, or his family, or who might not be related at all? She'd practiced in her mind, but never out loud to Silas, and she knew in her heart she would just have to be in the situation to feel what was appropriate. It was not a stage show after all.

A tall, young man of about eighteen opened the door. Juanita tilted to one side as she started to speak. Silas grabbed her elbow to steady her.

"Can I help you?" he asked from behind sad brown eyes. His flop of thick, brown hair was cut shorter above the ears and neck than was standard in the California countryside. A thin mustache decorated his upper lip while a goatee with an auburn tint sprouted from his chin. He wore knee-high work boots, rough wool pants, and a faded blue cotton collared shirt with sleeves rolled up. As he waited for them to answer, his look grew more quizzical.

"Are your parents here? Could we speak with them?" Juanita managed to get a few words out. Silas nodded, taking her hand.

"My mother is. Who may I tell her is calling? You know, it's not a convenient time. We've just had a death in the family."

"We are very sorry for your loss. We just need a moment." Juanita managed while standing straight, finding her authoritative posture and voice.

The boy turned, closed the door softly, and left them standing on the porch. They glanced at one another.

Would someone return or were they being dismissed? A death too recent, the house's inhabitants too fragile.

"Maybe a Southern man and a Californio is too much," Silas muttered. He never called himself a former slave, always a South Carolinian or a Southerner. Juanita had noticed it years before and thought it self-preserving. What would she call herself? Surely not a Californio. No one even knew what that was anymore.

The door opened and a woman, youthful but looking aged by anguish, stood there. Silent. She stared for several moments longer than expected. Her shining black hair and brownish skin revealed plenty of time doing outside work. But instead of what was probably normally a healthy complexion, her eyes were red-rimmed, her cheekbones stood out too sharply, and her lips were cracked and thin.

"Yes? May I help you? Are you customers who just heard? Have I met you before, ma'am?" She peered at them, an ingrained habit of politeness visibly propelling her through her grief.

Juanita held out her hand. "I'm Juanita Castro de la Cruz and this is my friend Silas Holloway. We heard a Joe Brennan lives here with his family. Is Mr. Brennan home? We'd like to speak with him."

"Oh, oh." The woman started to crumple and Silas stepped through the threshold to catch her.

"Ma'am, can we come in and get you seated?" he asked in an obsequious tone. Juanita had never heard him speak so. It revealed not only his past, but the intrusion they were making in these strangers' lives.

The woman nodded and called out, "Samuel!" The young man with the goatee flew in from the back of the house.

"Oh, Mama, let's sit you here. Thank you, sir, but you need to leave. Perhaps you can send us a letter for whatever you need. Get some water, Peter. Hurry!" he yelled over his shoulder, taking his mother from Silas and leading her to the sofa.

"No, no, Samuel. It's all right. We need to talk with these

people. Please have a seat," she said, offering two worn reddish chairs with curling wooden arms.

A small table stood between them, bearing a bouquet of daisies. Faded, yellowing wallpaper with an ornate diamond pattern covered the walls, and an iron stove sat in the corner. The room was dark thanks to the thick curtains, but it was warm and comfortable, feeling as if it had been lived in for some time. Family portraits in simple frames dotted the wallpaper. A basket of socks and pants needing mending sat in one corner, while another under the table held unfinished needlepoint. Altogether, it made for a stark contrast to the latest fashion in Isabel's home, comfortable or not.

"What?" Samuel said. Anger and protectiveness suffused his deep voice.

Suddenly, as Juanita looked at the young man, it all was clear. A rushing sound filled her ears, and her chest constricted until she could barely breathe. Thank goodness she was already sitting down. She clenched her dress in her fist and blinked hard, trying to maintain her composure.

"I think we should leave now, Juanita." Silas reached his hand to her across the table. "We can come back at a better time."

But the mother sat upright from the original slump, took several swallows of water and excused her children. "I'd like to speak with these two, alone. I'm fine. Please finish your chores. Samuel, get to that firewood."

Her authoritative tone demonstrated she'd regained her composure and the children complied, Samuel more hesitant than the younger boy.

"What is your business with Joe?" she asked.

"Are you Mrs. Brennan? We're looking for a Joe Brennan but aren't sure if this is the right place. Tall, auburn-haired, says he's an orphan from Ohio. Is he your husband?"

She nodded and her eyes filled with tears, brimming over so one cheek was immediately wet. She brushed at them, then reached to the quilt on the back of the sofa and drew it in to use as a handkerchief, hugging it to herself as if she were a child with a favorite blanket.

"I'm sorry but we just lost Joe over a fortnight ago. The cholera got him. Healthy one week, went to Los Angeles to advise on their new sewer system, came back sick and gone so quickly. It was a shock. Just came out of the quarantine ourselves. Had a service for him last Sunday. Had to bury him in quarantine with even the minister at a distance."

She stopped abruptly, sat up straight. "But that's not what you came for is it? You're here looking for your son? Yes, he called himself an orphan from Ohio, but he wasn't. He was from right here. He grew up on a rancho not far down the El Camino." She stopped. "The Castro Rancho," she whispered. "Miss Castro, Joe would be absolutely beside himself to see you at our door. He's been searching for you for years." And she collapsed in sobs, then pulled herself up as though to embrace her.

Juanita had prepared herself for yet another disappointment, yet another false lead or roadblock. It had never occurred to her to prepare for the disappointment of locating Joaquin but then being too late.

Her heart thumped, a flush filling her cheeks as she stood to embrace this lovely, sad woman. Joaquin's wife. The mother of his children, including the son who looked so much like him a part of her had known from the first moment that they'd knocked on the right door. She let the unusual tears slide down her cheeks, making no attempt to hide or brush them away. She hugged the woman fiercely and led her to sit together on the couch. An indescribable combination of grief and regret and joy overwhelmed her. She gazed over at Silas in awe.

What a rare gift he was witnessing, and had helped facilitate. She knew he was touched by discovering these relatives but also thought of the rare reunions among former slave families broken apart by cruel masters. No such reunion was possible for him, or thousands like him among the Black diaspora out of the southern states.

The women held each other, silently, staring in wonder, then finally both talking at once. There were so many questions.

"What do you mean he looked for me for years? I've been looking for him. Mostly in the mining areas. I put ads in papers and telegram offices. There were a few false leads. I didn't know his surname. I'm sorry I sent him away at only fifteen, telling him to become American. Those times were difficult."

The woman nodded. "I'm Elizabeth, his wife. We have four children and one grandbaby too." She told them she knew little of Joe's childhood, and then, how just two years ago, he'd revealed his true identity.

"He kept it a secret all that time? From you?"

"Yes, but he was a good man. It was just the name, and origin that he hid. And his search for you."

"Seems rather important," Silas interjected. Juanita glared at him and he mumbled, "Sorry. Not my place."

"Haven't we all used false names and identities at one time or another?" Juanita asked. "I so wish we'd found you and Joaquin earlier." Her voice trailed off.

Elizabeth sat up, brushed her tears away for a final time. "I don't know many details, but I believe my husband was looking for a poor widow. He told me he went to your sister's ranch. They were struggling, clearly. Probably about 1858, maybe early '60's. Your brother-in-law was rude, chased him off. Said you were a thief, were dead or up to no good. Said he should forget you. Joe never saw your sister. What kind of uncle says such horrid words to a young man searching for his mother?"

Elizabeth suddenly placed her hand over Juanita's. "Miss Castro, Mr. Holloway," she said, a brightness in her tone. "Please stay for supper. I want to show you something. I'm not sure what I'll tell the children. But the truth, I suspect, is best. Don't you agree?"

After some time alone in another room, the family emerged and began preparing supper. Juanita took it all in like a muleteer who'd survived on the trail with no food or water for days, then came upon a mountain spring and drank and drank until almost sick. These were her grandchildren, here was their daily experience, their home. She wanted to absorb every scrap and weave it into a quilt of their lives she could sleep in. Joaquin had sat in these very chairs just weeks ago. Raised his children here. The tragedy of just missing meeting her grown son was devastating. So hard to accept. Yet, here in front of her were the people he loved.

She watched as they prepared the simple meal of stew, vegetables, and fresh bread. Young Peter's thick eyebrows danced under his mop of curling, unkempt hair with every twist in a story he narrated. Samuel, the tall boy, kept casting suspicious glances her way; he presented himself as the man of the home, protecting his fragile mother, but she suspected he was the most devastated by his father's death. The boy between Peter and Samuel was called Joseph and was a quiet, shy child on the precipice of the teen years. He listened to his mother, watched his eldest brother's every move, and swatted, irritated, at his younger brother, but didn't say a word. Juanita surmised he was in shock, rattled by his older brother's strange behavior and frightened by his mother's tears. This boy almost telegraphed his thoughts to everyone. *What will become of my family now? What happens with Papa gone? Is he really gone or just on another trip? Surely, he'll be back soon.*

"Oh, and there's one other, Miss Castro, Mr. Holloway," Elizabeth said as the boys were setting the table. When they were finished, she ordered them to scrub their hands out at the water pump.

"Please call us by our given names," Juanita said quietly as she sat on the planked bench bordering the long kitchen table, a single chair at each end. "Juanita. Silas."

"Yes, of course," Elizabeth said absently, focusing on her dinner preparations, looking out the window she'd finally opened to the afternoon light. "Oh, here she is."

She opened the door to a young woman with a toddler at her feet. The little girl held up a chubby hand to knock.

"'Buela, I knock," she said, indignant she'd lost her chance to perform.

"Oh yes," Elizabeth said and closed the door.

They waited quietly until they heard a light tap.

"Who is it?" Elizabeth called.

"It's me, 'Buela, you know."

When Elizabeth reopened the door, the child seemed put out her grandmother was so confused. Elizabeth feigned great surprise.

"Look who's here. It's Rosie and her mother. Come on in, honey, I want you to meet our guests. This is our daughter, Beatriz, and our granddaughter, Rosie. My son-in-law is on his shift up at the mine. We'll see him in a few days."

Juanita gave another cough of surprise at the name, admonishing herself not to start crying. What was wrong with her? Tears never escaped her eyes. She shook the young mother's hand with both of hers, resisting temptation to give this unsuspecting woman a full hug.

"Beatriz, I'm your grandmother," she said. "My sister is Beatriz and my aunt is a Beatriz. It's an important name in our family. Your family."

This Beatriz scooped up the toddler and sat her at the table. Then she gave her mother a piercing glare before delivering the same to Silas, then Juanita.

"What on earth is going on? Who are these people?" she asked her mother. "Carpetbaggers trying to take advantage. Papa's grave is not even cold and you let these strangers in? Samuel? Mother clearly is not well."

Everyone stared at the empty chair at the table's head.

"That's enough, Beatriz," said her mother sharply. "Your father would have wanted to hear these folks out. Be polite and we'll listen to their story. Now, pass the kettle bread around."

An uneasy silence ensued as the family filled their plates with green beans and thick slices of juicy tomatoes and bread from the Dutch oven, then ladled up bowls of thick stew filled with carrots, onions, potatoes, and small beef chunks, all simmered together to form a bubbling, brown sauce.

The little girl broke the silence. "Delish, 'Buela. More, Mama."

"'More please,' Rosie. Mind your manners. 'Buela has guests," her mother said.

Elizabeth ladled more stew into the child's small bowl. "Miss Castro, Mr. Holloway, please tell us how you come to us. About what you know of Joe."

Juanita did not correct the formality this time, understanding the seriousness with which this woman was introducing them to her children. She set her soup spoon down, wiped her mouth with the thick cotton napkin and began her story.

She told of her childhood on the Castro Rancho, of her grandparents and parents, the loss of the ranch, the changing times in Alta California. The family listened without interruption— Elizabeth saw to it with a pointed glower here and there. Her daughter set the toddler with a cloth doll and toy horse to occupy her on the woven, oval rug at the fireplace, embers still glowing from cooking the bread.

Juanita explained how she fled the ranch to run a mule train to make a living, eventually building a hotel. Where she and Silas worked together now.

"But what does all this have to do with us? With our father? What Beatriz were you talking about? Do you want to take the drilling equipment business? It's not worth much anymore," the daughter said bitterly. "The land's protected. Papa saw to that."

"No. I have two hotels, a fire clay extraction company, logging tracts, orchards and gardens, a mule delivery service. I have plenty of businesses and no interest in yours."

Juanita had to be blunt so they would feel less threatened. But most importantly, she had to go to the heart of the matter. Tell these strangers her most difficult secrets. The pain of her past.

And so, she told them everything. Of Malachy sweeping her into a passionate love affair, of him leaving her pregnant. She told them of bearing her son while disgraced in an abandoned Santa Barbara mission alone, of returning to the family fold with the understanding she would help her father manage the enormous ranch when her grandmother passed. Of the cow plague, Don Pedro's death and his debts, then Malachy returning to buy the ranch, making a point to humiliate and torment her family. How she had decided to send Joaquin away because she feared the whole family would be thrown out into war-torn Alta California with not a penny to their name, no skills but ranching, she and Joaquin the only ones speaking English.

"My mother had become very confused, her only certainty a determination to be buried in the family cemetery next to my father. I married off my much younger sisters to get them out. Joaquin grew tall, auburn-haired, and began to resemble the owner. I realize, now, I should have figured out something else for Joaquin close to home, maybe at another rancho. He was so talented at breaking horses. He had the touch, the vaqueros said. But you must understand our relatives basically disowned us because I lost the Castro ranch.

"And it was chaos in those years, with governors changing, war, the US taking over. We were no longer Mexico, nor Spain, and that, in itself, was a terrifying mystery. What would become of us Californios? I'd grown up rich in land but nothing else. We had no US dollars, little Mexican silver. We were traders. Joaquin was the fourth generation on that ranch. The changes in our land, our country, language and culture, our reduced circumstances after a well-off existence for generations . . ."

She couldn't help but study the faces around the table, searching for a hint to how the family perceived the story. At least they all listened intently.

"I didn't handle it well," she said. "I panicked. I sent Joaquin to the gold diggings to make an American man of himself. To become 'Joe' and never speak Spanish unless absolutely necessary. My grandmother had predicted a sea change with yanquis taking over, and I could feel it in the air, in my bones, too. We'd lost, more deeply than anyone could imagine. It became all about survival."

The air hung heavy. Only the quiet chatter of little Rosie with her toys had interrupted the story and now she was asleep on the rug, curled around her cotton doll, a soft snore rattling from her lips.

"Before you say anything, I must apologize for what I did. I've regretted it every day since. I broke my own heart and fear I hurt him. When my mother passed, I buried her next to my father, then left. The ranch owner told me they'd received letters from the gold fields but his wife had destroyed them. I believe Joaquin wrote me, but I never received his letters. I was furious and distraught. What he must have felt when he got no response." She looked down at her hands, swallowing to prevent her voice from cracking, tears from forming.

"I searched up and down the diggings for years. I finally settled in Sonora but have always looked for him, posting announcements, following rumors. But I didn't know what last name he used, if he had stayed in gold country. Silas here," she paused smiling at him, "my . . . my husband, contracted a Pinkerton detective. Silas guessed he'd used the Brennan name."

Silence. So thick Juanita felt she might fall into it and drown. Would this family believe her? At the same time, Silas' hand was squeezing hers so hard it hurt. When she looked at him, she saw tears filling his eyes, felt his breath catch. Had she just married him right there in front of these strangers? He looked astonished.

What a fool she'd been with him too. All these years, all this posturing. If he really wanted to marry her, then so be it.

He was the man for her. Finding this family was such a gift, proving the depth of his love. Why had she denied him the marriage he desired? Complicated, yes, but secretly, possible.

She squeezed his hand. Then let go and pulled out a cloth-covered object from her satchel.

"I have a gift for your wall of photographs." She handed it to Elizabeth, who unwrapped it with care.

With a little gasp, she smiled. "Oh, there's Joe. He looks so young. Was when he worked for the railroad company. Thank you. We don't have any daguerreotypes of those years. How did you get this?"

Silas explained, leaving out the missed train and years of separation he and Juanita had endured before joining forces. There was plenty of time for that. But he did mention Juanita had known instantly it was her son.

"Thank you so much, and for the background. I believe you, Miss Castro. I'm not sure about my children. We'll have to give everyone time. We're still in shock at Joe's passing, grieving, you understand. I'm also trying to figure out next steps without him. But I have something to show you."

She pushed her chair back and left. Juanita looked across at the oldest son and the daughter, whose suspicious glares did not let up, and then at the boys. She and Silas held hands tightly underneath the table. She could feel his love propping her up, keeping her in this strange, unexpected moment, willing her to stay strong. To let her survivor sarape loosen just a bit, enough to allow the emotions, yes, the grief, but also the possibilities, the hope, in.

Elizabeth returned with official-looking documents in hand. She sifted through them to the final page. This time she sat in Joaquin's chair at the table's head, then held up the paper to show them before turning it back to read.

"The Brennan Castro de la Cruz Trust is officially initiated by Joe Brennan (Joaquin Castro de la Cruz). Mr. Brennan is establishing this land trust to protect 200 acres of his 300 acres to remain forever in the hands of his descendants. He is doing this in honor of his mother, Juanita Castro de la Cruz, and his grandparents, Pedro Castro and Juana Candelaria de la Cruz. True Californios. Mr. Brennan is taking this action at the birth of his first grandchild, Rose Josephine Trelawny Brennan, in recognition of his family continuing to thrive as California grows and prospers."

A little voice came sleepily from the rug. "Rose 'phine. That's me, 'Buela!"

"Yes, dear. That's you. Abuelo mentioned you in this paper."

The little girl smiled at her family, then grabbed her doll and curled up with it tightly in her fist.

Tears streamed down Juanita's face. Silas stretched to look more closely at the document as Elizabeth held it up again for everyone to see Joaquin's signature at the bottom. He wrapped Juanita in his arm and she cried into his shoulder rather than lose all dignity in front of these strangers, her family. She stayed with him for a moment, then looked back at her daughter-in-law, at each face around the table, seeing Joaquin in each one.

"Thank you for showing me," she said. "I'm overwhelmed."

Joaquin was always there loving her, just as she was loving him. The tragedy of not finding each other in time was excruciating, like a knife stabbing her. Yet this gesture of love, not only for her, but for continuing the traditions of land ownership and stewardship, valuing the acreage just as her family had, was immense.

Could they let her in? Could she be a grandmother to these

suspicious, grieving children? She hoped so, but at this moment, the knowledge Joaquin had never stopped being her son, never stopped being a Castro de la Cruz, swelled her heart with gratitude. He had been loyal to the end.

The broken family sat for a moment, smoothing their pants, dresses, and hair, nervous tics and confused energy escaping through the haze of shock, sadness, loss, gifts, and love. What a strange, devastating, and unexpected few weeks it had been for every one of them.

Rose stirred on the floor, rubbed her eyes and sat up. She wandered over to Juanita and Silas' side of the table.

"'Buela. I'm hungry. More stew, please. Can I sit by your friends?" And with her little, chubby hands, she pushed Juanita's hip so she'd slide over and climbed up between them, leaning into Silas' ribs.

"What's your name? You like 'Buela's stew? Want more too, mister?" she asked.

Little Rosie pointed to Silas to have more. He nodded and Elizabeth ladled into his bowl. Silas and Rosie ate stew together.

"It's good. 'Buela's a good cook, right?"

"She sure is," he agreed.

Beatriz squirmed uncomfortably on the bench. "No more games, Rosie. Come sit with me." The little girl ignored her mother.

Suddenly, the young man, Samuel, asked to be excused. Elizabeth sighed and nodded, appearing resigned this was all a bit much for her children to take in. Silas and the little girl kept eating, taking bites in turns.

"Your turn, Sila'," she giggled. "Now, my turn."

Silas waited, a smile fully covering his face, revealing the dimple, his white teeth shining after each swallow.

Beatriz swung her legs over the end of the bench. "Enough, Rosie. Time to go home. Thank you for supper, Mama."

She scooped up Rosie and marched out. Not a goodbye to anyone. The little girl squirming and whining in protest.

"I'm so sorry for her rude manners. This is quite an unexpected shock for all of us," Elizabeth said.

"We mustn't take any more of your hospitality. Are there rooms in New Almaden?"

Elizabeth insisted on escorting them to the Cinnabar Rooming House and introducing them to the owner, explaining her guests owned two hotels in the Central Valley. They thanked Mrs. Brennan for welcoming them and listening despite their difficult circumstances. She invited them to stop by for coffee the next morning for a little more conversation before riding back to the city. Sensing the same tension had followed them into New Almaden's rooming house, Juanita paid for two rooms.

"I'm exhausted, Silas," she whispered as they unloaded saddlebags off the horses. "Let's just sleep and talk tomorrow. Thank you for helping find my family."

She stood on tiptoe to kiss him while he squeezed her tightly. He nodded, and after walking up the creaky porch steps, they went opposite directions down the hallway to their rooms.

Silas always woke well before dawn, a habit from childhood when he needed to be watchful every moment possible. Today he was itchy and fidgety, still pondering yesterday's miraculous, yet sad, events while also focusing on his own dream of marrying Juanita. First, he'd consult her lawyer and find out if a legal route was even possible. If not, he envisioned a simple ceremony with Isabel officiating. He couldn't think of anyone else who was more suited, especially now he'd observed the bond between the women. Isabel would likely be his best ally in this escapade.

At daylight, he snuck out of the rooming house, completed a telegraph blank at the local office and the operator teletyped it out.

To: Thomas Ralston, Esquire
K Street, Sacramento

Your client will marry me STOP Can I, a South
Carolinian Black man, legally marry Juanita Castro
de la Cruz STOP Could you officiate STOP Please advise
STOP Telegraph back today if possible STOP

From: Silas Holloway
New Almaden Telegraph office

A quick reply was highly unlikely, but Silas was hopeful. He was still floating on yesterday's success at finding Joaquin's family, despite the mixed blessing of the discovery and her son's tragic demise. He knew Juanita was emotionally raw, so he did not mention the telegram to her as they strolled to the Brennan house, noticing mineshafts bored into the hillside above, swarming with workers like an ant colony.

"It's a lot for them to accept, Silas. I understand they might never want to see me, us, again," she said as they neared the porch.

He nodded and just squeezed her hand. "We'll see," he whispered. The house was quiet as they stepped past the withered geraniums, no sign of children present.

As she poured coffee and offered thick slices of cinnamon cake, Elizabeth revealed her daughter had been scandalized by the relationship between Juanita and a Black man. Wasn't he a slave? she'd asked. It's immoral and illegal for a mixed-race couple to marry, she'd said, and insisted little Rosie was not to interact with either of them. Silas sat, unmoving, in the velvet chair beside the fire.

"Mrs. Brennan," Juanita said, "perhaps I misspoke. Silas and I are not married but we do have such a relationship. He was emancipated and the war was over eight years ago. Slavery is what's immoral. After raising rice on a South Carolina plantation for a despicable owner, Silas, and many other Black Southerners, helped build railroads in Virginia and the Carolinas. He worked as a Pullman Porter for years serving white men on those trains. He is a free, independent, self-determined man, just as all of us should be."

"My sons and I don't care who your companion is. It's none of our business. Beatriz is more traditional. I'm sorry she was so cold, untrusting. I hope with time she'll be more accepting. Please visit us again. We have so much to learn about each other."

Juanita returned the invitation encouraging them to join the Castro family Christmas. They could meet more relatives, including another Beatriz.

"My brother-in-law never comes, but I have a good relationship with my sister, her children, and the little ones." She wished she could tell Elizabeth she supported Beatriz financially, but that was too personal. She didn't want to boast of her financial success to this new family member, though she'd clearly hinted the day before.

"How kind. We'll have to see. But I'd like to," Elizabeth said, then seemed to be gearing up to say something important.

"Before you two leave I want you to know, that ranch owner, the one you say was Joe's real father, showed up here, asking about another Brennan. Joe chased him away but not after a hot argument. It was out front, but I heard some of the conversation. At the time I was confused, not knowing any details. The man seemed curious, maybe wanting a relationship. I'm not sure. But I heard Joe say he was no family of his because he treated you, his mother, so badly. Said the man had forced his mother to send him away. Said he was ashamed they had any connection. To leave and never come back."

Silas moved to the sofa to sit next to Juanita. He put his arm around her. Elizabeth continued.

"He loved you and the ranch very much, ma'am. He poured every silver dollar he saved into buying land. I thought he was hoping for a quicksilver strike. But when he told me the truth, and about the trust, I understood. He did say it was ironic after years in the industry he had amassed the only three hundred acres in New Almaden with not one piece of cinnabar.

"Miss Castro, Juanita, it was as if he wanted to get your land back. He told me he never wanted his family to go through the loss, heartbreak, shame you all experienced. He was proud of being a Castro, even though he buried the truth."

Once again, Juanita was speechless. Tears pooled in her eyes and she wiped the back of her hand forcefully across her lids, as if she could stop the emotion with a brusque rub. Taking pity on her, Silas changed the topic.

"Mrs. Brennan, why was Joaquin, Joe I mean, in the photograph with the Big Four? Juanita always looked for him in mining towns and ranch areas. Where were y'all these past twenty years?"

"Oh, yes, of course you're curious. It's true Joe left the diggings for New Almaden's quicksilver, then started an equipment company with a fellow miner. They did well around the state and over in Utah Territory. That's when I met him. But there were ownership changes here in New Almaden, a lot of chaos, so we went up to Sacramento in the railroad years." She glanced over at the new photograph of Joaquin she'd placed next to the daisies on the side table.

"Mr. Judah was a mentor and took him in even without technical training. My Joe was a smart man though. He worked for the Central Pacific, but he didn't like the way they treated Mr. Judah. The hypocrisy and greed, all that wealth they accumulated, manipulating politics and laws for their gain. But they sure did build that transcontinental railroad."

Juanita tried to imagine Joaquin in a suit, drawing and figuring mathematical equations. She'd always pictured him in an icy stream shoveling rock and sifting through gold pans.

"Our son Samuel," Elizabeth said, "he wants to go to the university in Berkeley to study engineering. Says he wants to build the future railroads and telegraphs. He wasn't pleased when we left Sacramento City, but Joe wanted to be back on this land. The railroad bosses looked down on him because he lacked a formal education. He was bitter about it."

While Silas and Juanita digested the story, a door creaked behind them and Samuel appeared with an object in his hand. He looked so much like Joaquin, who was only a few years younger when she'd sent him away.

"Mama. Miss Castro, I have something to show you." His eyes were red as if he'd been crying. "Miss Castro. I think this might belong to you. My father gave it to me when I turned eighteen. He said it should keep me safe on my travels and had kept him safe. He didn't say much, except it was a family bible, part of his history. I didn't pay attention, didn't open it, just put it in my drawer."

When she saw what was in his hand, she covered her mouth to hide a gasp. So many unexpected confessions and memories.

"But I looked through it just now," Samuel said. "You wrote in this when he was born, right? In Santa Barbara? I didn't believe you. I thought you two wanted to take advantage of us losing our father. But I think maybe you're telling the truth."

Juanita felt her heart pound in a flutter at her throat and could not stop the tears as he handed her the pocket bible. She turned to the final pages and found the one she'd inscribed. She swallowed before reading it aloud, her voice catching.

"*'Joaquin Castro, born to Juanita Castro de la Cruz, Mission Santa Barbara, December, 1834.'* I named him Joaquin in honor of my grandmother Maria Joaquina Altamirano Pacheco. I admired her independence and business sense. She was a great Californio and made the Rancho Castro very successful on the old El Camino Real. My grandfather gave me the bible before he died, when I was only nine. This bible holds many family stories I hope to tell you some day."

She flipped through to the beginning pages, caressed the frail paper lightly with her fingers, then closed it slowly, holding it for a moment more.

"This is not mine, Samuel. It's yours," she said softly. "Your father gave it to you. Just as my grandfather gave it to me. He said it would protect me. I gave it to Joaquin when I made a mistake and sent him away. I'm glad it did keep him safe enough to meet your mother and have this family. The Castro family bible is yours."

And through his tears, Samuel nodded and smiled, ever so slightly, at his grandmother.

Promises

September to October 1873

To: Silas Holloway
New Almaden Telegraph Office

Congratulations STOP 1872 California Civil Code no longer criminal penalties of $10,000 or 10 years prison for officiating STOP However still not legal STOP As attorney I cannot STOP Good luck STOP

From: Thomas Ralston, Esquire
K Street, Sacramento

Silas collected the telegram as they left New Almaden. Having promised no more secrets, he explained what he'd sent early that morning and showed her the scribbled receipt from the operator.

Juanita hugged him quickly, nodding at attorney Ralston's rapid response, but she did not want to discuss their relationship now. She was consumed with grief, while also assessing her altered family situation and worrying about Isabel's injuries and safety.

"I'm still stunned by what we found here. It's overwhelming. Let's get to the city and check on Isabel," she said, her practicality shining through.

Isabel was feverish and confused, her wound raised and red, pus oozing around the stitches. Ines already was providing constant care, changing the dressing frequently, bathing her and managing the medicines. The doctor had been by several times applying tinctures and prescribing tonics to fight infection.

"Madam Platt is suspicious of them all," Ines whispered as she fluffed the pillows and smoothed the sheets in the massive mahogany bed holding the inert Isabel. She dipped a cloth in a basin filled with floating ice chips and patted the madam's forehead. "I'm not sure if she's in her right mind, but she says these tongs and doctors want to drug her. Not sure what a tong is. Glad you're here, Miss Juanita. Is she your relative?"

Isabel stirred and opened her eyes slightly. Then wider when she saw Juanita and Silas in her private chambers. She tried to push herself upright on the pillow only to sink back into the feathery covers.

"I'm not gonna get foggy. Gotta stay clear-eyed. Need to go out soon and show 'em all I'm just fine. Those bastards not gonna to take me down." Was there a slight slur in her words?

"Now shush, Isabel. Rest," Juanita said. "Ines will not leave your side. You've got Josiah and your best men at your hotels, right? We will check on whatever worries you. Rest now."

Isabel stretched out her hand, waving her fingertips at them to beckon them closer. "Ines is just perfect. So gentle. The best part is she knows no one in town. Loyal to you, Juanita, means they can't corrupt her. Thank you. I mean it. Now tell me what happened in New Almaden."

Silas and Juanita stayed for a fortnight in a guest chamber at the back of the mansion. The house was so large it was easy to go unnoticed, but they were still discreet. They visited Isabel together but went in and out of the mansion separately as they checked on Isabel's hotels, speaking privately with the man in charge at each location.

Juanita also consulted with Lizzie, who now managed all the girls, albeit in four different bordellos. She'd never gone out on her own as Isabel had once feared. Installing her in a leadership position probably had helped insure her fidelity.

The Barbary Coast was in full swing on certain streets and back alleys. Isabel complained about the city's notorious lack of police, which meant she now employed her own private squad of henchmen to keep her operations secure. Not sure where they were the night of the masked ball when Isabel was attacked, Juanita grumbled to Silas, but she said nothing to her injured friend.

Lizzie's charges appeared healthy, clean, and well cared for. Isabel's philosophy of providing finer living standards than her competition seemed to encourage the prostitutes who worked for her to avoid riffraff. But there was plenty of business to go around in the Port of San Francisco's underbelly.

One night, dressed in a dark cloak reminiscent of her days exploring the Mission neighborhood, Juanita took Silas with her to inspect Pacific Street and a Barbary Coast Dance Hall. They could barely peek in past private security guards but saw, through cracks in one shanty's pine walls, the "pretty waiter girls" serving drinks and dancing with male customers. Silas pointed at a woman slipping her hand into a target's pocket and tucking pilfered greenbacks into her bosom.

They walked on, sticking to the shadows all the way through

Chinatown with its opium den street and an all-night shop peddling laudanum. They avoided Pacific's dangerous block between Kearny and Montgomery but still peered down it as they passed. Not daring to stay out too long, they quickly slid down Grant to Washington, then over to Portsmouth Square where Isabel's coachman waited to take them back to the mansion.

After the hotel visits and nighttime exploring, Juanita felt confident Isabel's legal businesses were thriving and the brothels were operating in as clean a manner as could be hoped. She assured her friend that Ines could stay as long as necessary. If Isabel wanted more assistance, she would send Jacinto or Manuel immediately. Isabel turned her down but told her to watch the telegraph deliveries and postal stops as she would send updates.

"I do have one request now I'm a bit stronger," she said one night. "Will you and Ines dress me so I can go out tonight? Make an appearance at each hotel. I need to be seen, to get the word around town that I'm fine, workin', and not one bit frightened, nor weakened, by the attack. Y'all understand?"

They dressed her in a thick red silk with pleated ruffles and a long train, a black choker at her neck and ribboned streamers in her hair. They covered her in a plush cloak with a wide hood which allowed her curls to frame her face and hide her cheek gash, still scabbed and swollen.

"Can the Pullman Porter escort me for these visits?" she asked Juanita, who said she needed to ask Silas himself.

He agreed. Isabel offered him a fine hotel bellman suit and he escorted her on the new cable railcars down the hill to the waterfront hotels. She insisted on riding the latest horseless transport everyone in San Francisco raved about these days.

They stepped in to each hotel lobby, promenaded through

the chandelier-bedecked restaurants, checked on the reception staff and kitchen employees, then moved on to the next establishment. Silas held her arm tight when he felt her fade and moved quickly to the waiting cable car. Then back up the hill to the Golden Nugget and then to the Diamond Crown.

When they finally made it back to the mansion, Isabel was exhausted but grateful for their assistance. She was hopeful her visibility and show of strength had sent a clear message to San Francisco.

"Now the *Daily Chronicle* can print I'm back," she said triumphantly. Madam Platt was not going anywhere.

In private matters, once the madam's successful tour of the city was complete, Juanita relented to Silas' request that Isabel officiate a private marriage ceremony. Naturally, the flamboyant Isabel, who complained she felt like a prisoner stuck in her private chambers, loved the idea and got to scheming with Ines. The mansion's grand library with hand-carved floor-to-ceiling bookshelves stuffed with leather-bound books was the perfect venue, she said. The only additional witness would be Josiah, the old Black butler who'd worked for her since her first days in the city. They were to wear elegant attire.

"Just something simple, please," Silas requested privately. "Juanita is barely agreeing to this, so let's not overdo it."

"I don't think you'll scare her away, Silas," Isabel told him. "Thank God, she finally realized how lucky she is to have you. After all these years, I think I know what she can tolerate. I promise to keep her dress simple, but not too plain," she said with a laugh, sending him off to the tailor for a fitting.

Silas' suit featured a maroon, knee-length coat atop black trousers accented with a gold vest and purple cravat. Isabel saw Silas wince at the extravagance, but once he was wearing it, he admitted he looked elegant. "Only the best for the two of you," she said.

For Juanita, she ordered a white, gossamer silk dress with lace accenting the neck, fitted bodice, wrists, and hemline. Juanita, too, was embarrassed by such exquisite fabrics, but had to admit she looked younger and prettier than she had in years—even bore a slight resemblance to her youthful self before all the troubles.

"Ha, I just knew you'd been a beauty in your youth. Could've been one of my girls," Isabel winked, as her forthright crassness embarrassed her friend. *Oh dear, what did I agree to? Juanita thought.*

At the appointed hour, she and Silas met outside the tall library doors. Juanita felt a bit ridiculous, and could see Silas did too, but they smiled, shyly, admiring each other in finer clothes than either had ever worn.

Then a solemnity overtook them. He reached for her hand.

When Josiah and Ines pulled open the heavy doors, the couple walked past pinkish marble columns and over thick Persian carpets toward the immense fireplace. Isabel stood beside a massive bay window in a ribboned, ruffled gown in her favorite shade of green, a chair to her side in case she felt weak. Though the swelling had subsided, she still had an ugly wound across her cheek. She would likely have a permanent scar.

Isabel had instructed them to arrive in the late afternoon, just when the sun touched the glass and brought direct sunlight streaming in from the southwest. Chandeliers swayed above the five, illuminating the frieze circling the top of the fourteen-foot-high ceiling and marble mantel over the fireplace.

The room's rich decor made Juanita uncomfortable, but then she reminded herself they were in Isabel's home. Since Isabel was leading the ceremony, the lavishness fit. Juanita was pleased to see, however, Ines' influence in the delicate bouquets of summer wildflowers decorating the mantel and every side table.

Isabel gestured for them to come forward. Josiah and Ines stood at their sides. There were no rings, no religious blessings or family members. Just an ornate room filled with sunlight, love, and friendship, sunflowers, daisies, lupine, and yarrow.

Isabel, for once, was soft spoken and kept her speech short. She asked if they promised to love each other in sickness and in health, and if they would support each other in difficult days as well as bountiful times. After they assented, with shining eyes, she told them as far as everyone in the room was concerned, they were officially, legally, forever married.

"Forget what the ridiculous law says, I know love when I see it. I know its tremendous power in difficult times, such as we've all faced, and are upon us again. Partnerships such as y'all have provide stability, reassurance, and companionship during challengin' moments. Those are rare, and to be treasured. What is permanent here? Not much, but love, friendship, and commitment to one another, to our fellow mankind."

She stopped, squeezed their hands as if she were finished. But Juanita had known her long enough to wait for a bit more.

"Let me just add, before we retire for my favorite celebration treat," Isabel said, smiling so widely it pinched her stitches, and she blanched. "I am quite serious that people, such as y'all, who've suffered through enormous tragedy and societal shifts, who've endured the excesses and errors of history, of man's greed and cruelty, deserve some happiness.

Y'all are regular people forced to survive through extraordinary effort in extraordinary times. Your grit and resilience, your capacity to build and love and give to others, despite such hardship, is truly commendable. Such people like y'all, Juanita and Silas, deserve a little peace and comfort for your weathered souls. Congratulations! Now let's get to the champagne and oysters!"

They departed the day after the ceremony, wanting to return to regular routines and the quieter country life, where they could sift through all that had occurred on this unusual trip. So much had changed in just a few weeks. So much to think through.

Juanita had a son to mourn and a new family to treasure. She had an unusual concern for her San Francisco friend, and, perhaps, an intensified understanding with Silas. She didn't believe their relationship would be any different because of the simple ceremony, but for Silas it was important in building his new life. She understood that now. Happiness emanated from him like a mist of goodwill as they cantered east to Sacramento, then south toward home.

She'd always been one with the earth, seeking solace from its permanence, finding strength and purpose in active stewardship over the land. Discovering her son valued the same was a revelation, truly a gift she'd never dreamed possible.

"Silas," she said, calling over as they jounced in the saddles, almost in unison. "Even though I'm heartbroken we couldn't find Joaquin, alive," she paused and swallowed to collect herself. "Even though his family lost him, and we've lost him, at the same time I know who he was. I know he grew into a good man who loved deeply, and was loved."

Silas smiled and nodded. "True. That's a good family there."

"Yes. And I look forward to getting to know them. I hope they'll let us in. The young Samuel, he's smart, sensitive, sounds like he's ambitious. He reminds me so much of my son."

Silas nodded. They rode on in silence until Juanita spoke again,

"You know, I always focused on just locating him, but I see now discovering who Joaquin was, what he built, his own family, is what's really important."

And that was just it. Juanita's heart, her deepest self, had accepted a new way of being, beyond only self-reliance. One that understood human connection was critical for leading a meaningful life.

She loved the land passionately, but the people on it, the ones who partnered with you due to an unbreakable bond, who cared for your well-being, they were what emboldened you to face life's uncertainties. They were who gave you purpose, and gave you strength, and enabled you to adapt to the unfamiliar, resiliently.

She smiled across the horses' manes at Silas, feeling connected to the past, yet also fortified to face the future, strengthened by a renewed bedrock of love and family. More armed than ever to confront any obstacles California would undoubtedly cast their way.

Acknowledgments

Like most historical fiction authors, I am deeply indebted to those who honor the past—historians, archivists, librarians, museum volunteers, PhD researchers, and both fiction and nonfiction writers. We are especially fortunate when individuals who live through extraordinary times document their experiences, preserving them for future generations. While *Unfamiliar Territory* is a work of fiction, primary source diaries, journal entries, letters, and journalistic reports were invaluable to my research. For readers interested in firsthand accounts of 19th-century California, I recommend a few favorites: *Two Years Before the Mast* by Richard Henry Dana Jr.; *Eldorado* by Bayard Taylor; *The Shirley Letters from the California Mines* by Louise Knapp Smith Clappe; *They Saw the Elephant: Women in the California Gold Rush* by Joann Levy.

Creating a high-quality book requires guidance from dedicated professionals, and I am deeply grateful to those who lent their expertise. My exceptional editor, Andrea Robinson-DiNardo, provided astute conceptual insights, meticulous line edits, and thoughtful advice on book design. Larry Habegger contributed important suggestions with thorough copyediting and keen input on design elements. *the*BookDesigners, Ian Koviak and Alan Hebel, did a fabulous job designing the cover and interior layout with their usual creativity, professionalism, and honest guidance. It was a treat to work with mapmaker, Joe LeMonnier, to create a geographic representation of Juanita's Gold Rush world.

After nine years of a public writing life, I knew it was time to upgrade my website. Reagan Grant-Jackson of Reagan Aerial Design was the perfect person for the task. She is not only highly creative but also incredibly efficient, and a joy to work with. Many thanks to the friends and family who, in addition to Reagan, provided thoughtful feedback on book cover and interior design options: Carolyn Prowse Fainmel, Perrin Brew Stewart, Brian Stewart, Susan Loudenslager Smith, Greg Smith, Angela Phillips, Beverly Kitson, Sarah Payne, Ben Davis, and Pam Wilson.

A writer's solo journey is enriched by not only professional expertise but also through encouragement from those who believe in the vision. Heartfelt thanks to my husband, David Payne, who has supported my writing dream from the moment I first dared to express it. To longtime friends who have also become writers—I appreciate how we support each other professionally, while still making time for hikes and long lunches. Hugs to Perrin Brew Stewart, Jessica Sheffield Zamora, Tracie White, and Kathy Nielsen. I am also grateful for the camaraderie of fellow authors from Central Coast Writers, of Monterey, California, whose understanding of the process has been a unique source of support: Nancy Middleton, Scotty Cornfield, Nicki Ehrlich, Christine Sleeter, Alison van Diggelen, and Robert Walker.

Many thanks to family members, who patiently tolerate me disappearing behind a closed door, cheer me on, and celebrate each milestone: David Payne, Sarah Payne, Dwight Payne, Ben Davis, David Smathers Moore, Kim Grose Moore, Steve Payne, Laura Payne, Ardis Breslauer, Al Breslauer, and Roland Payne.

A heartfelt thank you to friends, readers, book clubs, booksellers and librarians who champion my books, recommend them to others, and—most memorably—never stopped asking, "Which way did Juanita turn on the El Camino?" To every reviewer—your words are like gold. Reviews are difficult to collect but essential to an author's success. I deeply appreciate each one.

Finally, to finish where I began, this book is dedicated to the memory of my mother, Katrina Moore Smathers, and my grandmother, Katrina Hincks Moore—women who faced the challenges of their times with grace and grit. I just know they would have liked Juanita and been so pleased to see her story, and her era, come to life.

About the Author

Mary writes fiction for both adults and children. *Unfamiliar Territory* is her second work of historical fiction. Her debut novel, *In This Land of Plenty*—a family saga set against the backdrop of California history—was popular with book clubs and earned multiple awards, including the 2021 Fiction Book of the Year from BiblioLab's Indie Author Project (California), and a Readers' Favorite Gold Medal for Western Fiction. She also has published a collection of contemporary short stories, *Fertile Soil: Stories of the California Dream*, and a bilingual children's picture book series, *Tropical Tales*.

Before dedicating herself to writing, Mary had a fulfilling career in California public education, serving as a teacher, administrator, teacher trainer, grant writer, and educational entrepreneur. She played a key role in founding three education companies and a public charter school. She now divides her time between California's Monterey Peninsula and Costa Rica's Pacific Coast, where she continues the Castro/Brennan family saga and expands the *Tropical Tales* picture book series.

For more information, including how to contact Mary for book club and school presentations, visit: www.marysmathers.com.